WHAT MAKES SAMMY RUN?

RANDOM HOUSE 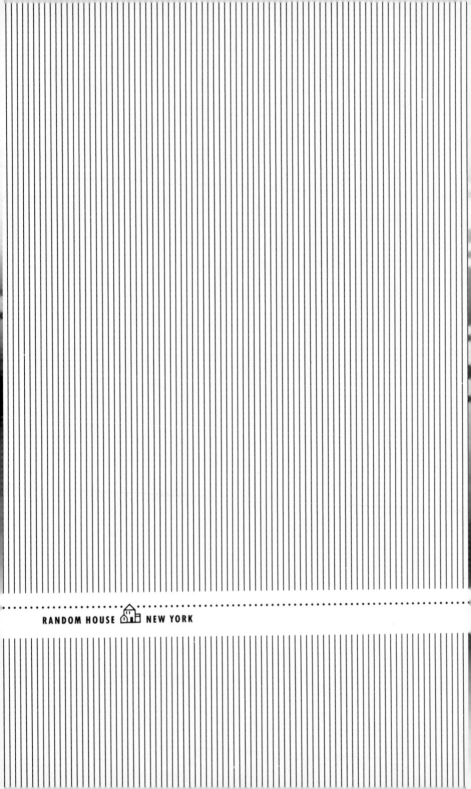 NEW YORK

What Makes Sammy Run?

Anniversary Edition

. . . .

BUDD SCHULBERG

The novel *What Makes Sammy Run?* was originally
published by Random House, Inc., in 1941. Copyright
1941 by Budd Schulberg. Copyright renewed 1968 by
Budd Schulberg. The short stories, "What Makes
Sammy Run?" and "Love Comes to Sammy Glick" were
originally published in *Liberty* magazine. The Afterword
was originally published as "What Makes Sammy Keep
Running?" in *Newsday* on August 2, 1987. Copyright ©
1987 by Budd Schulberg

Library of Congress Cataloging-in-Publication Data
Schulberg, Budd.
What makes Sammy run? / by Budd Schulberg.
p. cm.   ISBN 0-394-57618-7:
1. Title.
PS3537.C7114W45   1990   813'.52—dc20   89-3996

Manufactured in the United States of America
9 8 7 6 5 4 3 2
First Edition

Designed by J. K. Lambert

For Saxe Commins, the "Max Perkins" of Random House, devoted midwife to the birth of this book and the first to predict for it a future that a neophyte novelist thought uncharacteristically extravagant.

And for my children and grandchildren across the generations,

B . S .

CONTENTS

INTRODUCTION
TO THE MODERN LIBRARY EDITION

The choice of What Makes Sammy Run? *for
the Modern Library, giving it the prestige of "a
modern classic," was a milestone in the life of
the novel, and prompted the following
Introduction:*

In the spring of 1941, when my first novel was published, I did
not expect it to have much of a sale. While expressing a good deal
of personal enthusiasm for it, my publishers warned me that works
of fiction concerned with Hollywood were notoriously poor sellers.
So I simply hoped that a few thousand readers would appreciate
it for an honest and serious effort to throw some light on one of
the less glamorous but not insignificant phases of Hollywood life.

Consequently—even after John O'Hara, a friend in need and
in deed in those days, had tried to warn me—I was almost totally
unprepared for the reaction to my book. Whatever else it was, it
was not mild. People were, in several senses, wild about *Sammy.*
Some hailed it as a long-awaited expedition into darkest Holly-

wood. I found myself acclaimed for honesty, insight, courage. Lest this sound faintly megalomaniacal, I hasten to add that people also hated my book. Some said it was the most disgraceful, vulgar, callow novel they had ever read. They attacked it not only as a slander on Hollywood, but on the human race, and I found myself denounced as a sensationalist, a falsifier and even (since we were still living in the afterglow of the finger-pointing thirties) a Fascist! There was something about the book that evoked nothing but lavish praise, violent condemnation and incessant controversy. Only one journal, however, managed to reflect both sides. *The Daily Worker* first hailed the book as a masterpiece of social realism, and then, just one week later, faced about to lambast it as a bourgeois canard on Hollywood's "progressive forces."

The complaint of most novelists is that their literary firstborns suffer inattention and cruel neglect. If I had any complaint, it was that Sammy suffered just the opposite. Overnight the novel which I had hoped might please a few thoughtful readers had become a *succès de scandale*. Sammy, to push my French vocabulary to the wall, was a *cause célèbre*. Damon Runyon welcomed him into the inner circle of all-time all-American heels. The title became a punch line for radio comics and tabloid captions. Winchell revealed to a breathless nation "the true identity of Sammy Glick." Next day the Hollywood producer who had been positively identified as my model passed my table in a restaurant and pointedly looked the other way. Meanwhile at least three other Hollywood producers had been similarly and just as positively identified. My favorite Hollywood pubs suddenly were full of people who would corner me with an inevitable "No kidding, I won't tell a soul, but isn't Sammy really ———?"

In vain I heard myself repeating, like a record revolving in a worn groove, that Sammy was composed in the manner of all fictional characters, out of the writer's recognition of similar and overlapping traits in various individuals who have passed within his circle of observation. Believing frontispiece disclaimers to be empty gestures, I omitted the old wheeze that "any resemblance is purely coincidental." If you wanted to think that Sammy Glick was your boss or your nemesis or yourself, that was for you. As Somerset Maugham had written, in behalf of all the writers accused of literary assault and battery, "No author can create a character out of nothing. He must have a model to give him a starting point." I had no lack of models when I first began sketching Sammy for a series of short stories in 1937. Fresh from college, and inclined to talk too much for a writer anyway, I happened to give a quasi-friend and quasi–screen writer a literal answer to his casual cocktail-party question "What're you working on?" In my innocence I described a little film story I was blocking out. A few days later I had the good fortune to read in a movie column of the sale of my little idea, credited to the fast-moving passerby who had seemed to be listening so sympathetically. I say good fortune, for this mishap launched me both on a hobby and a career. When I complained of my misadventure to fellow scenarists, they shrugged it off with the observation that my wound was a mere scratch compared to any number they had suffered. I began to wonder if every scrupulous screen writer didn't have a Sammy in his life.

I put down everything I heard about the credit hounds, the shoplifters who had learned how to loiter around the idea counter. Notes on at least two dozen quicksters went into my workbook. That's why I can never honestly affirm or deny when I'm asked, "Wasn't it really Willie Blank?" It was and it wasn't. What I had, when I read through my notebook, was not a single person but a pattern of behavior. The job was—as the job of writing always is—to recognize that pattern, to humanize it and then to try and understand it.

Another kind of reader Sammy was apt to hear from was the fellow who said, "Of course we know that Hollywood has its Sammy Glicks. But why must you write about them? After all, we also have plenty of decent, generous and gifted people. Why don't you write about *them*?" If you think of the novel as a kind of literary census-taking, with so many chapters devoted to so many "decent" people and so many words to so many heels, they are right, of course. There were French philistines, passing as literary critics, who protested against Flaubert, "Why does he devote a whole book to a selfish, willful, immoral, hysterical woman like Madame Bovary? Do we not have fine, upstanding, respectable women in the provinces more worthy of immortality?" Not by the widest stretch of vanity am I presuming to have written a *Bovary* or to shine in the reflected brilliance of the French master. But the crime of which he was accused—indeed for which he had to stand trial before a court of justice!—raises a similar question of literary morality. And not only is Flaubert's answer my answer, but that of every serious writer from Defoe to Faulkner: I committed this character to public attention because I found significance in him (or her). Such heroes and heroines of negativism as Julian Sorel, Emma Bovary, George Babbitt, Julian English and Sammy Glick are symptoms that warn of some malaise in their society. I tried to suggest Sammy's as "a way of life that was paying dividends in the first half of the twentieth century." It would be comforting to believe that the inverted morality of the book is outdated. I am frequently asked, "Are there still Sammys in Hollywood?" And the answer must be "Of course," though such naked aggression as I have treated may be hopefully on the wane. But the Sammy-drive is still to be found everywhere in America, in every field of endeavor and among every racial group. It will survive as long as money and prestige and power are ends in themselves, running wild, unharnessed from usefulness.

An extra-literary criticism that *Sammy* has had to face—and which I would like to head into directly here—is that of anti-Semitism. An odd axis of reactionary hush-hushers and propaganda-minded Communist litterateurs raised quite a hue and cry along this line. I said at the time—and even the genocidal forties has not altered my opinion—that I despised anti-Semitism not because I happen to be Jewish myself but because I have always opposed Neanderthalism in any form. I hate it when a Negro is barred from his rightful place in a state university. I hate it when an American of Jewish ancestry is turned away from a hotel or, more important, from a job with some great national firm. I hate it when Russian writers of high talent like Babel or Pilnyak,

Zoschenko or Pasternak are silenced or obliterated for the crime of writing their own themes in their own way. Social cruelty and stupidity, for whatever reason and whatever ends, is Neanderthalism. I would be unhappy about any writing of mine that contributed to it in the slightest degree. But I did not feel guilty of this, even when my book was published in the crucial year of 1941, and if I thought so today, after the hardest kind of thinking on the subject, I would not consent to its reappearance. It is true that the principal character in this book is about as unpalatable a character as ever came down the pike. It is also true that I have made this Sammy Glick a Jew. But as Dorothy Parker said in her review, "Those who hail us Jews as brothers must allow us to have our villains, the same, alas, as any other race." The attack on Richard Wright's hero-villain-victim Bigger Thomas in *Native Son* was strikingly parallel. In defending both his book and mine against the charge that we had played into the hands of racists by making a member of a minority group something less than a knight in shining armor, I wrote, "I believe that for any single reader (of *Native Son*) who came away with a feeling of revulsion for the Negro race, ten closed the book with a deepened understanding of the conditions, the processes that turn a Bigger Thomas from a strong, ambitious, socially useful human being into a hunted animal that kills and hides . . . I planned and hoped that my book would have a similar effect." While admitting the fear that bigots might be able to turn my book against my own people and the democratic ideal, I said this could only be done "by wrenching characters out of their cultural sockets and paragraphs out of their continuity."

One way of distorting the intent and meaning of the book is to overlook the fact that every one of Sammy's victims is also Jewish: his idealistic father, his gentle brother, the easygoing Al Manheim, the gifted, impractical Julian Blumberg and the fading producer Sidney Fineman. Just as the Jews, in other words, have no monopoly on the Sammy Glicks, Sammy himself cannot and should not be interpreted as the personification of an American Jewry that has also given us Brandeis and Gershwin, Baruch,

General Rose and Irving Berlin, not to mention Benny Friedman, Hank Greenberg and Barney Ross. There was no passage in this book that I worked over with greater care than:

It struck me that Julian and Sammy must have been just about the same age, twenty-two or -three, probably brought up in the same kind of Jewish family, same neighborhood, same schooling, and started out with practically the same job. And yet they couldn't have been more different if one had been born an Eskimo and the other the Prince of Wales. And there were so many Julian Blumbergs in the world. Jews without money, without push, without plots, without any of the characteristics which such experts on genetics as Adolf Hitler, Henry Ford and Father Coughlin try to tell us are racial traits. I have seen too many of their lonely, frightened faces packed together in subways or staring out of thousands of dingy rooms as my train hurled past them on the elevated from 125th Street to Grand Central, too many Jewish *nebs* and poets and starving tailors and everyday little guys to consider the fascist answer to *What Makes Sammy Run?*

All right, if the fact of Sammy's Jewishness is a false and thoughtless answer to the question, then what *does* make Sammy run? Of all the questions about the book that have been put to me through the years, this is the only one I find irresistible. It is not so much the novelist as the frustrated sociologist in me that stops for this one. In fact, one of my favorite sociology professors at Dartmouth once greeted me with, "Well, I see you got most of our Socy 1 course into *Sammy*. I'll be interested to see what you'll be able to do with Socy 2." The Dartmouth sociology department, which uses *Sammy* as a textbook, recently sprung on its seniors this final-exam question, "What Makes Sammy Run? (Discuss for one hour.)" I couldn't help wondering what mark I would have received on that one myself.

But it is less important for the novelist to solve his questions than it is to frame them in such human terms that each reader will be incited to come up with his own answers. One reader, Dr. Franz Alexander, head of the Psychoanalytical Institute at the University of Chicago, wrote his answer into a provocative book,

The Age of Unreason. Finding the ultra-aggressive, ruthless and belligerently self-centered type rather common among second-generation Americans from impoverished immigrant families where the father has lost his prestige due to his inability to cope with his new environment, Dr. Alexander writes:

A common solution is that the son usurps the father's place in the mother's affection as well as in economic importance and acquires an inordinate ambition. He wants to justify all his mother's hopes and sacrifices and thus appease his guilty conscience about his father. He can do this only by becoming successful at whatever cost. Success becomes the supreme value and failure the greatest sin because it fails to justify the sacrifice of the father. In consequence of this all other defects such as insincerity in human relationships, unfairness in competition, disloyalty, disregard of others, appear comparatively slight, and the result is a ruthless careerist, obsessed by the one idea of self-promotion, a caricature of the self-made man and a threat to Western civilization, the principle of which he has reduced to absurdity. I am impressed by the accuracy with which Schulberg has described this type, a victim of cultural conditions, and how well he has portrayed the hero, Sammy Glick, the "frantic marathoner" of life, "sprinting out of his mother's womb, turning life into a race in which the only rules are fight for the rail, and elbow on the turn, and the only finish-line is death."

It pleased me that he recognized Sammy as a victim. In the process of writing my book I discovered that while I had begun in a mood of pure hatred, I felt myself, toward the end, caught up in a compassion for Sammy's obsession that threatened any moment to cross over the line into sentimentality. Perhaps that is why I have never gone on to a sequel, as originally planned. But whether I write it or not I have a habit of stopping to wonder, every once in a while, just what Sammy is doing this very minute. I see him now with his antiques and his collection of French Impressionists, slowed down somewhat, considerably refined and comparatively mellowed. He's probably been analyzed, and his second marriage, made for sounder reasons than his first, may last if he's careful. He wants children now; he has a vision of patriarchy. He has been told that he must find a new set of values to fill the moral vacuum in which he throve and strove. In throwing over the ways of his father without learning any sense of obligation to the Judeo-Christian-democratic pattern, he had nothing except naked self-interest by which to guide himself. Instead of being "between pictures," like some of those he overcame in his rush to the top, he may be said to be between patterns of social responsibility. And I believe this is true not only because he happens to be a second-generation product of the slums, but because our American culture as a whole may be in a state of dislocation. We are a babel of heterogeneous moralities. We are dizzy with change. We are Sunday Christians and summer Democrats. No wonder Sammy Glick (including all the Sammy Glicks who would never allow him into their clubs) has found the moral atmosphere so suitable and the underfooting so conducive to his kind of climbing. Yes, Sammy is still running, I'm afraid, and the question still is, How do we slow him down? Perhaps the answer involves an even bigger question: How do we slow down the whole culture he threatens to run away with and that threatens to run away with us?

Why all this moralizing about a book frequently described as racy, fast-moving and principally an entertainment? Well, there's an old saying—or there ought to be one—"Scratch a novelist and you find a moralist." Where is the tension in any novel to be found, after all, but in the discrepancy between the writer's knowledge of what is and his vision of what ought to be?

New Hope, Pa.
January 1952

WHAT MAKES SAMMY RUN?

CHAPTER 1

The first time I saw him he couldn't have been much more than sixteen years old, a little ferret of a kid, sharp and quick. Sammy Glick. Used to run copy for me. Always ran. Always looked thirsty.

"Good morning, Mr. Manheim," he said to me the first time we met, "I'm the new office boy, but I ain't going to be an office boy long."

"Don't say ain't," I said, "or you'll be an office boy forever."

"Thanks, Mr. Manheim," he said, "that's why I took this job, so I can be around writers and learn all about grammar and how to act right."

Nine out of ten times I wouldn't have even looked up, but there was something about the kid's voice that got me. It must have been charged with a couple of thousand volts.

"So you're a pretty smart little feller," I said.

"Oh, I keep my ears and eyes open," he said.

"You don't do a bad job with your mouth either," I said.

"I wondered if newspapermen always wisecrack the way they do in the movies," he said.

"Get the hell out of here," I answered.

He raced out, too quickly, a little ferret. Smart kid, I thought. Smart little yid. He made me uneasy. That sharp, neat, eager little face. I watched the thin, wiry body dart around the corner in high gear. It made me uncomfortable. I guess I've always been afraid of people who can be agile without grace.

The boss told me Sammy was getting a three-week tryout. But Sammy did more running around that office in those three weeks than Paavo Nurmi did in his whole career. Every time I handed him a page of copy, he ran off with it as if his life depended on it. I can still see Sammy racing between the desks, his tie flying, wild-eyed, desperate.

After the second trip he would come back to me panting, like a frantic puppy retrieving a ball. I never saw a guy work so hard for twelve bucks a week in my life. You had to hand it to him. He might not have been the most lovable little child in the world, but you knew he must have something. I used to stop right in the middle of a sentence and watch him go.

"Hey, kid, take it easy."

That was like cautioning Niagara to fall more slowly.

"You said rush, Mr. Manheim."

"I didn't ask you to drop dead on us."

"I don't drop dead very easy, Mr. Manheim."

"Like your job, Sammy?"

"It's a damn good job—this year."

"What do you mean—this year?"

"If I still have it next year, it'll stink."

He looked so tense and serious I almost laughed in his face. I liked him. Maybe he was a little too fresh, but he was quite a boy.

"I'll keep my ear to the ground for you, kid. Maybe in a couple of years I'll have a chance to slip you in as a cub reporter."

That was the first time he ever scared me. Here I was going out of my way to be nice to him and he answered me with a look that was almost contemptuous.

"Thanks, Mr. Manheim," he said, "but don't do me any favors. I know this newspaper racket. Couple of years at cub reporter? Twenty bucks. Then another stretch as district man. Thirty-five. And finally you're a great big reporter and get forty-five for the rest of your life. No, thanks."

I just stood there looking at him, staggered. Then . . .

"Hey, boy!" And he's off again, breaking the indoor record for the hundred-yard dash.

Well, I guess he knew what he was doing. The world was a race to Sammy. He was running against time. Sometimes I used to sit at the bar at Bleeck's, stare at the reflection in my highball glass and say, "Al, I don't give a goddam if you never move your ass off this seat again. If you never write another line. I default. If it's a race, you can scratch my name right now. Al Manheim does not choose to run." And then it would start running through my head: What makes Sammy run? *What makes Sammy run?* I would take another drink, and ask one of the bartenders:

"Say, Henry, what makes Sammy run?"

"What the hell are you talking about, Al?"

"I'm talking about Sammy Glick, that's who I'm talking about. What makes Sammy run?"

"You're drunk, Al. Your teeth are swimming."

"Goddam it, don't try to get out of it! That's an important question. Now, Henry, as man to man, What makes Sammy run?"

Henry wiped his sweaty forehead with his sleeve. "Jesus, Al, how the hell should I know?"

"But I've got to know. (I was yelling by this time.) Don't you see, it's the answer to everything."

But Henry didn't seem to see.

"Mr. Manheim, you're nuts," he said sympathetically.

"It's driving me nuts," I said. "I guess it's something for Karl Marx or Einstein or a Big Brain; it's too deep for me."

"For Chri'sake, Al," Henry pleaded, "you better have another drink."

I guess I took Henry's advice, because this time I got back to the office with an awful load on. I had to bat out my column on what seemed like six typewriters at the same time. And strangely enough that's how I had my first run-in with Sammy Glick.

Next morning a tornado twisted through the office. It began in the office of O'Brien the managing editor and it headed straight for the desk of the drama editor, which was me.

"Why in hell don't you look what you're doing, Manheim?" O'Brien yelled.

The best I could do on the spur of the moment was:

"What's eating you?"

"Nothing's eating me," he screamed. "But I know what's eating you—maggots—in your brain. Maybe you didn't read your column over before you filed it last night?"

As a matter of fact I hadn't even been able to see my column. And at best I was always on the Milquetoast side. So I simply asked meekly, "Why, was something wrong with it?"

"Nothing much," he sneered in that terrible voice managing editors always manage to cultivate. "Just one slight omission. You left all the verbs out of the last paragraph. If it hadn't been for that kid Sammy Glick it would have run the way you wrote it."

"What's Sammy Glick got to do with it?" I demanded, getting sore.

"Everything," said the managing editor. "He read it on his way down to the desk . . ."

"Glick read it?" I shouted.

"Shut up," he said. "He read it on his way to the desk, and when he saw that last paragraph he sat right down and re-wrote it himself. And damn well, too."

"That's fine," I said. "He's a great kid. I'll have to thank him."

"I thanked him in the only language he understands," the

editor said, "with a pair for the Sharkey-Carnera scrap. And in *your name.*"

A few minutes later I came face to face with that good samaritan Samuel Glick himself.

"Nice work, Sammy," I said.

"Oh, that's all right, old man," he said.

It was the first time he had ever called me anything but Mr. Manheim.

"Listen, wise guy," I said, "if you found something wrong with my stuff, why didn't you come and tell me? You always know where I am."

"Sure I did," he said, "but I didn't think we had time."

"But you just had time to show it to the managing editor first," I said. "Smart boy."

"Gee, Mr. Manheim," he said, "I'm sorry. I just wanted to help you."

"You helped me," I said. "The way Flit helps flies."

Ever since Sammy started working four or five months back he had done a fairly conscientious job of sucking around me. He hardly ever let a day go by without telling me how much he liked my column, and of course I'd be flattered and give him pointers here and there on his grammar, or what to read, or sometimes I'd slip him a couple of tickets for a show and we'd talk it over and I'd find myself listening to him give out with Glick on the Theater. Anyway, he had played me for a good thing and always treated me with as much respect as a fresh kid like that could, but right here, as I watched that face, I actually felt I could see it change. The city editor hadn't hung a medal on his chest but he had put a glint in Sammy's eye. You could see he was so gaga about his success that he didn't care how sore I was. That was the beginning.

"Don't you think it's dangerous to drop so many verbs?" he asked. "You might hit somebody down below."

"Listen," I said, "tell me one thing. How the hell can you read when you're running so fast?"

"That's how I learned to read," he cracked, "while I was running so fast. Errands."

It made me sore. He was probably right. Somebody called him and he spun around and started running. What makes Sammy run? I pondered, looking after him, what makes Sammy run?

||||||

For the next couple of months Sammy and I didn't have much to do with each other. I thought maybe by being tough I could teach him a lesson. I'd just hand him copy without looking up, and I quit trying to develop his mind. But after a while that began to seem a little silly. After all, here I was a grown-up drama editor having a peeve on a poor kid who was just trying to get along. It wasn't dignified. So next time he stopped by I suggested that we bury the hatchet.

"Two bits says I know where you'd like to bury it," Sammy said—"in my head."

I had to admit that was quite a temptation, but I managed to overcome it. I guess I've always been a gentle soul at heart. I've never been able to walk past a street fight between two little newsboys out to murder each other over a three-cent controversy without trying to stop it. On off moments when I wasn't drunk or working hard I suppose you would have to call me an idealist. I'm not boasting about this. In this world which is run with all the rules and restrictions of a rough-and-ready free-for-all, it is always a little embarrassing to find yourself still believing in such outmoded principles as the golden rule and brotherly love.

So I began piously, "Now, Sammy, after all, I'm almost old enough to be your father . . ."

"Don't give me that," Sammy said. "My old man was twice as old as you when he kicked the bucket five years ago."

"Oh, I'm sorry," I said. "I hope you won't mind my bringing it up. But I'll bet I know what he'd say if he saw you today. He'd say, 'Sammy, in the long run you'll get further by being nice to people because then when you need them, they'll be nice to you.' "

You should have seen Sammy's face laughing at me. "Mr. Manheim," he said, "that spiel really rings the bell on my old man. That's what he'd be telling me, all right. Because you want to know what my old man croaked from? Dumbness."

"That's a fine way to talk about your father," I said.

"Can I help it if that's what he died of?" Sammy asked. "He didn't know enough to come in out of the rain and he died of a disease that seems to run in my family—dumbness."

"That diagnosis doesn't sound exactly scientific," I said.

"To hell with science," he said. "All I know is that my old man kicked off because his brains were muscle-bound, and my old lady and my half-brained brother suffer from the same thing."

I could see that all this talk was definitely a blind alley. Most Jewish families are pretty strong on filial love, but Sammy wasn't what you'd call a loving son. So I switched to my sociological approach.

"Sammy," I began wisely, "society isn't just a bunch of individuals living alongside of each other. As a member of society, man is interdependent. Not *in*dependent, Sammy, *inter*dependent. Life is too complex for there to be any truth in the old slogan of every man for himself. We share the benefits of social institutions, like take hospitals, the cops and garbage collection. Why, the art of conversation itself is a social invention. We can't live in this world like a lot of cannibals trying to swallow each other. Learn to give the other fellow a break and we'll *all* live longer."

I felt pretty pleased with myself after I said that because I was convinced that it was one of the most sensible things I had ever said. But I might as well have been talking to a stone wall. In fact that might have been better. At least it couldn't talk back.

Sammy's answer was, "If you want to save souls, try China."

I suppose the reason Sammy was getting my goat was because he was the smartest and stupidest human being I had ever met. He had a quick intelligence, which he was able to use exclusively for the good-and-welfare of Sammy Glick. And that kind of intelligence implies stupidity, for where other people might have one blind spot, Sammy's mind was a mass of blind spots, with only a single ray of light focused immediately ahead.

But fat with tolerance, like a Quaker, I decided to break Sammy down with kindness. I had two for *Of Thee I Sing,* so I gave them to him and told him to take his mother or his girl.

"Girl," he sneered, "you don't see me with any girl."

"That's a terrible loss to the opposite sex," I said.

"What good would a girl do me?" he said. "All they do is take up time and dough, and then if they happen to get knocked up they go yelling for their mothers."

"In other words," I said, "you're above sex?"

"Hell, no," he said, "I've got a pal who gets me fixed up every Saturday night. Gratis."

"Isn't it romantic?" I sang the words of a current song. "Now that we've got that settled, do you still want the ducats? Take 'em home and surprise your mother."

"My old lady at a musical show?" Sammy said. "The closest she ever got to a real show was hearing the cantor sing 'Eli Eli.' "

"Then take her out and give her a treat," I said. "About the most fun you can have in the world is showing people who aren't used to it a good time."

"Jesus, you're a sentimental bastard," Sammy said. "Most of the Hebes I know drive me nuts because they always go around trying to be so goddam kind. It ain't natural."

"Remember what I told you," I said. "Don't say 'ain't' or you'll be an office boy forever."

"Fat chance," Sammy said, and hurried off.

When I saw Sammy the next day he didn't even mention the show, so I finally had to ask him.

"I didn't expect you to thank me for those tickets," I said, "but I thought you might tell me what you thought of it."

"Good show," he said.

"Good show," I screamed. "One of the greatest American plays ever written and all you can say is, 'good show!' "

"I wouldn't mind having half of what Kaufman and Ryskind have," he added.

That's a little more like it, I thought. "I'd settle for half their talent myself," I said.

"I don't mean talent," Sammy said. "I mean profit. That show must be cleaning up."

"Go on, beat it," I said. "Disappear."

A little later I happened to meet one of the rewrite men, Osborne, at the water cooler. He was a sweet old gray-haired duck who was gradually working his way down from the hundred-a-week ace reporter he had been before the War.

"Hello, Osborne," I said, "I thought you were going to drop around when you wanted a couple of tickets for some musical. The offer still goes."

"Thanks, Al," he said, "but I didn't want to bother you, so me and the little woman just took one in ourselves. Last night as a matter of fact."

"What did you do that for?" I said. "Two seats at the box office must have set you back plenty."

"As a matter of fact," Osborne said, "it isn't as bad as it sounds. I happened to get a bargain on two seats right up in front. And since it happened to be our twenty-seventh anniversary, I thought it wouldn't hurt to splurge."

"Someone bootlegging in the lobby?" I said.

"No," he said, "I bought them from one of the kids. Name's Glick, I think. Sold me the two of 'em for four bucks."

That made me burn. Four dollars was a lot of money to Osborne.

I didn't wait to run into Sammy again. I sent for him as soon as I got back to my desk.

"So you thought the show last night was pretty good," I began.

"I've seen worse," Sammy said.

"I didn't know you were such a tough critic, Mr. Glick," I said. "You make George Jean Nathan sound like a blurb writer."

"I just know what I like," Sammy said.

"That's quite a trick," I said, "knowing what you like without even having to see it."

"What do you mean haven't seen?" Sammy said in a tone of injured belligerence.

"Wipe that indignation off your face, Sammy," I said. "I mean I've been talking with Osborne."

He took this without a sign of embarrassment. Ability to absorb insults and embarrassment like a sponge was turning out to be one of his greatest accomplishments.

"Oh," he said, "I would have told you only I didn't want to hurt your feelings."

"Don't be so goddam thoughtful," I said. "If you didn't want to see the show, why didn't you tell me?"

"I didn't find out until the last minute that I couldn't go," he explained. "So instead of wasting them I gave them to Osborne."

"There was nothing wrong with that," I said. "Except for one little detail. You didn't give those tickets to Osborne. You soaked him four bucks for them."

"That's one way of looking at it," Sammy said. "On the other hand you could say I saved him the three and a half more he'd've had to pay at the box office."

"*You* could say it," I said, "but you're the only one who could say it. Why, there's even a law against profiteering on complimentary tickets. You could go to jail for this."

Sammy found this threat merely amusing. "All right, mister," he said. "Don't shoot. I'll come quietly."

"You've taken four bucks from Osborne just as sure as if you've picked his pocket," I said sternly. "Why don't you be a good kid and pay him back? He's having his troubles, too."

"Sure, I'd give him his lousy four bucks back," Sammy said. "Only it's too late now. I spent it."

I didn't notice him looking down at his shoes as he spoke, but I guess he must have because I found myself staring at them too. They were brand new the way only shoes can be new, stiff and shiny and still in the window. They were a highly polished yellow-brown leather that made up in gloss what it lacked in quality, small neat shoes that came to a point too stylishly narrow for everyday use.

"So those are the shoes I gave you," I said.

"They were on sale down at Hearns," he said, with no hint of apology. In fact, he seemed really proud of what he had done. He looked down at his shoes, reveling in their newness and added, "You know what, Mr. Manheim, these are the first brand-new shoes I ever had. It's about time, too. I was fed up with wearing my brother's hand-me-downs."

"Sammy," I said, "for Christ's sake, if you needed shoes that bad you could have told me. I'm not exactly Rockefeller, but I'm always good for a little touch if it means going without shoes."

"Thanks," Sammy said, "but you never find me going in for favors. I found out long ago that was a sucker's trick. It leaves you wide open. This way you're sore for a while and I don't owe you nothing."

"Don't owe me anything," I said. "When are you going to learn two negatives cancel each other? If you don't owe me nothing that means you do owe me something."

"O.K.," Sammy said agreeably, "so I don't owe you anything."

I gave up. It was like trying to convince Capone to exchange his machine guns for water pistols. I simply became resigned. It was just as if a wildcat were loose in the office and if I happened to see it crouching on the water cooler I would say to myself that new copyreader certainly looks queer. Only Sammy Glick was a much more predatory animal than any wildcat. For a long time I thought that the phenomenon of Sammy Glick was my own little secret, but after a while I began to find that the whole office was afraid of him. I know that sounds wacky. Hardened newspapermen being afraid of a snot-nosed little office boy? But that's really what it added up to. Even Osborne, the Christ-like rewrite man who always had a good word for everybody, confided to me one day, "I don't know what it is about that kid, he's a hard worker and I think he's good to his mother but he gives me the creeps."

And the managing editor who carried on the tradition of hard-boiled journalistic bosses to the best of his loud-mouthed and soulless ability put it this way:

"I'd kick his little ass for him—if he'd only leave it in one place long enough."

"If he gripes you that much why don't you can him instead of wanting to hand him a raise?" I said heartlessly, though I knew my conscience wouldn't keep me up nights because there must have been thousands of kids in the city waiting to step into his job and I had seen enough of Sammy not to have to worry about his ever starving to death.

But the managing editor just smiled and said, "No, I hate his guts just as much as you do, but I'm not running a popularity contest; I'm running a business office and Sammy's strength as a copy boy is as the strength of ten."

"You've got me wrong," I said. "I don't hate his guts. He's just another worm you haven't got the heart to step on. What the hell makes you think he's big enough to make me waste my time and energy hating him?"

"If he matters that little, why in hell are you getting your bowels in an uproar?" he asked me, and I had to admit that the logic of that stopped me cold.

Since Sammy burst into the office over a year before, I had tried every method I could think of to overcome him. I had tried fatherly criticism. I had guided him with the impersonal and professional tolerance the master craftsman shows the apprentice. I had humored him. I had patronized him with sermons on the goodness of man. I had insulted him. I had given him the silent treatment. I had smothered him with kindness. I had used psychology and I had resorted to frenzied ridicule. Once I had even taken a poke at him. And after twelve months of Sammy Glick I was still behind the eight ball. I can't exactly explain it, but every time I looked at him now I got a crazy helpless feeling, the way you feel in drunken dreams when the Phantom of the Opera is coming after you and the faster you try to get away from him the more you run toward him. I couldn't understand it. In the first place I hadn't even figured him out, and in the second place I couldn't understand why I felt I had to figure out an inconspicuous little copy boy, and in the third place I couldn't figure out why

I gave a damn in the first two places. I know that sounds nuts now but that's the condition I was in when Sammy was running my tail into the ground.

But the wear and tear of our relationship was entirely one-sided. Sammy seemed to be absolutely blooming. Without giving an inch in the personal tug of war he was waging with the world, he was coming into maturity. Only it wasn't what is generally thought of as maturity. It was his own special brand, Sammyglick maturity. No mellowing, no deepening of understanding. Maturity to Sammy merely meant a quickening and a strengthening of the rhythm of behavior that was beginning to disconcert everybody who came in contact with it. Because he seemed to escape all of the doubts, the pimpled sensitivity, the introspection, the mental and physical growing pains of adolescence, he was able to throw off his youth and take on the armor of young manhood with the quick-changing ease of a chorus girl. His alert little ferret face began to take more definite form, the thin neat lips permanently set, the nose growing larger but still straight and sharp, giving the lie to the hook-nosed anti-Semitic cartoons, a nose that teamed up with the quick dark eyes and the tense, lined forehead to give an impression of arrogance and a fierce aggressiveness, which, when you included the determination of the pointed, forward-thrust chin, produced a face that reminded you of an army, full of force, strategy, single will and the kind of courage that boasts of never taking a backward step.

|||||||

The first sure sign I had of Sammy's growing up was when he came to me with the announcement that he now felt himself ready to conduct the paper's radio column. Of course, the fact that the paper had never had a radio column didn't seem to discourage him in the least.

"And just what makes you think you're prepared to be an expert on matters Marconi?" I said.

"What made you think you were an expert on the theater?" he said.

That made me pause.

"That's got absolutely nothing to do with it," I said. "I had plenty of reasons."

"Name one," said Sammy.

I don't know why the hell I was letting a twelve-buck-a-week half-pint bulldoze me, but there I was. "Well, for one thing," I said, "I always liked the theater. I've seen lots of plays."

"Well, I've listened to the radio plenty too," Sammy said.

"That doesn't mean anything," I said. "Everybody listens to the radio."

"That's why there oughta be a radio column," Sammy said.

It struck me funny. Here was this office boy applying for the job of writing a radio column that didn't exist, and he actually had me on the defensive.

"Listen," I said, "do you realize you have one hell of a nerve interrupting me in the middle of my work to ask me a thing like that?"

"O.K.," Sammy said, "go ahead and put your own selfish interest ahead of the paper's good."

It made just enough sense to exasperate me into going on. That was getting to be one of Sammy's favorite tricks. He could go so far that your curiosity was pricked because you wouldn't believe anybody could get that brazen.

So instead of simply giving him his walking papers the way I should have, I accepted the challenge. "What are you talking about, the good of the paper?" I said. "What's the good of the paper got to do with it?"

"You know the paper needs a radio column," Sammy said. "But you're such a dog in the manger you're afraid it might cut into your column and that's why you're against it."

"What's the good of fighting with me about a radio column?" I said. "Everybody knows the old man doesn't want it because he says why should we plug a setup that's cutting our advertising."

"But millions of people are listening in all day long," Sammy argued. "That'd mean new readers for the *Record*. And I'll bet the column would land us plenty of radio ads. So if you'd put in a good word for me with the boss . . ."

"Listen, Sammy," I said. "That is, if you ever do listen, which I doubt. In the first place, I don't care about radio columns, and in the second place, there are half a dozen boys I could name in this office I'd give the job to before you, and in the third place, even if you were the radio master mind of the century I'd be damned if I'd help you get it, and in the fourth place—or have you had enough places?"

"I don't know," Sammy said. "I guess if you've heard one place you've heard them all."

Three or four weeks later I was sitting around in Bleeck's one night with the boys after turning in my column.

The telephone rang and Henry answered it and said it was for me. "It's your pal, Sammy Glick," Henry said.

"Good evening, young man," I said, feeling mellow on four or five highballs.

"It's a good evening for me all right," Sammy said. "But I don't know about you, Mr. Manheim."

I didn't like the tone of that "Mr. Manheim."

"What's up?" I said.

"Your dinner," Sammy said, "when you hear what's happened."

For a moment or two it was touch and go as to whether or not I burst a blood vessel right there in front of all my friends.

"Come on, spill it, you punk," I said. I was so sore I was talking like a gangster in the movies.

"The boss says your column is two sticks short," Sammy said.

"For Chri'sake I haven't even finished it," I said. "I just came down to grab a couple of drinks before wrapping it up. Tell him he can stop worrying. I'll be right up."

"He's not worried a bit," Sammy said. "And you don't have to either. Everything's under control. I took care of it."

"You?" I said. "You?" I repeated. "What do you mean you?" I said stupidly. I knew he had me. I could tell.

"Sure, Al," he said, just as if he had always called me Al. "I dashed off a four-inch radio column to fill, and the boss liked it."

"Oh, he's seen it already!" I said. "Then why the hell did you bother to call me? Why the hell don't you just take over my column? Why the hell . . . ?"

"I just wanted to help you," Sammy said simply.

"Sure," I said, "Joe Altruist," and I hung up.

That night I dreamt about Sammy Glick. I dreamt I was working in my office, minding my own business and peacefully writing my column, when all of a sudden I looked up and screamed. Everybody in the office looked like Sammy Glick. There must have been thirty or forty of them, and every time one of them passed me he'd say, "Hello, Al, I'm the new drama editor"; or "Hello, Al, I'm the new city editor"; or "Hello, Al, allow me to introduce myself, your new publisher, S. Glick," and, finally, when I couldn't stand it any more, I started to run, with all the Sammy Glicks behind me and I got into the elevator just in time and heaved a sigh of relief when, so help me God, who do I see driving the elevator but Sammy Glick, and when I finally get out onto the street, sure enough there's nobody but Sammy Glick waiting for me, thousands of Sammy Glicks all running after me.

It was a relief to wake up, because I figured that nothing that ever happened between me and Sammy could top that one. From now on Sammy Glick was sure to be an anti-climax and I was saved. That just goes to show you how little I still knew about my friend Glick.

The pay-off began next morning when the managing editor hovered over my shoulder just after I had started my column.

"From now on write it thirty lines shorter all the time," he said in the same tone of voice he'd ask for a stick of gum.

"What do you mean thirty lines shorter?" I said.

"I mean," he explained, "that from now on it should be thirty lines not as long as you've been writing it."

"This is a little sudden," I said, "but it's O.K. by me if you can give me one good reason why this amputation's necessary."

"Listen closely and hold on to your seat," the city editor said. "From now on we're using Sammy Glick's radio column."

"You mean Sammy Glick the copy boy?" I said.

"No, I mean Sammy Glick the radio columnist," he said. "His stuff looked all right today."

"I read it," I said. "Maybe you'd like to know he copied that first paragraph from Somerset Maugham?"

"Maybe that's where you need to go for your stuff," he said.

So that's how Sammy got his start. It was hard to believe, but you didn't have to pinch yourself to know you weren't dreaming. All you had to do was turn to the amusement page of the *Record*, and there we were, side by side, "Down Broadway" by Al Manheim and "Sammy Glick Broadcasting." I always suspected that Sammy sold the editor that title so his name could be in fatter type than any by-line could possibly be. That may not be one of the things you or I would think of doing but it meant plenty to Sammy.

The funny part of it was the kid's stuff wasn't bad. He was just smart enough never to crib from the same writer twice. He was glib. When it came to wisecracks he rolled his own. I had gone through so many emotions with Sammy that I felt as if I had to have my emotional valves ground but now I was reaching the stage of loathing him so much I was beginning to admire him. Every other copy boy in the place was just a nice guy. At least if you bent over, they'd ask you to stand up and turn around before stabbing you. But Sammy Glick was teaching me something about the world. Of course, I hadn't found out what made him run, and, lucky for him, I had no idea just where he was running. And if I had, I suppose I might have spent the rest of my life serving time for committing premeditated mayhem. And I suppose there's no use kidding myself. Somehow Sammy would have capitalized on that as he did everything else. It looked as if Sammy Glick had the drop on this world.

As a columnist, Sammy had no scruples about printing what he overheard. He always managed to get on the inside with the key secretaries. He had a well-developed talent for squeezing news out of victims by pretending he already had it. He had no qualms about prominently featuring what he knew to be lies and then printing the truth a day or so later in an inconspicuous retraction at the bottom of the column.

He even found a way of turning those retractions into a good thing. For instance, if some big shot happened to demand a correction, Sammy would call him by some private nickname and say, "Sorry, Jock," or "Pudge" or "Deac, thanks for the help." He learned to play all but the most complex and suspicious minds like a harp. He pumped and he promised and he did small favors. He managed to get near the best of them and he picked up much of his hot news from the worst. He overcame the fact that he had absolutely no literary ability whatsoever by inventing a lingo which everyone mistook for a fresh and unique style when it was really plain unadulterated illiteracy. But all of these achievements were overshadowed by one stupendous talent; his ability to blow his own horn. He blew it so loud, so long, and so often, that nobody believed all that sound could possibly emanate from one person and so everyone really began to believe that Sammy Glick's name was on everyone else's lips.

There was the occasion of Sammy's birthday party which was also (though I always suspected him of tying these together conveniently to make a better story) the anniversary of "Sammy Glick Broadcasting."

I hadn't been on exactly chummy terms with Sammy for quite a time now but one afternoon he came up to me at Bleeck's and, without taking his ten-cent cigar out of his mouth (this was a new addition to the evolving personality of Sammy Glick), he said, "Hello, Al, can I buy you a drink?"

I didn't like the idea of his buying me a drink, so I offered to play him the match game to see who got the check and I lost. There's no use making myself out a hero about this. I was pretty generally considered the King of the Match Game down at Bleeck's and I didn't like the way Sammy was starting to beat me.

After I finished my drink I started to edge away, but Sammy was too quick for me.

"Say, Al," he said, "next Monday is my birthday, and since you sorta gave me my start I thought maybe you'd like to have dinner with me and my girl, at the Algonquin."

"Gave you your start!" I said. "I did everything I could to get you canned."

"No kidding, Al," he said, just letting that roll off him. "I know birthday parties are old-fashioned, but I want you with us at dinner Monday night."

"Monday night?" I said. "Sorry, Sammy, I'm a working man; I've got a show Monday night."

I couldn't think of a show Monday night, but, by God, I was going to find one.

"Then how about Sunday?" Sammy said.

"Well, it's more fun to have your party on your actual birthday," I said, "so why don't you just go ahead without me? I'll—sort of be there in spirit," I added, a little lamely.

But Sammy always was too practical to go in for anything as philosophical as that. "No," he insisted, "I wouldn't think of having my party without my old pal Al, so I'll just change it to Sunday night."

We met in the Algonquin lobby. Sammy was standing with a spindly-legged, too thin, sickly-pale, vague little girl. She could have looked like an angel, only her face was made up like a Fourteenth Street chorus girl, heavy red lipstick and eye shadow and too much powder and orange rouge. I wanted to take my handkerchief and wipe it all off. The poor little kid. The blue eyes and the frail body and the sad beauty were hers. They grew out of the shadow of the tenement right up through the crowded sidewalk.

"Miss Rosalie Goldbaum," Sammy said, "meet Mr. Al Manheim, who has the column next to mine."

"Oh, Mr. Manheim, Sammy has told me so much about you," Miss Goldbaum said.

Sammy took Miss Goldbaum's arm and mine and guided us

through the lobby to the restaurant. He caught the headwaiter's eye with an air of practiced authority. He smiled down his cigar. For the occasion he had bought himself a new pair of $7.50 black flanged shoes at the London Character Shop.

Dinner was what I would have called uneventful. Sammy was too busy looking around for celebrities to pay much attention to either of us. Miss Goldbaum was shy, strangely unsophisticated, full of self-conscious smiles and silence. Except when she talked about Sammy. And I encouraged her. For her heart was so full of Sammy that I began to wonder if I had overlooked one of his virtues. Perhaps this was another side; he was a kind and thoughtful lover and slowed down to a walk for Miss Goldbaum.

"You know, Mr. Manheim," she said, "writing that column isn't what Sammy really wants to do."

"Of course not," I said, "they forced it on him."

"He just does that to make a living," she said.

"It's a damn shame," I said, "this materialistic world crushing a beautiful soul like that."

"It really is," she said. "Because he writes me the loveliest things. I just know that some day he's going to be a really great writer. Because he's really a poet."

"He's a great man," I said, expecting God to strike me dead any second. "You're a lucky girl."

"You're telling *me*," she said.

There was a lull. Sammy was staring across the room at George Opdyke, the three-time Pulitzer Prize winner. I was about to say he was lost in thought, but Sammy was never really lost, and he never actually thought, for that implies deep reflection. He was figuring. Miss Goldbaum edged her undernourished white hand into his. Sammy played with it absent-mindedly, like a piece of silverware.

"Gee," Miss Goldbaum burst out again, "honestly, sometimes when I look at Sammy I just can't believe it, and him just a little kid right out of the East Side like me."

"You're a lucky . . ." I began and then I caught myself and ended feebly with, "Yeah—a diamond in the rough."

She was becoming tiresome. Her tight little world was bursting with Sammy Glick. All her craving to live and her blood rushing to possess and to be maternal found expression in this one smart little guy. I wondered if she had known Sammy that time a year or so ago when he had proudly pronounced his independence of all women, except for what he could get gratis on Saturday nights.

I liked her and pitied her and didn't want to hear her any more.

About that time Opdyke had finished his coffee and was passing our table and just at the moment that I was going to nod to him, for I knew him slightly, Sammy suddenly surprised me in a loud voice:

"Hey, Al, I thought you said you were going to introduce me to Opdyke."

Of course that was the last thing I had intended to do but it was too late because Opdyke had already stopped the way anyone does when he hears his name. He paused a moment, just long enough for me to get the introduction out and Sammy had had his way again.

Miss Goldbaum looked at Opdyke with some reproach, as if to say, You can't horn in on this, it's *our* birthday party.

But you should have seen Sammy go to work. He offered Opdyke a cigar and said, "I sent you a column of mine a couple of months ago giving you a pretty good plug. I always wondered how you liked it."

Opdyke looked at him questioningly. "I'm afraid I couldn't tell you," he said, "I get quite a few clippings in the mail."

That would have been enough to discourage you and me, but all it did was give Sammy a better idea of how to proceed.

"You know, Mr. Opdyke," he said, "I was always hoping I could meet you so I could tell you how much I liked *The Eleventh Commandment.*"

This time Opdyke came to life a little bit. "Really," he said, "I thought everybody had forgotten that little one-acter. I wrote *Eleventh Commandment* when I was just getting started."

"It's just as good today as it was when you wrote it," Sammy said. "I happened to read it just a couple of weeks ago. You'd be surprised how it stands up."

"Is that a fact?" Opdyke said, rather pleased.

I could see what Sammy was doing and I had to hand it to him. If there's anything every successful writer loves, it's to hear praise for some obscure failure which he is still convinced is one of the best things he ever wrote. That was Opdyke's Achilles' heel, just the way it probably was Dreiser's and Shaw's and Sinclair Lewis's, and Sammy had found it.

The next thing I knew Opdyke was actually sitting down with us. "This protégé of yours is a real student of the American theater, Al," he said.

Protégé. I winced. And I didn't have the heart to tell him what I was beginning to realize: that Sammy, knowing that Opdyke usually hangs out at the Algonquin, had probably been doing a little research on the playwright at the public library.

For the next fifteen minutes, Sammy was in his element, busy being sophisticated and artificially gay, trying his best to outwise-crack Opdyke.

After Opdyke left, with a hearty Glad-to-have-met-you for Sammy, Miss Goldbaum started to yawn and I mumbled something about having a lot of work to do before hitting the hay, and Sammy looked at Miss Goldbaum and said, "We both appreciate your celebrating this way with us." She nodded happily. Yes, her Sammy said it exactly right, and the birthday party was over. The last I saw of them they were walking down the steps to the subway arm in arm and she was looking up at him. He was nineteen years old.

||||||

On the way home I stopped in "21" and had a drink by myself, somehow hoping to find the answer to Sammy Glick at the bottom of my glass. I didn't want to hate Sammy too quickly because I wasn't a hater by nature. I usually tried to find some reason for liking everybody. That had always been my favorite luxury in life, being able to like everybody. I suppose that could be traced back to my heritage, in a small New England town where life was always peaceful and friendly, and where my father, the town's only rabbi, had led a life of community service and true Isaiah-like vision that had won him Middletown's approval and genuine respect. When I enrolled at the good little Methodist college in our town, I still expected to follow my father's footsteps and go on to rabbinical school, but four active and enthusiastic years in college dramatics changed my mind for me and that's how I happened to wind up in front of the footlights instead of the altar. My father's life message of tolerance was imbedded too deeply in the undersoil of my adolescence for any Broadway cynicism to wipe away entirely, and sometimes at the most ridiculous moments the words of my father would return to me, phrased in the dignified Biblical language that had become his everyday speech, though I believe the wording was his own: "Try to love all your fellow men as you do your own brother, for the Lord placed all men upon the earth that they might prosper together."

So that's what I sat there saying to myself that night as I downed my Scotch and tried my very best to love Sammy Glick along with all the rest of my fellow men. Under the potent influence of Scotch and my father I began to feel downright repentant. Almost maudlin, in fact. Here he was a young kid just trying to get a good job and now that he had got it and was beginning to grow up he'd have a chance to relax and become one of the boys. Manheim, get a grip on yourself, I cautioned myself unsteadily. Stop seeing dark clouds behind every silver lining. You're going to love Sammy Glick, Manheim, I lectured, you're going to remember what your dear dead father told you and love Sammy Glick even if it kills you. Why, Sammy's hospitality tonight is a beautiful gesture. It's the beginning of a golden friendship.

You will have to forgive me for that because I was a little drunk by that time, and then too when it came to a knowledge of Sammy Glick I was still in the first grade.

But I skipped a couple of grades after I saw Winchell's column next evening. There it was, right at the top, the boldface print laughing up at me:

> When rising columnist Sammy Glick celebrated his twenty-first birthday at the Algonquin last night, George Opdyke and colleague Al Manheim were on hand as principal cake eaters . . .

You didn't have to be a mastermind to figure out how Walter got that item, or where those two extra years came from. So when Sammy blew into the office I gave him one of my searching looks.

"I see where George Opdyke got himself a plug in Winchell's column this morning, Samuel," I said.

"Yeah," Sammy cracked, "you should have been there."

"Listen," I said, "you've got enough gall to be divided into nine parts."

"Aw, don't be sore, Al," he said. "I can't hide in this nest forever. I gotta spread my wings a little."

"Then you must be a bat," I said, "because that's the only rat I know of with wings."

"Why, Al," Sammy said, "I'm surprised at you. I always thought you were my friend."

He really meant it too. Trying to hurt his feelings was like trying to shoot an elephant with a BB gun. It simply tickled him.

"You're physically incapable of having friends," I said. "All you can ever have are enemies and stooges."

That rolled off my tongue just like that, without thinking much about it, but I remember looking back on it in later life as one of my few profound observations.

"Sammy," I continued, "try to learn before it's too late. Don't be cheap. Cheapness is the curse of our times. You're beginning to spread cheapness around like bad toilet water. That item about George Opdyke's celebrating your birthday was one of the cheapest things I ever saw."

"Sure, it was cheap," Sammy said. "After all, I got better publicity free than you could have bought for big dough. You can't ask for anything cheaper than that. And what are you squawking about? It didn't do you any harm either."

"You don't have to convince me," I said. "I know you're a philanthropist. But while you were about it why didn't you mention Miss Goldbaum? She's the only one who would have got any joy out of seeing her name linked with yours in print. Why didn't you give her a break?"

"Wise up," he cracked, "she gets her break three times a week."

"You—stink," I ended lamely, so sore I couldn't even try to be clever.

"Okay, I stink," he said, walking off, "but someday you'll cut off an arm for one little whiff."

CHAPTER 2

For the next few weeks I tried to avoid Sammy, even though he had his desk in the adjoining cubicle. I was beginning to wonder if this office wasn't too small for the two of us, and I was afraid to put that suspicion to the test for fear of losing the best job I'd ever had. Of course, all that time I knew I was living in a fool's paradise because nobody on earth could sit within ten or twelve feet of Sammy day after day without becoming emotionally involved in some unexpected phase of his activity.

One day a frightened young man with an unassuming, intelligent, unhandsome face behind glasses came in with a manuscript under his arm and inquired for Mr. Glick in a voice quavering with inferiority.

He said his name was Julian Blumberg and he had a small job in our advertising department, and, and his life's ambition was to become a writer and, and, er—he had written a radio script and, and, er—er since Mr. Glick was such an expert on radio writing, would he be so kind as to read Blumberg's manuscript?

I expected Sammy in his own pungent vernacular to go into the physiological details of where Mr. Blumberg could dispose of his manuscript, but Sammy was playing a new role today, and that's what made me sneak up and grab a choice seat in the orchestra. Sammy had decided to be flattered.

"I should be very happy to help you," he said, in a new and different tone.

That was one of the moments when I could feel something happening to him, a new step, something big. So help me God, I could feel something loud and strong pumping inside that little guy, like a piston, twisting him up and forcing him on.

After Julian Blumberg went back to his advertising department, Sammy sat down and read his stuff. He was smiling when he turned the first page, and when he hit the third page he laughed out loud.

"Hey, Al," he said (he used to yell over to me whether I answered him or not), "this is good stuff, funny as hell."

"Mmmmmmmm," I said.

He read through the rest of it, laughing and loudly commenting, and then, never being able to keep anything to himself, he popped over to my desk and slapped Blumberg's manuscript down.

"Whataya know about that?" he said. "A brand-new angle."

"Yeah?" I said doubtfully. "What's it about?"

"It's a comedy with a helluva twist in it," Sammy said. "It starts out where the guy won't have anything to do with the dame. So *she* kidnaps *him*. But he still says no dice and gets her arrested. In court it looks like curtains for her till they clinch and decide to get married, which saves the dame, because he's the only witness and a guy can't testify against his own wife. Pretty nifty, huh?"

I didn't pay much attention to the story, but I was surprised to find Sammy so interested in somebody else's work and I told him so.

"Say, that's nothing," Sammy said, "I even have a better ending for him. The same Judge that was going to sentence her suggests that he have the honor of marrying her. So they hold the wedding right in court, and how's this for the last line: the Judge says, 'Case dismissed.' "

"Yeah," I said, "that's swell, but I don't see what it adds up to for you."

"Oh," he said, "I'm not thinking about myself. I just like to see a young kid get ahead."

That was all I needed to watch the further development of the Blumberg-Glick affair with suspicious interest.

Sammy Glick's pale young genius returned the following week. Sammy shook his hand firmly, but I noticed that he didn't exactly boil over with enthusiasm as he had with me.

"You have an idea here," he admitted to the poor guy. "Of course it's rough and it needs developing, but maybe with a little work we could fix it up."

"You mean you'll help me?" said the dope.

"I think I can pull something out of it," Sammy said modestly, "and then I'll give it to my agent."

"Say, I didn't expect all *this*," the dope said.

I thought Mr. Blumberg was going to break down and fall on Sammy's neck for joy. I never saw a man so pleased about getting chiseled in all my life.

When the guy had gone, practically bowing out backwards, Sammy turned to me and said, "Say, Al, who's a good agent for me?"

"Jesus, Sammy," I said, "haven't you any shame? First you muscle in on Mr. Blumberg's perfectly good story. Then I hear you tell him you've got an agent."

But Sammy was in no mood for cross-examination. This was the chance he knew he had been waiting for and he was as preoccupied as a good quarterback figuring out the next play.

"Who's a good agent for me?" Sammy repeated. "This story is too good for radio. I'm going to sell it to Hollywood. I even got the title all doped out: *Girl Steals Boy.*"

"As soon as the agents hear you're interested in Hollywood, they'll be coming at you from all sides," I said, trying to keep a straight face. "But you might do worse than Myron Selznick."

"Is Selznick any good?" Sammy asked with a naivete that was to pass all too quickly.

"I think so," I said. "At least he's good enough for Carole Lombard, William Powell, Norma Shearer and a couple of dozen other stars."

"Is he any good with stories?" Sammy asked.

"Pretty fair," I said. "He's supposed to average a couple of grand a week out of them."

"Maybe I'll give him a try," said Sammy.

"Why, Sammy," I said, "I never heard you so retiring before. I'm sure Myron Selznick will never forgive you when he hears how you hesitated about giving him your business. If I were you, I'd put in a long-distance call to him right now."

If Sammy knew I was kidding, he certainly didn't let on. "Where can I reach him?" he asked.

"Myron Selznick and Company, Beverly Hills, California, is all you need," I said.

I was laughing. But Sammy wasn't laughing. Sammy never looked more serious in his brief, serious career. "By God, Al," he said tensely, "I think you've given me an idea."

Then, while my face must have drained white with shock and disbelief, I was privileged to overhear one of the most astounding conversations in the history of the telephone.

"Hello, operator," Sammy said, "this is Mr. Glick. I wish to speak with Mr. Myron Selznick in Beverly Hills, California, person-to-person."

While he waited for his call to go through, we didn't say anything, he too intense and I too stunned. I just looked into his face, waited for his voice and wondered. His face was beginning to settle into a permanent sneer. I had begun to hear it in his voice too, an incredible contempt for other human beings, not only for those like me, the secretaries, the copy boys and the men on the staff who were unfortunate enough to be his everyday acquaintances, but for strangers too, the back of a taxi driver's neck at which he yelled instructions, people he pushed out of the way in a crowd, the anonymous operator just now . . .

It stemmed partly from the confidence he was taking on like fuel at every new station, but there was something more, some angry, volcanic force erupting and overflowing deep within him.

"Hello, Mr. Selznick? This is Mr. Glick calling from New York . . .

"Sammy Glick! I just wanted to let you know I've decided to let you handle my story . . .

"No, of course you never heard about me. But you're going to—plenty . . .

"Don't give me that maybe stuff. The most surefire story sale that's come to Hollywood in years, and he tells me maybe. Well, I've got a couple of maybes of my own, Mr. Selznick. Maybe I won't even show you that story. Maybe I'll give another agency first crack at it instead . . .

"Oh, I'm paying good money for a long-distance call just to make jokes, I suppose. Well, if that's the way you feel. Good-bye . . .

"Yes, it's right here on my desk, but I'll be damned if I'm going to send it to you until you show a little more interest . . .

"Oh, that's different. But you've got to read it as soon as you get it. Because the idea is so hot I don't want to give anybody time to steal it . . .

"And one more thing, I want you to call me as soon as you finish it. Call me collect here at the *Record,* if you don't like the expense . . .

"Now you're talking my language. *Girl Steals Boy* will be on your desk the day after tomorrow. So long, Myron."

Sammy hung up, took out a handkerchief and wiped the sweat off his forehead. Then he put his handkerchief back in his pocket, took it out again and wiped his head some more.

"Whew!" he said. He slumped in his chair like a fighter after the final bell.

I stared at him. I felt as I did when I stared at a photograph of the man who walked across Niagara Falls on a tightrope. With such a stunt I could have absolutely no sympathy, yet I was held fascinated by its crazy boldness. In Sammy was everything I hated most: dishonesty, officiousness, bullying. But I felt I wasn't only staring at him with dislike, I was staring at him with actual awe for the magnitude of his blustering.

He sat there smiling as I came over to him.

"Sammy, were you scared?"

I asked him that because the phone call was completely outside my sphere of experience. It was like asking a man how it felt to start out in a rocket to the moon. Even though superficially we were similar, both columnists, both Jewish, both men, both American citizens, both awake for the same brief moment in world time, I stared at Sammy now, asked my question and waited for the answer like a mystic trying to reach another world.

"Sammy, were you scared?"

"It's a funny thing, Al," Sammy said in the most quiet voice I had ever heard in him, "I'm scared now, all right. Goddam scared. I got scared the second I hung up. But I wasn't scared when I called him. I didn't even think about being scared."

I leaned forward. I felt closer to him than I ever had before. For just a moment his guard was down.

"What were you thinking about, Sammy?"

He murmured as if he were talking to himself.

"I was just thinking about me. I just kept thinking nothing but me. I just kept saying Sammyglicksammyglick over and over inside my head and it kept growing louder SAMMYGLICKSAMMYGLICK-SAMMYGLICK. I guess that don't quite make sense, does it?"

Oh, yes, I thought to myself; oh, yes, that makes sense all right. It makes the most fearful horrible frightening sense I ever heard.

Sammy rose and snapped out of it.

"Come on down to Bleeck's," he said. "I'll beat the pants off you in the match game."

"The hell you will," I said, and we walked down together and he beat me. And, as we played and drank together, I kept wishing I could really hate him because I was in no-man's-land now and there was a terrible sense of frustration about not being able to hate him as much as he deserved.

Weeks passed without Myron Selznick ever returning Sammy's call. I watched closely for some sign of disappointment in Sammy but there was none. He went right on crowing around the office like a bantam cock. I began to picture Sammy twenty years from now, growing bald and mellow, making mild jokes about the impetuousness of youth. It was a tremendous temptation not to exult. Well, Sammy, my boy, so you finally bit off more than you could chew?

Soon I was glad for my restraint. Because it was so wrong to imagine that Sammy could ever stop running this early in the race.

I remember Sammy rushing in, triumphant and jumpy, as if he had stolen the cheese and avoided the trap. He had.

"Shake hands with God's Gift to Hollywood," he said, grabbing my hand before I had time to stick it in my pocket.

"Don't use the name of our Lord in vain," I said. "You mean you sold that story?"

"Five thousand bucks," he said.

"Go home and get a good night's sleep," I said. "You'll feel better in the morning."

"We should have had a better price for it," he went on, "only this was my first story."

It was screwy, it was Horatio Alger, it was true.

"It's a disgrace," I said. "Only five thousand. I'd be ashamed to take it."

"Well, that's just a starter," he said, "and there's plenty more ideas where that one came from."

"You mean from Julian Blumberg?"

"Aah," he said, "that schlemiel had nothing on the ball but a prayer. He's lucky I bothered with him."

"Like Miss Goldbaum," I said quietly.

There. That's what it needed. All of a sudden I was hating

Sammy Glick. Ah, that felt better. It was satisfying. No more being annoyed or disturbed or curious or revolted. There isn't a decent emotion in the lot. But this felt like it was on the level, good-to-the-last-drop one-hundred-percent-pure hate.

As if things weren't bad enough, the next morning right between a spoonful of soft-boiled egg and a bite of toast I read something in the film section of the morning paper that brought on acute indigestion. You didn't have to be an FBI man to detect the subtle hand of Mr. Glick.

TEN GRAND FOR BOY GENIUS

Sammy Glick, youngest radio columnist and ranking favorite for national boy-genius honors, has sold his first screen story to World-Wide for $10,000. Titled Girl Steals Boy, *story is supposed to go into immediate production as one of big budget pictures on World-Wide's program. It is the first of a series World-Wide has contracted for, according to Mr. Glick. Mr. Glick was undecided whether to accept any Hollywood offers or to remain in his position on the* Record, *he said last night. Collaborating with him was Julian Blumberg.*

What I can't understand, I thought, is how Julian ever managed to get mentioned at all. I was very bitter. I didn't know whether to be painfully jealous of Sammy Glick or congratulate myself on not being like him. I'm afraid I did both.

Sammy was in and out of the office the next few days, very important and mysterious, conscientiously neglecting his work.

"You still here?" I said. "I thought you had gone to Hollywood."

"No," Sammy said, "you know how it is, once you get newspaper ink in your veins."

"Sure," I said. "In other words you haven't got a job in Hollywood yet."

"No," Sammy said, "not yet."

Then one day Sammy didn't show up at all. Maybe he's sick,

I thought at first, but I quickly discounted this optimism. Guys like Sammy Glick don't get sick unless it helps them out of a contract or lands them an insurance payment. The afternoon passed and still no Sammy. Maybe he was murdered by Julian Blumberg, I dared to hope. But I knew better. Julian undoubtedly had talent, but he didn't have the nerve to kill time.

While I was wondering, Sammy came in, or rather, he made his entrance. He wore a new suit. He also wore a new expression. I took one look and I decided I liked it even less than the old one. He wore a blue-check tab-shirt and a red carnation in his button-hole. His shoes screamed newness. Brown alligator. He caught my look. "Set me back fifteen bucks," he said. I took a step back and drank him in. He took out his cigarette case and offered me a Parliament. Sammy Glick, my Sammy Glick, my little copy boy. America, America, I thought, God shed His grace on thee and crown thy good with . . .

"Hello, obnoxious," I said.

"I came in to say good-bye," Sammy said.

"Good-bye," I said.

"I'm not kidding," he said. "I'm off for Hollywood."

"I'll bet you got Irving Thalberg plenty worried," I said.

"If he's not he oughta be," Sammy said. "I've got a hunch Hollywood is my meat."

"How did this happen?" I said. "Metro wire that they just couldn't struggle along without you another day?"

"Not exactly," Sammy said seriously. "My agent sold me to World-Wide on the strength of that story."

"And that's strength," I said. "How about Julian what's-his-name? Does he go too?"

"No," Sammy said simply, "World-Wide just wanted me."

"Well," I said, "our gain is World-Wide's loss."

"No more peanuts for me," Sammy said. "From now on it's two hundred and fifty bucks a week, starting a week from Wednesday."

Five guys whistled.

There was a short pause, during which time I composed a short history of Sammy Glick, complete from twelve to two hundred and fifty a week, analyzing it from the sociological, psychological, philosophical and zoological points of view. It was America, all the glory and the opportunity, the push and the speed, the grinding of gears and the crap. It didn't take nearly this long to think. It went zingo, just a look, a blank look.

"See you in the Brown Derby," Sammy was saying.

Then I got nostalgic, I was always a soft guy, so I said:

"Sure kid, and remember, don't say ain't."

That was too good for Sammy. He didn't like it. He was going to be one of those big shots who didn't like to be reminded. There seem to be two kinds of self-conscious self-made men, those who like to dwell on the patriotic details of their ascent from newsboy or shoe-shiner at two bucks and peanuts a week and those who take every new level as if it were the only one they ever knew, rushing ahead so fast they are ashamed, afraid to look back and see where they've come from. One is a bore and the other is a heel. Sammy may have had other faults, but he had never been a bore.

I watched Sammy walk out of the office that day, and then I stood at the window and watched his new shoes and his new hat cross the sidewalk and disappear into a taxi, and then I leaned out the window and watched the taxi go ducking in and out through traffic like a broken-field runner.

Like Sammy Glick, I thought, as I watched the cab at the next crossing jump out ahead of the car that should have had the right of way. There was a shrieking of brakes, a raw angry voice, and Sammy's cab was away, around the corner on two wheels, though I stayed at the window a long while staring after it.

CHAPTER 3

F

or months after that, whenever I thought of the way Sammy
Glick had blown in, over, and through our office, I was overcome.
I tried to flatter myself into thinking that mine was a moral
disgust, but of course it was much more than that, or would you
call it much less? Left in the draft of Sammy's speed I had caught
a bad case of jealousy. From here on I may be accused of having
the soul of a shopgirl, but I might as well admit it: Long before
Sammy Glick had been shot through my life like a bullet I had
had Hollywood on my mind. I had wanted to go for all the usual
reasons: I was anxious to investigate the persistent rumors that the
"streets paved with gold" which the early Spanish explorers had
hunted in vain had suddenly appeared in the vicinity of Holly-

wood and Vine. I was half convinced that Southern California was really the modern Garden of Eden its press agents claimed it to be. And like all the other writers outside of Hollywood I had seen enough of its product to convince myself that I could do no worse.

Of course I never mentioned this to anybody and, if it hadn't been for the unexpected whim of some Hollywood mogul, I would still be pounding a typewriter for the *Record*. I don't really know how it happened yet, for the only fiction writing I had managed to do was a story in the *Post* last year and another more recently in *Cosmo,* and neither of those would have set the world on fire, or Edward J. O'Brien either, for that matter. I guess one of the Monarch execs must have just got the idea of rounding up all the drama columnists in New York and when they pulled in the nets, there I was, floundering with the rest.

The day after the news broke that I had "surrendered to Hollywood" (though it certainly hadn't been much of a battle), a girl's voice came quavering over the telephone to me.

"Hello, Mister Manheim," she said, "I'm awfully sorry to bother you this way and you probably don't even remember me . . ."

"Who is this?" I said.

"Miss Goldbaum. Rosalie Goldbaum. You met me that night with Sammy Glick?"

It wasn't a question but there was a question mark at the end of her voice. It was a shrill voice, shrill but dead, like a high note on a cheap piccolo.

I had to tell her a lie, which was that I was glad to hear from her again.

She said thank you and then there was a pause. I thought she had hung up.

"Hello?"

"I'm still here," she said.

"Anything wrong?" I said. "Something the matter?"

"When I read you were going to Hollywood . . ." she started. "When I read that, I wondered . . ."

She must have been crying.

"I mean I've got to see you," she said.

Oh, Christ, I thought. "Meet me at the Tavern at seven," I said.

I got there fifteen or twenty minutes late because I stopped to have a couple of drinks to take the curse off my rendezvous. She didn't even know enough to find herself a table and wait for me. She was just sitting on a bench by the door. I hadn't realized that first time how scrawny she was. When she took her coat off, her shoulder blades stuck out. Her eyes were red and soggy. When I took her hand and said Gladtoseeyou, it was soft and rubbery, like a half-blown balloon.

Her eyes looked scared and she said too quickly, "Oh, it was awfully nice of you to come."

"We'd better get a table," I said, and we walked to it without saying anything more. I put my hand lightly at her elbow to guide her and our eyes searched each other's for a moment. There was something too intimate and uncomfortable between us.

"How've you been since I saw you last?" I said as we sat down. "You're looking swell."

It was stupid and it sounded flat so I let it go at that. I looked up at her and waited. It was her move.

She looked down at the menu a moment as if wondering whether to order first or plunge right into it.

"You're going to Hollywood," she told me. "You'll see Sammy Glick."

Queer how she could have been so close to him and yet always use his full name. As if it already had achieved the rounded significance of an F. Scott Fitzgerald or a Sinclair Lewis. Somehow I sensed I shouldn't wisecrack. So I compromised.

"I can," I said cagily.

"Will you, would you, Mr. Manheim, see him for me?"

"Sure," I said, "when I run into him, I'll tell him you said hello."

That was cruel, for I knew it was more than that. But it was the quickest way I knew of finding out.

"It's not that," she said. "I want to know how he is. I want to know . . ."

"But you must get all that in his letters," I broke in. "What more could I do?"

"Find out why he's stopped writing," she blurted out. "He used to write, once in a while, anyway, when he first went out. But not any more. He just won't answer any more. Not even a postcard in months and months."

She dried her leaking nose with her napkin.

"I know it's tough on you, Rosalie," I said, "but maybe it isn't as bad as you think. It's never a cinch to get set in a new spot. Why, he's probably up to his ears . . ."

Can you imagine, me defending the slob? But I never was much of an actor and it didn't sound convincing.

"But you don't understand, Mr. Manheim," she interrupted. "It was all arranged. He promised to send for me the second week he was out there. I was so sure I even quit my job. I got rid of everything I couldn't take along. I was all set. He told me not to worry, he'd send for me in a couple of weeks more. Until finally, he just stopped writing."

"Oh," I said, losing my appetite.

"He said the only reason we couldn't go together was he didn't have the train fare. He was going to send me his second week's salary."

Her head moved with her mouth in nervous little jerks. She was getting all excited again just remembering what he had told her.

"So now I don't know what to do," she said.

"Skunk," I said.

"Oh, you've got to tell him I don't understand," she said, hurrying to keep ahead of her tears. "Ask him why, please ask him why."

She was crying. The waiter was standing over us impatiently. It was embarrassing. "Want yours with onions?" I asked.

She blotted her eyes, her nose and her cheeks with her napkin. I don't know why she had to wear mascara. Maybe it made her feel better able to face things but she didn't have a face for mascara, and when it started to run she had the forlorn look of a doll with the paint streaking off in the rain.

"I shou'n't've come," she whimpered, "only Sammy was always telling me you were his closest friend."

I almost choked on a mouthful of steak. My God, that was probably true!

On the way out I slipped her twenty-five bucks. Just to salve my conscience for being considered a friend of a jerk like Sammy Glick. She sneaked it into her purse as quickly as possible, as if her hand was trying to put something over on the rest of her.

"Give me your address in Hollywood so I can pay you back when I find another job," she said.

"Forget it," I said, "you can pay me back next time you see me."

We shook hands and she held mine a moment as if dreading to break away even from the slim protection I represented, pressing my hand hard to keep from crying again. I looked after her as she turned down toward Broadway and the crowd swallowed her up. I couldn't help wondering what New York would do to her now that Sammy Glick had used her and thrown her away.

|||||||

All the way out on the train my mind still felt damp with Miss Goldbaum's tears. So as soon as I got set in Hollywood, or as set as a bewildered stranger ever gets in this town, I gave Sammy a buzz. He talked so loud I had to hold the receiver at arm's length. It was like a loudspeaker.

"Hello, chump," he yelled, "welcome to Los Angeles, the city of Lost Angels."

"What do you mean, *chump?*" I said, already resigned to the fact that time had not mellowed Mr. Glick.

"I was having a drink with your producer the other night," he said. "He was boasting about getting you for a hundred and fifty a week. Why the hell didn't you let me know you were coming? I could have fixed it for you."

I told him I thought I could manage to struggle along for a while on a hundred and fifty dollars a week.

"Jesus, Al," he laughed, "you know about as much about Hollywood . . ."

"As Rosalie Goldbaum," I said.

That would have stopped the average heel, but not a man who had a genius for it like Sammy.

"Listen, Al," he said, "I haven't got time to talk about that now. Why don't you run over here tomorrow around lunchtime?"

I said I would and he gave me that glad-hand business. "Okay, Alsie-palsie. Glad you're gonna be with us, keed."

I spent that afternoon and the next morning wandering around the studio that had employed me, trying to find out why. Then I hurried over for my audience with Little Caesar. I told myself at the time that I was only eager to see justice done by Miss Goldbaum, but there was a lot of curiosity mixed up in it too. Morbid curiosity. Like wanting to pull a bandage off to see an infection you know has spread.

There was his S A M M Y   G L I C K in gold metal lettering, screwed onto the door of his office with a certain permanence. Inside, I found that I had only gained admission to his secretary, who was occupying an office that seemed somewhat larger than our city room. I told her I was an old friend of Sammy's, which is what you would call a white lie, and she told me that Mr. Glick would be tied up in a story conference for the next half hour.

An hour and twenty minutes later Mr. Glick made his appearance. The first thing I noticed was that he wasn't wearing a tie. Instead he wore a big yellow scarf with horses racing around the edges, and a big yellow handkerchief to match, which dangled rakishly over the pocket of a sports coat you could have played checkers on. He reeked of toilet water. He was certainly a long way from the thin, pale, eager little kid who used to say, "Thank you, Mr. Manheim." At least superficially. He had one of those California tans. He had filled out a little, but he still looked fast on his feet.

We sat down in his office. On his walls were a couple of

autographed pictures of stars, and several of him, one playing tennis, and another playing genius on the set with the director and principals. He swung his feet up on his desk and I noticed his camel's-hair socks and tricky shoes, leather strips woven like a Mexican basket, with a space left for the toes to stick out.

"These are swell shoes for working," he said. "Lucky Hamilton, the director of my first picture, brought them back for me from Mexico City. The Greasers call them *huaraches.* I'm a sucker for shoes."

I never could get excited about clothes, so there didn't seem to be much to say. But you never have to worry about conversation with Sammy Glick around.

"Well, how's the chain gang back in the office?" he said. "Still working so hard they haven't got time to starve to death?"

"They all wanted to be remembered, Sammy," I said.

As if I actually believed that Sammy would ever remember anybody who couldn't do him some good.

"Great old gang," he said meaninglessly, and then, more himself: "But once you get the Indian sign on these producers out here the dough comes rolling in so fast you can use it for wall paper."

"Miss Goldbaum wants to be remembered too," I said.

Sammy stopped running for a moment. He looked at me, and I knew he was wondering how much I knew.

"I want to talk to you about that, Al," he said. "But how about grabbing a little lunchee first? Where do you want to go, the Derby, the Vendome, or Al Levy's? Those are the only restaurants in Hollywood."

He picked the Vendome because that's where everybody was going then.

We drove over in his yellow Cadillac roadster. I couldn't see how he could afford a car that big as soon as this.

"I couldn't," he explained. "I grabbed it up from a ham actor who bought it on the strength of a contract he was going to get. As soon as I heard that fell through, I beat it over to see him and showed him how it was cheaper for him to let me take the payments off his hands than for him just to give the car back to the dealers again. It's only gone sixteen hundred miles. Just saved me the trouble of breaking it in."

It was funny to see him taking the Vendome in stride too. He was on speaking terms with everybody, the parking attendant, the hatcheck girl who could have been a stand-in for Jean Harlow, the headwaiter who led us to a table from which he flourishingly removed that restaurant symbol of rank, the RESERVED sign.

The moment Sammy sat down he started looking around to see who was there. He waved to a bald, bulky middle-aged man across the way with a high-blood-pressure complexion.

"Didn't expect to see you up this early, Harry," Sammy yelled across.

"I still don't know whether I'm up or not," the man laughed back.

"That's Harold Godfrey Wilson," Sammy said proudly. "He's one of the top screen writers in the business. Twenty-five hundred a week. He threw a terrific party last night. Everybody had to come as their pet aversion."

"I could just have sent you."

Sammy reminded me of one of those willing club fighters who laugh when they get hit. "Same old Al," he grinned, "still trying to get a rise out of me."

A group of women came by, of all ages and sizes, but all dressed much the same, in chic dark dresses, fantastic hats, silver foxes and lots of jewels. Sammy leaped to his feet like a Boy Scout at the sound of the Star-Spangled Banner.

"That was Louella O. Parsons," he said when he sat down after exchanging a few pleasantries. "The first thing I did when I got to town was call her up and give her an item for her column. That's a good habit to get into because every couple of times you can slip her a story about yourself too. That's one of the main tricks in this town, to keep them reading about you."

I could see we had come to the wrong place to talk about Miss Goldbaum, but I finally managed to work her back into the conversation again, while Sammy was drinking his coffee with B & B.

"Well, how is she, Al?" he asked.

"Swell," I said, "just swell. High and dry."

"I couldn't help it," he said. "I'm sorry, Al. I swear to God."

He was still a kid in many ways. He sounded actually frightened. And the sad part of it was he was really telling the truth when he said he couldn't help it.

"The trouble with me is that I was too softhearted with Rosalie," Sammy said. "I never told her I was going to bring her out here. She just took it for granted and I didn't want to hurt her."

"That's your weakness all right," I said. "You're just killing her with kindness."

"What could I do with Rosalie out here?" he said. "Rosalie's one of those nice Jewish girls whose main idea in life is to stay home all the time and start having kids right away. And this is a town where you've got to keep circulating. She'd go nuts inside a month."

"As far as I'm concerned," I said, "she must have been nuts to be able to love you in the first place. But since she doesn't seem to take the same view of it I do, the least you could do is let her down easy with a nice letter and enough money to tide her over till she's on her feet again. Give the poor kid a break."

And then, for no reason at all, I added, "Give everybody a break."

I seemed to have tapped the tiny pool of Sammy's better nature. For, as I said, he was still a kid then. The crust hadn't completely hardened.

"How much would you send," he asked, "if you were me?"

"I shudder at the thought," I said, "but I'd give her every cent I could spare. After all, she quit her job to come out here."

"How would fifteen hundred do?" he asked.

I had the feeling that this was more a grandstand play for me than kindness toward Miss Goldbaum. I didn't see how he had that much money put away on his present salary and told him so.

"I've been playing casino with my producer Joe Rappaport," he said. "The drunker he gets the bigger he bets. He's a cinch for a couple of hundred every time we play."

Getting fifteen hundred dollars not to have to live the rest of your life with Sammy Glick was my idea of a bargain.

"O.K.," I said, "I'll write her that that fifteen hundred is on its way, just in case it slips your mind."

"I sprinkle rosin on my mind every morning," Sammy said. "Nothing ever slips up there."

The check arrived. I reached in my pocket to pay it, but the waiter had already handed Sammy a pencil and he signed it.

Then Sammy made one of those bumblebee exits, buzzing from table to table on his way out.

Driving back to the studio Sammy felt more expansive, now that he had disposed of the Goldbaum question.

"Got anything to work on yet?" Sammy asked.

"At the moment I'm very busy working on the producer's secretary," I said, "trying to convince her that it's his duty to call me in and let me know what I'm being paid for."

"As long as you have a six months' contract," Sammy said, "you can afford to warm your ass for a while. You don't have to start impressing them till around the fifth month."

"But I didn't come out here to sit on the bench all season," I said. "I want to learn everything I can about screen technique."

"Screen technique is a pushover," Sammy said. "All you've got to do is read a couple of good scripts. I'll let you read mine. Then you can compare it with the finished product. It's being cut and scored now. They'll be previewing in two or three weeks."

"You mean *Girl Steals Boy?*" I said. "All finished already?"

"Already?" Sammy said. "They'll be shooting my next one in a couple of weeks. When they really make you start writing out here they don't fool. I had to do my last one in three and a half weeks. One day I even dictated twenty-seven pages of screenplay. What I always say is, writing either comes easy to you or it doesn't."

"That reminds me," I said, "what ever became of Julian Blumberg?"

"Oh, he's around," Sammy said casually. "Drove out in an old heap four or five months ago. I've been trying to get him a job. But it's pretty tough because the studios aren't hiring junior writers in mass lots the way they did a year ago."

"What are junior writers?" I wanted to know.

"Well," Sammy said, "nobody's exactly sure, but I'd say they're writers who aren't given anything to write, and if they do write something of their own they can't find anybody to read it."

By this time we had reached his studio. "I would drive you back to Monarch," he said, "but I'm working on a football story and I'm running a couple of college pictures in the projection room this afternoon. Just to make sure it isn't too similar."

"Which I suppose is a polite way of saying you're looking for something you can lift," I said.

He seemed actually pleased that I saw through his feeble euphemism. He grinned. "You'll be all right out here," he said. "You learn fast."

That was one thing you had to give Sammy. He made no bones about it. At least with me. He was glorifying the American rat.

He put his arm around my neck intimately as we got out of the car. "Here's a hot one Lombard told me," he said, and he giggled it into my ear.

"I heard that three weeks ago at Bleeck's," I told him.

But he was impregnable. He took it with his own peculiar brand of *joie de vivre*. I found myself realizing that he had cut a lot of warts off his personality since I had seen him last. He was in the first grade of the charm school. I wouldn't be surprised if there were a great many people out here who actually thought he had it already. People who didn't know him very well. That is, people he hadn't got around to using yet.

"Well, keep in touch with me, Al," he said. "Call me and we'll make a night of it sometime."

Being a timid soul unless I'm cornered, which is what I was most of the time with Sammy, I didn't bother to point out that it might be his place to call me. I just said, "Thanks for the lunch, Sammy," or something equally useless and then I watched him hurry across the street and up the studio steps. His form was smoother and his stride wasn't as jerky as it was in the old days on the *Record,* but he was still running all right. And from the way he was hugging the rail it looked as if Hollywood was the perfect track for him. I was always a man of simple ambitions, but one of them was to be around when Sammy crossed the finish line, wherever that would be.

When I got back to my cubbyhole of an office, I shoved down the window to keep out the sound of the machine shop across the way, plunked my feet on the desk and pondered what kind of a world it was which could give Sammy a reputation on the basis of one story he hadn't written, while its real author couldn't even get himself hired as a junior writer.

I was still pondering two hours later when the secretary of the producer I was still trying to see called to say that I might as well not wait any longer this afternoon as he was tied up in a story conference. Out of sheer desperation I asked her if there wasn't anything else a person could be in a story conference besides *tied* up, but she didn't even chuckle. So then I sat down and wrote a very businesslike letter to Miss Rosalie Goldbaum advising her to forget Sammy Glick but not to forget to write me whether she got that fifteen hundred or not. I told her to find herself a good clean hardworking boy and not to pine for Sammy, for he was one of those geniuses who could only be married to his work. I just marked that down under the heading of kindness, then. That was because I didn't know as much about Sammy Glick then as I do now, or about the world either. It was funny as time went on how the more I learned about one the more I understood about the other.

Those first few months in Hollywood were the loneliest I've ever known. You'd think a writer on contract to one of the biggest studios in Hollywood would be thrown into that merry-go-round of social life the fan magazines and the columns like to tell you about. Unless you have an unusual talent for knowing everybody, it isn't so. It seemed as if the few friends I knew in Hollywood from the theater crowd had all gone back to the land, to Bucks

County or Cape Cod or one of those places. After a couple of weeks I moved out of the Hollywood Plaza into a big, pink, reasonably priced apartment house called the Villa Espana. I spent desperate and lonely hours in my office at the studio mulling over the story they had finally given me to read, an action melo-drama about smugglers, come-on girls and the coast of Florida. I knew that Sammy Glick would have thrown it back in their faces and demanded something more in keeping with his artistic tem-perament, but I supposed the producers knew their business and, as it turned out, this story did have the makings of a fair C picture. But it was dismal, ditch-digging work, and I felt more alone than ever because the producer didn't even seem to care how I was doing. The only word I had for weeks and weeks was the pro-ducer's request, via interoffice communication, to keep turning in pages.

At night I usually had supper at the Vine Street Derby, always hoping to run into someone I knew, and then I'd stroll down Hollywood Boulevard, stopping in at one of the joints for a drink, or browsing around in Stanley Rose's bookstore listening to the conversation, or maybe dropping in at a movie. After a while I felt as if I were wandering around a small town, because there never seemed to be anything to do and I began to notice the same faces drifting by night after night.

The only friend I made in those early days was an unknown playwright who had the office two doors down from mine. He told me he had come out to Hollywood about a year ago because the doctor had told him his four-year-old daughter's sinus trouble was going to get serious if he didn't get her out to a warm, dry climate. When I met him he was just beginning to get jittery because his option was coming up in a couple of weeks and he didn't seem to think he could get a job anywhere else if they let him out. He said the reason he was scared was because he hadn't any credits. Anybody who goes a year in Hollywood without getting a single screen credit, he said, might just as well shop around for another profession.

I asked him how it happened that none of his pictures had

reached the screen, and he explained that the first script he wrote had been shelved because at the last minute they couldn't get the actor it had been written for, and the second one never reached first base because it was a topical subject and one of the other studios beat them to it, and the third one was stymied because it couldn't get by the Hays Office. I didn't see why that should hurt him if the producers had liked his scripts, but he took a more pessimistic view of it. He said by the time a year had gone by, all they would probably remember is that he had worked twelve months without getting anything on the screen and that would be the pay-off.

I tried to cheer him up, even took him and his young wife out to dinner one night, but when I came to my office the following Monday morning he was gone. He left a note for me saying the worst had happened, and that I had taken some of the curse off those last few weeks and that he was driving back to New York to see if he couldn't get an advance on a new play he had started. A couple of years later I saw one of his plays that the Federal Theater was doing in Los Angeles, but I've never seen him again. It's queer to think how many little guys there are like that, with more ability than push, sucked in by one wave and hurled out by the next, for every Sammy Glick who slips through and over the waves like a porpoise.

After he left, I tried to think if there was anyone else in town I knew, and I suddenly remembered Henry Powell Turner, the poet, who had been a senior when I was a freshman at Wesleyan. I remembered how excited we all were at school when we heard that the book-length poem on the history of New England which he had read to the Literary Society while he was still in college had been awarded the Pulitzer Prize. I had met Henry again on his way out to Hollywood several years ago and he had told me, by way of making conversation, to be sure and look him up if I was ever out that way.

The operator told me that Mr. Turner had a confidential number, so I finally wired him at his studio and asked him to call me. I didn't hear from him until several weeks later when I picked up the phone to hear a cultured woman's voice say, "This is Mr. Henry Powell Turner's secretary. Mr. and Mrs. Turner would like to have the pleasure of your company at dinner at seven-thirty this Wednesday evening."

What I remember most about the Turner manse was that it was a five-dollar taxi ride from the Villa Espana, that you could see the Pacific Ocean from its front lawn, and that it was the largest example of the worst kind of architecture I have ever seen. Hollywood Moorish.

I had always thought of Henry Powell Turner as my ideal of what a great poet should look like. I could remember him as a student, built along heroic proportions, six feet three and over two hundred pounds, with blond curly hair and the kind of chiseled, classical good looks that always remind me of the way epic Greek poets looked—or ought to have looked. And even when I had seen Turner last, four or five years ago, he was still a romantic figure to me, erect and hearty as ever, with his wild yellow hair turning a more dignified gray at the temples.

When I saw him again this time, in that huge, cold living room, with the expensive furniture and the high ceiling, there were only a few strands left of the old youthful yellow among the thinning, straightening gray, but he was hardly more dignified because he was already well on his way toward the state of drooling intoxication which I later discovered he managed to achieve with monotonous regularity each evening.

I met his wife, a gaunt, high-strung woman, prematurely gray, with a boyish figure in low-cut red velvet. They asked me the usual polite questions during cocktails, and conversation died once or twice at dinner, though Turner and I did our best to squeeze the most out of our common interest in Wesleyan. That's about all I remember about that dinner, except that it was served with an irritating pomp, and that Turner shattered whatever illusions I had left about him by telling one of those long dirty stories for which the only justification would be the tag line at the climax, which they never seem to reach. At the finish he laughed so loud that he finally broke into a coughing fit which he managed to soothe with loud gulps of sparkling burgundy.

When we rose from the table, his wife, ghostlike all through dinner, finally disappeared, and I found myself cooped up with him and several bottles of Bellows Scotch in his imposing study. I spent the next three or four uncomfortable hours in trying to follow him through his various stages of drunkenness. In the first, he recited some of his lyrical poetry. In the second, he mocked his own poems with dirty limericks composed extemporaneously, "which," he laughingly informed me three or four times, "I have seen fit to create in line of my duties as Hollywood's Poet Laureate." In the next he reviewed his chief conquests of the current season with a glint that brought me back to the lurid tales we used to swap in our adolescence. And of course he reached the final stage full of teary nostalgia for the glories of his youth and eloquent resolutions to return to New England and his Muse, "as soon as I finish the MacDonald-Eddy script I have to do when I get back from my vacation."

I finally managed to escape around one in the morning, after we had topped off the evening by killing the second bottle of Scotch and singing a Wesleyan song. I must have been more upset than I realized when I left there, because by the time I reached my room and started to undress, the vision of Henry Powell Turner before and after was still with me. Only now what I had taken merely for boredom or disgust came into sharper focus as I began to be stunned by the horror and sense of mental nausea most of us feel when we're forced into ringside seats for great personal tragedies.

So I buttoned my shirt again, put my tie back on and called a cab. For I had decided that the only way to forget the wreck of my epic poet was to make an evening of it. I asked the cab driver where a man could get a drink and a couple of laughs at an hour like this and he drove me to the Back Lot Club.

You have to stay up till two o'clock to realize what a small town Hollywood is. It goes to sleep at twelve o'clock like any decent

Middle Western village. The gay nightlife you dream about there is confined to private houses and the handful of hotspots which enjoy special privileges for which they are taxed in a very special way. At least that's the way it was when I first went out there before Judge Bowron and his reformers had won the Battle of Los Angeles and began to fumigate the City Hall.

The Back Lot was a noisy, gaudy example of what most people seem to imagine all Hollywood is after dark. But except for an occasional celebrated face, it might have been any night spot in any American city. It was a montage of hot music, drunken laughter, loud wisecracks and hostesses like lollypops in red, green and yellow wrappers. The music took the old sweet melodies and twisted them like hairpins. It was a symphony strictly from hunger, to which everybody beat their feet in a frenzy of despair, trying to forget luck that was either too good or too bad, festered ambitions or hollow success. It made me realize again how true jazz music was, how it echoed everything that was churning inside us, all the crazy longings raw and writhing.

I had a few drinks while I looked the place over, and then a few more while my angle narrowed from a full shot of the crowd, to a group shot of the ladies who floated through the semidarkness on the loose, to a close-up of one particular hostess, large, but well-proportioned inside her tight satin evening gown, with a reddish glint to her hair combed strikingly back from her face and falling gracefully to her bare shoulders, where it emphasized the creamy whiteness of her skin. I watched her hips slip up and down as she moved among the tables and it wasn't until she lingered at one of them to chat with a little blonde co-worker that I realized who the little blonde's escort was. Sammy Glick.

It was one of those moments when I would have greeted the devil as a long-lost brother if he had only been willing to sit down and have a drink with me. And, in the mood I was in, the redhead was something of an attraction too. It didn't make sense, but my friends have always considered me a disgustingly normal person, and it was normal if unprincipled to get the idea that Sammy might be able to supply the kind of good time I was looking for.

Sammy had been doing a lot of drinking but he wasn't drunk. That didn't surprise me, for it was hard to imagine him ever letting his defenses down long enough really to lose control. As soon as he spotted me he leaped up, yelling, "Well, if it isn't little Alsie-palsie," and threw his arms around me. It was strange to think that Sammy probably liked me as much as he could like anybody in the world. I think that was because anybody who took life the way Sammy did, gangster, dictator or screenwriter, was doomed to be lonely, and even though Sammy knew I could read him like the top line of an optometrist's chart, he also knew that he could relax with me because I wasn't willing or didn't know how to use him for a ladder the way he used me. And at moments like these when he slowed down to a trot I sensed a flash, just the tiniest sparkle of appreciation for the way he had climbed on my shoulders to leap over the wall, and a hint or two of the old respect that he felt in those early days on the *Record* when I was still trying to teach him not to say ain't.

"Al," he said, "this is one of those lost angels I was telling you about, Sally Ann Joyce."

He put his arm possessively around the little blonde and grinned at her. She took this as her cue to laugh. She seemed too young to look so tired around the eyes.

"Honey," he said, "I want you to meet one of the sweetest guys in the world. Al Manheim.

"And last but never least, you can see for yourself," Sammy said, indicating the redhead, "is Billie. I don't think I know your last name, honey."

"Rand," Billie said, moistening her large lips and trying to look pleased about the whole thing, "Billie Rand."

"Rand," Sammy laughed, "the name is familiar, but I can't quite place the body. But I bet you can guess where I'd like to place it."

Sammy led the laughter, which they joined automatically. I pushed Billie's chair in for her and as she looked up over her shoulder to smile into my face she didn't seem to mind my staring down her dress.

"What are you trying to do, Al," Sammy said, "give us an imitation of a tourist at the edge of Grand Canyon?"

Sally Ann and Billie giggled dutifully again, though I wasn't sure whether they thought it was that funny or not. We drank a couple more rounds, while Sammy told the girls what pals we had been in New York, and it was funny to see how he could carry himself away with his own salesmanship. By the time he was through he made it sound as if the only reason I had come to Hollywood was to be near him.

"Maybe you boys want to be alone," Billie said, knowing that was always good for a laugh.

It was, but of course Sammy managed to top it.

"Don't give up, girls," he said. "Haven't you heard we're ambi-sextrous?"

The last time the waiter set our drinks up again he told us the bar was closing in ten minutes.

Sammy pushed the table away rudely. "Let's get out of this hellhole," he said. "You're all coming up to my apartment." He took one girl under each arm, calling to the boss on the way out: "Don't worry about your girls, Pop—I'll see that they get to bed early."

The boss gave a fake laugh and tried to make his voice sound as friendly as possible, "Glad you came in, Mr. Glick. Come back again."

I was feeling pretty woozy from all that liquor and the smoke, but I remember wondering as I hit the open air how many people in this world would tell Sammy they were glad he had come—in that same tone of voice.

Sammy's apartment was in the fashionable Colonial House just off the Sunset Strip. The names of the tenants underneath the mail boxes at the entrance read like a list of Hollywood's most eligible bachelors.

Sammy's place was one of the smallest in the building and even that must have been way beyond his means for those early days, but he wrote off only part of the expense to shelter, the rest to prestige.

The apartment was furnished with an elegance that didn't seem to fit Sammy, at least not yet, with a bedroom that opened off a long living room with a fireplace at one end. Sammy brought out Courvoisier. I wondered where he picked up all those little tricks, and then Billie and I started playing records and doing a little slow dancing, while Sammy and Sally Ann took over the big couch.

As we danced, hardly moving together, I heard the sound and silence of held kisses, several shrill, half-giggled *Sammy, don'ts!* and then Sammy started giving her the business about putting her in the movies. It was hardly more than kidding, and Sally Ann knew it, but you could tell from the way she kidded back how much that meant to her. It was all so naked that I wished I were drunker or not there. It was no secret to anybody that she was working out on him and he was working out on her, each one wanting something and not quite admitting it. Some people call that the Hollywood tug of war, though that concept is a little narrow. Hollywood may be one of its most blatant battlegrounds, but it is really a world war, undeclared.

There was a long silence while we made a gesture at dancing and then Sammy and Sally Ann started for the bedroom with their arms around each other. They could have slipped out with us only half-noticing them, but Sammy could no more do things by halves than J. P. Morgan could run for president on the Communist ticket.

"If anybody asks for me," he cracked at the door, "tell them I'm tied up in a conference."

Billie started to laugh, but it was just force of habit, and I didn't crack a smile, so he must have thought he wasn't being funny enough and tried again.

"Well, be good, Al," he said, "and if you can't be good, be careful, and if you can't be careful, see that it gets a good agent."

Then we were left alone and I suddenly felt very lousy. Maybe I'm a Puritan, but there has to be somewhere you draw the line and this was always it for me. I have always been one of those who held that whatever sex may have been to our primitive ancestors, it has become an experience for us that at least deserves the same privacy we give to taking a bath. Sinking to the couch with Billie, I remembered a similar revulsion years ago when I walked into a college fraternity the morning after an all-night house party and found half a dozen drunken cards cheering and egging on a preoccupied couple on the living-room sofa.

"What are you thinking about, honey?" Billie stage-whispered, though she could never be the quiet, seductive type. She and this whole set-up were about as subtle as Wallace Beery's acting.

I wasn't exactly surprised to find that Sammy approached the most elemental emotion in life with all the sensitivity of a slaughterhouse worker slitting a steer's throat, but somehow that last crack at the bedroom door had sliced too close to the bone, and it wasn't very pretty. With one razor-edge phrase he had cut me down to his level, and it was going to take me some time to rise again.

But one thing you had to say for Billie, she was very kind in her way and always patient.

|||||||

I felt as if I had just closed my eyes when a sense of motion in the room opened them again. Through sticky eyes with the eyeballs burning holes in the lids, my host slowly came into focus, dressed for the day and apparently on his way out. As I sat up and started to rub some of the sleep out of my eyes, I could see that Sammy was all washed and shaved and looking irritatingly fresh. My face felt like an old shoe that had been left out all night in the rain, shrunk and stiff in some parts, swollen and mushy in others. But Sammy's face looked fresh from the laundry.

I looked around at the half-empty glasses, the cigarette butts and the other desolate remains, and asked, yawning, "What time is it?"

"Eight-thirty," Sammy said.

"Eight-thirty?" My stomach went roller-coasting down. "What the hell you doing up at eight-thirty?"

"I have a date for breakfast," Sammy said.

"Not . . ." I began.

"No," Sammy said. "That was last night. This is business."

Then I realized only Sammy and I were left.

"Where are the girls?" I said. "In the other . . . ?"

"I got them out of here around five," Sammy said. "While you were passed out. I don't like to see them when I get up. They get in my hair."

"But eight-thirty!" I mumbled. "What's doing at the studio at eight-thirty?"

"I'm picking up a friend for breakfast before I check in," Sammy said. "As a matter of fact you know him. Julie Blumberg."

"Blumberg," I muttered. "Oh—Julian . . . ?"

"He's been trying to write some originals," Sammy said, "so I thought I ought to help the poor kid out and take a look at them."

I was too groggy to see anything wrong with that picture so I just let it pass. Sammy advised me to call the studio and say I was sick and then climb into his bed for the rest of the day. He was being kind, but even in my condition I could sense the way he was gloating over his superior powers of recuperation. He made me think of some horrible grinning robot.

"You did all right for yourself," he said. "I'll buzz you next week and we'll do a repeat."

Then he looked at his watch, saw he was late, cursed his dawdling and was off on a run.

So there I was, spending the day, of all places, in Sammy Glick's bed. When I woke again around four I had a bad taste in my mouth and a worse one in my mind and all I thought about was getting out of there as quickly as possible.

I went straight from Sammy's to a Turkish bath, where I abandoned myself to steam and sweat and where I had nothing to do for hours but stare at the ceiling and dwell upon the discovery that Sammy Glick at work was hardly more terrifying than Sammy Glick at play.

CHAPTER 4

I suppose it's too bad that people can't be a little more consistent. But if they were, maybe they would stop being people. They might become characters in epic tragedies or Hollywood movies. Most of our characters on the screen are sandwich men for different moral attitudes. We will have the young man who stands for Honest Government and Public Service while his brother is a low-down Wallower in Wine, Women and Corruption. In the last reel the good brother has to be killed off so the bad brother can be regenerated. Regenerated. That is one of Hollywood's favorite words. This may be heresy, but I have yet to meet anybody who ever got himself Regenerated. I don't see any one-hundred-percent-pure heroes running around loose either. All people seem to do is the best they can to get along and have a good time; and if that means keeping what they've got, they're liable to become fascists; and if it means trying to get what they need and don't have, there's a good chance of their learning the *Internationale*.

If I were trying to tell this as a picture story instead of just putting it down the way it happened, my hate for Sammy Glick would have to be exalted into something noble and conclusive. I mean if he passed me on the street I would have to cross over to the other side and sooner or later we would come to grips, probably on the edge of a cliff. But that doesn't seem to be the way we're made. Most of us are ready to greet our worst enemies like long-lost brothers if we think they can show us a good time, if we think they can do us any good or if we even reach the conclusion that being polite will get us just as far and help us live longer.

I'm afraid all this is just an apology for admitting that the next time Sammy called me, a couple of weeks after that first soirée, I didn't hang up on him. In fact, I didn't even refuse his invitation. And without that slackening of moral fiber I would never have had an excuse for knowing him better. For there was no use kidding myself any longer. I wanted to know him. Not that I ever expected to solve the mystery of What Makes Sammy Run. But I had been much too involved with Sammy already ever to be able to forget him. Or even want to. He rankled. He was like a splinter festering under my skin. If I broke off now, I had the feeling his memory would go on torturing me. I had the crazy feeling that only by drilling into him, deeper and deeper, could I finally pass through him and beyond him and free my mind of him at last.

Or maybe all I am trying to say is that he was slowly driving me nuts.

"Hiya, sweetheart," he said, "don't you love me any more?"

"As much as ever," I said.

"How's tricks over at that sausage factory of yours?"

He always made you feel that any confession of failure was on a level with admitting that you had a yen for nothing but female dogs and ten-year-old corpses. So all I gave him was a cagey "Okay, I guess."

"You guess! Don't talk like a schlemiel, you schlemiel. Sounds like you're letting them push you around."

"Being pushed around can be quite a luxury," I said. "At Atlantic City you have to pay for it."

"Don't worry," he said, "you'll pay for it here too. Remind me to give you a couple of pointers on How to Win Friends and Influence Producers when I see you tonight."

"Tonight I am going to get into bed and read," I said.

"Listen, dope, there's only two things bed is good for. And one of them isn't reading."

I told him to try me some other time as I was already half undressed. As a matter of fact I did have my tie and shoes off.

"If you're half undressed that means you're also half-dressed, right?" he said. "So get those gunboats out of dry dock and get the hell over here. We're unpacking and deflowering a new crate of virgins that just came in. I told Billie we might look in on her later too."

I felt the knot which held me to the bedpost slipping a little bit. I had come to admire Billie considerably.

"Not tonight, Sammy," I said. "I'm right in the middle of a book."

He had to know what book and I told him. "*Fontamara.* By Ignazio Silone."

"Who the hell is Ignats Silone?" he said.

"For my dough one of the greatest writers in the world," I said.

"No kidding!" He was interested. "Has he got a good story?"

"One of the greatest stories I ever read," I said. "All about how a ragged little group of peasants rise against Mussolini."

"Well, for Chri'sake, who do you think's gonna make a picture about a lot of starving wops? In the first place, you'd lose your whole foreign market and . . ."

As soon as I could get a word in I told him I knew it didn't have a chance for pictures.

"I don't know why the hell I waste my time with a crazy bastard like you," he said. "You're shell-shocked, you don't add up. What good do you think it's gonna do you to crap around with stuff like that?"

Very much on the defensive, I admitted that I liked to read.

"Sure," Sammy said, "I never said I had anything against reading books . . ."

"The publishers will be relieved to know that," I tried to insert, but Sammy was too quick for me and was already rounding the bend of his next sentence.

"But as long as you're going in for it there's plenty of good, dead authors that'll hand you terrific picture plots on a silver platter. Why, I knew a guy who made a nice little pile out of one of De Maupassant's stories just the other day. And all he had to do was switch the hooker from a French carriage to a Western stagecoach. If you were smart you'd try to hit on something like that and write yourself an original."

I found myself thinking that wherever De Maupassant was I hoped he was unaware of what was going on. He had too little faith in mankind as it was.

"Hello, where the hell are you?" Sammy was saying. "Have you hung up?"

"No," I said, "but only because I have no conscience."

"That's what you get for being a rabbi's son," he said, "a conscience. Going through life with a conscience is like driving your car with the brakes on."

I'm not sure why I switched and said I'd come. It might have been the lousy day I had had at the studio. My producer had thrown out my first script and put another writer on with me. His name was George Pancake. I hate to sound obvious, but Pancake couldn't have been over five foot five and looked as if he shaded two hundred pounds. He had the body of a wrestler and the face of a fag. The boys in the office across the hall told me Pancake was a credit hound, one of those writers who practically have convulsions over sole screen credits, so I knew I was in for trouble. The first thing Pancake said when we started talking it over was that he thought it would go faster if he did all the writing, as I obviously hadn't caught on to what producers want. Then he started dictating a new line as fast as he could talk and it suddenly hit me that he wasn't just coming on the story at all. He must have been working on it for weeks without my knowing it. When that dawned I felt so low I knocked off early, went home and called a masseur. There is something about a massage that makes it a better gloom-chaser for me than getting plastered. But it didn't quite sweat the mood out of me and just as I was about to climb into bed with my rebellious peasants and my blues I had a notion that a little of Billie and Sammy Glick might not be such a bad idea, if only to get my mind off my own *tsurus.*

I sat at Sammy's little bar a few minutes, while he stood behind it making drinks and telling me what a riot his next picture was turning out to be. When the doorbell rang I started to answer it, but Sammy told me to sit still and let his Jap get it.

"My Jap's in the kitchen going crazy carving cheese into flowers," he explained. "I think he's a fugitive from the WPA Artists' Project."

We heard the door open and a woman's voice say, "Hello, Naga."

"This," Sammy said mysteriously, indicating the door, "is the most terrific thing I ever met."

I looked up as Sammy turned to meet her. She came toward us with a mannish, swinging stride, like a good woman golfer following her ball, hatless, coatless, not even carrying a bag, with both hands thrust deep into the pockets of a smartly tailored suit.

Sammy went for her with open arms, rocking back and forth as he hugged her, half kidding, half on the level. I stood on the sidelines, conscious that I was seeing a new kinetic element in the life of Sammy Glick. This was no faithful poodle like Rosalie Goldbaum or a cute little doll like Sally Ann Joyce. She was arresting, but no beauty, at least not stamped from the Hollywood mold. She looked the type that always gets picked to play the leading man in girls' school productions. She was in her middle twenties, tall, maybe five-eight, and neatly put together though there was something about the masculinity of her carriage and gestures that scared you off. Her skin was tanned and seemed to have been pulled too tight across her face, revealing the bone structure. Her lips seemed even fuller than they were in her lean face. She left her eyebrows pretty much alone and I noticed that her nails were cut short and unpainted. She might have done things with her hair, which was walnut brown, but she just combed it back into a thick coil.

"Hope I haven't kept you waiting," she said. "I spend my entire day trying to duck my producer and then I have to meet him in the hall on my way out. Ever try putting over a story you know is falling apart as you go along? Great way to lose weight."

Her voice was low-keyed but not husky, and her words raced ahead of each other as if hurrying to keep up with a mind that was always crowding them.

She maneuvered neatly out of Sammy's embrace and turned to me. "My name's Sargent."

Her eyes were dark and restless, with large shiny pupils that made me nervous. She extended her hand, and when I took it I wasn't surprised to find her grip intimidating.

"Kit," Sammy said, "I want you to meet one of the sweetest guys in the world, Al Manheim. Al, this is Kit Sargent, my favorite screen writer."

He put his arm around her shoulder. It wasn't quite long enough to make the gesture look graceful.

"Kit is doing the next Gable-Loy."

There was almost as much pride in his voice as if he had the assignment himself.

"Oh, you're Catherine Sargent!"

I felt like Merton-of-the-Movies blurting it out that way, but I suddenly realized this was the gal all the critics were nominating a couple of years back to write the great American novel. I could still remember that first book of hers, *The Sex Express*, which penetrates the mind of a flapper after her day is done and the depression has set in, when she's floundering in a backwash of neuroticism and mental disease. I also remembered the author's photo on the jacket, a picture that made her look a little more elegant than she looked now but which caught nicely her cool smile. Under it was a blurb by Dorothy Parker which ran something like: "Miss Sargent, fresh from Vassar, takes us on a fascinating and frightening journey . . ."

I told her how her book had hit me.

"I'm glad you thought so," she said.

I suppose that was modesty, but it made me feel like a dope. All she had to do to make me feel that way was just stand there and smile through me. Because we really haven't learned to take female superiority in stride, I resented it.

"Her book must have been all right," Sammy said. "It sold twenty thousand copies and got her a sweet five-year ticket."

"How did you like it, Sammy?" I asked.

"What I read of it was terrific," he said, "but I couldn't get through the first chapter. Let's get out of here. Let's go over to the Back Lot and make like crazy."

His humor hadn't improved but he was beginning to develop a surefire delivery, with some of the knack of the fast-talking comics. I laughed and he was encouraged.

"We're going to find Billie and have like a bacchanale." The way he pronounced it, it rhymed with ukulele.

We got into his yellow Cadillac. Sammy raced the car too fast in first and threw it into second with naive abandon.

"I can go sixty in second," he said.

He only reminded you once in a while that he was in his early twenties. It was frightening to think what he would be like when he really grew up.

When we reached the Back Lot the band was beating it out and the music came at us like a Santa Ana wind.

"Will this be all right, Mr. Glick?" asked the headwaiter, showing a lot of teeth in what was supposed to be a smile.

"No," Sammy said, "I want that one over there."

He pointed to a table practically in the middle of the dance floor, with a RESERVED sign you couldn't miss.

"I'm very sorry, that one is reserved, Mr. Glick."

"Balls," Sammy commented.

"Really, Mr. Glick, you know if I could . . ."

"Balls, you just hang those signs out to try to give the joint a little class."

Kit started for the ladies' room. "Let me know how it comes out," she paraphrased. "I'll be in Number Three."

People were beginning to look around. I tried to act as if I weren't with Sammy, for I hate headwaiter scenes.

"If I don't get that table," I heard Sammy say, "you'll never get me in here again."

I could imagine what the headwaiter would like to have told him. But we got the table.

We sat there without anyone taking our order for a minute or two and then Sammy looked around and yelled, "Hey, waiter, gasson, what do you have to do to get a menu in this place—send in your agent?"

The waiter hurried over, grinning as if he loved being beckoned that way.

"Never talk to waiters like that," Kit said.

"Can I help it," he said, "if I only went one year to finishing school?"

"It isn't manners," she said like a sensible schoolteacher quietly disciplining a small boy, "it just isn't smart."

I thought of the time I first told him not to say ain't. He took this the same way, a little peeved but making mental notes. I noticed he was never too much of an egotist to take criticism when he knew it would help. It was part of his genius for self-propulsion. I was beginning to see what Kit had for Sammy. Of course she stood for something never within his reach before. But it was more than that. Sammy seemed to know that his career was entering a new cycle where polish paid off. You could almost see him filing off the rough edges against the sharp blade of her mind.

"I want a Scotch and soda," said Sammy. "And don't bother sticking your thumb . . ."

He caught himself and made a nice recovery. "Have you two made up your minds?"

I said Scotch and soda too.

Kit said Scotch and water.

The waiter had only taken a couple of steps when Sammy called him back. "St. James, if you have it," he said.

He tried to make it casual, but he couldn't quite get away with it and I knew he must have picked that up since our last outing.

The band broke into a rhumba. Sammy rose and reached out his hand for Kit.

"I feel like dancing," he said with a cigar in his mouth.

"You don't know how to rhumba," she said.

"I can do as good as the rest of these jerks," he said, and his voice carried.

"I hate a bad rhumba," she said. "There's something about a bad rhumba that's indecent."

"What do you think the rhumba is," Sammy said, "a spring dance?"

As he pulled her to her feet, not roughly but forcefully, he noticed a swarthy, sideburned Latin who was dancing under the impression that he was Veloz. "That guy looks like a leading man in a dirty picture," he laughed. Then he broke into song, singing through his teeth and his cigar, with an exaggerated Jewish accent. "I'm a Letin from Menhettin . . ."

"Now look," she said, "either dance with me—or the cigar."

Sammy was a crude dancer, but he wasn't like so many bad dancers who can't make up their minds. Because he wasn't self-conscious about it and forced her to follow all his mistakes, he got away with it. It wasn't exactly a thing of beauty, but you had to hand it to him, he had a sense of rhythm. Back in the New York office if anybody had told me that three years later I would be sitting in a Hollywood night club watching my copy boy dance the rhumba with one of those Vassar smarty-pants I would have called the Bellevue psychopathic ward to come down and take him away. But now that I was actually at a ringside table watching it happen, I couldn't make myself feel too surprised. He had about as much interest in dancing the rhumba as he had in writing. But I had begun to take for granted his ability to do everything just well enough so it wouldn't break his stride.

She was dancing under wraps but looked as though she really enjoyed it, even with Sammy. But not he. He looked desperate and busy. He was working at it, he was working at having fun. Recreation never seemed to come naturally to him. In fact the only activity that did seemed to be that damned running. I don't think he ever drank because he liked the taste of whiskey or frequented the Back Lot through any craving for hot music. He just went through the motions of relaxing because he was quick to discover and imitate how gentlemen of his rank were supposed to spend their leisure. It wouldn't have surprised me if this even extended to sex. He seemed to be a lusty little animal, but I think if Zanuck offered to give up his job to Sammy on the condition that Sammy never touch a woman again our hero would have gone impotent before you could say general-manager-in-charge-of-production.

The waiter set our drinks up again. They went on dancing. I kept an eye on Billie doing a little drink promoting at the bar. They came back to the table because the floor was getting too crowded, and the waiter went for another round.

Kit fixed a cigarette to her long holder and eyed the dance crowd with frowning amusement.

"Kirstein says the way people dance with each other is the real barometer of any country's society," she said. "Just look at ours—no more group spirit—every man for himself, covered with sweat and trying to push all the other couples off the floor."

Trying to follow her and watch Sammy at the same time was distracting. I noticed that Sammy hadn't been listening. He was preoccupied with somebody on the other side of the room.

She turned her head for an instant, caught on and gave him a patient smile. "Go ahead," she said, "go over and see him, you're practically over there anyway."

Her voice was that of a mother trying to practice child psychology on a delinquent child.

He rose, thrusting his cigar through his lips, and there was something pugnacious about the way he clenched it between his teeth in the corner of his mouth. It stuck out in front of him like a cannon leveled at the world.

"I'll try to get him over for a drink," he said.

He didn't circle the dance floor to reach the other side. He walked straight across it, pushing his way through the dancers.

"Who's he sucking around now?" I said.

"A good-natured lush called Franklin Collier," she said. "He was married to one of the big silent stars, I forget-her-name. When she got tired of him she packed him off to Iceland to make a picture. He surprised her and everybody else in town by not only coming back alive but bringing *Pengi* with him."

Pengi was the epic that was so beautifully acted by a cast of penguins, one of the sensations of the twenties.

"Is Collier a good . . ."

She had the disturbing habit of beginning to answer your questions before you had finished asking them.

"He's always had a flair for outdoor pictures," she said. "He's sort of a one-man Last Frontier. But when it comes to stories, I don't think he knows his ass from a hole-in-the-script."

She didn't use those words the way women usually do, conscious they're making you think they're talking like men, but having to get a running start for every word not considered fit for ladies or dictionaries.

Sammy returned with a tall man in his late forties, with a red face and bald spot, slimly built except for a pot belly which made me think of a thin neck with a large Adam's apple. He wasn't navigating too well under his own power and Sammy, almost a head shorter, guiding him to our table, looked like a busy little tug piloting a liner into port.

"Mr. Manheim," Sammy said with his best Sunday manners, "I want you to meet not only one of the greatest producers in town but one of my favorite people."

I almost expected Mr. Collier to start making an after-dinner speech. I thought that was going a little too far, even for Sammy, but Mr. Collier took it very gracefully, or perhaps it was only drunkenly. He seemed to be bowing, but it turned out he was only aiming his bottom cautiously at the seat of the chair. The waiter brought his drink over from the other table and Collier stared into it with an expression that might have been either thoughtful or thirsty.

"Now what was I just saying, son?" Collier began.

"What Mr. Rappaport told you about my work," Sammy prompted.

"Correct," Collier said. The only effect his drinking seemed to have on his mind was to throw it into slow motion. "Rappy tells me you did a hell of a job on *Girl Steals Boy,* Glick. Hell of a job."

"We'll know better after the sneak," Sammy said. "And we'll know best when we see whether Mr. and Mrs. Public buy tickets."

Later Kit told me Collier's favorite beef was that writers didn't care what made money and what didn't as long as their stuff went over with the Hollywood first-nighters. And Sammy didn't sound as if he were exactly stabbing in the dark.

Collier looked around at us in triumph. "If only more of you writers talked that language!"

Then he turned back to Sammy as if he were going to kiss him. "Well, you and I could talk pictures till all hours of the morning. But I'm in a spot, son, hell of a spot, and maybe a bright young kid like you can help me out. I've got Dorothy Lamour for a South Sea picture that's supposed to start in six weeks. It opens at the Music Hall Easter week. It's got a surefire title, *Monsoon.* All I need now is the story."

Sammy jerked the cigar from his mouth as if it were a stopper checking his flow of words. "South Sea story! You're looking for a South Sea story! Well, of all the goddam coincidences I ever heard of!"

Hold your hats, girls and boys, I thought, here we go again.

"Don't tell me you've got one!"

"Have I!" Sammy yelled. "Is this a break for both of us! I've only got the greatest South Sea story since *Rain,* that's all."

It was so convincing it even made me wonder if he hadn't been holding out on us.

"I'll tell you something about me," Collier said happily. "I never made a mistake in my life when I played my own hunch. Something just told me you might come through on this."

He took a little notebook from his pocket and wrote in a large, precise, drunk-under-control hand: Glick—*Monsoon.*

"You folks won't mind if Sammy tells us his yarn right here?" he asked us.

"Go right ahead," Kit said, "maybe we can even get the boys to play us a little South Sea music."

I tried to figure out how she felt about him, but it wasn't simple. She was as eager as I to put him on the spot, but I don't think she was hoping to see him go on his trim little can the way I was. I think she was just pushing him off the high board because she enjoyed the spectacle of seeing him straighten out and get his balance before knifing into the water.

It made me panicky just to imagine myself out on that kind of limb, but Sammy didn't even look ruffled. As the boys in the band started working again, he said, in a voice buttered with boyish sincerity, "Listen, Mr. Collier, I'd love to tell you the story now, but it wouldn't be fair to you. When you hear this story I want you to hear it right. Now what if I came out to your house next Sunday? . . ."

He had sidestepped his tackler beautifully and was off again. Sammy not only had his lunch date Sunday but Collier was urging him to come early and try the pool.

Sammy hardly let Collier get out of earshot before he asked his question.

"Neither of you happen to know of a good South Sea story I could use? I'd split the sale with you."

I stared at Sammy as if I were practicing to be an X-ray machine. I just couldn't seem to take him easy. Kit was leaning back, relaxed, but with her eyes busy, as if she were enjoying a football game in which she wasn't rooting for either side.

"Sammy," I started to say and then I stopped because I knew I couldn't think of anything equal to the occasion. So all I finally said was *"Sammy Glick,"* using it like a swear word.

"A little birdie tells me that lunch is going to cost him just about ten G's," Sammy said.

"This time you've lost me," Kit confessed. "How can you sell anything while you're under contract? The studio owns everything you write."

"Everything I write *after* I began working for them," Sammy said coyly. "It wouldn't be fair for the studio to own everything I wrote before I came to Hollywood, would it? So who has to know when I wrote my South Sea story?"

All he had to do was say *South Sea story* once more and I'd begin to believe he had really written one. The only answer I could think of was, "What South Sea story?"

"Don't worry," Kit assured me, "he'll have it. It would be different if he had to write the greatest South Sea story since *Rain* overnight. But he has three whole days."

"That reminds me," Sammy said, "what's *Rain* about?"

"Holy Jesus," I said with reverence.

"Sammy, now I *know* you're a great man," she said. "What other writer in the world could compare his story, which he hasn't written, with a classic he's never read?"

"I didn't have to read it," Sammy explained. "I saw the movie. But I was such a little kid that all I can remember is Gloria Swanson shaking her cute little can in a minister's face."

"That's the plot all right," she said. "What more can I tell you about it?"

"Come on, Kit, stop the clowning, give out with *Rain.*"

Sammy was through playing for the evening. She began to tell Maugham's story. She told it well. You could feel the machinery in his mind breaking it down. I kept my eyes on his face. Sharp, well-chiseled, full of the animal magnetism that passes for virility, his skin blue-complexioned from his close-shaved heavy beard adding five years to his appearance, he was almost handsome. If it wasn't for that ferret look. In moments like this when he was on the scent of something you could see the little animal in him poking its snout into a rabbit hole.

Just as she was reaching the climax, where the good Sadie starts giving way to the old Sadie again, Sammy suddenly leaned forward and cut in.

"Wait a minute! I got an angle! I've got it!"

There was an old junk dealer in my youth who used to collect all our old newspapers to grind into fresh pulp again. That was the kind of story mind Sammy was developing. Without even warning us he launched into one of the most incredible performances of impromptu storytelling I have ever heard—or ever want to.

"All you gotta do to that story is give it the switcheroo. Instead of the minister you got a young dame missionary, see. Dorothy Lamour. Her old man kicked off with tropical fever and she's carrying on the good work. You know, a Nice Girl. Then instead of Sadie Thompson you got a louse racketeer who comes to the Island to hide out. Dorothy Lamour and George Raft in *Monsoon*! Does that sound terrific? So Dotty goes out to save George's soul and he starts feeding her the old oil. Of course, all he's out for is a good lay, but before very long he finds himself watching the sunrise without even thinking of making a pass at her. The soul crap is beginning to get to him, see? He tells her she's the first dame he ever met he didn't think about that way. Now give me a second to dope this out . . ."

I told him I would be much more generous than that, I would gladly give him several decades, but he didn't stop long enough to hear me.

"Oh, yeah, how about this—just about the time George is ready to break down and sing in her choir every Sunday morning they get caught in a storm on one of the nearby islands. They have to spend the night in a cave huddled together. Well, you can see what's coming, she can't help herself and lets him slip it to her. When they realize what they've done they both go off their nut. He goes back to his booze, shooting his mouth off about all dames looking alike when you turn them upside down, and Dotty feels she's betrayed her old man, so she goes to the edge of the cliff and throws herself into the ocean. But good old George manages to get there in time and jumps in after her. Then you play a helluva scene in the ocean where you get over the idea that the water purifies 'em. Jesus, can't you see it, George coming up for the third time with Dotty in his arms hollering something like: 'Oh, God, if You get us outa this—I'll work like a bastard for You the rest of my life.' And you're into your final fade with Dorothy and George married and setting up shop together, in the market for new souls to save."

Sammy looked at us the way a hoofer looks at his audience as he finishes his routine.

There was a moment of respectful silence.

"Of course," Sammy explained, falling back on the official Hollywood alibi, "I was just thinking out loud."

"But where," I said, "does the monsoon come in?"

"Jesus," he said, "I'm glad you reminded me. What the hell is a monsoon?"

"A monsoon is a sequel to a typhoon," Kit explained.

"Only bigger," Sammy interpreted. "So the monsoon'll have to be coming up all the time they're in the cave. It'll be a natural for inter-cutting. Symbolical. When she does her swan dive from that cliff she lands right in the middle of it. That will really give the rescue scene a wallop."

"I'm glad you added the monsoon," Kit said. "I couldn't quite see how an ordinary ocean would purify them. But a monsoon makes it convincing."

"What do you think of it, Al?" he said.

"I don't know much about art," I said, "I only know what I like. I think it stinks."

He looked at her with a question mark. "I think Collier will buy it," she said seriously.

Sammy turned on me with a leer not quite hidden in a smile. "That shows what you know about story values, Al."

His shell of egotism hadn't quite had time to harden yet, but he was already beginning to show annoyance when his picture judgment was questioned. I wasn't especially interested in qualifying for the job of Sammy's future yes-man so I pressed my point.

"I didn't hear Kit say anything about the story. All she said was that you might sell it."

"Well, what more do you want me to do with it?" Sammy said. "Win the Nobel Prize for literature?"

"Haven't you learned yet never to argue with Sammy about himself?" she said. "That's one subject on which I'm convinced he's infallible."

"But why should you want to encourage crap like that?"

"You don't really think what we say has anything to do with it when there's so much more encouragement at the other end, good at any bank?"

Her voice was crisp and confident.

I decided that I would always prefer to have her on my side.

"As long as they sell South Sea pictures before they know what they're going to be about," she continued, "the kind of ad-libbing Sammy just gave us will be a work of genius."

"Sammy's story is a work of genius," I said, "like Shirley Temple is my child bride."

"Look up the word *genius* in the dictionary sometime," she said.

Sammy was lining up the plot on the tablecloth. "How the hell can I get George to find out she's drowning?" he said.

I stuck a cigarette in my mouth and Kit promptly lit it for me.

"Feel like dancing?" she said.

For some reason it reminded me of a night down in the Village when a man invited me to dance. I wanted to go on talking with her, but I knew I would feel foolish having to take her in my arms. I don't think I ever had that reaction to a woman before. I tried to beg off on the grounds that it would leave Sammy alone. But he said, "Go ahead, dance. You know me, Greta Garbage, I von to be alone."

As we rose Sammy's hard, stubby fingers snapped staccato.

"Know who Dorothy's mother oughta be?" he said. "An exotic little savage her old man converted. So when she starts going for George she's just reverting to type!"

"Don't you think that psychology stuff is a little highbrow?" I said over my shoulder, and we were out there on the floor, set to music.

I felt like a kid at his first dance. Scared of getting too close to her. I held her at arm's length literally and otherwise. She was so damned cool and well-groomed. Not only her clothes, but her face and her mind. I had a screwy temptation to mess her up a little bit, muss her hair, mix her up. She had it all down so pat. When it came to understanding our little friend I felt she had a couple of laps on me. My dancing wasn't too good because I was conscious of not being able to think of anything to say.

Finally, she had to start it. "How long have you been out here?"

"Not so very long," I said. "I don't know, maybe a month."

"Suppose it isn't fair to ask whether you like it or not?"

"I'm making twice what I was in New York, and the climate's a whole lot better. Why shouldn't I like it?"

She smiled at me with so much understanding it was humiliating. "Don't worry, hardly anybody does at first."

"How about the eminent author of *Monsoon*?" I said.

"They're different," she said.

I told her I could only see one Sammy Glick at that table, unless the last couple of drinks had caught up with me.

"I meant all the Sammy Glicks," she said.

"There is only one Sammy Glick," I insisted. "I know. I met him when he couldn't have been much over seventeen. Why, I've practically seen him grow up and . . ."

"I doubt that," she cut in. "I don't think Sammy Glick was an adult at birth, but he must have become one very soon afterwards."

"I hope you aren't right," I said. "For his parents' sake. But I had Sammy working out on me every day for years. And I'm willing to swear on my option that he's a unique contribution to the human race."

"I hate to disillusion you," she said, "but he has plenty of soul mates running in the same race."

"I won't believe it till I see it, God forbid," I said. "One Sammy Glick in my life is all my constitution will stand."

"I've known Glicks before," she said. "My first producer out here was a Glick. And so was the agent I just got rid of, Barney Burke."

"God rest their souls," I said.

"Of course, I will admit Sammy is an unusual model," she said. "With a special hopped-up motor. But he's put out by the same people."

The only topic we had in common was Sammy—and I was afraid of pushing that too far because I wasn't sure how things stood with them. The conversation hit an air pocket.

She could dance, all right. She danced the way professional models walk, with a haughty effortlessness. The only trouble with her dancing was it made me feel pretty much the way her talk had. She followed so well she seemed to anticipate me. At times it was really hard to tell whether I was doing the leading or not.

The music stopped and I made a false start toward the tables, but it was only a beat between numbers and she started dancing with me again.

"I love to dance," she said. "But no one ever seems to think of taking me dancing."

"It's a funny thing," I said, "I've always liked to dance and yet I've always been lousy at it."

"You're not a lousy dancer," she said, "you're fair. I like to dance with fair dancers. For some reason they're usually better guys."

The music blared. Billie promoted. Sammy figured. The crowd pushed, and we pushed back, in time to music.

We danced along silently and I wondered what we were going to talk about next. Until she suddenly said, "I guess you're his best friend, aren't you?"

There it was again. Beginning to haunt me. The wording of a familiar Jewish phrase came back to me: My worst enemy shouldn't have such a best friend!

"I don't know," I said. "Maybe I am. Maybe I am at that. Only I don't think friendship is one of Sammy's fortes."

"He only has one forte," she said, "himself." She didn't say it bitterly: solemnly.

We were hardly dancing now, just standing there in the middle of the floor, feeling the music and getting to know each other.

The band struck its intermission chord. "Thanks," I said. "Let's go back and see how W. Somerset Glick is getting along."

She laughed. "Even Houdini couldn't turn *Rain* upside down!" We laughed with each other again. More than the remark deserved. I couldn't help taking her figure in as I stood aside to let her lead the way, single file, to our table. Not as masculine as I thought. Athletic, but not so much the Babe Didrickson type as the Helen Wills.

"The music's getting on my nerves," Sammy said as we sat down.

I was surprised to hear he thought he had them.

"What d'ya say we blow 'n' go back to my joint? I wanna try my story on you."

"You remember us," I said, "we were here for the first show."

"Oh, hell that was just roughing it out," he said. "Now I've really got it licked."

||||||

Half an hour later Kit, Billie and I were seated on Sammy's modernistic gray suede couch watching him like an audience. You had to hand it to him. He was always improving. I mean, he was becoming more and more expert at being Sammy Glick. The way he was telling this story, for instance. He wasn't outlining it, he was acting it. What the story lacked in character and plot his enthusiasm and energy momentarily overcame. As I watched him perform I realized why he was repeating it. This must have been the only way he could write, telling his story over and over to people who supplied a line here, an idea there, until the story began to take shape like a snowman forming hastily under many hands. Instead of listening I found myself sifting the qualities which made his kind of storytelling possible.

First, no qualms. Not the thinnest sliver of misgiving about the value of his work. He was able to feel that the most important job in the world was putting over *Monsoon*. In the second place, he was as uninhibited as a performing seal. He never questioned his right to monopolize conversation or his ability to do it entertainingly. And then there was his colossal lack of perspective. This was one of his most valuable gifts, for perspective doesn't always pay. It can slow you down. I have sat in my office and said to myself, There are twelve million of your fellow Americans unemployed this morning. Who the hell are you? If that kept me from writing a line all morning it might mean I had perspective. Or thinking how the world was fifty million years ago and all the men who had their chance at living in it and what that had to do with the big pay-off scene in *Nick Turner—Boy Detective* I was supposed to turn in by five o'clock. That's perspective too. Or just staring up into millions of stars at night till you become molecular. Perspective is a fine thing. It can make you very unhappy. I couldn't imagine Sammy ever unhappy. Or happy either. I wondered what emotions he did have. Perhaps only a burning impatience to be further, further on.

Billie liked the story because she could just see Raft and Lamour playing the parts.

Kit started to tell Sammy how to put a picture story together. "The scenes can't be like a lot of people gathered at random, Sammy, even if they're colorful people. A good picture should be like a family tree. Every scene giving birth to the one that follows."

You didn't have to have much of an imagination to see the tentacles of Sammy's mind closing around that idea. I could almost hear him explaining his theory of film continuity to Collier that Sunday.

When my turn came I said, "Sammy, I still don't think the vehicle is worthy of you, but the acting is devastating. But deafeningly."

I wasn't exaggerating. The worse the story became, the louder it seemed to get.

"Just the same," Kit said, "there must be something in that technique. Adolf and Benito have been doing it for years and look where those boys are. What a marvelous pair of Hollywood phonies they'd be! Can't you just see them taking over a story conference?"

Sammy seemed rather flattered by the comparison.

"She's right, Al," he said. "Here's a little motto your Uncle Sammy made up himself—hang it up in your office—I'll give it to you free: Work hard, and, if you can't work hard, be smart; and, if you can't be smart, be loud."

"You sound like Moses," I said, "proclaiming the Ten Commandments from Mount Sinai."

"Moses was a sap," Sammy said. "Look at the joke they made of those Commandments of his. They've been playing him for a sucker for three thousand years. At least mine work. For instance, just to wise you up a little bit, take the first story conference I ever had out here."

He took that first conference, all right. We had a very vivid picture of the producer, the supervisor, another writer and Sammy trying to dope a good, quick way for the boy and girl to meet at the opening of the picture.

"The supervisor keeps throwing out but the producer plays tough. All he says is *corny, stinks* or *1902.* The other writer is a Caspar Milquetoast with an expression on his face like he's really thinking. Looks like he needs an enema. I'm thinking too, but not about the scene. I'm thinking I know from nothing about what I'm supposed to be doing and any minute the producer who's no deadhead is going to find it out.

"Then Milquetoast starts mumbling something under his breath. Like this, see?" Sammy tried to give us his interpretation of a timid soul. It was a difficult part for him. " 'I wonder if it's a bad idea to have the landlady show the boy into a room she believes vacant but actually is still occupied by the young lady?'

"This time the producer don't even bother to say no. Maybe he doesn't even hear him at all. Everybody just goes on thinking. The poor schlemiel looks around waiting for a reaction and ends up talking to himself. 'Yes,' he says, 'I guess it is.' " The poor schlemiel turned out to be S. Henley Forster who has had more books reprinted in the Modern Library than any living American writer.

"The dope probably doesn't know it, but he showed me how to smack a story conference. I sit there a couple of seconds till I'm sure I have the producer's eye. Then I start opening my eyes and sucking in my breath like I'm just discovering America or something. Then I start getting to my feet, slow, like this, looking at everybody as I rise. Significantly.

" 'Wait a minute!' I yell. I can feel them all moving in.

" 'Jesus H. Christ I've got it!'

"They look like I've slugged 'em over the head with sandbags. The boss doesn't even say swell or let's have it. I can feel I've got 'em already. Jesus, what a feeling!

" 'Here's the boy,' I says, 'wandering through the rain in a strange city looking for the cheapest room he can find.' "

Even for us Sammy turned his collar up and started trudging through the rain.

" 'The landlady, a terrific old character, leads me up the rickety stairs. "You're in luck, young man," she says to me, "there was somebody in this room but she had to be out by six o'clock. I can't afford to run a free mission around here." ' I'm not giving you the dialogue, you understand, just ad-libbing, but you can see where the dialogue can be terrific. Now we got suspense, see? We've got a lonely kid that the audience is crazy about already and we've got them wondering about the lovely young girl who's just been turned out into the cold.

" 'Now the door swings open. I walk in. All of a sudden I look up and stop. Dead in my tracks. Staring . . .'

"That's where I paused," Sammy told us. "Let 'em have a moment for the scene to sink in.

" 'The camera swings over and what do you think we pick up?—our girl, half-dressed, just as little on as the Hays Office will let us get by with. She looks up—like a tigress—fighting for shelter. We're right into a helluva situation. It's a terrific moment.

I keep looking at the girl. She keeps looking at me. Everybody in the audience knows the battle I'm fighting. How the hell can I take this room tonight and throw this tragic little waif out into the gutter?' "

Sammy paused again, looking at us dramatically, just as he had for his producer. " 'The landlady is talking to me, telling me she'll have the girl out of there right away. I don't even hear her. And then, do you know what I say? Without taking my eyes off the girl I ask the landlady, 'How much does she owe you?' And when she tells me, I just say, 'It's paid,' just like that, 'It's paid . . .'

" 'And if you don't think that's the most terrific opening you ever had on any picture let me out of my contract and I'll go back to my old job of managing editor of the New York *Record*!' "

Sammy turned his collar down again, indicating that the curtain had fallen. "Jesus, I murdered them. The producer jumped up and kissed me. Then he had me tell the whole thing through again. Then he asked the supervisor and the other writer what they thought of it. I wish I could have had a picture of that poor schlemiel's puss when he told the producer he agreed with it completely."

Sammy's laugh invited us to join in at Forster's expense. His excuse for dwelling on the story was its lesson for me. But from the relish with which he re-enacted his crime you could see how the experience fattened his pride. It made me realize more sharply than ever what a peculiar phenomenon his pride was. He was prouder of the method with which he had triumphed than if he had thought of the original suggestion himself.

"Now I know what I have to do to become a successful screen writer," I said. "Take elocution and singing lessons."

I tried to kid about it, but I was really depressed. For if making the grade out here meant going through the song-and-dance that Sammy had just presented, I felt I might as well start applying for hand-outs at the Motion Picture Relief.

But Kit reassured me. "You may not believe it, but there are some writers out here who really write. I've seen them do it on honest-to-god typewriters, with my own eyes. Dudley Nichols, for instance. He and John Ford have just done a job called *The Informer* that made me want to wash my mouth out with soap for all the nasty things I've been saying about Hollywood."

That was the first time I had ever heard anybody make Hollywood sound like a job, instead of a happy hunting ground where the customary weapons were a fabulous gall and a mouth energetic and loud. I was settling down beside her, ready to hear more, when Sammy came over and dropped his arm around her.

"I can't understand it," he said, "a smart wench like her—just lousy with ideals."

Out of his mouth that word sounded like something from a foreign language.

"You know she's on the Board of the Screen Writers Guild," he said. "She even got me to join her lousy organization."

It disturbed me not to be able to get a line on what they thought they were doing with each other. You could hardly call it an intellectual companionship. And yet if it was love it was a new kind on me. I think I had collected enough evidence to prove to myself that the only love Sammy Glick was capable of was a violent passion for his own future. And why a dame in her league wanted to play around with a swift little rodent like Sammy Glick seemed to be one for Dr. Freud.

"Look at the time," I said. "How about it, Billie? Maybe you and I ought to drag each other out of here before he starts charging us rent."

Kit showed Billie into the bedroom to get her hat and coat. I didn't know why I should have felt annoyed that she knew her way around so well.

Sammy and I had a nightcap. I must have been a little further gone than I thought, to tell him about my studio troubles with Pancake.

Sammy responded like a fireman hearing the alarm. "Let me show you how to give that guy the finger," he said. He wanted to help me. There was real benevolence in his voice, of his own peculiar brand.

"If you turn in one treatment with both your names on it and that fat swish lets the producer know he did all the writing, you're dead. If you want to play it cozy, write a treatment of your own without letting Pancake know and then get to your producer alone and tell him you thought Pancake was so far off the line it seemed faster to straighten it out yourself. That way you've got a chance of scaring him into bouncing Pancake off the picture and grabbing yourself a solo screenplay credit."

I couldn't see myself doing it, and I told him so. I wasn't sure whether I would ever make a screen writer or not, but I had no illusions about my powers as a politician.

"Don't be a sap," he said. "You've heard of the survival of the fittest."

I admitted that I held with the theory of evolution, but in a somewhat more complex form.

"You can give it all the fancy names you want," he said, "but when you come right down to it it's dog eat dog."

Somehow, I had been hoping that Kit was going to leave with us. But she had made herself very much at home. She had even let her hair down. I never understood before what a nice figure of speech that was. Instead of the large, neat knot that gave her that brisk, efficient look, it fell down over her shoulders now, softening her face, making her look relaxed, almost girlish.

"So long, sweetheart," Sammy said to me. "We'll be previewing some night next week. I'll give you a ring when I find out what night and we'll all get together."

There he stood in the doorway of his classy apartment, in his early twenties, in his expensive shoes, in his brand-new flashy jacket, in his brand-new Horatio Alger mind, but still looking like a kid off the streets who had sneaked in and put on the clothes he found in the closet. My best friend. My worst enemy shouldn't have such a best friend.

|||||||

Back in my room, Billie and I had our moment and then as the passion drained, our bodies returned us to what we really were, casual acquaintances.

The longer the silence lasted the further apart we drew. Finally she said, "What're you thinking about, honey?"

"Oh, just a lot of things, Billie," I said. "Nothing much, I guess."

"You know," she said, "I like it with you a lot. You're sweet."

There was nothing ever sordid about sex with Billie. The way she talked about it, it might have been surfboard riding or mountain climbing, anything she happened to be good at and enjoy.

"Billie," I said, "don't answer this unless you want to. How many men have you been with?"

The question wasn't intended to startle her, but the casualness of her answer startled me.

"Well, when I was fourteen," she said, "I tried to keep track of all the boys I knew. And when I was fifteen I tried to keep track of all the boys I kissed. And when I was sixteen—but now I've even lost track of that."

She chuckled as if she had told a joke on herself.

"Billie, what do you think of Sammy Glick?"

She pulled the sheet up to her neck. "Oh, I don't know. He's a pretty smart feller, all right."

"You know what I mean," I said. "How do you feel about him?"

This time she really seemed to think it over. "All I know," she said slowly, "is that I'd hate to go to bed with him."

The principal furniture in Billie's mind was a good-sized bed. "Why, Billie?"

She hesitated, giggling with the embarrassment of anyone out of the habit of probing ideas. "Oh, I don't know exactly," she said. "I've always liked to do it because it's just about the most fun you get out of life and because—I bet you laugh at me for this—it's always seemed like the friendliest thing two people can do in the whole world. That's why I've never wanted to turn pro. But—I know this sounds crazy—but somehow I've always felt that if I ever went to bed with *him*—even if he didn't pay me—I'd feel like I was doing it for money."

I kept turning that over in my mind as I was falling asleep and the more I played it back the surer I was that Billie, in her own sweet horizontal way, had said something more searching about Sammy than anything I had been able to hit on yet. And I had been working at it ever since the little copy boy burst into my office and launched his undeclared war against the world.

CHAPTER 5

Y ou could see the beams of the giant searchlights ballyhooing Sammy's preview plowing broad white furrows through the sky. "There it is," Sammy said as we turned off Sunset toward the Village. The words came out of his mouth like hard, sharp-sided pebbles. "Jesus."

He meant those lights up there were spelling Sammy Glick. There was no other word for the sound of pride mouthed with apprehension.

There wasn't much talking. Sammy's mood always provided the backdrop for the rest of us, and he was nervous. Even when he tried to cover it with wisecracks, they were nervous wisecracks.

"What kind of a house is this?" he said.

"A tough one," Kit said. "They only laugh when it's funny, not when it's supposed to be funny. And they never cry when it's maudlin. Only when it's pathetic."

"Jesus," Sammy said.

"And they're preview-wise," she warned. "They've had so many previews out here that they all sound like little DeMilles. They complain about the angles, and the smoothness of the dissolves, and they even tell you what to cut."

"The bastards," Sammy said, "they better think my picture is funny. I know it's funny. I counted the laughs myself. One hundred and seventeen."

The theater entrance was full of excitement that came mostly from women who were attracted to the leading man, and men resentful or regretful that they would never go to bed with anybody like the star, and unimportant people who idealized their envy into admiration and kids who wanted to have more autographs than anybody else in the world.

All the lights were on in the theater and everybody in the audience had his head turned toward the entrance. It looked crazy, as if the screen had suddenly been set up behind their backs. They were all watching for the celebrities to fill up the loge section that had been roped off for them. I realized why Sammy had rushed us through dinner. He wanted to be sure and get there before the lights went out.

The three of us started down the aisle together but we had only gone a couple of rows when we lost Sammy. When I looked around, Sammy was practically in the lap of a dignified, gray-haired man, with a pink, gentle face, which was a little too soft around the mouth.

"That's his producer," Kit said as I was about to ask. "Sidney Fineman." I looked again. Fineman was one of the magic names like Goldwyn and Mayer.

As we waited for the lights to fade, we talked about Fineman. He was one of the few real old-timers still on top. He had written scenarios for people who have become myths or names of streets like Griffith and Ince. He was supposed to have one of the finest collections of rare books in the country.

"And it isn't just conspicuous consumption," she said. "His idea of how to spend one hell of an evening is to lock himself in his library alone. He built a special house for his books at the back of his estate."

The more she told me the more curious I was that a man like Sidney Fineman should want to work with Sammy.

"Fineman isn't the man he was fifteen years ago," she said. "He had just as much taste as Thalberg and more guts. Hollywood was his girl. He loved her all the time. He had ideas for making something out of her . . ."

I could see Sammy out of the corner of my eye. He had finally worked his way down to our aisle. He was leaning over two or three people to shake hands with Junior Laemmele.

"But that's all gone," Kit was saying. "The Depression killed something in him. Not only losing his own dough, but the big bank boys like Chase and Atlas moving in on his company. He began to get an obsession about the Wall Street bunch working behind his back. He started playing safe. Now he's just one of the top dozen around town, making his old hits over and over again because he's scared to death that the minute he starts losing money they'll take his name off the door. He's convinced Sammy is a money writer. And I have a sneaking suspicion who convinced him."

Sammy ducked into the seat beside me as the credit titles came on. I watched his face as his name filled the screen:

ORIGINAL SCREENPLAY

by

SAMUEL GLICK

There is no word in English to describe it. You could say gloat, smile, leer, grin, smirk, but it was all of those and something more, a look of deep sensual pleasure. The expression held me fascinated because I felt it was something I should not be allowed to see, like

the face of the boy who roomed across the hall from me in prep
school when I had made the sordid mistake of entering without
knocking.

Then Sammy leaned over and whispered something in my ear
that will always seem more perverse than anything in Krafft-
Ebing.

"Just for a gag," he said, "clap for me."

The most perverse part of the story is that I did. There were
my hands clapping foolishly like seal flippers. The applause was
taken up and spread through the house, not what you would call
a thunderous ovation, just enough of a sprinkle to make my hands
feel like blushing. It wasn't bad enough that I had become
Sammy's drinking companion. I had to be his one-man claque. My
applause couldn't have been more automatic if Sammy had previously hypnotized me and led me into the theater.

As I stared at that credit title I had a feeling that something
was missing. But it wasn't until the screen was telling us who
designed the wardrobe and assisted the director that I remembered what it was. Julian. Julian Blumberg, the kid who made the
little snowball that Sammy was rolling down the Alps. Granting
that Sammy had written, God knows how, the screenplay alone,
the worst it should have been was original story by Samuel Glick
and Julian Blumberg preceding the screenplay credit. But there
it was, all Sammy Glick, no Julian Blumberg.

On impulse, but a better one than before, I leaned over and
asked Sammy whether he noticed anything funny about that
screen credit and when he didn't, I enlightened him. It was like
lighting a candle in Mammoth Cave.

"That first story we did all went in the ashcan, Al," he said in
a thick whisper. "I had to start from scratch. I know it's a tough
break for the kid, but that's Hollywood."

"The hell it is," I said. "That's Sammy Glick."

Kit said a sharp *shhhhh.*

As the picture was opening I was wondering whether I would
have agreed with Sammy about Hollywood before I met her.

The picture wasn't anything that would come back to you as

you were climbing into bed, or even remember as you were reaching under the seat for your hat; it was a good example of the comedy-romance formula that Hollywood has down cold, with emphasis not on content but on the facility with which it is told. It was right in the groove that Hollywood has been geared for, slick, swift and clever. What Kit calls the Golden Rut.

But in spite of the entertainment on the screen I preferred the show going on in the adjoining seat. I never saw a man work so hard at seeing a picture. "Eleven already," he said to me a couple of minutes after the picture started, and I realized he had a clocker in his hand and was counting the laughs. And each time they laughed he jotted down feverishly the line or the bit of business. And every time they didn't he'd mumble, "It's that goddam ham—he's murdering my line," or "That's a dead spot they can kill when they trim it."

I just sat there watching him learn the motion-picture business. He was an apt student, all right. He learned something about pictures in five months that I'm just beginning to understand after five years. Hollywood always has its bumper crop of phonies but believe it or not Sammy was one of the less obvious ones. He was smart enough to know that the crook who cracks his jobs too consistently is sure to be caught. His secret was to be just as conscientious about the real work he did as about the filching and finagling.

The picture got a good hand as the lights came on again. I turned to follow Sammy up the aisle but Kit grabbed my arm.

"Out this way," she said. "It's better."

She indicated the emergency exit on the side. It led us to an alley that ran around the theater. As we walked through the darkness toward the street, Kit said:

"I always like to duck out before anybody asks me how I liked the picture."

"Even if you did?"

"It isn't that simple. Hollywood has a regular ritual for preview reactions. When they know they've got a turkey they want to be reassured. And when they have one that's okay they expect super-latives."

She illustrated her point by telling the old Hollywood story about the three yes-men who are asked what they think of the preview. The first says it is without a doubt the greatest picture ever made. The second says it is absolutely colossal and stupen-dous. The third one is fired for shaking his head and saying, "I don't know, I only think it's great."

"Just the same," I said, "I'm impressed. To tell the truth I didn't know Sammy had it in him."

"Don't misunderstand," she said. "I think it's a damn good movie. The only thing I have against those guys is that they're like the old Roman Caesars—every piddling little success becomes an excuse for staging a triumph. And I just don't happen to enjoy being dragged along behind the chariot."

When we reached the street Sammy was standing with half a dozen men bunched on the curb in front of the theater. They all seemed to be talking at once, though Sammy was doing his best to drown them out. Kit pointed out the others besides Sammy and Fineman, the director, the cutter, several other executives and the cameraman. A couple of others were hovering around the edge, mostly listening and reacting. Fineman and the director seemed to be having an argument. The director was yelling that if they yanked his favorite scene they could take his name off the picture. Sammy was supporting Fineman.

We watched a boy bring out a ladder and climb up efficiently to change the lettering on the marquee, and then Kit said, "These sidewalk conferences are liable to last all night. Let's go and have a drink. He can meet us there."

My mind kept remembering the way she had made herself at home at Sammy's as we left that night. It was crazy to let it annoy me because I hadn't even made up my mind yet whether I liked her or not. I liked the way her mind drove at things but there was something disconcerting about the way she kept you from getting too close to her.

As we started for the parking station, she turned around and called to Sammy briskly, "The Cellar."

An anemic young man in a shabby overcoat was waiting at the car. I knew him, but I couldn't place him until he began to talk. Of course it was Julian Blumberg.

He was unable to hide the terrible effort it was for him to approach me. You could see it was an act of desperation.

"Mr. Manheim, I don't think you remember me . . ."

His eyes seemed to be forever crying. He kept cracking his knuckles, shifting his balance and looking everywhere but at me. The Jewish language has the best word I have ever heard for people like Julian: *nebbish*. A *nebbish* person is not exactly an incompetent, a dope or a weakling. He is simply the one in the crowd that you always forget to introduce.

"Of course I do," I said. "Glad to see you."

I tried to make it sound hearty. He extended his hand as if he expected me to crack it with a ruler. I could feel the perspiration in his palm.

When I introduced him to Kit he gave her a preoccupied nod and then, as if he had been sucking in his breath for it a long time, he blurted out what he wanted to say to me. As with so many timorous people when it finally came out it sounded brusque and overbold.

"Mr. Manheim, I've got to see you right away."

"Sure, Julian," I said, "can you tell me what it's about?"

He looked at Kit suspiciously. "Alone," he said. "I want to talk to you alone."

His voice begged and demanded at the same time. I suppose I should have been sore, but it was hard to miss the undertones in Julian's rudeness.

"All right," I said, "will it take very long?"

The determination valve suddenly seemed to loosen and the bluster leaked out of him. "Gosh, Mr. Manheim, I know I'm being a nuisance but I wouldn't think of bothering you like this unless . . ."

"How long would you say it would take?" I interrupted impatiently.

"It's—there's quite a lot to tell. I'd say a couple of hours."

I looked at Kit. "Why don't you two go ahead?" she said. "I don't mind being alone."

That was the trouble, I knew she didn't mind being alone.

"I'll tell you what you do, Julian. It'll keep until lunch tomorrow, won't it? How about dropping around at the studio? Twelve-thirty okay?"

He was so grateful it was painful. He backed away like an awkward courtier, hoping he wasn't being too much trouble and thanking me again.

"Who is that damp little fellow?" Kit asked as she pressed her foot on the starter.

I still didn't feel I knew her well enough to tell her the story of *Girl Steals Boy*. So I just said he was a writer Sammy and I knew in New York who was out here looking for a job.

"No wonder he looked worried," she said. "There were exactly two hundred and fifty of us working today. The Guild keeps a daily check-up. And do you know how many screen writers there are? Nearly a thousand. With carloads of bright-eyed college kids arriving every week—willing to do or die for dear old World-Wide at thirty-five a week."

|||||||

I don't really believe that liquor will cure all the ills in our society. But two or three healthy slugs often cure our curious inability to know each other. Unless we know people well, we sit around with our words and our minds starched, afraid of being ourselves for fear of wrinkling them.

Down in the Cellar, after the first couple of drinks, I could feel us loosening up with each other. It wasn't in anything we said, it was just that we seemed to like each other better and we both knew it.

We entertained ourselves for the first few minutes watching

how different people came down the stairway and posed on the final landing before entering the room.

When we had had enough of that game we found ourselves playing a new one called How I Met Sammy. She asked me first. I amused her for ten or fifteen minutes with a quick enumeration of the highlights of Sammy Glick's *Mein Kampf,* but doing a Will Hays on the more extravagant of his achievements.

"I met him during the revolution we almost had last year," she said. "When Upton Sinclair was running for Governor."

I said I had heard about it but had never paid much attention to it.

"Then you really missed something," she said. "The panic was on when Upton Sinclair won the Democratic nomination by announcing that he was going to End Poverty in California."

"I always thought Sinclair was just another of your California crackpots," I said.

"Oh, his script had plenty of holes all right," she said, "but I think it would have given the people a better run for their money than Merriam's—which hadn't changed a line since *Birth of a Nation.*"

"Well, where does Sammy Glick come in?"

"He's practically banging on the door now," she said. "At the height of the campaign World-Wide had a sudden loss of memory. It's funny how a little thing like the Bill of Rights can slip your mind once in a while. They demanded that every employee contribute a day's pay to the Merriam fund. That was something I thought even honest Republicans should resent, so I told them where to go, in my prettiest profanity.

"A couple of days later I was sitting there in my office minding my own script, when a total stranger burst into my office as if his pants were on fire."

"I'm Sammy Glick," he said.

And waited as if that were all the introduction he needed.

"Whatever you're selling," she said, "I'm not in the market for anything. I'm very busy."

"You've got me wrong," he laughed. "I'm the new writer just moved in across the hall."

"How chummy," she said. "If you're ever short drop over and borrow a cup of dialogue."

Because she had never heard of Sammy Glick she tried to discourage him by turning back to her typewriter.

"That's a honey," he laughed, moving in. "I'll hafta remember that one."

As she turned around she found herself looking into his face.

"Mr. Glick," she began sweetly, "I suppose I ought to be hospitable and welcome you to Writers' Building C. And now that I have will you get the hell out of my office and let me work?"

She had chased her share of brassy guys out of the office, ad-space salesmen and small-time agents and the usual studio lounge lice. When sarcasm didn't get them, a little pungent cussing would. But this one was different. He settled down on the edge of her desk and looked over her shoulder.

"I hear you're working on Dancing Debs," he said. "That oughta be a swell credit."

She rose, covered her typewriter, stuffed some of the papers on her desk into a big envelope and slung her coat over her shoulder.

"Where you goin'?" he said.

"Where I can work," she said.

"Hey," he said, "don't let me chase you out. I just dropped in for a friendly chat. Thought I'd give you a tip that the front office knows you're the only writer on the lot who hasn't come across for Merriam."

That was the way the pressure went. Nobody was ever called into an executive office and told to shell out or get out. That job was taken over by the stooges. The yes-men had a field day with their "all-for-your-own-good-old-fellow" stuff, coercion by innuendo in the best Hollywood style, pouring it in the victim's ear as if he were being told the latest studio gossip.

Next morning Kit reached the lot a few minutes before nine-thirty and had coffee at the studio diner before going to work.

Sammy was there, having breakfast and making verbal passes at the waitress. When he saw Kit he slid over to greet her as if their first meeting had been love at first sight.

"Which way do you come in the morning?" he asked. "Maybe you could pick me up."

"I come by way of Boulder Dam," she said. "I'm sure it's a little out of your way."

He took this as a joke and started reading the Megaphone with her. Of course the lead edit was about Merriam and Sinclair. Sammy began to read it out loud. She picked up the paper and paid her check. He followed her out. She walked faster, ignoring him. He trotted along beside her desperately.

"Look, you're a smart girl, you read the papers, you know how the cards are stacked against this nut Sinclair . . ."

She managed to lose him by turning into a convenient ladies' room.

As she came down the hall he appeared at his doorway. She tried to shut the door in his face but he slithered through like a cat.

"No kidding, Katie—is that what they call you, Katie? I'm worried about you," he said. "Now why don't you let me get on the phone and tell Dan Young . . ." Dan Young was the studio manager who had sent out the notices about the day's pay. Sammy reached for the phone.

Kit looked at him curiously.

"How long have you been in California?" she said.

"Four days."

"So you've learned enough about the issues of the campaign in four days to become a political adviser," she said.

"How long does it take you to find out that the sun rises in the east?" Sammy said. "One good look."

"What do you know about Merriam?"

Sammy's answer came prompt and glib. "He's for law and order. He's a friend of the industry. He's a right guy."

"If the people push over the Merriam machine," she stated quietly, "it's my guess they'll find enough corruption crawling around under there to keep all the starving lawyers in California busy the rest of their lives—digging it out."

"So what?" Sammy said. "Everybody knows about Jimmy Walker. And he's the best mayor New York ever had."

"I'm afraid you flunk in citizenship," she said. "Didn't you ever have to take Civics?"

"Sure," he said. "What a laugh. The teacher giving us all that crap out of a book when all we had to do to learn about politics was watch the Tammany guy on the corner."

She looked at him. She had a temper and she knew she was going to have to lose it, but she didn't want to lose it for a moment or two. Anything on a large enough scale, even a pest, can be arresting.

"And how about Upton Sinclair?" she said. "What do you know about him?"

"He's a Bolshevik," Sammy recited. "He's out to cut up all the big dough in the State so everybody has the same. He wants to shut down the studios and start a revolution."

"Do you know he's the regular Democratic candidate?" she said.

"What are you trying to give me?" Sammy said. "Merriam's running for the Democrats and Republicans both. Sinclair's running for the Communists."

"This time," she said, "you've been learning your politics on the wrong corner. Sinclair got the heaviest vote in the history of the Democratic primaries. The regular party machine is behind him. And the Communists are running their own candidate."

Sammy looked at her as if she were crazy. "Okay, okay," he said. "All I know is either you plunk for Merriam around here or you're a dead pigeon."

That was where the smooth pavement on Kit's patience ended. "Goddam it," she yelled, "comes the revolution I only want one favor of Comrade Sinclair—to line you up against a wall and shoot you myself—and if you don't get out of my office by the time I count up to one, I won't even wait for the revolution!"

She told it vividly and I could see it happening: Kid Get-Ahead being dropped right down in the middle of Hollywood's most violent controversy, taking a couple of turns in the air and landing on his feet, with all the instinct for self-preservation of a scrappy kitten.

"I really lost my temper," she said. "You'd have thought that would have been the end of it."

"Oh, no," I said. "Not me. Sammy's built too much like a boomerang. The harder you throw him out the faster he comes back."

"I've never seen anything like it," she said. "Two hours later he was trying to get me to have lunch with him. That afternoon he called me on the phone about the Merriam business again. I hung up on him and he called me right back and said we were cut off. Finally, I went to Sidney Fineman, who was my producer then, and told him I wasn't being paid to vote for Merriam but to turn in the best script I could. And that a leech across the hall that called itself Sammy Glick was pestering me so much about my day's pay to save the industry that he was ruining the chances of one of its pictures to show a profit. Sidney was sympathetic. He made it pretty clear that he wished he could resist the pressure himself.

"Of course, I felt a little guilty about snitching on my neighbor that way. Even a neighbor like Mr. Glick. But the next time we met in the hall he had a smile not only from ear to ear but all the way round the back of his neck."

"Thanks, baby, for the plug you put in for me."
All she could do was look and sound bewildered.
"You musta told some of the top guys I was after your dough for Merriam. That's what I need. That gets 'em talking about me, see. Hell, every punk on the lot has laid it on the line for Merriam, so that adds up to nothing. But this way they all hear about it. Next time they hear the name Sammy Glick it rings a bell in their brains."

"I'll bet he was wetting his pants he was so scared his name might never ring those bells," I said.

"I doubt it," she said. "I don't think Sammy knows how to be afraid. He'll probably learn it out here, because this place is full of fear. But when he does I think something will have gone out of him. Like a tomcat I had castrated once."

"Were you afraid?"

"When I was holding out on that Merriam thing? Of course. Terrified. All my heroics were strictly on the surface. Maybe that's where heroics always are."

"And was Sammy right—about your being a dead pigeon?"

"No," she laughed. "They wouldn't even fire me, thank God. In other words those threats turned out to be a super-colossal bluff."

"That's a helluva way to start a friendship," I said. "I thought mine was queer. But yours is absolutely bughouse."

"Maybe friendship is the wrong word," she said. "I used to wonder why I kept seeing him after the Merriam affair blew over. I think it was the sense of excitement I seemed to feel around him. I don't know, he does something to the air you breathe, intensifies it. Haven't you felt it? Know what it reminds me of sometimes? A shrill note held too long. Makes you want to scream."

"I didn't know you ever let anything get you like that," I said.

It was spoken with an irritation that made her smile. "It bothers you." There was that disconcerting habit of stating unnecessary questions as facts.

I hadn't realized how much it bothered me until I began to talk about it. "Everything about you and Sammy bothers me. That night I left you at Sammy's, for instance. That bothered the hell out of me."

We looked at each other until we weren't acquaintances any more. After the pause, she didn't change the subject, only the direction of it.

"I'm sorry for him."

"Sorry for him! Sorry for Sammy Glick?"

"I have a crazy theory about that," she said. "You know the cripple who peddles papers outside the Derby? We're sorry for him because a germ he didn't have anything to do with got inside him and twisted him out of shape. Maybe we ought to feel the same way about guys with twisted egos."

"But the kid with the papers is helpless."

"So is Sammy," she said. "In his own way. Ever have him tell you anything about his childhood?"

Her Sammy Glick was a new conception and I paused to see what I could do with it.

"Try to think of it this way," she instructed. "There was an epidemic raging in that neighborhood of his—more contagious than polio—and he caught one of the worst cases on record."

There was just time enough to file the idea for further reference, for Sammy was coming down the stairs, making a triumphal entrance with Sidney Fineman. Sammy lingered to shake hands around the first table. You could tell from the faces that he was being congratulated. By some inexplicable telepathy, news of his success had preceded him. It seemed to me to be black magic, for the people congratulating him had been at the Cellar when we arrived. It had Kit stopped too. She said that one of the things which distinguished the old Brown Derby on Wilshire was the way guests at one end of the room could hear distinctly every word being said at the other, because of the trick acoustics of the dome-shaped ceiling. And that it always seemed as if all Hollywood must be covered by one of those Derby ceilings.

Fineman and his party found a table and Sammy continued his victory march down the aisle until he reached us. From the moment he sat down, the conversation continued to be about Sammy Glick, but in a different key. It was Variation on an Old Theme by Glick, *allegro con spirito.*

It would have been deadly if Sammy hadn't been hopped up with success. He sprayed us with words like a verbal machine gun. He described every detail of the evening just as if we hadn't been there at all.

"I'm over the hump," he said. "From now on I can write my own ticket. But I'd be a fool to move in yet. Why not wait till it's held over a third week at the Music Hall and starts to clean up in the sticks? By that time I'll be able to spit in the boss's eye and make him like it."

I had never seen him so wound-up before. He seemed to have memorized every word of praise he had received all evening. He told us how the cutter had said that even though the picture ran eighty-five hundred feet it moved so fast it could stand that footage. And what the theater manager had said. He went on talking about Sammy Glick with such flaming enthusiasm that so help me God I could feel the excitement beginning to catch in me.

The effect was hypnotic, like hearing a record over and over again: *So I told Fineman . . . I'm in a terrific spot . . . My picture . . . I said . . . I . . .*

He talked at you with so much force it was hard to eat. You felt he was sticking his face right into your plate and the words into your mouth. If you have ever seen Henry Armstrong fight you know how Sammy was learning to talk, leaning against you, never letting up, swarming all over you as he forced you back and back.

I watched for an opening and when Sammy had his mouth full of his last bite of steak sandwich I made a motion that we adjourn.

"I hafta wait for the reviews," Sammy said. "They mean a helluva lot."

Hurrying importantly down the stairs was a beefy middle-aged man whose clothes were dapper, if not his body. Nine-tenths of his silk handkerchief was hanging out of his breast pocket. His eyes seemed too small for his large face, and too close together. He looked like a confidence man, but a confidence man who had risen to the position of employer of other con men.

I noticed that Kit and Sammy stopped talking to watch him, that people at other tables were doing the same thing. Kit kept her eyes on him as he entered the room. "You can stop worrying about that review, Sammy," she said. "You're in."

"Jesus," Sammy said. "I gotta read it."

The note of anxiety that had been there before the preview was back again. He was off to Fineman's table on the double-quick.

I was mystified. "I've heard about portable telephones in here," I said. "But when you start getting wireless messages . . ."

"This is like every other spiritualist trick," Kit said. "Very impressive until you go behind the scenes."

"Let's go," I said.

She led me off on a little verbal tour through Darkest Hollywood.

"All I had to do was watch the guy who just came in. Gabby Hanigan, who runs the *Megaphone.*"

"What do you mean, watch him? Who're you, the girl with the X-ray eye?"

"All it takes is practice," she said. "I've been watching Hanigan come in after previews this way for years. When he's written a rave he's giving you the big hello all the way down the stairs. But you can always tell when he's thrown the hook into you because then he just gives it this . . ." Her hand made two quick fluttery motions and stopped. "So this time it looks in the bag. Gabby was waving to Fineman like a Boy Scout the moment he came into sight."

She was right. Sammy came trotting back with a proof copy of the review. He rolled it out on the table for us with a flourish.

"Read that," he said crisply, and he shook his head as if further expression failed him. "Tuhriffic."

It was. You could almost hear the headline screaming: "GIRL" CINCH B.O. SMASH. Kit began to read it out loud, with an ironic inflection which Sammy was too intoxicated to appreciate. It read like a press-agent blurb. It drooled over Fineman's showmanship, the acting, the directing, the photography. It didn't say anything about them except that they were all wonderful. And Sammy had a whole paragraph to himself. He was hailed as a brilliant addition to the ranks of Hollywood writers. The reviewer seemed especially impressed with his craftsmanship and originality.

"Sammy," I said, "tell me the truth. Is Gabby Hanigan your father?"

"Father, hell," he said. "That plug is going to set me back two hundred smackers."

I said I hadn't realized the *Megaphone* was that kind of sheet. I mentioned the word *bribe*.

"What do you mean bribe?" Sammy said. "They just came in a couple of days ago trying to sell me a full page ad and when I told them I'd think it over and let them know after I read the review, they said not to lose any sleep over it."

"I beg your pardon," I said. "I didn't mean to jump at conclusions."

I was mystified again. And with good reason. How could Sammy get so upset about a review that was already in the bag?

"There you have your finger on my favorite Hollywood foible," Kit said. "I don't know how many times I've sat in this very room with producers who were absolutely sweating blood to read a review they had already made sure of. And not only that, but gloat over it like children when it finally arrived."

I said I couldn't believe it. But Sammy could. "That's not so crazy as it sounds," he explained. "This Hanigan guy is nobody's fool. I hear he likes to cross you up once in a while, just to keep you guessing."

"Why the hell does Hollywood let him get away with it?" I said.

"Because there are still too many people out here more interested in boosting their own stock than in making pictures," Kit said. "As long as they're around we'll have our Hanigans and our canned reviews instead of the real, slugging criticism that might do some good."

Sammy was signing the check. "Come on, smarty pants," he said. "Reform the industry tomorrow. Tonight we celebrate."

||||||

The Triangle Club wasn't Monte Carlo, but it was the best Hollywood could do. You had the old thrill of being stared at through a peephole and feeling privileged as the door swung open. This was partly for the effect, partly because gambling was illegal in Los Angeles and they had to slip the city machine something for protection. It was the place the top producers liked after working their guts out until midnight, hoping to slow down with champagne cocktails, five-dollar steaks and a couple of grand tossed away at roulette before trying to catch up with a little sleep that was as restful as a Vorkapich montage.

They knew Sammy here too. More people were stepping up to grab his hand. They all seemed to know he had a hit. That was the Hollywood grapevine clicking again, the thing about it that impressed me most—a gigantic industry involving thousands of people situated in a boom town with a village psychology. Take out the cyclamen drapes, the lush carpet, the mirrored bar, and all the rest of the trappings, and you would have the village beer joint. For hardly anywhere else could Sammy have become so quickly known or his exploits so discussed.

I don't remember much about that night except that Sammy kept buying us champagne and blew five hundred bucks at the crap table (and told everyone it was a thousand) and Kit tried to explain that it wasn't really a loss because a guy called Veblen said we make our reputations by how much money we can publicly throw away, and I tried to get her to come home with me which even surprised me and made me realize how much champagne Sammy must have bought, and I lost my week's salary at blackjack which is strictly a sucker's game, and I began seeing Sammy's face exploding around me like a pinwheel, and when I asked myself *What makes Sammy run?* a woman's voice answered *How many times are you going to ask me that?* and I said, "Pardon me, but I don't think we've met," and the answer came, "Of course we have, you've been to my house for dinner," and even then she had to repeat it several times before I could realize that the woman in my arms was Mrs. Henry Powell Turner and that somehow the Triangle Club had disappeared and the walls that were spinning around belonged to my room at the Villa Espana.

CHAPTER 6

ifteen minutes early, Julian's hesitating voice trembled up to me from the reception room. I hated to keep him waiting because I know how it is when you're down; the most trivial slight becomes persecution. But I didn't want to leave too soon in case my producer called. Writers usually cover up for each other, but I couldn't trust that bitchy streak in Pancake.

When I went downstairs I found Julian looking even more miserable than the night before. "It's awfully nice of you . . ." he began.

"Let's see," I said, "where shall we eat?"

I ran through the usual list automatically. "Like Chinese food?"

Anything, he would eat anything.

"Good," I said, "there's a pretty good little Chinese place around the corner."

A Chinese joint is usually a good place to talk, because it's almost always empty and the waiter is so busy reading his language paper in the back that he barely has time to drop his plates and run. It's easier to talk around waiters who seem more interested in something they can't wait to get back to.

I ordered egg foo yong and cold pork and Julian thought a while and decided he would have the same and I yelled after the waiter to throw in a bottle of sake. Then I waited for Julian to begin.

He leaned forward uncomfortably, nervously cracking his knuckles.

"Don't crack your knuckles," I said. "It's bad for your hands."

He dropped his hands into his lap in embarrassment.

"I know," he said. "Blanche keeps telling me."

"Who's Blanche?" I said.

"Oh, gee, I'm awfully sorry to bother you about all this, Mr. Manheim," Julian said. "But that's what I wanted to talk to you about. Blanche is my wife. And she's going to leave me."

I hadn't even known he was married. Why do poor little *nebs* like Julian always have to be the first ones married?

"We've been married three years," he said. "Blanche and I were engaged all through high school. We've always been crazy about each other. And now . . ."

His voice trailed off like a distant radio station fading and I had to wait for it to come back again. "Now she says she's going back to New York."

I was sorry, very. But I was sorry about so many things I couldn't do anything about.

"But you could," he said. "If you could only talk to Mr. Glick. After all he'd listen to you—you're a good friend of his."

Please, Julian, I thought. When you say that, smile.

But that would have been asking too much of him at the moment. It struck me that Julian and Sammy must have been just about the same age, twenty-two or -three, probably brought up in the same kind of Jewish family, same neighborhood, same schooling, and started out with practically the same job. And yet they couldn't have been more different if one had been born an Eskimo and the other the Prince of Wales. And there were so many Julian Blumbergs in the world. Jews without money, without push, without plots, without any of the characteristics which such experts on genetics as Adolf Hitler, Henry Ford and Father Coughlin try to tell us are racial traits. I have seen too many of their lonely, frightened faces packed together in subways or staring out of thousands of dingy rooms as my train hurled past them on the elevated from 125th Street into Grand Central, too many Jewish *nebs* and poets and starving tailors and everyday little guys to consider the fascist answer to What Makes Sammy Run? And yet, if the same background that produced a Sammy Glick could nurture a Julian Blumberg, it wasn't an open-and-shut case of environment either. I filed a mental note to mull over Kit's idea again, that Sammy's childhood environment was the breeding ground for the predatory germ that thrived in Sammy's blood, leaving him with one of the most severe cases of the epidemic.

"Sammy Glick!" I said. "You don't mean to tell me that your wife and Sammy . . . ?"

"Oh, no," he said. "I don't mean that. But I swear to God, Mr. Manheim, even that wouldn't be as bad. It isn't my wife that Glick's stolen—it's my—my whole life."

I wished his eyes could have been angry, but they weren't. They only cried.

"Wait a minute," I said. "If you're talking about the credit for that story, I'm with you. But I don't see what I can do about it, Julian."

"Oh, that isn't it," he said. "That story doesn't matter, Mr. Manheim."

"My name's Al," I said.

"I'm sorry," he said. "But that was just the beginning. Jesus, if I could only have my job in the ad department back and go on writing my novel at night. I can't even write any more, Mr. Manheim. Honest to Christ, if I had a little more guts I'd throw myself off that bridge in Pasadena."

His voice threatened to get away from him.

"Hold it," I said. "You better eat that while it's hot. There's nothing lousier than cold Chinese food.

"Then begin at the beginning. Take your time. And telling me how upset you are won't do either of us any good. Try to hold yourself down to the facts."

I poured the sake and he wet his lips with it. When he began again he dropped his voice to a flat monotone to keep it steady.

It seems that Rosalie Goldbaum wasn't the only one waiting for a letter when Sammy went west. Sammy was supposed to lay the groundwork for Julian and let him know the moment he found an opening. So Julian kept his little job in the ad department, waiting for Der Tag. *But the only news of Sammy he ever had was via Parsons' column. Finally, Blanche made him sit down and write a letter. It was long, plaintive and unanswered.*

One night he came home from his job to find Blanche packing. For the vacation in the Catskills she had been wanting? No, to California, to Hollywood.

"But Blanche!" he said. "We haven't heard from Sammy Glick. How can we go to Hollywood?"

Blanche was short and lean, toughened in the same tenements that Julian had passed through so curiously untouched.

"Sit down and eat your dinner before it gets cold, Julie," she said. "We're going to California in the secondhand car I bought with part of the story money this afternoon. We're going to pay a little visit to that friend Glick you were all the time telling me was doing so much for you."

"Blanche, you sound mad. Don't be mad at me," he said.

"Oh, don't be silly, I love you," she said furiously. "If I didn't love you it wouldn't get me so sore to see you let a gonif *like Glick make a dope out of you when I know you could be a fine writer. Now sit down and eat so you can get through and help me pack."*

They had three blowouts, their radiator cracked from overheating crossing the Continental Divide, Julian drove a hundred miles out of their way one night when Blanche fell asleep and when they arrived in Hollywood Sammy wouldn't see them.

They called the studio every day for a week, but Sammy was never in. They couldn't reach him at home because the studio wouldn't tell them where he was living. They frequented places they couldn't afford, hoping to run into him. It wasn't until their money had dwindled to the margin Blanche had laid aside in case they had to drive East again that Julian managed to get Sammy on the other end of a telephone.

Sammy dispensed with the overtures. His voice grated: "Listen, shtunk, for Chri'sake who the hell told you to come out here?"

"But Mr. Glick, I thought . . ."

"The hell you did. If you thought you would have stayed home. Didn't I tell you I'd send for you when the time came?"

"Yes, but I didn't think it would take . . ."

"Listen, kid," Sammy's voice suddenly soft-pedaled. "Don't think I'm having any cakewalk. As soon as I get set I'll be able to fix you up, but right now they've got me going around in circles." He paused, trying to suck Julian in on the laugh. "I guess we're just a couple of kids who didn't know when we were well off, hey, Julian?"

Julian thought of the trip home, of the lousy job, and Blanche. "Mr. Glick, I told Blanche you wouldn't give me the runaround. There must be some way you could get me in. Not even as a writer. Maybe the story department could use a . . ."

"Look, do you wanna be smart?" Sammy told him. "Get the hell out of this lousy town and back to New York. You won't have a prayer around here until the fall anyway—the summer's always slow . . ." Then his voice tensed and quickened. "Listen, pal, they're calling me for a conference. I'll shoot you a wire the first time anything looks hot—now be a smart guy like I toldya. Have a nice trip back." And he cut Julian off.

I don't know how he looked when he really hung up that phone but the secondhand version he gave me in the booth of that

Chinese restaurant was the closest I ever want to come to it. His pale blue eyes were pink-rimmed and his skin looked too thin to hold his face in. It was not a weak but a sensitive face, which seemed to be characterized by the gentle curve of a delicate nose.

"For days I didn't even have the nerve to tell Blanche I had talked to him," Julian said. "I knew what she would say and I felt like a big enough sap already. You know, love is a funny thing, Mr. Manheim. There never was anything small or selfish about Blanche, and yet I think things would have been better between us if I could have come home with that writing job."

So he spent three weeks riding the street cars and the buses and trying to get by the studio reception desks. His Hollywood wasn't that exclusive night club where everyone knew everybody else. He learned that Hollywood extended from Warner Brothers at Burbank, in the valley beyond the northern hills, to Metro-Goldwyn-Mayer, twenty-five miles southwest in Culver City. He found a new side of Hollywood, the ten-man-for-every-job side, the seasonal unemployment, the call-again-next-month side. The factory side. He learned how many Julian Blumbergs there were, who found nothing but No Admittance signs, for every Sammy Glick who opens the lock with a wave of his cigar like a magic wand.

It wasn't until he had made the rounds of all the major studios and began ringing doorbells on Poverty Row that he had his first nibble. A shoestring producer told him he had bought the stock shots from Hell's Angels and Wings and needed an airplane story with no more than three principal characters, in as few interiors as possible.

He worked all week and when the producer told him he seemed to be on the right track he put in another feverish week, finishing a thirty-page outline of a tight little melodrama. The producer's secretary (who was also his entire staff) asked Julian to leave the manuscript with the assurance that if it were approved he would be hired. Two weeks later it was returned in the mail, with a brief, formal note.

An unemployed writer in the hotel put him wise. Julian had fallen for a familiar Poverty Row economy gag. The producer encourages as many as a dozen aspiring writers to work on his idea. They knock themselves out over his story for two or three weeks in return for nothing but the vaguest of promises. Then the producer comes out of it with enough free ideas to nourish the one writer he finally hires.

When Julian heard this there was nothing to do but make a full confession to Blanche and throw the suitcase into the back seat again.

The drive back took them three days longer than they expected because of a short in the battery and the piston rings' wearing out. They had the trip budgeted so carefully that they reached Blanche's parents' apartment in the Bronx with exactly forty-three cents.

"So you can imagine how we felt when we read this telegram," Julian said. "Mother said it had been waiting there several days. I saved it as a souvenir of my Hollywood career."

His mouth smiled, but nothing happened to his eyes. "It's turned out to be the only item in my collection."

He handed me the over-fingered, often-folded telegram. I read it, and then I read it again, and then again. It was like hearing Sammy Glick's voice in the room.

DEAR JULIAN. HERE IS GREATEST BREAK OF YOUR LIFE. HAVE SCREEN-WRITING JOB FOR YOU. ENCLOSING MONEY FOR IMMEDIATE AIRLINE TRIP TO HOLLYWOOD FOR YOU AND WIFE. WIRE COLLECT WHEN I SHOULD MEET YOU AT AIRPORT. YOUR PAL

SAMMY

So the day the Blumbergs arrived from Hollywood in their broken-down jalopy they were flying back again via TWA. Sammy was waiting at the airport. He threw his arms around Julian like a brother. Five minutes later they were in the car Sammy had hired, rushing back to town.

Julian's mouth was dry with excitement. He thought he was heading straight for the studio.

Twenty minutes later he found himself in Sammy's apartment. Sammy wasn't losing a moment. He sat Julian down, handed him a script and told him he could start working.

Julian began reading obediently, too busy to notice Blanche's suspicions. What kind of a job was this that kept them from the studio? she wanted to know.

"Lots of writers work at home," Sammy said. "I told them I thought it would go faster here. And to tell you the truth—you aren't exactly on the payroll yet, Julian."

"Oh," said Julian.

"Not exactly?" said Blanche.

"I'll come clean with you," Sammy said. "The studio canned the writer who was working with me because they seemed to think I could get along better alone. But I find I haven't got time to knock the script out myself so I thought it would be a swell idea to get you out here to give me a hand. And as soon as you have a couple of scenes under your belt it'll be a cinch for me to get you a regular job by showing 'em what you can do. Meanwhile you can move in with me and I'll loan you twenty-five a week to keep you going till you're on your feet."

It didn't sing like the telegram. But at least it was an in and even Blanche was willing to ride along.

Julian rolled up his sleeves without knowing the difference between a fade-in and a stand-in. He stayed up all that night reading one screenplay after another, getting the feel of it. By morning he discovered that he was able to find holes in the script that grew out of the bizarre collaboration of S. Henley Forster and Sammy Glick. Twenty-four hours after he arrived he was rewriting the first scene and he kept batting out scenes for the rest of the week in eighteen-hour stretches. The plan was for him and Sammy to write alternate sequences. Only Sammy was always being called to conferences at the studio that lasted most of the day. But he explained to Julian that he was still carrying the brunt of the work as he was going ahead and laying out the ensuing scenes. In his mind.

In the frenzy of those first days Julian began to feel he had been writing scenarios all his life. When Sammy read his work all he said was, "This stuff sounds okay," but Julian noticed that he didn't waste any time racing off to the studio with it.

Blanche and Julian took the day off and discovered Hollywood was a small town on a large scale with simple, modest houses separated by small, neat lawns. It was Julian's last day before he was to take his place with Sammy at the studio. They rode to the end of carlines, holding hands and giggling like kids. They felt as if they were taking the first deep breath since they arrived. It was fun to remember that this was late winter, with the green trees and the warm sun. Blanche wondered happily how long it would take for this crisp heat to dry up Julian's sinuses. They even stopped in to ask the rent of one of the cute little stucco bungalows on Orange Grove Avenue. Fifty dollars a month with a small yard of their own and two orange trees, tiny ones but each with a real orange.

Sammy was waiting for them when they got home. With a face full of bad news. "Tough luck, kid," he said. "I'm afraid your scenes didn't go over like I thought they would."

He let Julian feel just lousy enough before adding:

"But I haven't lost faith in you. In fact just to show you where you stand with me I'm going to throw in ten bucks a week extra with that twenty-five."

That was more money than Julian had ever made before, enough for him and Blanche to take a flat of their own in one of the cheap apartment houses above Hollywood Boulevard.

Sammy started calling Julian his secretary. He was doing all his work at the studio now, but he thought it would be good practice for Julian to go on writing through the script and promised to go over his scenes with him and give him pointers, to help him learn the trade.

When the script was finished and Sammy was waiting for his next assignment, Julian didn't like to sit around without writing so he started working on an original called Country Doctor because he thought it would help Sammy plead his case at the studio. He was almost too frightened of Blanche's beautiful and brutal candor to tell her the story, but she surprised him by saying, "Julian, if you were only as smart as you knew how to write! It doesn't matter how *much money there is in this story as long as you make sure it says—By Julian Blumberg. So the big shots will finally find out my pupsie is a writer."*

Julian wrote easily, and it was his sort of stuff, simple and human, and he had it finished in a week. For the next three days he wondered whether it was good enough to show to Sammy. He had decided it wasn't when Sammy came to him and said, "Say, I read that yarn of yours Blanche showed me. It's pretty fair—got a couple of nice moments. I'll see what I can do with it."

"Well," Julian said, "weeks went by and it looked like he'd forgotten all about my story, so I started helping him with his next screenplay because there didn't seem to be anything better to do. And then one day Blanche happened to be reading through the trade papers and found this:

He handed me a ragged little clipping. I was beginning to feel like a district attorney. "Exhibit B," I said.

Sammy was running through the room again as I started to read: "Sammy Glick makes it two in a row as his latest original, *Country Doctor* . . ." and handed the squib back.

What a two-scene that must have been, Julian's stammering request for an explanation—Sammy hammering back at him:

"Listen, Julie, don't be a schlemiel all your life. Everybody thinks I'm hot at the studio right now. So I saw a chance of smacking them for a bonus that means twice the dough they'd pay a Julian Blumberg." He made the name sound like a cussword. "Jesus Christ, what the hell have you got to bitch about when I'm putting the money in your pocket?"

"But it isn't fair . . ."

"No fair," Sammy mimicked. "Like they say in sissy schools. No fair! For Chris'sake, grow up, this isn't kindergarten any more, this is the world."

That was one of the most philosophical observations Sammy ever made.

I was beginning to feel like a groggy fighter waiting for his manager to toss in the towel and Julian seemed to sense this, for he said, "Well, there isn't a whole lot more to tell, Mr. Manheim . . ."

My God, more! I thought. If what he had been telling me were supposed to be fiction I would have broken in ten minutes ago to tell him his story was hopeless hyperbole. But you could tell Julian was telling the truth. It's strange that a writer as gifted as Julian could be so stupid that he was incapable of telling anything but the truth. I believed him because truth is never hard to recognize. Nothing is ever quite so drab and repetitious and forlorn and ludicrous as truth.

"I guess you must have thought I was a little shell-shocked when you saw me after the preview last night. Well, maybe I was. Because that picture was the biggest shock in my life, Mr. Manheim. How do you think you'd feel going in to a movie cold and suddenly starting to realize you're hearing all your own scenes?"

Oh, God, I thought, I'm going to explode. Sammy Glick is a time bomb in my brain and it's going to go off any moment and blow me to bits.

"The whole picture," Julian was saying. "All those scenes I thought I was just doing for practice—actually showing on the screen—all mine—every line, mine—you know what I felt like doing, Mr. Manheim? I felt like jumping up right in the middle and screaming. I wanted to tell everybody there that the only line Glick wrote on *Girl Steals Boy* was the by-line on the cover. I felt like telling all of them that now I know why he had me fly out in such a hurry—because when he got the other writer bounced he knew he couldn't stay on the picture alone—he didn't dare."

"Why didn't you?" I said. "I suppose you'd've been rushed to the psychopathic ward, but it would have been worth it."

"I just got sick to my stomach," Julian said. "I mean actually throwing up, in the men's room. And when I came out Blanche made me talk to Sammy right away. I've seen Blanche mad, but I've never seen her like that before. I thought it might be better to wait and see Sammy in the morning. But she said either I saw

him right then and there—or she'd go home and move out. You
see, Blanche is a funny kid, Mr. Manheim. To look at her you
wouldn't think she was anything but a nice, frail little Jewish girl.
But . . ."

"So you did have a talk with Sammy last night?" I said.

"I caught him for a moment in the lobby on his way out,"
Julian said sadly.

*"Sammy, you've got to listen to me! How could you do this to
me, Sammy? Telling me they didn't like my scenes when they
used . . ."*

*Sammy looked around the lobby coldly, saw the little group
nearby surrounding Sidney Fineman.*

"I don't want to discuss it here."

"But Sammy, I can't go on this way. Blanche . . ."

"I said shut up."

*Then he looked up and added, "Thank you very much. I'm glad
you enjoyed it."*

*Julian looked around. A gray-haired gentleman with a smiling
pink face was joining them. He slipped his arm around Sammy with
fatherly affection.*

*"Looks like we have a hit, son," he said. "And everybody's
talking about the writing."*

*"Thank you, Mr. Fineman. Julian, I don't suppose I have to tell
you who this is—Sidney Fineman?"*

"I'm very glad to meet you," said Julian.

*"How do you do," said Fineman. Julian felt he was being cordial
and oblivious to him at the same time. "How did you like the
picture?" It was hardly a question the way Fineman put it, more
like the perfunctory How-are-you in passing an acquaintance on the
street. And it demanded the same kind of "Fine-thanks" answer.*

*There was a pause. Julian was hesitating. Wondering if Blanche
was watching him. Repeating to himself what he knew he ought
to say. Fineman was waiting. Sammy was staring at him like the
bully in the classroom whose eyes say "See you after school."*

"Very much," Julian said.

"Fine," said Fineman. "There are a couple of things I want to talk over with you, Sammy. Will you excuse us?"

And Julian was left standing there alone in the lobby, not knowing what to do until he spotted Sammy's friend, Al Manheim, in the crowd. Even then he might not have introduced himself if Blanche hadn't insisted that he go over and try to tell him the whole story.

"And God knows you have," I said. "So what are all the fireworks between you and the Missus?"

"That's the part I haven't told you," he said. "The part that's just happened."

"Oi vay!" I said.

"You see, Sammy was over to see me at half past eight this morning."

Now I remembered another morning that Sammy had been up at the crack of dawn after an all-night party to keep an appointment with Julian—leaving me behind in his apartment to dwell on my biliousness and his sudden interest in Julian's welfare.

"He was awfully friendly. He said he was still convinced our destinies lay together and was willing to raise me to fifty a week to convince me. He said he had just sold Mr. Collier a story called *Monsoon* without having anything down on paper. But he had to have something written by the time he saw him again, and he thought we might knock it out together over the weekend. And, oh yes, he told me that there are plenty of ghost writers in this town who make more dough than lots of pretty well-known B writers. Well, I wasn't wild about the idea, but fifty bucks is fifty bucks, so he made me promise I'd call at his office at three o'clock this afternoon and give him my answer. Then I told Blanche. She went nuts. I told her with fifty bucks a week we could rent that cottage on Orange Grove we wanted. But you should have heard her."

"To hell with the cottage! Maybe it would help pay the rent if I walked the streets too. That's what that great pal of yours wants

*you to do. Only worse. I'm beginning to feel I'm living with a ghost.
Look at you, you're even beginning to look like one, so pale, and
losing weight and stammering worse than ever. It's this lousy job.
You want to go through more nights like last night? You think it's
worth fifty dollars a week to vomit your supper in the toilet?"*

"Next time I won't get so upset," Julian said. *"Now I know how
I stand. I'm a ghost writer, and meanwhile . . ."*

"Meanwhile," Blanche said in a voice that gave Julian the shiv-
vers, *"if you let him shmeikle you into this, I'll be in New York.
I'll catch the bus tonight."*

The waiter came to take the plates away.

"You haven't eaten anything," I said.

"I'm not hungry," he said. "I can't eat."

Then I realized that I had hardly eaten anything either.

"Will you help me," he said, "Al?"

"I don't know," I said. "All I know is that I'm going to try."

"I thought because he was a friend of yours," he started to say.

"Here's a nickel," I said. "Get Blanche on the phone. Tell her
she was right. Tell her that whatever happens you two are sticking
together. And tell her that somebody who's never met her but
knows her awfully well sends his love."

Then I called Pancake, whom I hadn't been able to clip from
behind in spite of Sammy's coaching, and told him I would be
unavoidably detained from the studio this afternoon. I realized
this meant giving him a free-kick at my posterior, but if you can't
take an hour off to help a guy with something on the ball, you
begin to wonder just what the hell you think you're working your
ass off for. And other questions equally searching.

|||||||

The receptionist's pencil poised over the pad of studio passes.
"Mr. Glick. Who shall I say is calling?"

Since Sammy was waiting for Julian the chances are he'd only
brush me off. I didn't like to do it, but I had to figure what Sammy
would have done if he were in my spot.

"Mr. Blumberg," I said.

I walked down the corridor to his door, slowing up as I reached it because I was scared. Here I was going out of my way to do something I hated more than anything else in the world. Avoiding controversies has always been an obsession with me. The only times I could digest were when I was liking everybody around me. *Will you please tell me why you had to get yourself into this?* I thought. *Who the hell do you think you are, Sammy Glick's conscience?* I wasn't so far off at that. As I stood there turning the knob I knew that my best excuse for knowing Sammy Glick was as a kind of self-appointed first-aid station, trying to revive the victims he left behind him as he kept hitting-and-running his way to the top.

When I walked in on him he gave me a hollow "Hello-Al," looked around for Julian, questioned me with his eyes, and caught on.

"Your collaborator isn't coming," I said. "He's on his way over to see his wife. To tell her she doesn't have to leave him. Because you're going to promise that the next picture he writes he not only gets paid for but gets his name on."

Sammy had looked at me in a lot of interesting ways since that first meeting, but I had never seen anything like this before. I have never had a gangster pass death sentence on me with his eyes, but now I know what it is to see not only friendship but even recognition iris out of them, the pupils contracting and ossifying till they looked as if they could be plucked out and fired through a shotgun.

"Aren't you satisfied just being a Boy Scout? Whatta you wanna do, get your Eagle Badge too?"

The Sammy Glick I met when I first came to Hollywood was a cream puff compared to the one with whom I now found myself caged. He was still in his early twenties but no sign of youth remained. The little knives of ambition had already begun to cut lines into his face and the way he hunched over his cigar somehow suggested middle age.

"Sammy," I said, "at the rate you're going you'll die of old age before you're thirty."

He planted himself so close to me that I instinctively backed away. His voice spat in my face. "Listen, you son of a rabbi. When I want sermons I don't have to listen to amateurs. I can buy tickets for the big shots in the racket—like Wise or Magnin."

I tried everything I could think of to break him down, flattery, nostalgia, the brotherhood of man, the camaraderie of the newspaper game and even, as a last resort, the need of Jews to help each other in self-defense.

"Don't pull that Jewish crapola on me," Sammy said. "What the hell did the Jews ever do for me?—except maybe get my head cracked open for me when I was a kid."

What makes Sammy run? The childhood, Kit had said, look into the childhood.

Sammy took his eyes from me only for a moment, but it brought relief. He looked past me, almost thoughtfully, as thoughtful as a man rushing through life like Sammy could ever be.

"Jews," he said bitterly and absently.

"Jews," he said, like a storm trooper.

That was all he said but I knew it was much more than that. I knew he was speaking his hate and his fear and his rage of anything that had or would ever stand in his way.

He paced around me impatiently. "Let me tell you something for your own good," he said. "Wanna know why you're a flop out here? Because you pay too goddam much attention to other people's business. When I was a kid I felt kind of gypped because I couldn't go to college and make the basketball team. I was a helluva basketball player once. But when I look at you I think maybe it's a good thing I didn't get my mind all cluttered up with crap at that. I may not know a lot of cushy words, but, by Jesus, I know about life. Take Darwin, for instance. I didn't have to read any books to know all about the survival of the fittest."

I felt lousy. We were in the same room all right but we couldn't seem to connect. I knew I was making a mess of it, that all I was doing was convincing him that I was a lunatic. And not even a dangerous one. I think he actually felt that he was going out of his way to be kind to me. And I suppose he was, according to his lights, those crazy blinding lights of his.

"What do you mean fittest?" I said. "Who's more fit to write screenplays, you or Julian?"

His hand tightened around his cigar the way his voice did around his words.

"Listen, pal, you'll be doing yourself a big favor if you get out of here. Because I'm liable to be in a position to do you some good one of these days. And when I am I don't want to have to remember what a jerk you're making outa yourself."

"I don't leave this office until Julian's taken care of," I said.

The statement was not as heroic as it sounded because it wasn't given quite enough voice. It wasn't fear that stifled me, but a terrible sense of inadequacy.

That was something Sammy never had to worry about. His whole body was behind his voice. Even when everyone else was silent he used his voice as if he were yelling down a crowd.

"You can tell Julian for me," he said, "that if he don't like the fifty bucks he can crap in his hat, pull it over his head and call it curls."

That phrase has its ghost writer too, I thought, for it was a folk cry of the New York gutters I had heard before. But Sammy spoke it with a terrifying eloquence.

I said all the four-, five- and seven-letter words I could think of, most of them outside in the corridor, after the door had slammed behind me. I stood there trying to begin thinking what to do next. I don't know whether I thought first of Kit and then saw her name on the opposite door or vice versa. Like most inspirations, the impulse probably followed the stimulus so rapidly that it seemed to be snatched from the sky. I don't know why I hadn't thought of her before. She knew how to be just as tough as Sammy in her own way. I had to admit that the characteristics that had made me hesitate about her were the ones that might do Julian the most good.

The secretary told me she was very sorry, but Miss Sargent left word for her to admit no one this afternoon, not even to put calls through.

I said this was an emergency and must have made it pretty strong for the secretary asked, "Is it a matter of life or death?"

"Both," I said.

This seemed to bewilder her sufficiently to stir her to action. A moment later the door to the inner office swung open and Kit appeared, dressed in tailored slacks, with a pencil stuck in her hair and no makeup.

"Sorry to pull the big-shot stuff on you. But all you have to do to start a salon around here is leave your door open."

We shook hands and she signaled me into the office. It was full of smoke and an atmosphere of being worked in. At the desk, which was littered with typewritten notes, sat a stenographer still writing in her shorthand pad.

"While we're talking it might not be a bad idea to start typing up that last scene, Ellen," Kit told the stenog. "Be ready for you again in fifteen minutes."

She led me to the couch and told me to sit down.

"Don't mind my standing up," she said. "I've been pacing up and down this office so much all day I can't stop. I feel like Charlie Chaplin still going through the motions after he leaves that factory in *Modern Times*."

She demonstrated his nervous reflex-action gag.

I asked her what she was working on.

"On something really respectable for a change," she said. "*Young Tom Jefferson*. You know Tom has always been my secret passion. I've been after them to make a Jefferson picture since the day I checked in here—but they were always afraid of it for the British market. Then I had the brainstorm of getting an English star like Howard to play the part. So it looks as if it's going through—if I can only hammer out the goddam story line."

She glanced at her watch, and her tone changed.

"But this isn't what you came in to talk about," she said, "so

I better give you the floor. Because I really will have to run you out of here in fifteen minutes."

She paced while I talked. I was watching to see if the revelation would shock her, but her only comment when I finished was, "I've been wondering who was doing Sammy's stuff. That Blumberg kid looks sad enough to be a real humorist."

"I've just been in talking to Sammy," I said. "No dice."

"I'm afraid you're too nice a guy to do much good in this world," she said. "It takes a cold bitch like me to get anywhere with him."

"Oh, I wouldn't say that," I said.

"I know you wouldn't," she said, "you'd only think it."

She perched on the couch beside me for a moment.

"You're not the iceberg you'd like to have us think you are," I said.

She smiled at me as if she was going to laugh and then remembered she didn't have time. "How much time have I got to make an honest man of Mr. Blumberg?"

"Blanche is about to give him up as a lost cause any moment," I said. "Could you get to Sammy this afternoon?"

"Sorry," she said. "I make it a rule never to let anything cut into my work. I don't even take calls from the Guild office. The only way to get ahead in this business is to do one thing at a time."

"Sounds a little like Sammy," I said.

"A little bit of Glick would be a good thing in all of us," she said. She caught my look, and smiled. "I know, a very little bit."

"I could call you at home tomorrow," I said. "Want to give me your number?"

"That's not time enough," she said. "You've given me a tough assignment. Tell Blanche to cool off and hang on. I'll give you a ring when it's under control."

She saw me to the door without any last-moment embarrassments, told Ellen she was ready for her and shook hands with me again.

"So long, Al," she said. "Sorry I have to rush you off this way. Don't let Julian's worries throw you."

When I looked back her door was closed and her swift, low-pitched voice was already beginning to dictate again.

I helped Julian talk Blanche into unpacking her bags and then I returned to the wars with Pancake.

Kit didn't call me for ten days. But when she finally did she said:

"Tell that bashful genius of yours to be at the studio at nine in the morning, ready to take off his coat, hang his inhibitions behind the door and go to work."

"What did you have to do, promise to marry him?"

"You know better than that," she said. "Sammy is only infatuated with me and respects me. Marriage is one of the trump cards he has to hold until the pot is big enough."

"And Julian actually has a real job?" I said. "And gets paid real money? And doesn't do his writing as if in training for the German underground?"

"One hundred dollars a week," she said. "No contract, just week to week, but that doesn't matter as long as he's teamed with Sammy. Sammy's option was lifted for another year and I have a hunch he won't let Julian stray very far from him."

"A hundred bucks a week!" I said. "That isn't hay. Even if Sammy is getting three or four times that much."

"If the ratio of talent to bombast is only one to four," she said, "talent is coming up in the world."

"I guess you're right," I said. "We should be thankful for small miracles. Like having a credit line read—by Sammy Glick *and* Julian Blumberg. How the hell did you swing it?"

"The Guild's supposed to protect writers from unfair practices," she said. "Not only from employers—but from other writers."

"A very pretty sentiment," I said. "But since when was Sammy a sucker for sentiment?"

"From the moment I promised him Julian would get up and tell all at the next membership meeting. One of the planks in our Code is to stamp out ghost writing. Ghosting is the writers' Fate Worse Than Death."

"But the Guild isn't recognized, is it?" I said. "You haven't any power. So what good will your public confessional do?"

"Hollywood consists of half a dozen studios and half a dozen restaurants," she said. "And as you probably know, writers are talkative fellows. And when six hundred writers start saying the same thing . . ."

"I see," I said.

"So did Sammy," she said.

I said it seemed odd for her to put the screws on Sammy that way after the compassion she was expressing for him just the week before.

"That's like saying because we know the cause of a disease and feel sorry for its victim, we shouldn't quarantine him," she said.

I thought: I was the one who felt sorrier for Julian. And Kit was the one who did him some good.

"Okay," I said, "I'll cry uncle."

"Not until you join the Guild," she said. "After all, you've had a practical demonstration in your own home."

"I haven't got anything against the Guild," I said. "But, oh, hell, I guess I'm an individualist."

"So is Al Smith," she said, "and he belongs to everything from the Grand Street Boys to the Liberty League."

"Pancake tells me that screen writers shouldn't have a Guild because they aren't employees."

"He didn't happen to say what they were?" she said.

"Artists," I said.

"Tell that to the producers," she laughed.

"When am I going to see you?" I said.

"I'll give you a ring before the next Guild meeting," she said. "Maybe we can all go together."

"Jesus," I said, "I seem to meet nothing but B-girls out here."

She laughed. "I guess we're all B-girls for something."

"Well, thanks a helluva lot for going to bat for the kid," I said. "It was damn nice of you."

"Forget it," she said in that same tone of voice that always made me feel a little foolish and a little peeved. "The Guild is always at your service. See you, Al."

As soon as she hung up, I dialed Julian's apartment to break the news.

"Hello, Julian?" I said.

"Hello, sweetheart—come on over and drink to the future of a writing team that's going to make Hecht and MacArthur look like a couple of office boys."

"What the hell are you doing there?"

"I just came over to tell Julie I've decided to give him a break," Sammy said. "From now on he's going to be my collaborator. You ought to see him, he's tickled to death."

"You better get a grip on yourself," I said. "One of these days that generosity is just going to run away with you."

After I told them I was too busy to join their party (Sammy was blowing them to a spread at La Maze), I walked over to Barney's Beanery, listened to a once-famous vaudeville team who were singing once-famous songs for tips and tried to drown my reaction to Sammy's most recent philanthropy in Barney's onion soup.

CHAPTER 7

ammy had little chance of disturbing my dreams those next few months, for the studio was having one of its periodic drives to cut overhead—which seemed to mean shaving stenographers' wages first and gradually working their way up to firing small-fry writers like me—so I had been working like a bastard trying to hang on. The *Megaphone* had labeled my first effort *Fair Meller*, and even though I had refused to take an ad, that seemed to be giving it the benefit of the doubt. The situation was so tense that I got the jitters every time an inter-office memo arrived, for fear of being informed that I was no longer employed.

Kit would call me two or three times a month, but that was nothing to gloat over, since all it was ever about was her goddam

Guild. I was still carrying the membership card around in my pocket unsigned. I got a rise out of her when I told her that I liked a lot of people, but I liked them one at a time, not all bunched together.

I finally went, of course. For almost five hours I sat with three or four hundred others in a badly ventilated gymnasium listening to speeches without even the consolation of sitting with Kit because she had to be up on the platform. I felt that if the Guild had a place in Hollywood it had yet to discover what it was. The low-paid writers wanted the Guild to be a real bread-and-butter union, and the congenial five-hundred-dollar-a-week guys thought what writers needed most was a communal hangout like the old Writers' Club where they could sit around and get to know each other. The twenty-five-hundred-dollar-a-week writers with famous names seemed to be most interested in increasing their influence in picture productions and spoke fine, brave abstract words about the scope of the medium and dignifying the position of the screen writer. The meeting seemed a little too much like a caterpillar separated into several parts groping blindly for each other.

When Kit called again about six weeks later I said, "Don't tell me, let me guess; another meeting?"

She said, "The Guild situation is getting hot. Some of the boys are beginning to criticize it because it's too much like a union—and some because it's not enough."

I told her I didn't feel like a meeting tonight and she said to meet her at Musso's on the Boulevard at seven, so we could get there around eight-thirty. Kit had left word for Sammy to meet us for dinner, but as we were sitting down the headwaiter gave us the message that he was tied up with Franklin Collier in a *Monsoon* conference.

"How's he getting along?" I said.

"There hasn't been anything like it since the rise of Irving Thalberg," she said. "But he's been very unhappy."

"You're breaking my heart," I said.

"He and Julian could go on being a successful team for a long time," she said. "I suppose if he saved his dough he could retire before he was thirty. But that isn't enough for him. He can't stop there. Being bracketed with Julian is driving him crazy."

"Where's it going to end, Kit?"

"That's his cross," she said. "Always thinking satisfaction is just around the bend. Not so different from the whippet with his mechanical rabbit."

"That's good," I said. "I want to remember that."

"A whippet," she said. "That's what he's always reminded me of, from that first moment he came in to put the bee on me for Merriam."

"That's funny," I said, "I always thought of him as an animal too—only a ferret."

"I wonder if that's the difference between the male and the female reaction?" she said lightly.

"You think more like a man than any woman I've ever known— and most men."

"If you think that's a compliment, you're crazy," she said. "Every time a man discovers that a woman thinks, the only way he can explain it is that she happens to have a male mind. You just don't know me, Al. I'm feminine as all hell."

"It looks as if the only way I'll ever know you," I said, "is for the Guild to hold meetings every night."

"That reminds me," she said. "We ought to be on our way."

I tried to grab the check but she was too fast for me. I told her I didn't like the idea of having a woman take me to dinner, but my defense of the old-fashioned ways only seemed to amuse her.

"Why should you pay it?" she said. "I asked you, didn't I?"

||||||

The meeting had a tenseness, which could be felt in the hall like air pressure, as the president began to speak of the Guild's need for allies in its fight for recognition and the logical step of joining the Authors' League of America.

Until that moment the Guilders had kidded themselves into thinking that they were one big happy family. But the president had hardly finished when angry gentlemen were screaming to be heard. Their anger seemed almost inexplicable to me. You would have thought that the president had recommended joining the Communist International, instead of the conservative Authors' League. We must remain a purely Hollywood organization, they yelled. We must not fall under the domination of outside forces. We don't want to slip into the clutches of Eastern racketeers and Reds.

One of the loudest attacks on the Authors' League plan was made by a man with a paunchy body and a paunchy face. I recognized Harold Godfrey Wilson, whom Sammy had pointed out to me that first day at the Vendome. As far as I could remember, all that the president had suggested was that the Guild look into the question of what kind of assistance it could obtain from the Authors' League. But for some reason, that made Mr. Wilson apoplectic. He began by telling the story of his life, how he had come to Hollywood in the early twenties, working as an extra, then as a gag man, gradually fighting his way up to become one of the most important writers in the industry, and now, by God, no bunch of Broadway snobs, who thought they were too good for Hollywood, was going to sit around the Algonquin and tell him what to do.

I didn't have a chance to hear much of Kit's rebuttal because that was just about the time Sammy came in. He was wearing a wrap-around camel's-hair coat with a yellow scarf. He stood there in the doorway a moment and then he picked me out on the aisle and took the seat I had been saving for him.

The chair in front of him was empty and he turned it around and stuck his feet up on it. I couldn't help noticing the shoes. They were new again. A style I had never seen before, without any laces at all.

"You oughta get yourself some of these, Al," he said. "Cromwells. You can't buy them out here, but if you give them your measurements they'll send them to you from New York. I've got a standing order for a couple of pair a year."

I just pointed toward Kit on the platform. "As long as the Guild is a democratic organization," she was saying, "there aren't any differences we can't take in our stride. And we can go on being a democratic organization just as long as we all stick together; don't let anybody scare us and hammer out our program right here on the floor."

She seemed to have caught the mood of the membership because her plea for unity got the best hand of the night.

"Looks like Kit is our Joan of Arc," I said.

Sammy looked around at his fellow members with very little love. "Sure," he said, "she knows how to get to them, all right. But they're nothing but a bunch of sheep. Throw one good scare into them and they'll run out of this place so fast you'll think it's on fire."

"With a pair of Cromwell shoes in the lead," I said.

Up till that moment, though I had to admire what Kit was trying to do, and though I thought unions were a good thing in general, I didn't see much need or much chance for a screen writers' organization. But now I was defending it. I suppose if Sammy had expressed a preference for Heaven, I would have launched into a defense of Hell.

|||||||

The day I was laid off at the studio I felt so low I decided I had to see Kit. Whoever answered her phone told me I could reach her at Mr. Glick's, and when Sammy's Jap informed me that the master had gone to Palm Springs for the weekend I felt still lower. I called Billie.

I had never seen the old part of Los Angeles so we went down to Olivera Street, the narrow market with its tourist stalls which is all that remains of the early Spanish town, where marimba bands play their gay and melancholy tunes in front of sidewalk cafes, tamales are sold like hot dogs and you get the impression that every Mexican in the world is trying to sell you a souvenir.

It was a little too much like a set on the back lot to make me very happy at first, but a couple of slugs of *tequila* made a difference. Billie, who seemed to be in love with all men nicely, began to teach me the rhumba, and she used her few words of Spanish on the waiter and after burning my stomach with *enchilada* and my brain with more *tequila* I was holding her large plump hand and saying, "Billie, hey Billie, listen Billie, d'ya love me?"

"Sure, honey," she giggled. "You're cute when you're drunk."

"I'm not drunk, Billie," I said. "I know every word I'm saying. If you don't believe me I can tell you everything we've said since we sat down. Okay. So I'm not drunk. I'm just serious, that's all. I'm in love with you, Billie, seriously, and if you don't believe me I'll call you tomorrow and say the same thing when I'm sober."

"Don't be serious, honey," she said. "Love is much nicer when it isn't serious."

"But goddam it, I love you," I said loudly. "I want to marry you."

As I reached my hand out to hold hers and make it more convincing, I turned over my half-filled glass.

"Look at that," I laughed as the thick liquid rolled slowly across the table. "Looks just like lava. No wonder I feel hot. I'm drinking lava."

"You're in love, Al," she said. "You're in love with somebody, all right."

"Whatta you mean?" I said. "What are you talking about I'm in love with somebody?"

"It's a funny thing," she said, "but whenever a fella gets feeling good and wants to marry me, I know he's in love with somebody."

What the hell makes her know so much about love, I wondered. She may never write a book about it, but speaking strictly physically, spiritually, romantically and psychologically she must know more about love than Havelock Ellis and Bertrand Russell put together.

"I'm not in love with anybody," I said. "But if I were in love with anybody it would be with you, sweetheart. Because, well, hell, you're old-fashioned. You may not know it, baby, but you're the nineteen-thirty-six version of the old-fashioned girl—the nineteen-thirty-sex version," I added and broke myself up.

"Mmmm a tango," she said with her whole body behind it.

"I think I'll just sit this one out," I said. "Go ahead, Billie, I'd only be in your way. Just let me sit here and watch."

Later, a voice that seemed to come from behind me said, "Al, you'd better pay the check. They're closing up."

"My God," I said, "Billie, you scared me. Jesus, I've been sleeping. I must have been sleeping for hours!"

"We only finished dancing a second ago," she said. "You were just starting to close your eyes."

"But I've been dreaming," I said. "Know who it was about? Sammy Glick. He was climbing up a rope and I was chasing him, only the rope didn't seem to be tied to anything—just going straight up in the air. And every time he got near the end, it just kept getting longer. And then I fell off . . ."

"Señor, your check," the waiter said in a tolerant but wanting-to-get-home voice.

While I was waiting for the change I said, "Billie, I don't think I ever asked you before. Do you know what makes Sammy run?"

She looked at me puzzled, not knowing whether to take it seriously or humor me.

"That's all right," I said, "take your time. I've been at it for years."

"Do you know?" she said.

"Of course I don't know," I said. "But I'm working on it, little by little. You know what I need, Billie? A subsidy from the Carnegie Foundation. Then I could have a whole staff helping me. Because it's a big job, Billie. Once we know what makes Sammy run it will be a great thing for the world. Like discovering the cause of cancer."

"We better go home," Billie said.

"Billie," I said, "can you keep a secret? I think Kit is the only person in the world who knows what makes Sammy run. And she's such a coldhearted bitch she won't tell."

|||||||

When Kit called me for the next meeting I was either not myself or too much myself. I said, "I should think you could get a girl at the Guild office to take over some of this secretarial work for you, Kit."

"What is it, Al?" she said. "You sound sore at me."

I'm not sore, I thought. I think I'm falling in love with you. There is a very subtle difference.

"I guess I'm just in sort of a mood today," I said. "I think maybe I'll pass this one up, Kit, if it's all the same with you."

As usual I browsed around Stanley Rose's until I had an appetite and then as usual I went next door to Musso's.

"Evening, Mr. Manheim," the waiter greeted me. "Going to the Guild meeting tonight?"

Amelio was a good union man himself who would find no inner peace until Hollywood was an organized town. I said I was, in order to avoid indigestion over my chicken wings, for Amelio was the restaurant's indisputable forensic star.

On my way out I got it again. I stopped to say hello to three writers who always ate at the same table by the door. "Want to have a drink with us?" they asked. "And then we'll all go over to the meeting together."

I told them I would probably see them over there.

I started walking down the Boulevard and turned in at the narrow alleyway leading to Henkel's Art Gallery. The gallery was in a funny little bungalow with an easygoing, out-of-this-world atmosphere, which featured surrealist and abstractionist stuff and Mr. Henkel, blond, middle-aged, dumpy and vague, who spoke about art with a cigarette in his mouth so rapidly and indistinctly that I was rarely able to understand him, though occasional phrases always sounded significant.

I had only been in Hollywood a short time, but I was already beginning to meet people everywhere I went. This time it was my erstwhile collaborator, Pancake.

"Well," he said, "it seems there are some writers left who are still more interested in the better things than in forming a union like a bunch of plumbers."

I looked at my watch. I could still make it if I hurried. "As a matter of fact," I said, "I just came in here to kill a couple of minutes before going over with the rest of the plumbers."

I must have arrived only half an hour late because the meeting hadn't begun yet. People were still standing around in little groups, talking. I picked Sammy out right away. He must have swallowed a magnet when he was a little boy. I started over. He was with Harold Godfrey Wilson and a tall, lean fellow who would have had the face of a typical Yale man if it hadn't been for the pale, sick skin and the tired patches under the eyes.

Sammy proudly introduced me to Lawrence Paine, whose name had been on some of the finest pictures Hollywood had turned out. I remembered that he had won the Academy Award for the best screenplay a year or so ago.

They went on talking about the Guild. "I'm all for the Guild," Paine said. "But I'll be damned if I like how it's being run. They're letting too many people in. What the hell, every lucky bastard who happens to sell one story isn't a screen writer. The producers won't take us seriously until we limit the membership to writers who've been employed at least a year, or get a thousand dollars a week."

"If this bunch of Reds have their way we'll be marching down Hollywood Boulevard in their May Day Parade," Wilson said.

"What do you mean, Reds?" I said.

"Well, maybe not Reds," Paine said. "Harold here always gets a little excited. But they're goddam parlor-pinks and that's just as bad. It's up to the responsible element to save the Guild."

"Excuse me, Mr. Paine," I said. "I just joined the Guild on my way in tonight and I admit I don't know too much about it. But it seems to me you want to save the Guild by kicking out the little guys like me. And they're just the ones the Guild ought to be helping the most."

"Apparently not all the lower-bracket writers feel the way you do about it. Young Sammy here is with us, aren't you, Sammy?"

Young Sammy was with them, all right. Young Sammy was

applying for the job of bugle boy in the proud little army that marched under the banner of $2500 a week.

After they wandered off Sammy shook his head and said, "Al, you'll never get anywhere that way. Those guys have an *in* with some of the biggest producers in town. They know what they're talking about. They don't get twenty-five hundred a week for nothing."

"You will," I said.

"Twenty-five hundred a week," he said.

I could feel him going crazy inside when he said it.

"What are you making now, Sammy?" I asked.

"A lousy five hundred," he said. "But it isn't the dough. Hell, as long as I stay single I can manage on five hundred all right. But the producers use five-hundred-a-week writers to wipe themselves with, Al."

Kit was right, I thought. You couldn't blame a man for having a clubfoot, or a tapeworm in his mind.

"You're only a kid," I said. "You'll get your twenty-five hundred, you crazy son-of-a-bitch. I'll bet you get it before you're thirty."

"You know you can get good credits out here for years without getting in the big dough," Sammy said. "But I've been thinking about it. I've been looking over guys' shoulders while they hit the jackpot. Know how they do it? On the outside. With a hit play, for instance. That's how these producers think. They see something they like in print or on the stage and right away their tongues are hanging out to pay the writer three or four times as much as the guys trying to make a rep in their own business."

"What makes you think you can write a play?" I said.

"Hell, plenty of dopes write plays," he said.

"Talented dopes," I said.

"Talent can get you just so far," he said. "Then you got to start using your head."

The meeting was being called to order. There seemed to be a larger crowd than last time. It looked as if the Guild was on its way.

"What have you been doing for yourself?" Sammy said.

I didn't give him the usual optimistic crap because I wanted to hear what he would say. I told him after my option had lapsed I had gone without a job for a couple of months and finally had landed at National, a little action-picture lot, on a flat-deal basis at a thousand bucks a script. Which means that you work twenty-six hours a day trying to get your dough as fast as possible.

"Any time limit on rewriting?" Sammy said.

I couldn't remember any.

"Then they've got you by the balls but good," Sammy said. "Once you get your grand they can keep you on the picture as long as they like."

"I know," I said, "but what the hell can I do? Maybe that's a job for the Guild."

"If you ask me," Sammy said, "the Guild has one foot in the grave—and it's goosing itself with the other. Maybe you ought to write a play too."

The funny thing is I had been writing one. I had been writing one for three years. It was about a rabbi like my father and anti-Semitism in a small town and the fundamental quest of simple men for dignity, fraternity, peace and beer on Saturday night. I wanted to make the content of the play everything that I had seen and felt, and the form everything I knew. And I didn't want to tell anybody about it until it began to come alive to me. Because it seems to me too many writers drain their excitement and energy away in conversation.

"I've been working on one for a couple of years," I said.

"Don't futz around with it too long," Sammy said. "Try to peddle it. They buy lousy plays for pictures every day. And six months from now the chances are that they won't remember what kind of *dreck* it was. All they'll remember is that you are a play-wright and look at all the lousy playwrights out here in the big money."

|||||||

I don't know whether Sammy had the play already written the night we talked about it or whether he ran right home and dashed it off after that meeting, but it couldn't have been more than a couple of months later that I received an engraved invitation in the mail. Mr. Samuel Glick was requesting the pleasure of my company at the opening of his three-act comedy-drama *Live Wire* at the Hollywood Playhouse.

Sammy Glick, prominent scenarist and playwright, I thought tenderly and hatefully, my little Sammy Glick.

I was still admiring the tasteful typography of his announcement when Sammy called.

His voice was full of exulting raucous chimes out of tune.

"Hiya sweetheart, how're they hanging? Well, are you all set for your greatest evening in the American theater?"

I said I had his invitation.

"It's shaping up something terrific," he said. "Everybody says it looks like the biggest opening this town ever had. I gave Fineman and Frank Collier a row each and they even promised to join my party at the Troc after the show. I sent Irving Thalberg and Norma Shearer a couple of ducats and they haven't sent them back, so it looks as if they're in the bag too."

"How do you get away with all those tickets?" I said. "What did you do, buy out the house for the night?"

"To tell you the truth," he said, "I got a little dough in the show myself. I talked my agents into backing it with me fifty-fifty. I hadda brainstorm, see? I told them the best goddam way in the world to hit the producers for six figures was to put the show on right under their noses with a helluva fanfare. My agents can smell big dough a mile away. They went right out and grabbed a first-class Broadway producer to front for us."

"Sammy," I said, "you're a smart guy. At least if you've made a mistake so far I haven't noticed it. So why in hell do you want to go telling me all this for?"

"In the first place," he said, "you're a good guy."

He said it with absolute derision. "I never held it against you for putting the clip on me for Rosalie or Julian. If that's your pleasure, go ahead. I just figure your brain's a little soft, that's all, but it's okay by me. I still like you. You're good for me. If I tell you something in confidence you don't shoot your mouth off to the first big shot you meet to try to get an *in.*"

If he had hated me I might have had some satisfaction out of it. But he had more important people to hate.

"And in the second place, what the hell if they do find out? I'd just tell 'em it shows how much confidence I got in my own work."

"And in the third place you're so goddam pleased with yourself you have to tell somebody and I'm the best listener you've got," I added.

He chuckled. "I love you, you fresh bastard," he said.

"By the way," I said, "what kind of a play did you dig up for the occasion?"

"A million laughs," he said. "I knocked it out in exactly four weeks and everybody who's seen it says it's sensational. There's so much excitement about it that my press agent Stan Dickey says he's having an easier job getting space for it than for *Once in a Lifetime.*"

"You need a press agent like Fred Astaire needs dancing lessons," I said.

"You oughta get hold of Dickey yourself, Al," Sammy said. "He knows his way around. People are suckers for the printed word, Al, and that even goes for the top guys. They believe what they read, even when they're on their guard. If they read it often enough. I've had Dickey plugging me ever since I took Julie into the studio with me. I made a smart deal with Dickey. I told him he could keep working for me as long as he gets my name in there at least three times a week."

Sometimes it made me sore when Sammy talked that way, sometimes it just made me wonder how the hell *homosaps* got that way, sometimes it left me sick to think what a tremendous burning and blinding light ambition can be where there is something behind it, and what a puny flickering sparkler when there isn't. Sammy's flame was deceptive because you were always looking at it through the powerful magnifying glass of his own ego.

But when the telephone wires failed to transmit the magnetic current it was like standing off and looking at a small, cold star. This time, listening half to what Sammy was saying now, half to everything he had ever said to me before, I thought of Sammy, distinguished and dead at fifty, a front-page story which Stan Dickey had written and Sammy previously okayed, with governors and bankers and people in high places as honorary pallbearers and everyone mourning the loss of a captain of industry, an Elk, a self-made man and a Great American.

"Al," he said. "Here's the reason I called you. Do you wanna be a really good guy?"

"What do you want me to do?" I said.

"Take Kit off my hands tonight."

"Sure," I said, "I guess that's okay with me. But what's the story?"

"I'm taking Rita Royce," he said.

He said it in the same tone of voice as the first time he ordered St. James Scotch. Rita Royce was one of the better known of the new crop of aphrodisiacs, a sort of streamlined Theda Bara.

|||||||

Kit pushed open the door of her Ford convertible. She was wearing a short fur jacket over a white evening gown that emphasized her tan. She had her hair a different way, up on her head in a smooth roll, and it was almost a shock to see how feminine she could look when she wanted to.

She said, "Hi."

"What's with you and Sammy tonight?"

She answered me by imitating a hypothetical gossip in the audience. "Doesn't Rita Royce look simply divine? Isn't the young man with her Sammy Glick, the one who's supposed to be so brilliant?"

There wasn't any bitterness in it at all. She made you see it the way it really was, amusing and just a little pathetic.

"I'm surprised he didn't pair you with Gary Cooper," I said. "It would have been good publicity."

"He did want to palm me off on some glamour-boy who's supposed to be on his way up at Metro," she said. "But I'm afraid I'm something of a chauvinist about actors. Even intelligent ones. In fact, sometimes they're worse because they know more words to use about themselves. So I held out for you."

"I'm deeply grateful to you, ma'am," I said. "Otherwise I might not have been on hand for the unveiling of another milestone in my best friend's career."

"His milestones are coming so fast," she said, "they're like telephone poles through the window of a train."

Sammy had asked us to his apartment for cocktails before dinner. I have never shown the slightest inclination to sketch, but when Sammy came strutting toward us in a new full-dress suit, his chest puffing out his stiff white shirt like a pouter pigeon, with his hair slicked, a blood-red carnation in his lapel and a look on his face as if he had just swallowed his producer, I wished for one moment my fairy godmother would turn me into Toulouse-Lautrec. Even the customary patent-leather evening shoes weren't good enough for him tonight. He had discovered dancing pumps, those dainty, ultra-evening slippers with the pointed toes and the little black bows.

The cocktail session was fun to watch. It was fun to see Sammy trying to use manners to match his dress clothes. Funny to see him trying to form sentences without his four-letter words, leaving his conversation ridiculously stilted. And poor Rita, who seemed as if she might be a good kid under all those layers of glamour. If only she didn't have to try so hard to live up to that amazing body of hers.

Rita raised her glass and read her line as if it were the only one she was going to have in the picture and she had to make it remembered. "To our young genius—success."

I caught Kit's eye as we drank and we smiled at each other guiltily. As Rita drank she fell back on that hackneyed bit of business of smiling up over the rim of her glass with her eyes fluttering. You could feel sorry for Rita and like her, or embarrassed for her and dislike her, depending on your disposition at the moment.

Sammy acknowledged her toast with one of his own. "We can't drink to your success, because that's already established. So we'll drink to its continuance."

I could count back the years on one hand to the time when I was teaching the young genius and littérateur not to say ain't.

As I sat on the edge of Sammy's fancy desk sipping my drink I couldn't help noticing his clippings. There were items about Sammy from papers all over the country, mailed to him by a clipping service. When Sammy caught me looking at them he came over and shoved a paper under my nose.

"See this?" he said coyly.

It was the *Hollywood Megaphone*. I began to read the lead editorial in the corner. The editor was taking potshots at the Writers Guild again. "What makes these wild-eyed members of the Screen Writers Guild think they can get away with biting the hand that feeds them?" it asked. "We are not against the Guild. We are for this industry. If the Guild were for this industry too, instead of trying to ruin it by joining up with the Eastern playwrights who hate Hollywood and always have, we would be for the Guild too."

"What is all this fuss about the Authors' League?" I said. "What possible good would it do the Guild to ruin the industry?"

"Where are you reading?" Sammy said. "I meant at the bottom of the page—with the red circle around it."

It was half a dozen lines headed: GLICK THUMBS DOWN $75,000.

Sammy Glick, local boy-wonder scribe, puts thumbs down on major studio offer of 75 G's for his play Live Wire, *it was understood last night. Prefers to hold picture deals off until curtain goes up for first time at Playhouse Fri. night.*

I always love those journalistic outs—it was alleged, it was learned in semi-official circles, it was understood. "Who was it understood by," I said, "except you and Stan Dickey?"

Sammy slapped me on the back, playfully but jolting me, and his laugh was a little too loud for the evening-clothes atmosphere.

"One of these days remind me to rub you out," he gagged. "You know too much."

We drove to the theater in a sleek black Lincoln Sammy had hired for the occasion. As we got out, there was a little flurry of excitement around Rita, started by a plump young lady in slacks and a gangling, scabby-kneed girl who shoved their autograph books in her face while Sammy stood looking on, drinking it in. One frantic little fan, taking no chances, even wanted Kit's autograph. "You don't want *my* autograph," Kit told her.

The child insisted that she did. Kit looked at me helplessly, took the pencil and scribbled her name. The child stared at the page, puzzled a moment, cried out feverishly, "That was nobody!" ripped the page out, crumpled and threw it away and fought her way into the middle of the next circle.

As we took our seats photographers were prowling up and down the aisles hunting celebrities. Sammy and Rita were trying very hard to seem interested in what each had to say and watch the cameramen out of the corners of their eyes at the same time. When the flashlight boys finally sighted them Rita tilted her head with just the right come-on smile without seeming to realize she was being photographed at all. But Sammy took it big. He looked at that camera like a lover. The man who took that picture may have been just another publicity hack but that picture of his was worth saving as a real photographic study. In fact I clipped it out of next morning's paper for that collection of *Sammyglickiana* I am going to turn over to the Smithsonian when the species finally runs itself into extinction. The most striking thing about that photograph is that it isn't so much a picture of two people sitting together as two individual portraits that merely happen to be side by side. Rita is staring off at an imaginary leading man with a wistful gleam in her eyes. And Sammy is looking right at you, sneering joyfully. The head is cocked slightly at an angle, like an alert Boston bull. The eyes gloat. The sneer comes only from the mouth, which veers ever so slightly off center.

This photographic study was captioned: Lovely Rita Royce Shares Spotlight with Samuel Glick As Young Playwright's Comedy *Live Wire* Wins Acclaim at Last Night's Opening. With Them Is a Friend.

The unidentified Friend, of course, with his head turned away from the camera watching Sammy Glick, is myself.

The play was what Sammy needed, all right. It was one of those things about two red-blooded guys who are always scrapping and loving each other, in this case a couple of announcers in a radio station getting each other in and out of jams with enough gags and surprises and general hell-raising to keep the audience sufficiently amused. I was thinking how much the play was like its author, nothing really there to offer, but slugging the onlookers into submission with sheer noise and velocity, and back of all this I kept thinking something tells me this is awfully familiar and then the show was over and someone in the house, probably Stan Dickey, started to call Author, Author, and the cry was picked up and Sammy was taking a bow and all of a sudden it's a big success and I'm sitting next to a hit playwright and everyone's stepping over me to shake his hand, and he's modestly denying that he must have worked very hard on it, saying it just seemed to come to him, five or six nights' work and everyone's amazed and pleased and someone, not Stan Dickey any more, for by now it's spontaneous, says a new genius has come to Hollywood and Sammy says, "Oh, I wouldn't say that exactly."

We waited in the car while Sammy went backstage to congratulate and get congratulated by the cast, and when he returned he was not the same as when he left us a few minutes before. I'll be damned if even his voice hadn't changed. It seemed lower and more dignified. He wasn't just one more of those bright five-hundred-dollar-a-week boys any more. No more worries about being classed with Julian. He was ready for big time. No more trying to wangle invitations to Harry Godfrey Wilson's clambakes. He was already thinking of asking Wilson and Paine and McCarter and the rest of the upper crust over for a little stud poker himself soon.

Of course Sammy wasn't going to waste any time establishing his new social position. In fact we headed straight for the Trocadero, where Sammy was throwing a celebration party for himself. He seemed almost more elated about bagging the Finemans and the Colliers for it than he did about his play. I guess it was just as important at that.

We were there before any of the others, so we went into the bar to wait. Sammy ordered champagne cocktails and then Rita said, "Excuse me, I have to comb my hair," and went out to the ladies' room. She could say, "Pass the salt," and make it sound exotic. "I'll chaperon you," Kit said, as she rose and followed her out.

It was funny to watch Rita parading through the room like a peacock and know she was only going to the can. Funnier to watch Kit striding after her. It was a gait better suited to slacks than evening gowns. But I actually preferred Kit's figure. Rita's voluptuousness looked as if it might turn into fat some day if she didn't watch herself. But Kit made you feel she was always going to be this way, hard and slim.

Sammy looked after them appraisingly. "There's the difference between handsome and luscious," he said.

I wouldn't give him the satisfaction of letting him know I agreed with him. I just sat there with my wine, feeling righteous and jealous.

Sammy said, "Well, Al, you're the only one who hasn't told me what you think."

"I think it's just like something else I've seen," I said.

He started to say, "That's so much horse—" and then he remembered he was a prominent playwright. "After all no play can ever be entirely original."

"That's true," I said. "They can only be entirely unoriginal."

"You're crazy as hell, Al," Sammy insisted. "Just because you know I didn't happen to do any of the actual writing of that stuff with Julie you got it fixed in your mind that I can't write."

My mind skipped from Julian to the newspaper office to plagiary and then all of a sudden it came to me.

"My God! *The Front Page!*"

Even then he wouldn't give in until I had traced the parallel, scene for scene.

"Okay, pal," he said. "Maybe I did follow the construction of *Front Page.* Only I changed the characters. And I jazzed it up a little more."

"Those people didn't know what a genius you are," I said.

He looked around furtively. "Listen, Al," he said. "Before it didn't matter. I was only playing for marbles. But if you do any talking about this I'll killya—so help me Christ, I'll run you out of this town for good."

Then he suddenly dropped his voice and smiled at me, but fiercely.

"Jesus Christ," he said, "I know I'm no angel. I'm only human like anybody else. But if I ever get to be one of the head guys out here you won't find me forgetting my pals like some of these other bastards."

"Last time we had an argument," I said, "you seemed to think I was too dumb to do you any harm. Why the hell should I tell anybody what a bastard you are? Let them find out for themselves."

He relaxed, even patted my hand reassuringly.

"Okay, pal," he said. "I'd trust you like my own mother. It's just a funny thing about this racket—the bigger you are, the jumpier you get. Only just remember, what I said about loyalty still goes."

I'll remember it all right, I thought. How could I ever forget a combination as unique as loyalty and Sammy Glick?

Rita came back, gradually, stopping at three tables en route.

"Sammy," she said, "when are you going to write a play for me?"

"When he can find one," I said.

"I don't want to write for you until I feel something great," Sammy said, "something that's—you."

She moved closer to him.

That's the only real play you'll ever get from him, I thought.

Kit rescued us by announcing the arrival of Sammy's guests.

The Trocadero was the place to be seen that season, a chic, handsomely tailored night club with creamy walls, subtle illumination that retouched the women's faces like fashionable photographers. A startling south wall made entirely of glass looked out and down at the houselights and the street lamps and the red neon smears of Hollywood, Los Angeles, Beverly Hills, Culver City and the rest of the sprawling communities in the long valley between the Hollywood Hills on the north and the ridge dotted with oil wells sloping up behind MGM, fifteen miles to the south.

Sammy sat at the end of his long table, surrounded by Rita, his Finemans and Colliers and his new sense of authority, being witty and charming and intelligent. I think I even heard him expressing an interest in rare books for Fineman. The chances were he had had his secretary doing some research for him on the subject. A moment later he was leaning toward Collier, discussing the technical problems he must have faced in trying to photograph penguins in their native environment. That was a new gift Sammy was beginning to acquire. He was learning to abandon the direct sledgehammer approach. It was still there, of course, but he was learning how to camouflage it. He was developing an amazing ability to appropriate and broadcast ideas and cultural attitudes which he never held long enough to absorb. I heard him discussing a current best-seller with Mrs. Fineman, which I would have bet anything she had read and he hadn't, but that didn't stop him from doing most of the talking about it, employing a razzle-dazzle literary double-talk technique that had good, simple Mrs. Fineman on the run.

I was glad to find out Kit didn't like these parties either.

"What always amazes me," she said, "is that with all the turnover in Hollywood from year to year, almost from month to month, the faces in here never seem to change."

I looked around the room to see whom I was with. Kit pointed out to me the famous free-lance Hollywood photographer, Katz, a feverish little dwarf of a man who would look undressed without his Graflex and whose degree of interest in you as a photographic subject had become an accurate test of your rating in the industry.

"Last time I was here," Kit said, "someone pointed out to Katz that Major Adams was in the room—remember, one of the men who practically founded Hollywood, I guess, worked with Griffith for years and probably did more for pictures than any other producer before Thalberg? They say he's down-and-out now but some of his old gang keep him going. Well, Katz barely looked up from his reloading. 'Who, Adams?' he said. 'He's nobody. Anyway, I gotta save my bulbs for the Tom Brown–Anita Louise party coming in later.' And he said it so loud that poor old Adams turned around."

We watched the people together, being very catty of course about the little ingénue with gold stars pasted on her bare shoulders. And the beautiful young juvenile singing into her ear the words of the popular song they were dancing to. And the look of aloof superiority that came over the dancers' faces for the rhumba, flashing their heads expertly from side to side, so conscious of the figure they were cutting on the floor. And the ex-hatcheck girl on her way to stardom with her magnificent (but dead) pan, swirling around the floor with a dashing and toothy screen villain whose face seemed to be set in a permanent sneer. And the foolishly oblivious couple, he a half-bald, red-faced grinner, fugitive from middle age; she a young, plumpish and pretty blonde with a silly champagne smile and a gift for abandon. And the almost-matronly woman who had taken rhumba and tango and charm lessons and the fourteen-year-old who should have been in bed instead of awkwardly trying to simulate the rhythm of the rhumba. And . . .

"What do you think our chances are of taking a powder?" I said.

She took the table in and smiled. "He who hesitates," she said, "is trapped here in the Black Hole of Trocadero until morning."

We rose together, conspiratorially.

"Don't bother to say good night," she said. "So we don't break up the party. Let's just say we're going out to get a little air."

Outside it was good just to stand there a moment and let the wind sweeping down the Strip from the sea blow the liquor fumes and the smoke and the chatter of simultaneous voices out of your mind.

We hopped a taxi back to the Colonial House to pick up Kit's Ford.

She nosed the car into the boulevard and paused. "Where shall it be?"

I said, "Any place that is quiet, serves liquor and is uninhabited by Sammy Glick."

She said, "I think I can fill that bill without too much trouble"; and we shot forward into the fast-moving traffic.

We drove up the steep winding road to her house near the top of the Hills. The night was clear and it seemed as if the world was full of nothing but little pulsing lights above us and below us. It was so beautiful you thought you ought to say something about it, but there was nothing good enough to say. I felt as if we were floating between two starry skies, flowing into each other at the horizon.

"Mmmmm," I said.

"Wait till you see it from the studio window with the lights out," she said. "Better than the Trocadero—and no cover charge."

It was a cozy and inviting little house, consisting of one main living and dining room with beams across the high triangular ceiling, and two small rooms, a bedroom and a paneled study besides the kitchen.

"I really rented the house for the porch beyond that window," Kit said. "In another month I'll be sleeping out there. You can become surprisingly fond of Hollywood from that porch."

She made highballs and we took them out there with us and leaned against the railing. It did top the view from the Troc. We could barely make out the neon lettering *Trocadero* half a mile below.

"It seems wrong to know he's behind those lights and not be able to see him or hear him," I said.

"Shhh," she smiled, "I think I can hear him."

We really paused and listened a moment.

"I think that's only the wind rushing," I said. "Though it may be him at that."

"He and Rita are dancing," she said, watching the Troc as if she could actually see them. "Skirting all around the edge of the floor by silent agreement, to make sure of being seen by as many people as possible."

We were elbow to elbow, leaning over like ship's passengers looking out to sea.

"What did you think of the play?" I said.

Instead of answering my question directly, she said, "I wonder what would happen if Sammy used all that energy and imagination to create something—not just to devise ways of reaching the top without creating anything."

We kept going in to refill our glasses and returning to the rail and the view again, not growing intoxicated but only more intimate.

"Kit," I said, "we've known each other almost a year now. We're pretty good friends. And yet all we know about each other is Sammy Glick. I don't think we've ever talked about anything else but Sammy Glick. He's an obsession with me—and I know a hell of a lot about him now I wouldn't have known without you—but, well—I'm beginning to feel he's a kind of defense we use against each other."

It was a mellow evening and the moon looked like something private that went with the porch and it was easy to talk.

I told her about leaving Middletown after my father died, going to New York with not enough money to last me over a month, pounding the sidewalks begging for a job, making a goddam pest of myself at every newspaper office in town because I was greatly in need of fifteen dollars a week. I told her how I used to get up at five o'clock to train racing pigeons before going to school and how, if I ever hit this town for any kind of money, I would like to have a small house out in the valley somewhere where I could have a pigeon loft again. I told her a little of how balled up I felt inside because there were times when I wanted to say what I had to say as honestly as possible, and times when I felt as ambitious as Sammy without being able to free myself from the sense of relationship with everybody else in the world, which made it difficult to do anything which I thought might cause them pain.

Maybe I talked her ear off so that she had to open up in self-defense. She spoke in a monotone, keeping her head profiled to mine, and I felt that what she was saying came not only from her brain and her mouth but rooted deep in her, intestinal.

"My father's goal was the United States Supreme Court. I guess he came closer than most people do to their goals because he finally did make the State Supreme Court. Through a lot of hard work and a lot of smart politics. I don't think either one alone would have been enough. My father and mother shared one life between them, which sounds very romantic except the life they shared was his, exclusively. Her job was to see that his diet was observed and that he was not allowed to be disturbed when he was working and that the men who could help him were adequately feted and the wives of his associates duly luncheoned and teaed. In other words, she performed all her duties as automatically as any soldier. If she ever had a thought of her own or a job of her own or even a conversation of her own, I never knew it. Poor Mother. Their marriage always made me think of a motorcycle with Father at the controls and Mother sitting in the sidecar, not asking where she was going but only if he was sure he was warm enough without the extra scarf she brought along."

"That sounds rather like a typical happy marriage," I said.

"Oh, terribly typical," she said. "But the happiness part is pretty much bunk. At least for the person in the sidecar."

She told me how it was with her father dead. "That was when I was sixteen. Arranging his funeral was the last function Mother had in the world. After that she was through. There wasn't anything left for her to do. And when she wasn't reminiscing about him there didn't seem to be anything for her to say. I was really fond of her. But I always remember what a relief it was to be back on the train on my way to school again. I felt sorry for her of course—but that didn't keep her from driving me crazy. After college Mother wanted me to go to law school. She had it all planned. I'd go into my father's old firm and we'd live together and she'd take care of me. To be very ruthless about it—what she really wanted to do was turn me into my father, so she would have a place again. Well, I decided I had to be ruthless about it. I was already started on my book and I wanted to be away from her—on my own. I couldn't see why the hell men should have a monopoly on independence any more. I made up my mind to stay out of sidecars. Have you ever thought of the difference between the two words spinster and bachelor? It seems pretty significant that spinster has a thought association of loneliness, frustration and bitterness. Bachelorhood is something glamorous—doesn't the sound of the word give you a sense of adventure and freedom? So I decided I'd be a bachelor. I don't mean sex orgies. Most girls go through that period, either with actual experiences or in their mind; they'll slow down after a while if you let them alone. I mean that when I met a man that appealed to me—well, you know how men feel about it. I didn't want to be a pushover, because then it wouldn't mean anything any more; look at the rabbits. But I didn't want to set up any barriers of fake coquetry either."

She paused and finished her drink coolly. "If that sounds too immoral just make believe I'm very tight—which I probably am."

I said, "It sounds plenty moral for my money."

"I think so," she said. "Not the Hays Office kind, of course. But under the bonnet of organized morality lurks a very filthy mind."

We made another pilgrimage inside for drinks and out to the porch again.

"When you were talking before," I said, "you know, about men that appealed to you? I couldn't help thinking about Sammy."

She laughed. "You mean the person we weren't going to talk about?"

I said keeping him out of an entire conversation was too much to ask. And now that he had come up, I wanted to know.

We were absolutely cockeyed, but completely coherent because that's the kind of mood we had set in the beginning.

When she didn't answer me I said again, "What's the real story on you and Sammy?"

"You don't really want me to talk about it," she said. "You know it'll only make you uncomfortable."

"Uncomfortable!" I said. "Why should it?"

"Okay, pal," she said. "But don't blame me if it makes you sore. As you probably guessed, our little corporal is pretty damn good in bed. Sex hasn't much to do with friendship or love or any other of those virtuous relationships. Most people know that, but they don't like to admit it. Well, the first day Sammy came into my office to save California from annexing itself to Russia, I was ready to tear him limb from limb and at the same time I had this crazy desire to know what it felt like to have all that driving ambition and frenzy and violence inside me."

She broke off, staring down tensely, her composure finally ripped.

"Jesus," she said quietly, "you get to know a man that way. And it's strange to see the same selfishness and cruelty and power working out there too."

There was a long pause. No embarrassment, just that she had finished.

Finally, she said, "Well, are you sore?"

"I don't know," I said. "But I'm glad you told me."

"So am I," she said. "You're a good guy to tell things to." She paused. "I feel as if I've opened a window and hung my mind out to air."

The wind was fresh and cool, rippling by like a mountain stream and we stopped to rediscover it.

"The Chamber of Commerce boasts about the sunshine and the palm trees and the Chinese Theater," she said. "And the things that have the most vitality they're always on the defense about—the long rains and the night winds."

In her white gown she reminded me of a sail as she pivoted to catch the wind squarely. She threw her head back and my eyes were drawn to the neck line curving up to her chin as if this were some intimate nakedness suddenly exposed.

"Kit," I said, and I bent to kiss her. She seemed preoccupied with something out there and oblivious of me. But as my mouth reached hers, she turned her head, casually, as if by accident, and my lips brushed idly against her cheek.

Nothing was said about that, nothing about that ever.

She inspected her glass and said, "Let's freshen our drinks," and we went inside.

"I'm worried about the Guild," she began as if we had been talking about that all evening.

I said I had seen the blast in the *Megaphone* that morning.

"That wasn't a blast," she said. "That was just the pop of Hanigan's little trial balloon. But Hollywood never likes to do things in a small way. Something tells me that when our blast comes, it will really be a production."

"What do you think will happen, Kit?"

"I don't know," she said. "I wish I did. All I know is that if it comes to a showdown over the Authors' League, a lot of Guild guys who have been using their heads and their voices may have to start using their guts."

"But there's no sense looking for trouble," I said. "If it just gets that bunch Sammy was sucking around sore at the Guild we'll never get anywhere."

"I'm not so sure," she said. "I'm beginning to wonder whether the only way the Guild can please them—is to go out of existence."

Just as a white evening gown was wrong for her, mascara, powder and lipstick were more out of place than ever when she pressed her lips together and set her jaw.

"We might as well recognize we have some of the most unique union members in the history of organized labor. Like Brother Glick, swimming around in that fish bowl of champagne down there."

Lights were going out all over Hollywood. As I watched, the two o'clock curfew erased the blazing neon longhand of the

Trocadero. Sammy Glick was probably leaning back in the plush seat of his rented Lincoln blowing cigar smoke into the face of the goddess millions of American guys of all nationalities were making love to as they fell asleep in flop houses, salesmen's hotels and college dormitories.

"Kit," I said, "let's have another drink. Let's drink to a helluva wonderful country—and a cockeyed time."

CHAPTER 8

That was the month everything happened. It started crazy right off the bat. I got a good job, the best I ever had. Kit swung it for me. After Masaryk died, it struck me that the story of his life ought to be a natural for pictures. His ties with American democracy gave it special significance for us, and with Mussolini shooting off his big guns in Ethiopia and Hitler his big mouth in Germany, an anti-fascist picture seemed like a good idea. I told Kit about it, and as usual she didn't show too much excitement, but a couple of weeks later she bowled me over with the news that she had passed the idea on to Sidney Fineman and he had given her a favorable reaction and wanted to see me.

Fineman said he had thought of doing Masaryk before, had

even registered it, in fact, but he liked my angle on it and put me to work. Fineman was a refutation of everything I had ever heard about producers. His office was large but in good taste, with real books in the bookcases and theatrical prints on the walls. He could express a thought without making you find the words for it and an emotion without resorting to profanity. He knew much more about Masaryk than I did. He didn't want to be yessed. He told me he could only hire me week-to-week but not to get panicky, that he wouldn't even ask to see what I had done for at least four weeks.

"Even then," he said, "I don't care if you only have a handful of pages as long as there's something worth going on with. The danger in this story is that it will be a series of lectures on democracy. Moving pictures haven't got time for sermons. Try to get in the habit of thinking in terms of pictorial action."

He gave me an example I'll always remember. Fineman once imported a famous playwright from Broadway at five thousand a week. The first job the playwright had to do was an opening scene in a picture where he had to establish that the husband was tiring of his wife. Fifteen thousand dollars later the playwright brought in a twenty-page scene. Fineman thought the dialogue was brilliant but way over length for the start of the picture. The playwright protested that you couldn't cut a line out of his scene without ruining it. Fineman showed the scene to his director, Ray MacKenna, one of the few men left in the business who got his training in the Mack Sennett two-reel comedy school. Mac sent the scene back to Fineman with one of his own. It was typed out on half a page. It read:

INT. ELEVATOR MEDIUM SHOT
Husband and wife in evening clothes. Husband wearing top hat.

REVERSE ANGLE
As elevator door opens and classy dame enters.

CLOSE SHOT HUSBAND AND WIFE
Get husband's reaction to new dame. Removes hat with flourish.

*Wife looks from dame to husband's hat to husband. Then glares
at him as we*

CUT TO:

Fineman chuckled at me over his curved pipe.

"Mac couldn't write a complete sentence," he said. "But that
was great writing—for the screen."

I couldn't wait to get out of his office and start writing the
greatest screenplay of all time. I hadn't felt like that since I ran
into an English teacher in college who had the effect on you of
a literary laxative. You felt you would have to run out of class
before it was over and rush back to your room and let it all out
of your system. Kit's enthusiasm for motion pictures had always
been a little hard to take. But now I remembered something she
had said somewhere along the line, "The most exciting way ever
invented to tell a story is with a moving-picture camera." I
couldn't wait to get into my office and begin telling it.

Sammy Glick may get everything else, I thought, but by God
this is a pleasure he'll never know, the joy of writing that first line
on the pad, which sounds so beautiful now and so lousy later, the
tremendous pleasure and labor of creating something you believe
in.

Sammy looked in around lunchtime. He wasn't dressed like a
writer. More like a fight champ or a sweepstakes winner. The
crepe soles on his white kid shoes seemed to be half a foot high
and the flower in his lapel stood out like a red light against his
white suede jacket.

"You look like a fugitive from *Esquire*," I said.

He had to laugh because it was supposed to be a gag, but I don't
think his heart was in it.

"Welcome to the big leagues," he said. "I hear you sold Fineman a bill of goods. I want you to know I put in a good word for
you. Hear you got a terrific story."

You could feel him selling your story back to you the same way
he would his own.

"I haven't got any story yet," I said. "Just a start, an idea."

"I bet it's terrific, sweetheart," he said. "I hope you make a million dollars."

Then he paused to look at me compassionately. "But I hear they got you working for peanuts. Three hundred and fifty a week."

I had to admit my disgrace, though I couldn't figure out how he found out so fast.

"I got a pipeline from the front office," he said. "Me and Dan Young's secretary are like this."

His hands performed an obscene gesture. "I mean Young's secretary and I. I wound up with her at the last studio Christmas party and she still thinks I'm in love with her."

"Sammy," I said, "I'm trying to work."

"Al, why don't you cut it out?" Sammy kidded. "Your sense of fair play is going to ruin the racket for the rest of us."

He dragged me to my feet affectionately. "Time to duck out for a little lunchee. I'll introduce you around the commissary. Cooped up in here all day isn't going to get you anywhere. You got to spread your wings a little bit."

I hesitated. I wanted to think about Masaryk. And when you ate lunch with Sammy Glick, there was only one thing on the menu, Sammy Glick.

"If you need a convincer," Sammy said, "I told Julian to save a couple of seats for us at the writers' table."

||||||

Julian hadn't changed. He looked a little healthier, he was wearing a new suit which was just like the old one and his handshake didn't seem so frightened, but you would never have taken him for a hit writer and that's what he was becoming. Studio environment seemed to have no more effect on him than his tenement neighborhood had. He and Blanche had never been so happy, he said. They had rented a little cottage overlooking the ocean near Topanga Canyon and they had a baby coming along in the fall. He was even getting his novel finished.

I said I couldn't believe it. Everybody said it was absolutely impossible out here to do any writing of your own.

"I know," he said. "That's what everybody says. But I don't understand it. Every Saturday, unless I'm doing a rush job, I leave here at noon. Blanche and I go for a long walk along the beach, I take a quick dip—I've been doing it since the first of March—and then I write until I go to bed. You couldn't want a better place to work than right there over the ocean."

Sammy hadn't even sat down with us yet. He was all over the place like a headwaiter. We could hear him yelling to somebody across the room.

"He spends two hours here every day," Julian said. "This is where he really goes to work. He's the commissary genius. I don't know whether you've noticed our screen credits or not but they always say—Story by Sammy Glick—Screenplay by Sammy Glick and Julian Blumberg. You know where he got all those story credits? Right here in the commissary."

The story of how he did it was so intriguing that we both forgot to order. Sammy would walk up to a director and say, "Spencer Tracy and Marlene Dietrich in *Titanic*. Do I have to say any more?"

Then he would just walk away from the guy, significantly, and leave it in his lap. The director has been desperate for a socko story all year. Tracy and Dietrich in *Titanic*. Jesus, it sounds like something. Natural suspense. And two great characters. Maybe Spence is a good two-fisted minister who tries to straighten Marlene out. Marlene is a tramp, of course. He's real. She's anything for a laugh. Then, even though the boat is going down you bring the audience up with a hell of a lift because Marlene suddenly sees the light.

Meanwhile Sammy bumps into a supervisor. "I was just telling Chick Tyler my new story," he says. "He went off his nut about it. Spencer Tracy and Marlene Dietrich in *Titanic*. Do I have to say any more?"

And he drops the hot potato in the supervisor's lap and runs again. The supervisor knows Sammy hasn't missed yet. And he's been trying to get a cast like that ever since he's been made a supervisor. So he drops by Tyler's table.

"Sammy Glick tells me you're hot for his *Titanic* story," he says.

"Yeah," Tyler says, "I think the kid's got something. And it's right down my alley."

By this time Tyler is practically thinking up the acceptance speech he'll make on receiving the Academy Award. "I could get a great picture out of that," he says. "Remember what I did with *Strange Voyage*? That's for me!"

All this time Sammy is hopping from table to table, pollinating his story like a bumblebee, catching them as they go in and out, asking everybody who can possibly help him if he has to say anything more and running off before they can answer. Everybody is now asking everybody else if they have heard Sammy's *Titanic* story. And by this time, through unconscious generosity, they have contributed to the story two characters, a beginning, middle and a climax. Now Sammy manages to cross the path of the General Manager in Charge of Production. Sammy has heard that he's been a little burned lately because people are saying he is losing touch with studio activities.

"How do you do, sir," Sammy says. "I suppose Tyler and Hoyt have told you my story for Dietrich and Tracy. *Titanic?* Everybody who's heard it seems very excited about it."

He has heard about Glick, of course, and he never likes to appear ignorant of anything. "Yes, I have, Glick," he says. "Sounds very interesting. I'm going to call you all in for a conference on it some time this week."

When they all get together, all anyone knows is that everybody else thinks it's great. And since everybody has gone on record, no one is willing to admit just how little about the story he knows. So the safest thing is to let Sammy get something on paper, which means that Julian has to start dreaming up a story called *Titanic* while the trade papers and Parsons naturally pass on to their readers what Sammy has told them, that everyone on his lot is saying his epic drama *Titanic* is absolutely the greatest vehicle either of those two great stars has ever had.

There was no bitterness or anger in Julian's story. It was full of mild wonder and deep resignation.

Sammy finally got around to us. He introduced me to everybody at the long table, selling me to them and them to me.

"I want you to meet a very sweet guy," he would say. "I want you to meet the sweetest guy in the world."

The talk around the table was almost all gags. Everybody seemed afraid to say anything unless he thought it would get a laugh. One of the writers had ordered wine and a young producer who had just been graduated from the writers' ranks asked him, "What are you Guild members drinking these days—producers' blood?"

It got a good laugh and you could hear him repeating it with variations. "At the Guild Board meetings they toast *Der Tag* with producers' blood. Hey, Joe, know what Brown is drinking . . . ?"

Everybody kidded about the Guild back and forth, but I felt that gagging was really the official court language and that underneath it all you could feel the friction growing.

"Just wait till we join the Authors' League, comrades!" Sammy shouted. "Then all us downtrodden writers can become producers and we'll punish the producers by making them get down on their hands and knees—and write!"

Some of the laughter was automatic, some frightened, some reactionary.

That was the month I will never forget because it seemed to sum up everything about Hollywood that was splendid and crazy and hopeful and terrifying.

You can choose your own adjectives for the front-page story in the *Megaphone* that was waiting for me on my desk one morning, for like everybody else I couldn't start my day without reading the little trade journals from cover to cover.

GLICK GETS $80,000 FOR
LIVE WIRE FROM WORLD-WIDE

——

RETURNS TO HOME LOT TO ADAPT

OWN PLAY AT $1250 A WEEK

That, as Sammy would say, was the convincer. I decided that the history of Hollywood was nothing but twenty years of feverish preparation for the arrival of Sammy Glick.

Sammy came in a little later, of course, making the rounds to take his bows. He was wearing a new outfit, gray checks of contrasting sizes for the coat and pants. And the flower which was becoming a fixture. "Sammy," I said, "I read the bad news this morning. May I be the first to console you?"

He thought I meant it as a gag. But I assured him I was serious. "I thought this play was going to put you in the two-thousand-a-week class," I said. "But I see you're only getting twelve-fifty."

I was right. All the excitement of that astronomical dough was over already. He was really eating his heart out about that extra seven-fifty. Of Hollywood's one thousand screen writers, there might be three or four dozen getting twelve-fifty. But the two-grand-a-week boys were really the inner circle. It was the difference between the Big League and Triple-A.

"They wanted me to sign a new contract," he said, "but I wouldn't do it. Why should I tie myself down?"

The Guild was asking its members not to sign contracts that bound them for more than two years, so that at the end of that time they would all be free to take a strike vote if that became necessary to win recognition for the Guild. That was called Article XII. It was going to be called a lot of other things before the month was over. Kit was a very persuasive girl, but I had never expected to see the day when Sammy would be loyal to his own mother, much less nine hundred fellow writers he was breaking his neck and his heart to outdistance. And I told him so.

"Hell, no," he said. "That's not why. If you ask me, the Guild has a helluva nerve telling us to do anything like that. If I signed a contract now it would probably get me there in a couple of steps, probably fifteen hundred and then seventeen-fifty. But I'm catching the express now, baby. I'm getting off at my station in one stop."

That day it seemed to me that when we were talking about the Guild's struggle for a foothold in Hollywood and Sammy's struggle for a stranglehold, we were talking about two different things. That only showed how much I had to learn about Hollywood and the Guild and, in spite of all these years and all my lessons, Sammy Glick.

A few days later the *Megaphone* had a new headline that they were so happy about, it sounded as if they could hardly resist printing HOORAY at the end of it.

OPPOSITION GROUP FORMS WITHIN GUILD!

Responding to a rising tide of resentment among Guild members against their Executive Board for selling out their autonomy to the group of Eastern racketeers and Reds who controlled the Authors' League, the news story chortled, the responsible element has formed a Committee of Five who have pledged themselves to rescue the writers' ship from the hands of the crackpots and adventurers and steer it back to the port of sanity again. The five distinguished gentlemen who were so unselfishly volunteering their time and prestige to rescue their fellow artists from destruction were Lawrence Paine, Harold Godfrey Wilson, John McCarter, Robert Griffin and—Sammy Glick.

Things had been moving so fast that it didn't even seem strange to me any more than this copy-boy punk of mine should be taking it for granted that he was one of the spokesmen for the Guild elite without, as far as I could detect, ever having written a line. As I watched Sammy at the big-shot writers' table in the commissary that noon, I kept wondering where the hell it was all going to end and how many pairs of shoes Sammy must have collected by now and whether he was twenty-four years old or twenty-five.

I caught up with Kit on our way out and we fell in step.

"Take a walk with me," she said.

We walked out past the sound stages and the machine shops and the labor gangs to the back lot. We walked past the New York street and up through the Latin Quarter of Paris until we came to a South Sea Island with a little beach leading down to real water. We crossed a little bridge to the island and sat down on the sand in front of a native hut. The hot April sun was just what the set designer ordered. I dug my hands into the warm sand and lay on my back, looking up through a palm tree supported with piano wire, at the cloudless sky.

"Where are we?" I said.

"This used to be Hollywood," she said with a poker face and voice. "Before the Depression."

"If a rescue ship comes by," I said, "hide."

She gave a little laugh that seemed to release her inside.

We both lay back and laughed in the sun, not so much at what we were saying but at the idea of being on a desert island together. She started to say something else and I got ready to laugh again but she crossed me up.

"Those sons of bitches."

"Who?" I said. I was still on our island.

"The Committee of Five," she said.

"What do you think?" I said.

"The panic is on," she said.

"Some of the boys seem to think they're just sucking around for better jobs," I said. "Others think it's the Executive Board's fault for pushing things too fast. You don't know what to think."

"I know what to think," she said.

"But what are they doing it for?" I said. "What do they get out of it?"

"I don't think you can settle that with one answer," she said. "Because they're all doing the same thing for different reasons. Start with Larry Paine, for instance."

Listening to her gave me the impression of watching a river moving too swiftly, cutting its banks down sharp and straight, uncompromisingly.

"Larry's a good writer. But a complicated one. There's nothing like a rich man's son who's done a little starving, just enough to scare him into becoming a self-made man. He's a recluse and the kind of a drinker who reaches for that bottle when he wakes up in the morning. Something's gone wrong. The way he laughs, for instance. It gets louder and harsher until I don't know what it becomes, but it isn't laughter. And those eyes, everybody notices those sunken, hurt eyes. He's been nursing his paranoia along for years. I think he really believes the Guild was organized just to deprive him of his individuality!"

She ran through the other four more rapidly. "Harold Godfrey Wilson is an old boozer who had written himself out ten years ago, and Jack McCarter is a young boozer who never had anything in him to write out and just coasted in behind Wilson."

Bob Griffin, she thought, was one of the most competent writers in the industry, naturally conservative but with a straight-from-the-shoulder integrity. "I think the only trouble with Bob is that he has read one too many editorials in the *Megaphone* about our being cannibalistically inclined toward producers and wanting to replace Louis B. Mayer with Joe Stalin.

"And I believe," she concluded, "that you can hazard a guess at Mr. Glick's motives. And that is the Sanity Five that has volunteered to lead the writers to their New Jerusalem."

"How much support do you think they have?" I said.

"Nobody knows," she said. "They still have ten days to work over the membership before the general meeting. None of us has ever been organized before. It's hard to say how we'll hold up. Sitting up there on the platform with the Board all year, I've had a chance to watch the membership react. They blow hot and cold. Maybe that's because they're high-strung and they're individualistic and, except for the handful of left-wingers, none of them knows a labor tactic from a sacrifice scene.

"And of course they haven't learned to work together. With longshoremen or fruit pickers that probably grows right out of their jobs. But with us it's just the opposite. We're pitted against each other. Two or three times I've worked on the same script with somebody else without either of us knowing it. That's like rubbing two fighting cocks together. I'd say it's fifty-fifty right now as to whether the Guild weathers the storm or not."

She looked at her watch. "Time to go to work," she said, and jumped nimbly to her feet. "Well, what do you say? Think we've destroyed enough of the industry for one day? Or shall we go back to the office and commit sabotage by writing the stinkingest scenes we possibly can?"

"I only hope Mr. Fineman doesn't think my treatment of Masaryk is sabotage," I said, as we started back toward the writers' building again.

Those were the Ten Days That Shook Hollywood. It was earthquake weather. Writers woke up excited or went to bed frightened. They fought battles of words in which the injuries sustained were nervous stomach and insomnia.

One of the first casualties was Julian, who dropped into my office on his way home that Friday evening.

"How would you like to come down to the beach for lunch tomorrow?" he said gravely.

I said I would like to but I had planned to come back to the studio because I wanted to get my treatment in before the end of the month and the rumpus all week had put me behind schedule.

"I've asked Kit too," he said. "There's something I wanted to talk over with you."

"Okay," I said, "I guess I can work late tonight instead."

||||||

We drove out in her car with the top down. We drove past Westwood Village, the home of UCLA, which is either the model for Hollywood's version of campus life or vice versa; past Sawtelle, the Old Soldiers' Home, where veterans of our more recent wars live out their days watching cars go by; past Santa Monica with its swanky swimming clubs and its public beaches, where bronzed and pretty girls in little bathing suits wear sailor hats and munch hot dogs as they skip barefooted across the blistering pavement to the sand. Then we turned north up the coast highway curving to the shore, bordered by matchbox cottages, snug and dilapidated, with names like Crow's Nest and Joe's Joynt.

Finally we reached a group of cottages which were a little newer, with the paint not yet eaten away by the salt air, and one of these was Julian's.

The house was clean and compact and shiplike. The long narrow dining room faced the sea, which was so close to us that big waves would shake the walls and send the surf swishing up below us. Blanche was one of those efficient little Jewish mothers who look as if that was what they were meant for from their first moment of puberty.

Julian was dressed more informally than I had ever seen him before, in a loose-fitting dungaree suit and beach sandals, but he would never look really sporty. In spite of his natural graveness, he did his best to be jolly through lunch, but his sensitivity was of too simple a kind to conceal his uneasiness.

Later, sitting on his porch overlooking the ocean, we heard the cause of it.

"You know," he said, "all the time that I've been working at World-Wide I've been working from week to week, without a contract. Two days ago," he continued sadly, "they offered me a seven-year contract. Beginning at five hundred dollars a week."

He stopped, sighed, put his pipe back in his mouth and looked out at his ocean.

All of us knew what he meant. There had been lots of rumors flying around World-Wide that writers were being offered unusually attractive contracts in order to tempt them into breaking the Guild provision. But I hadn't really believed it. This was the first actual case I had heard of. Kit and I had been called in to help Julian wrestle with his conscience.

I didn't say anything. I watched Kit.

"Unless all of us are free agents two years from now the Guild is licked," she said. "God knows, none of us want to strike. But if we aren't even in a position to threaten one, we're just charging a machine gun with our bare hands and we might as well fold."

Julian looked as if he were going to burst out crying. Blanche was upset.

"That's all right for you to say, Miss Sargent. You're all established. But Julian is finally getting a good start. And with our baby coming . . ."

Jesus, what a hell of a complicated world, I thought. Here is a kid who is finally getting the break he's been waiting for and deserves and he's dying to take it, and who the hell can blame him, and Kit, that coldhearted humanitarian, isn't going to let him.

"Julian might still be ghost writing if it weren't for the Guild," she said. "Of course, if we ever have a Guild shop in Hollywood, all the interests of writers will be protected; but the ones it will help most are the boys like Julian, who aren't able to take any kind of a stand alone."

"Then what does he pay his agent ten percent for?" Blanche said.

"Agents can help just so much. But when we were asked to take that fifty-percent cut my first year out here, the agents were swept along with the rest of us. You probably don't remember, but the crafts that were organized were the only ones that didn't have to take it."

Julian kept turning his head from Blanche to Kit as if he were watching a tennis match. I tried to make out which side he was on. He looked miserable when Kit spoke and even more miserable when Blanche retaliated.

"You know I'm for the Guild," he broke in. "I joined as soon as I was eligible. But, God, when I think of the difference between five hundred a week and losing my job . . ."

"Who says you're going to lose your job?" Kit said, almost angrily.

"Sammy," Julian said. "He had a talk with me yesterday. He told me what a damn fool he thought I was, if I didn't sign it. He said he had it confidentially from the front office that if I didn't sign it I'd never work for World-Wide again."

Oh, Sammy, you frantic marathoner, I thought, you bastard I used to hate and almost understand! You success!

"How can you possibly ask him to turn it down?" Blanche said.

Blanche is right, I thought. Blanche is right and Kit is right and never the twain shall meet.

"I'm not asking him to turn it down," Kit said relentlessly. "That's something you'll have to decide yourselves. All I can do is tell you what turning it down means."

Nebbish, poor Julian, I thought.

IIIIIII

When we left, the sun was taking its evening dip, slipping down into the ocean inch by inch like a fat woman afraid of the water.

Instead of turning back toward Hollywood, we started north, just driving anywhere with the top down and the sunset just beyond our reach. The ocean and the clouds were red when we started out, soon after deep purple with a splinter moon giving the night a subtle, indirect lighting. We drove up past Malibu, left the last houses behind. The beach had disappeared and in its place were turbulent rock formations jutting out into the sea. On the other side of the road stretched pasture lands and cultivated fields.

As we took a hairpin turn Kit said, "There's my little beach down there."

I saw nothing but steep rocks below us piling into the water.

"You can't see it from the road," she said. "The rocks are too high around it. I found it one hot day driving up to Frisco. It's a beautiful place to go swimming in the raw."

"How would you like to go in now?" I said.

She put her foot on the brake. "Okay," she said. "It might be warm enough."

"But how can we get dry?" I said, a little panicky. "We haven't any towels."

"I'll look in the rumble," she said. "I think I have some with my tennis stuff."

"I hope so," I said unconvincingly.

She found them. I almost broke my neck on the jagged path that angled down to the little beach that lay concealed and virginal below. Natural hydraulics working overtime for a couple of million years had scooped it right out of the cliffs.

"Quite an improvement on our last island," I said. "Unless that moon is being held up by piano wire."

"I've named it Glick's Lagoon," she said. "Because it's the last stronghold of individualism."

"Was Sammy ever down here with you?"

She shook her head. "I pointed it out to him once. But he didn't want to stop. No one ever taught him how to play."

We undressed silently, seeing each other only as silhouettes. She was ready first and didn't wait for me. Out of the corner of my eye I saw her moving swiftly toward the water, her tanned arms and legs and head blending into the dark, the rest of her body that had been concealed from the sun looking from the back like a white, tight-fitting bathing suit. She was long-legged, almost hipless, V-shaped from her waist to her broad shoulders.

The water was so cold it made my heart feel like an ice cube. I plowed madly, determined to stay in as long as she did. Her stroke was a smooth rhythmic crawl. She swam out beyond me and back and said, "Ready to go in?"

"Yes," I said with half a dozen *y*'s through chattering teeth. "But I'll have to dive down and find my feet first. I think they both dropped off."

"They'll probably come in with the tide," she said.

Five minutes later we were dressed again, warm and dry with towels around our heads and our bodies tingling. We sat there with our arms around our knees, catching our breath.

"What are you thinking about?" she said.

"Julian," I said. "How awfully sorry I feel for Julian."

"Poor little guy," she said.

"That's not the way you sounded a couple of hours ago," I said. "Jesus, you were cold-blooded. I almost felt like telling him to take that contract."

"That's what he asked us down to tell him," she said. "He was right on the borderline. One word of sympathy would have been enough to tip him the other way."

"I don't like it," I said. "I'll be damned if I do. This isn't just a character you can X-out and rewrite. This is a guy's life you're playing around with."

"Whatever we do," she said, "we have to do it all the way. If we want a Guild we have to fight it through. We can't have half a Guild. It's like a strike. You either scab or you try to stop the scabs. But you can't strike and feel sorry for the scabs at the same time."

"Why not?" I said. "The strikers only strike because they want something out of life they aren't getting. The poor scabs are in the same boat. I saw strikers beat hell out of a scab in my hometown once. He was just a desperate, hungry little guy. Being a scab wasn't his idea of what he wanted to do in this world."

"That's pity," she said. "Pity is always good for a couple of Christmas baskets for the poor. But that leaves three-hundred-and-sixty-four other days to take care of. Your attitude is very picturesque, from a distance. But try bringing it closer home. What do you think Sammy is but a desperate, hungry little guy?"

It was true. He was going around being desperate in a $150 tailor-made suit. He was hungrier than ever after five-dollar dinners at Marcel's.

"But Sammy is still in the Guild," I said. "I think you ought to try to get together with his bunch. Work out some sort of a compromise, maybe. It doesn't seem fair to put guys like Julian on such a spot."

"Sammy joined the Guild when it didn't cost anything," she said. "Everybody was doing it and it was absolutely safe. But now I think he's getting ready to jump. All he's waiting for is a nice, soft spot to land."

"Just the same," I argued, "his bunch is still a powerful minority in the Guild. I think you ought to give them the benefit of the doubt."

"The trouble with you," she said, "is that you're too goddam good. But I'll think it over. I'll put it up to the Board."

|||||||

The headline in the *Megaphone* the following Saturday read:

PREDICT CIVIL WAR AT GUILD SESSION TONIGHT!

But we didn't have to wait that long. All the writers on our lot—some fifty or sixty of us—were called together in one of the projection rooms just before lunch. And I can think of nothing better calculated to take away an appetite.

The atmosphere was electric. All of us seemed to be strung together with high-tension wires. The program began with Dan Young, the barrel-bodied, red-faced, profanely earnest studio manager, who seemed to feel that the story of how he had risen from truck driver right here at this studio to his present importance was a devastating argument for writers giving up the Guild foolishness and making the studio one big happy family. He even hinted that those who refused to participate in his family life (on his terms) would find themselves led by the hand to the studio gate and told never to darken his payroll again.

After he finished, to cautious applause, he introduced the next speaker, the white-haired boy of the happy family, whom he laughingly described as "a member of your own ranks who seems to have a little more sense than the rest of you."

Sammy Glick informed us that we would get further by voting the way the studio was asking us to. If he had used the first person singular instead of the plural he would have been right.

On the way out Sammy caught up with me and took my arm protectively. "Don't stick your neck out too far, Al," he said. "After all everybody's got to look out for Number One."

"Sure," I said, "but we can't all have a genius for it like you have."

I strolled back to the office with Kit. "We couldn't have done better if we had organized that meeting ourselves," she said. "That won more votes for us than it did for them. I was afraid a little pressure like that might run the boys out of the Guild. But it only seemed to pull them together. Now they're really sore."

"Where do you think Sammy is going to end up?" I said.

"It depends on what kind of a deal he can make with Young," she said. "He's probably holding out for general-manager-in-charge-of-production!"

||||||

The police department had taken the *Megaphone*'s prediction of civil war at the membership meeting seriously. Twenty or thirty policemen had planted themselves ominously around the hall to preserve law and order, staring curiously at the five or six hundred writers filling the auditorium.

Just before the meeting opened Kit stopped at my seat on her way to the platform and said animatedly, "Well, Al, it looks as if it's going to be run your way."

Then she was up there, facing the microphone. She ran her hand back over her hair once firmly, the way she always did before she began to speak. She spoke with an emphasis and implication of surprise that caught the membership immediately.

"For the past four weeks, which we will always look back on fondly as the Days of the Terror . . ."—she waited for her laugh— "there has been mounting confusion on the question of Guild autonomy. To satisfy those critics of the Authors' League amalgamation plan who honestly fear the loss of our independence, I propose that we vote tonight only on the *principle* of affiliation with the League, reserving the right to postpone official action on it until the membership is reassured that this does not mean the transference of Guild control from Hollywood to New York, Moscow, Mars or the dining room of the Algonquin."

I thought of our talk that evening at Glick's Lagoon. Now I knew what she meant by getting my way.

Lawrence Paine was recognized from the floor. Everyone leaned forward, expecting him to light the fuse that would set off the explosion. His gaunt, melancholy face was almost expressionless.

"I would like to second Miss Sargent's motion," he said and sat down.

Almost the entire audience rose spontaneously. The applause lasted several minutes. Dignified writers jumped up on their feet and whistled. They weren't cheering Paine. They were cheering the miracle of unity and peace.

The next move was a great piece of showmanship. "It is very appropriate," the President announced, "that the second motion we must vote on tonight will be made by a member who this morning turned down a major studio seven-year contract doubling his salary."

Julian walked onto the platform. His reception was deafening. It's a funny thing, I thought as I clapped with everybody else, we like to think of ourselves as the blasé, sophisticated people. And the first teaspoonful of emotion lays us right in the aisles.

He stood up there self-conscious and heroic and stiff with stage fright, a typewritten sheet of paper trembling in his hand.

"I move," he stammered, "that this meeting approve the action of the Executive Board in ordering us not to sign contracts binding us and our material for more than two years from today and that this Article XII remain in effect until the Producers' Committee opens negotiations with us for a minimum basic agreement."

This motion was seconded by none other than that courageous champion of the underdog, Samuel Glick. Now I am ready to face my Maker, I thought. For five years I've been waiting for Sammy Glick to make one positive gesture in the direction of the Brotherhood of Man. Now I can die in peace.

It might have been a positive gesture, but it wasn't exactly a modest gesture. That would have been too much. That would have been the regeneration stuff that has made so many pretty endings for the movies.

Sammy raised his hand importantly to halt the applause. "As the spokesman for our Committee," he said, "I wish to add that at a conciliation meeting with your Board just before we came in tonight, all differences were ironed out and our Committee pledged its support to the two motions on the floor. As loyal members of the Guild we are ready to carry out this pledge."

The audience sounded like a rooting section just after its team scored the winning touchdown. Sammy stood there at the mike longer than he had to, taking the bows. Suddenly everybody was loving everybody else. The cops must have thought the world had really gone nuts. They are sent to prevent screen writers from butchering each other and the crazy bastards do nothing but get up and make love to each other.

Everything after that was passed by acclamation. Someone got up and urged that all the Guild officers be re-elected as a gesture of our support, and we all yelled Aye. Then Kit took the mike again to propose that Paine, Wilson, McCarter, Griffin and Glick be added to the Executive Board, to demonstrate the Guild's concern for safeguarding the interests of the minority elements, and we all roared Aye again. The meeting was topped by an almost unanimous vote in favor of the two motions, and as much of the audience as possible adjourned to celebrate in the bar across the street.

We all piled into the gaudy little joint and turned an early May evening into a New Year's Eve midnight, only this time we really had something to celebrate.

Sammy and Kit and I buried the hatchet in a bottle of Scotch.

"Hey, Kit, what did I tell ya?" I kept repeating myself, being very gay and probably very boring. "This way everybody's happy. Isn't this just what I said oughta happen?"

Or I'd pound Sammy's sturdy little chest and tell him, "Sammy Glick, you ol' bastard, you know me. Don't I always tell you just what I think of you? Well, when you were shoveling it at the studio this morning, I says to myself: There goes the biggest sonofabitch in the whole goddam world. It's like the movie ads. Know what I mean, Sammy? See Sammy Glick in Ima Sonofa-bitch. Even bigger than last week, bigger 'n when he played Al Manheim for a sucker in the *Record* office, bigger every minute. But tonight! Tonight you really fooled me, Sammy. You finally came through and I'm proud of you. Hey, bartender, hit us all again and put your goddam money away, Kit, this one is on me."

And Sammy, drinking and kidding but never abandoned, "Well, Al, I'm really tickled to death. I think you and Kit had me pegged wrong about being against the Guild, but now that it's patched up I know our outfit's going to go places and I'm all for it."

My God, I thought, it almost sounds as if Sammy were actually going to stop running. Maybe he's decided he's gone as far as he needs and now he can cut off the motor and stop running people down. That thought made me very happy. It's wonderful what a few drinks of Scotch will do on an empty brain.

|||||||

The following day was Saturday and, after we knocked off at noon, Sammy took us to the swank tennis club he was very proud of joining. I couldn't see where Sammy had had time enough to attend to his private needs properly, much less learn tennis, but he had. We started volleying, and I thought this is one place where Sammy eats humble pie, but he started right off hitting them back one after another without much style but with plenty of confidence.

"When the hell did you learn this?" I yelled across the net.

"I just started taking lessons two weeks ago," he said. "From the best teacher in the country. Five dollars an hour. You ought to try him, Al."

"I don't have to," I said. "I've been playing tennis since I was a kid."

As a matter of fact, I looked very lousy. My eye was off and I was wild as hell.

"I'll play you for dough," he said, "and beat you."

I've always thought tennis is a better indication of character than handwriting or any of those other things they use. For instance, I liked to just get out there and slug the ball until I worked up a good sweat knocking most of the balls outside without paying too much attention to the score. Of the three of us Kit was the closest to a tennis player. She served her second serve just as hard as her first, chasing after her ball to the net and holding her ground with a good sense of volley and a stiff net game. Sammy was always reminding you of the score, especially if he were ahead. He played a smart, cautious game, getting everything back, making his awkward puny shots count by mixing up maddening lobs with shrewd little drop shots.

We played a couple of sets of doubles with one of the good club kids, whom Sammy promptly chose as his partner, and then Kit beat Sammy 6–3 and then Sammy turned around and beat me 10–8, in spite of the fact that I looked three or four times as good as he did and had him set point half a dozen times. I really think the margin between us was that he objected to losing more than I did. He had to win the little things just as much as the big ones; and the more I thought of it, the more incredible it seemed that he had backed down on his Guild position the way he had the night before.

|||||||

A few nights later I was sitting in bed reading when there was a knock on the door. I grabbed for my robe, surprised that anyone would be knocking, more surprised to find Kit.

"Well," she said, "now I've seen everything! Got a drink?"

She followed me into the kitchenette while I poured one for each of us.

"I'm afraid we congratulated ourselves a little too soon," she said. "Tonight Sammy and his playmates came to their first Board meeting. And it turned out to be their last."

I could feel it coming. I could feel him running again.

"Well, they walked out on us," she said. "Just got up and calmly announced they were resigning and walked out. Just told us what we could do with our pledges and took a powder."

She was still too overwhelmed to be really sore. It was the first time I had ever seen her really ruffled.

"My God! All of them?"

"All except Bob Griffin. He was absolutely furious. He said, 'Boys and girls, everything in Hollywood always seems to run to the super-colossal. I only regret that the Committee of which I have been an active member had to give you the most super-colossal double-cross I ever saw.' And he promised that he was going to stick with us to follow through the compromise program that the so-called Sanity Committee had pledged itself to. He was really magnificent. I had a hunch about him. You may not always agree with him but at least his convictions are never for sale. He ended up by saying, 'They say keeping pledges is a Rover-Boyish sentiment. I guess I'll just never grow up.' "

"Do you think Sammy and his pals were bought out?"

"I don't know," Kit said. "I'm too mixed up to think anything tonight. But I felt Griffin thinks so."

"What's the pay-off going to be?" I said.

She shook her head back and forth several times wearily. "Oh, hell, I don't know, Al. I guess it'll be interesting to see. If we live through it."

We didn't have to wait very long. The next morning there were rumors flying around about the number of Guild members who had already sent in resignations. First I heard ten and then I heard a hundred. Writers gave each other funny looks as they passed the stories around. *What do you think, pals?* they were asking each other silently, *think we're licked, think it's getting time to quit?* It was funny, that hot-and-cold business, the same pressure that made them so tough the day of the meeting was beginning to break them down now. Even though Sammy, Paine, Wilson and McCarter couldn't have had more than forty or fifty followers, their unexpected run-out had sprung a leak in the hull for fear to rush in.

And before the leak could be repaired it was torn wide open with another broadside.

Dan Young called us all into the projection room again. His big red face was wrinkled in a triumphant grin.

"Boys," he said. "If I thought that every writer in Hollywood wanted this Guild, believe me I'd be for it myself one hundred percent. But how do you expect us to take you seriously when you can't even agree among yourselves? Some of the biggest writers have quit already—and we understand more resignations are com- ing in every hour. Now what do you say we forget about the whole business—try to make World-Wide one big happy family the way we used to be?"

He paused and smiled again. "Okay, boys, that's all," he said casually. "You're going to be given resignation forms on your way out. You can turn them in to me any time within the next forty-eight hours."

He didn't say what would happen to us if we didn't. He didn't have to. Sammy Glick would attend to that, the Sammy Glicks.

We sat there passively, not thinking together any more, but each one alone and afraid, each one thinking of his own wife and his own script that was just beginning to come along so well and his own house in Beverly or Westwood or overlooking the ocean. We walked out as if those forms were the certificates of a disgrace- ful and contagious disease which each one of us thought he was the only one to have.

I tried to sign that form all afternoon. I knew I was a dope if I didn't, but somehow I just couldn't get around to it. I stuck a sheet of paper in my typewriter and started to write about Masa- ryk. But I found myself wondering what Masaryk would do if he had been asked to resign from the Guild. So I put on my coat and went home early. I didn't feel like seeing anybody so I got a little food out of the icebox and had supper alone, just me and that damned piece of paper.

Then I sat there in a ringside seat for the wrestling match between my conscience and my ambition, a fight to the finish, with a forty-eight-hour time-limit and finally I left them there on the canvas with a headlock on each other and called Kit.

"Kit? Did I wake you up?"

"No, I just got in. I was running some pictures at the studio. Two stinkers."

"Listen, Kit," I said. "I've been wanting to talk to you all night. I guess I'd like to be a hero and flush this goddam resignation blank down the drain. But there's no use kidding myself. I feel like a tug-of-war, the whole damned business, the rope and both teams pulling."

I expected her to give me a good shot in the arm, but all she said was, "I know, Al. It's very tough."

"Oh, Christ," I said, "I suppose I'm making it a lot tougher than it is, but I was just beginning to get the feel of this picture thing. This Masaryk job was—it still is exciting as hell, and Fineman is a swell gent; there's an awful lot I could learn from him. And yet I just can't see myself pulling a Sammy Glick."

"It isn't quite that bad," she said. "I'm afraid everybody's signing them, Al. I hear we have two hundred resignations already. I don't feel like telling anybody to go out and be a martyr."

"You didn't worry like that about Julian."

"That's different," she said. "That's when it looked as if we were going to win. We had to take that chance. And then, well, maybe I am being a little selfish about it."

That was a landmark. I would always remember it as the first sign of affection.

"Are you going to sign it, Kit?"

"No," she said. "But frankly, I'm in a much better spot. Three or four of my best credits all happened to come along this year. And they seem to feel that Keeler and I are clicking as a writer-director team. Of course, this may change their minds. But it does take less courage for me to hold out."

"In other words," I said, "you'd sign it."

"Al, I'm afraid that's a lonely battle you've got to fight out with yourself," she said. "But I wouldn't feel you were ratting out if you did. It's too late for that."

"Okay, Kit," I said. "Thanks. I'll think it over. See you tomorrow."

|||||||

When I went in to the studio next morning the form was still unsigned, but I had made up my mind. For a guy who didn't care six months ago whether the screen writers were organized into a

Guild or a sewing circle I had gone down the line for them every way I could. It had to stop somewhere. After all, I had come out here to be a writer, not a second John L. Lewis. So I took the paper out and scribbled my name at the bottom quickly, as if trying to keep myself from knowing what I was doing.

Then I went to work and I began to see my story again because my mind felt free for the first time in weeks.

Then Sammy Glick came in.

I hadn't talked to him since his famous *coup d'état*. I had passed him in the hall a couple of times and had thought of saying something insulting, but what was the use. I had said it all the day he marched in when I wasn't looking and invaded four inches into my column a long time ago. Anything I would have told him now would have just given him a laugh and maybe given me ulcers.

He came in with a smile stretching from his right ear to that flower he always wore in his lapel. I went on typing. He slung his leg over the corner of my desk. I looked up. In his hand was my resignation blank.

"Well, I see you're being smart for once," he said.

I tried to remember if Sammy had ever handed me a compliment before.

"That's just what I dropped in to check with you about," he said. "I didn't want to see you pull a sucker act like Julian."

"Hasn't Julian signed it?" I said.

"I'm washed up with that sap for good," Sammy said. "He's hopeless. He doesn't know to wipe himself."

Nebbish, poor Julian, a hero with quaking knees and a stomach full of butterflies.

"Well, now that you're using your head for something besides butting against a stone wall," Sammy said, "I think I can put you onto a good thing. Julian was beginning to get too much dough to work with me anyway. I need somebody in the lower brackets— to balance what I'm getting. So, while I was getting my massage this morning, it hit me like a ton of scripts. Why the hell don't I get Al? He needs a break and he's just what I need. So you're being transferred to our unit tomorrow. We're going to have a helluva picture—we just got word this morning that we can get Gable from Metro for the lead. It'll mean an A credit right off the bat. And, if you click, I'm liable to let you in on something really big that I'm not able to break yet."

"It's very nice of you to rearrange my life for me this way," I said, "but what about Masaryk?"

"Listen, my fine-feathered frand," he said, "between you and me and Louella O. Parsons you're just writing for the shelf. That anti-fascist stuff hasn't got a prayer. Why do you think Metro scrapped *It Can't Happen Here?* It's lousy for the English market. A producer who just got back told me that at lunch the other day. England doesn't want to get Hitler and Mussolini sore."

He yanked his lapel-watch out of his breast pocket. "Jesus, I better run—I've got a date with Frank, Frank Collier—to look at the rushes on *Monsoon.* The stuff is coming through terrific. Keep in touch with me, sweetheart."

The door slammed and he was off. I stood up and looked at that resignation blank. I studied the signature that Sammy had complimented me on placing there. I had a crazy impulse to make an airplane out of it and send it diving down into the studio street. But instead I just folded it double and began to shred it into the wastebasket.

|||||||

I really felt sorry for Mr. Fineman when he had to call me in and tell me I was being closed out. This was not his way. He felt guilty and powerless. "I'm afraid Masaryk is going on the shelf for a while and I haven't got another assignment for you at the moment."

He wanted to say more, but even if he had been able to, it would have been superfluous because the sympathy in his eyes, in his handshake, said it for him.

All I ever ask of a writer is that he deliver, he was trying to tell me. All I ask is that he loves to write motion pictures. That's the only kind of loyalty to the industry that means anything, and if that kind of loyalty comes through his work, whether he spends his nights in Main Street brothels or Writers Guild meetings is none of my business.

"But I want you to know I liked your work, and I'd like to do a picture with you some time. All the luck, Manheim."

For the next two weeks my agent tried to get me an interview at the studios, but everywhere he went he got the same answer: They weren't taking on new writers just now.

I sat by the phone like an extra boy hoping for that call from Central Casting.

When it rang a voice started talking a mile a minute.

"Oh, you dumb son-of-a-bitch, you glutton for punishment, you *momser* you."

"Where the hell are you, in a pay phone? Where you don't want to waste time saying hello?"

"Listen to him," Sammy said. "He's going down for the last time and he tries to make jokes yet. Well, Al, I don't know whether I'm just getting soft or whether I'm queer for you. But I'm going to give you one more chance."

"I didn't do it, mister, honest, don't hit me again," I said.

"Listen, Al," he said, "I don't see what you have to be so goddam cheerful about. I kept telling you. But you wouldn't listen to me. You had to stick your neck out like a giraffe. Now you really bitched yourself up. But good. But I've got some influence in this town now and there may still be an outside chance of cleaning you up. Now here's what I want you to do. Larry Paine is having a little get-together at his place tonight and I thought you might be doing yourself a hell of a lot of good if you came . . ."

This seemed to be a good chance to find out what the boys were up to. And of course there was the old curiosity as to how this was going to quicken the already mercurial pace of Mr. Glick.

Paine's home was an old plantation in Bel Air. The butler showed me into the bar, where I found the Four Horsemen, Paine, Wilson, McCarter and Glick, entertaining fifteen or twenty other writers. I spotted Lorna Flint, the old silent star who was in the writing game on a raincheck, George Pancake and my epic poet, Henry Powell Turner.

After two or three drinks, the party turned out to be a meeting.

Lawrence Paine called us to order and congratulated us on being the founding fathers of a new writers' organization, the Association of Photodramatists.

We, he informed us, were to have much the same aims as the defunct Screen Writers Guild, except that we would be a more select group, with a more discreet program.

Then Sammy nominated Paine as President, Jack McCarter seconded it and Sammy announced that he had been unanimously elected, although my right hand had stayed right in my pocket where it belonged.

Pancake nominated Henry Powell Turner for Vice-President. Turner rose, jowly and almost bald now, and I noticed how his fingers trembled as they reached to clutch the back of the seat in front of him.

"I regret that it will not be practical for me to accept this office," he explained. "For I am quitting Hollywood for good, to devote myself exclusively to poetry again, as soon as I finish my present assignment."

So the Vice-President of the Association of Photodramatists turned out to be Sammy Glick.

After Wilson and McCarter were honored with the remaining offices, we were all invited to sign up as charter members. Pancake signed with a flourish and handed me the pen.

"I thought you were opposed to writers' organizations?" I said.

"This one is different," he said righteously.

"You said it!" Sammy cut in. "These guys know what side their contract is buttered on."

He looked down the list officiously. "Where's your name?" he accused me.

"In my wallet," I said.

"What the hell is the matter with you?" he said.

"I've just been through one war," I said. "I don't think I could take another."

"There's not going to be any war," he said. "I got it all fixed."

"How about recognition?" I said. "The Guild's been battling over that for years."

"That shows you how smart your Guild is," he said. "We're going to be recognized right off the bat. I got it straight from Dan Young. What do you think of that?"

"I think that's very interesting," I said. "What were you and Young doing discussing the recognition of an organization that hadn't even been formed yet, much less elected spokesmen?"

"I thought it wouldn't do any harm to sound him out on the idea," he said.

"Do whom any harm?" I said. "So you and Young decided that it was wrong for the Guild with nine hundred members to represent all the writers in Hollywood, but all right for your Photodramatists with twenty members?"

"That's because they know we have the industry at heart," Sammy explained. "They know they can trust us."

"Oh," I said.

He put his hand on my arm intimately.

"Come outside a moment, Al. I want to talk to you."

We walked along the edge of the pool. Sammy's tone was conspiratorially important.

"You know I told you the other day I had something I wasn't ready to break yet? Well, it still hasn't quite jelled, but there's a good chance I won't be writing much longer. I'll be on the hiring end . . ."

Sammy paused to take a deep, proud draw on his cigar.

I wondered if this was the price of his sell-out tactics in the Guild. If he became a writer by using Julian Blumberg as a stepping stone, it seemed only fitting that he should become a supervisor by climbing over hundreds of other writers.

All I could think of to say was, "I'll be god-damned."

"Shut up and listen," he ordered. "If this thing goes through, I'm thinking of keeping a writer with me all the time. You know, someone who's loyal to me. What's the percentage in going down with the Guild when you can waltz into a set-up like that? So why not be smart for once and join an outfit that's strictly class?"

"Sammy," I said, "why not try *not* being smart for once? Just once."

Sammy's voice knifed cold through the night air. "Okay, Al, I was only trying to help you. But if you haven't learned by this time that it's every man for himself, it's no skin off my ass. It's your funeral."

Sammy thrust his hands into his pockets and started back to his Association of Photodramatists, taking long brisk strides with his head down as if he were bucking a stiff wind. It was the great-man walk he was developing.

|||||||

The next evening there was another little meeting in Hollywood. But this gathering was small for another reason, it was not a beginning, but an ending.

The Guild had called its members to a final reckoning. It wanted to learn whether it was still in existence. A handful of us stood around the door hopefully as the survivors straggled in. When the meeting began the room was so empty that the President asked us all to move up, so we wouldn't look so desolate. It was a sad and splendid little meeting full of the warmth and understanding toward each other that people have to dig deep in themselves to tap, which they only reveal when their farms have been washed away by flood or their homes blown off the earth by bombs or when somebody dies.

I looked around and smiled at friends I had never met or talked to. It was strange to see who the die-hards turned out to be. Some of those who had been the most belligerent and loudest were gone. But Bob Griffin was there, for some reason he would probably never be able to explain even to himself. And Julian, a shade paler than usual, faint from fright at his own courage, wanting nothing more from life than that little yellow house with the surf splashing up below it, martyring himself because he couldn't learn how to run, forward or backward.

Kit topped the evening off with a little hail-and-farewell speech that somehow managed to sound hard-boiled and idealistic at the same time.

"In four hectic weeks we have seen our Guild murdered by a small group of willful (for want of a better name) men with only one allegiance—to themselves. Our President has asked me to deliver the funeral oration but I'm afraid any elegy would be out of place because I have a feeling that the corpse is going to be very obstinate about being buried."

Afterwards Kit, Julian and I adjourned to Barney's Beanery to cry into our beer. In one corner of the joint somebody was playing a Louie Armstrong in a jukebox and in the other those two ex-vaudeville headliners were singing familiar songs that everybody has forgotten. And yet there was something nice and peaceful about the place.

The only discordant note was a recent discovery of Julian's that began to round out the picture of Sammy Glick, union member and all-around Brother of Man.

"Yesterday when I went back to clean out my desk—by the way, I'm no longer employed by World-Wide—I could hear Mr. Wilson shouting at the top of his voice—you know he has the office next to mine. Well, I couldn't make out what he was saying, but I thought I heard something about Sammy and it sounded interesting, so I used a trick I learned in that mystery picture we did: I put an empty glass against the wall and pressed my ear against it.

"Wilson was doing the worst cursing I ever heard. He was screaming his head off about the studio double-crossing him and calling Sammy every dirty name under the sun. After a while I began to get it. 'Son-of-a-bitch-bastard!' Wilson was howling, 'For ten years the one thing I want is to be a producer. I figure the best way to get my break is to lead the stampede out of the Guild like the studio wants. And then, when it looks like I'm all set, a little jerk who could be my son, God forbid, beats me to the punch!'"

It seemed a rather devious way of becoming a producer—but there it was. We all got hysterical at Julian's picture of Wilson foaming at the mouth because Sammy had appropriated the fruits of his treachery, but it would have been funnier if it hadn't contained so much horror, the horror of a foetus called Sammy Glick sprinting out of his mother's womb, turning life into a race in which the only rules are fight for the rail and elbow on the turns and the only finish line is death.

"Sammy is really revolutionizing Hollywood," Kit laughed. "It's getting so a man isn't even safe being a louse any more."

"Wilson ought to picket in front of Sammy's office," I added. "Sammy Glick Is Unfair to Organized Double-Crossers!"

|||||||

The next day I got a call from my agent. "Hello," he said. "How are you at dishwashing or making paper flowers? Because I'm afraid you'd better start looking for another trade."

"Is it that bad?"

"Tough," he said. "Very tough. Jesus, I didn't know you were one of the ringleaders of the Guild."

"Neither did I," I said. "So I'm really on the blacklist?"

"If there was a blacklist, I guess you'd be on it, all right," he said. "But they don't need anything like that in this chummy little business. All it takes is a couple of big shots happening to mention it over a poker game—or meeting in Chasen's and passing the word along. That's why you should have played ball."

"I know," I said. "I've been following the career of the greatest ballplayer of them all."

"What the hell are you talking about?" he said.

"About Joe DiMaggio," I said. "Skip it, pal." I guess I was just thinking I was back where I came from again, watching the kid run for a high one in the old Stadium.

|||||||

It was to be the last dinner before I caught the train for New York in the morning.

"Where shall it be for dinner?" I said. "Let's make it some place special."

"Oh, I think it's only fitting that you pay your respects to the

Derby," Kit said. "It's the Hollywood version of the farewell visit to the college chapel."

We sat in the Derby watching the people watch each other.

"It's a funny thing," Kit said. "If you watch an animal while it eats, it stops. But here in the Derby several hundred people pay and pay well for the privilege."

"And of watching everybody else," I said.

Everybody turned to stare at the foreign star who had just come in with her husband and her new lover. She walked between them with a haughty pride, the way one does with Russian wolfhounds.

"Look at that poor bastard," Kit said, pointing out the husband, a big director in Europe who hadn't been able to get a job here and who seemed to be laughing gaily at something the lover had just said.

"He knows everybody in the room read about his wife and that other guy in Parsons' column this morning, and he's feeling just terribly modern and Noel Coward."

"And lousy," I added.

I looked around the Derby, at the familiar faces, at the faces I had never seen before but which looked familiar because they fitted so well into the pattern, at the caricatures on the wall which seemed to be unconsciously mocking them all.

Then I suddenly heard a familiar voice.

"Saw your picture, Dave. Tuhriffic!"

I knew who it was before I spotted him, several tables down the aisle. No voice carried quite like Sammy's. He had stopped at Dave Roberts's table, draping himself over it to embrace the famous director.

"There he blows!" I said.

"Blows is right!" Kit answered.

"Tuhriffic!" Sammy was exclaiming. "You made me cry. You know what a tough audience I am and I swear to God when that little kid comes home Christmas morning and finds her doll broken, you got me"—he indicated the general direction of his heart and tapped it several times meaningfully—"here."

He gave Roberts's hand a tender good-bye squeeze and rejoined his own table. Rita was waiting for him, and a tall, elegant Englishman I had seen at the Larry Paine gathering, and a swarthy young man in a dapper stiff white collar and flashy suit.

"Who's he with?" I said.

"The one who looks like a bodyguard is something Sammy just dug up," Kit said. "Called Sheik Dugan. Sammy seems to be breaking him in as a high-class stooge. Out here they're as necessary a social prop as valets. The other one is Sir Anthony Abbott. Came over with quite a fanfare about being the greatest writer in England. So far the chief contribution he's made to Hollywood seems to be a five-goal rating for Zanuck's polo team."

"Remember that time you told me you knew a lot of Sammy Glicks," I said. "I thought you were crazy until I started thinking about that gang at Paine's the other night. They were all so different—a titled Englishman and a famous poet and an aesthetic nance and a tough, drunken ex-reporter—but they all really had the same idea Sammy had. They were all running. Sammy was just a little bit faster, that's all."

Kit nodded. "I wonder if the thing that makes Sammy so fascinating for us is that he is the id of our whole society."

"What do you mean?"

"Well, you know how the id is supposed to be the core of your basic appetites which the superego dresses in the clothes of respectability to present to the outside world? Somehow Sammy never had time to get dressed up the way all those others have, Wilson and McCarter and Sir Anthony, all their sammyglickness covered up with Oxford manners or have-one-on-me sociability or Christian morals that they pay their respects to every Sunday morning when they don't have too big a hangover. I think that's what first hit me about Sammy. He wasn't something trying to be something else. He was the thing itself, the *id,* out in the open. It might not be very pretty but there it was."

"So Sammy's got *id,*" I said. "And that's what keeps him running."

"Oh, I doubt if it's that easy," she laughed. "To find out why Sammy really runs so much faster than anyone else, you'd probably have to know what kind of infancy he had, and whether his kindergarten teacher used to slap him, and under what conditions he learned the facts of life, whether he ever suffered from malnutrition—the whole works."

"That's all I have to worry about when I get back to New York," I said. "Except for the little matter of finding a job."

Sammy had paid his check and was making an exit. He looked over at us, waved fleetingly and ran.

I watched Sammy at the entrance, standing under the big caricature of Franklin D., looking the place over as if he were about to stick it up, while his man Sheik was helping him into his brown suede overcoat. Then Sammy adjusted with casual care the green Tyrolean hat that his face would never suit, Rita floated out of the ladies' room and they were off.

"I wonder what shoes he's wearing now," I said. "Probably some little number whipped up by his official cobbler, with laces of human hair plucked from the heads of leading ladies."

"He must have twenty pair," she said. "What is that special yen for shoes?"

"Maybe he's trying to find a pair he can't wear out in a day," I said. "If I solve the mystery in New York I'll shoot a wire."

||||||

We were on our porch watching the lights black out over Hollywood again.

We talked about everything, about the Guild and about Sammy and about screen writing and about the revolt of the generals that had just begun in Spain, but it wasn't like any of the good talks we had had before, because words that night could only be a buzzing of irrelevance.

I kept noticing the wordless things, the casual, unladylike way she leaned over the porch wall, not caring what the wind did with her hair. The way the glow from the room behind us highlighted the bony handsomeness of her face; how long we were conscious of the closeness of our hands before they finally met, and then how much harder it was to talk.

And finally I said, "Kit, I've been trying to think of fancy ways of saying this for the past two hours. God, I've wanted you a long time! I guess you know how long, and I thought tonight . . ."

She looked at me and I saw how beautiful her eyes could be when they weren't being hard and I met the look, inquisitively, and she turned away to stare out at the lights far below.

"Hell, this isn't a roll in the hay for me, there's plenty of that around. This is, well, maybe the best way of saying good-bye . . ." There was a pool of nausea in my stomach that suddenly became anger. "After all, I'm not a Sammy Glick that hits and runs."

I thought she was going to get sore because I was, but instead she said, "Look, darling, I was never going to mention it again, but as long as you have . . . With Sammy there could never be any complications. You know how he is, monolithic, just tosses it off, never lets you get inside, no emotional entanglements to slow him down. But you, you're such a sentimental dope, you'd be calling me long distance before you passed Kansas City, wanting to make an honest woman of me."

She looked up at me, almost shyly, and grinned. "Or I'd be calling you."

That was all it needed and her lips seemed to be there waiting and I had a flash of that first moment we danced together when she had almost seemed to take the lead. It was the same struggle now, the impulses controlled so long finally pouring out in unexpected violence, and then suddenly she relaxed. "Feminine as hell," I could remember her saying, and I could feel myself holding her, feel her body accept my hands.

Then we were in the bedroom and I was fumbling impatiently with her dress but she stopped me, saying, "Don't, Al. Let me do it. I'll be right back."

I didn't understand then, but I did a minute later when she returned, her body trim and cool and confident.

"Hello," she said in a half-whisper and we looked at each other as she switched off the main lights.

There is always that fear of anti-climax, that it won't click, but from the first moment both of us knew that was something we would never have to worry about. It was the way she went at a script, or fought for the Guild or played tennis.

|||||||

Then she stretched to turn on the lamp near the bed.

"Hello," I answered and we both smiled, our new, intimate smile. She reached over and laid her hand on my shoulder affectionately. Sammy may go through every girl in Hollywood, I thought, but this is another pleasure he will never know, the give-and-take companionship, the overtones. Slip 'em a lay, I could hear him saying. Sure, I get in three times a week, gratis.

We must have been lying there a long time, for the electric lights had become part of the night before and the dawn was a pale blue canopy over our window.

"Kit," I said. "Maybe you were right. Maybe I would be calling you by the time I reached Needles. So why don't you save us both a lot of time by coming along with me? We'll get married when we get in."

She hesitated a long time, but I could tell she wasn't thinking it over, just trying to find the words to let me down easy.

"Al," she said, "you could stay here and let me support you until this thing blew over, but you'd be miserable. You wouldn't feel you had a place. That's the way I'd feel if I left here now."

"But God knows you could find plenty to do around New York."

"Yes, but I've spent four years trying to be a screen writer and I'm just beginning to learn how to be a good one. Now that *Jefferson* is clicking, I'm getting assignments that really give me a chance to do something."

We were as much apart now as if a bundling board had been there between us. "This is what I was afraid of," she said. "Starting something we can't finish. I thought you'd understand."

"I wasn't going to," I said, "but, oh, hell, if you were just willing to trail me around and wait for me to come home for supper—I suppose that wouldn't be you any more."

She clasped her hands in back of her head thoughtfully.
"I'm going to miss you," she said.

||||||

I sat there in the diner looking out at the pink-brown desert and finishing my coffee in peace when the steward handed me a Los Angeles paper.

I had caught the Hollywood habit of opening it straight to the film section. Sammy's picture was in the lead column, denying the rumor that he and Rita Royce were secretly married. "I respect Miss Royce tremendously," Sammy was quoted, "and we seem to have a great many mutual interests, such as the new play I'm writing for her." The words read like an old refrain: "But we're just good friends, very good friends."

And then I came to what Sammy would call the topperoo.

Mr. Glick, the column cooed, is the young miracle man who has just signed a writer-producer contract with World-Wide. "Last night on the phone he would only laugh modestly when I asked him to confirm my tip-off from reliable inside sources that this new contract will begin at $2000 a week."

I could just imagine that modest laughter. Sammy could only have one kind of laugh for $2000 a week and I was glad I didn't have to be around to hear it.

I sat on the observation platform thinking of the evening when two thousand dollars a week had only been a terrible passion sizzling in his belly and it was consoling just to lean back and let the distance between us widen tie by tie. I listened to the sound of the wheels carrying on their endless conversation with the tracks. At first their rapid chatter sounded like nothing but metallic and monotonous double-talk. But later, as my ear became accustomed to their language, I realized that they were asking each other, over and over again, What Makes Sammy Run? What makes Sammy run what makes sammy run what makes sammy runwhatmakessammyrun . . .

CHAPTER 9

I t may sound like sour grapes but it was good to get Hollywood and Sammy Glick behind me. The first day I hit New York I must have walked a couple of hundred blocks. It felt great even though I was broke and New York can be a lonely and ugly town for the guys without money. But I ran into some of the old gang right away, guys who were nicer to you when you needed it than when you didn't, and pretty soon I was back in the old groove, pounding it out for the *Record* again, beginning to work Hollywood out of my system.

I mean I was able to look at a guy without wondering whether he was a five- or a seventy-five-hundred man, and I could sit back in a movie and enjoy my fifty-five-cent dream without torturing

myself with the knowledge that the best scene in the picture had
gone the way of all censors or that the writing which was credited
to a famous Broadway playwright because he had a sole screenplay credit clause in his contract was really the work of half a
dozen busy little B-writers.

But best of all I congratulated myself on getting Sammy Glick
out of my life, or rather, getting myself out of his. Once in a while
I couldn't help reading about him, of course; one of the fan mags
would name him on its list of Hollywood's Ten Most Eligible
Bachelors, or he was off to Hawaii for a much-needed rest, and
I caught myself searching for his name in the columns from time
to time, but on the whole I was able to conduct my life as if he
had never been a part of it, settling down with the comforting
thought that he would never be again.

This thought persisted for almost four weeks. Then one night
some of us were sitting around the office a trifle on the alcohol
side and the conversation took a sudden turn for Sammy Glick.
One of the boys had just seen a picture of his, *Touchdown, Irish!*
a drama of Notre Dame's Four Horsemen, with exactly the same
plot as *Hold 'Em, Yale!* Sammy's football picture of the season
before, and of course we began to swap anecdotes of his days on
the *Record,* all told with a sense of indignation, humor and envy.
And then we got to arguing, God knows why, about where he
came from. There were votes for the Bronx and Washington
Heights and the Lower East Side and the usual bets were made.
We wondered how we could settle it, and then I had a brainstorm. Didn't we used to keep a file on all our employees?

Nobody knew, of course, so I yelled across to Osborne on the
copy desk, "Hey, Oz, don't we keep some sort of file on all the
guys that work here?" and Osborne wasn't sure, he had only been
on the *Record* a couple centuries, and I could hear the question
running through the room, "Hey, Jack, we got a personnel filing
system in the joint?" and Jack saying he had heard of something
like that, but he wouldn't know where it was.

We finally found a copy boy who had actually seen the file and
he guided me to a remote part of the building where I was left

to continue my quest for Sammy Glick. For this was part of the quest, though I was in no condition to realize it then as I thumbed foggily through the yellowing cards, thinking I was just ending a pointless, drunken argument when I was really stumbling onto the terrible mysteries of the child Sammy.

The cards shuffled slowly through my fingers, Gang, Gifford, Glennon, and then I reached Golden and wondered how I had missed Glick so I went back more slowly and then I discovered why. I had hardly been reading the names, mostly searching for that one quick syllable and the cards went Glennon, Glessner, Glickstein, only this time it registered and I yanked the card out, vaguely annoyed with myself at the excitement that came with it.

> NAME.....*SAMUEL GLICKSTEIN*
> OCCUPATION.....*Copy Boy*
> ADDRESS.....*136 Rivington St.*
> LAST OCCUPATION.....*Western Union messenger*
> PHONE.....*none*
> AGE.....*17*
> HT......*5'7"*
> WEIGHT.....*126 lbs.*
> PARENTS' NAME.....*Mrs. Max Glickstein*
> ADDRESS.....*Same as above*

I wondered when he had dropped that "stein" from around his neck. Something that Sammy once said about his father came back to me and I wondered what had happened to Max. I thought, just for the hell of it, of copying off the card, but that was too much trouble so I just slipped it into my pocket.

|||||||

It seems to be a human failing to accumulate a great many things in our pockets, all of them absolutely useless, but which we transfer conscientiously from suit to suit. That is how I happened to reach into my pocket the following Sunday and find the card still with me. Now, psychologists may say that I purposely brought the card with me that Sunday because of a subconscious determination to trace Sammy back to his roots. And the psychologists may even be right. It is very hard to say. All I know is that when I went strolling through Central Park that morning my only conscious purpose was to watch the ducks and feed the pigeons and get a little air, and that it was a genuine surprise to find SAMUEL GLICKSTEIN, Copy Boy, 17, in my hand when I reached for a cigarette. And when I turned casually out of the park and began strolling down Fifth Avenue, it was without the slightest knowledge of where I was heading.

But by the time I had walked down to 38th Street I was beginning to suspect. I thought of that scrapbook I had started. It was like putting a jigsaw puzzle together and some of the pieces were still missing. I was down to 34th Street, my mind trailing a ghost, the swift, fresh phantom of a pasty-faced copy boy, my body following foolishly after my mind.

Half an hour later I was walking into the world of his childhood, a foreign world of clotheslines, firetraps, pushcarts and pinch-faced children that stretches for too many blocks along the East River. I walked down Avenue A, down Allen, down Rivington, wondering at the irony of the fascist charge that the Jews have cornered the wealth of America; for here where there are more Jews than anywhere else in the world, millions of them are crowded into these ghetto streets with the early American names.

The Glicksteins lived between a synagogue and a fish store, in a tenement laced with corroded fire escapes and sagging wash-lines. It looked as if one healthy gust of wind would send its tired bricks tumbling down into the narrow street. The hallway gave off a warm, sweet and infinitely unpleasant odor of age, of decay, of too many uncleaned kitchens too close together. I found the name Glickstein on the mailbox, pressed the buzzer for 4C and started up the moldy wooden staircase that groaned protestingly as I climbed to the top floor.

A frail round-shouldered young man with sick skin opened the door as far as the safety-latch would permit. He looked suspiciously at me through the crack.

"Yes?"

Suddenly I was overwhelmed with the ridiculousness of this visit. I had an impulse to turn and hurry off. But it was too late. I had already begun to explain who I was, why I had come. As if I knew, as if I could.

"My name is Manheim," I faltered. "I . . . I knew . . . I'm a friend of Sammy Glick's from Hollywood."

"From Sammele!" I heard a woman's voice cry out. "Israel, quick, open up the door!"

As I entered, she rose from her seat at the window. The window was closed, so she could not have been sitting there for the air. After all these years she must have been still curious about what was going on down there in the street. The indoor complexion of her emaciated, wrinkled face was emphasized by the black lace shawl which she wore, peasant-fashion, over her head. My appearance seemed to frighten her, for she hurried over to me, looking up into my face with an anxiety that made me uncomfortable.

"Oi weh's mir, my little Sammele! Something has happened to him! Tell me, mister, please. He sent you to tell me, maybe?"

"No, no, Mrs. Glickstein," I said, wondering what had made me walk into this. "There's nothing wrong with Sammy, absolutely nothing, he's getting along fine."

"Please, I'm his momma—so if something's wrong with my Sammele I want I should know."

"Believe me, Mrs. Glickstein," I had to reassure her. "That's not why I came. Sammy couldn't be better."

"Ach," she sighed, slowly regaining her composure. "Excuse me, please. When I hear you come from Sammele I get so excited . . ."

"We haven't heard from Sammy in so long that Momma's been worried about him," the sallow-faced Israel explained.

"But Sammele's a good boy," Mrs. Glickstein added hastily. "Every month regular comes his check in the mail. Only he is all the time so busy he never has time for writing."

She looked at me and her face creased into the deeper wrinkles of a smile. "So maybe my son sent you, you should tell me something from him?"

Here I go again, I thought. Sammy's trusted friend bringing the message of devotion from the faithful son. Why do I always have to be defending the bastard?

"He said to be sure and tell you how well he's feeling," I heard myself saying. "He said that even if he hasn't much time to write he wants you to know he is always thinking of you."

In her excitement she had forgotten her customary hospitality.

"This is his brother," she said. "Israel." Israel nodded like an aged Jew in prayer. He was like an old, bent man with a young face. "Izzy, go in the kitchen and make some tea, like a good boy."

I watched Israel as he quietly obeyed his mother's orders. If physical similarity had anything to do with resemblance, he and Sammy would have looked very much alike. But I would never have recognized them as brothers, for Israel's face seemed to reflect despair and bitterness and the gentleness of resignation, and it was strange to see how these qualities had molded his face to one so different from the forward thrust of Sammy's.

The small front room was cluttered with ugly furniture. The warm, sticky smell I had noticed in the hallway downstairs was only the faint essence of the odor that hung over this flat, the smell of rotting woodwork and too much living in one place.

The street below vibrated with the harsh, raw noises of kids yelling at each other in a stoop-ball game, merchants driving their hard bargains, women shouting their gossip from stoop to stoop, radios turned up as loud as possible to drown each other out, automobile horns honk-honking to remind everybody that their marketplace, their playground, their social center, their arena, was still a street.

Mrs. Glickstein, sensitive with the suffering of thousands of years, guessed what I was thinking.

"Sammele wants we should move uptown," she explained, "but it is better here with the synagogue right next door, so I don't have to do no walking, and the Settlement House where Izzy works right around the corner, and everybody on the block I am such good friends with like in the old country."

Israel brought in the tea, in steaming glasses, and some salami and yellow bread. Mrs. Glickstein and Israel poured their tea into saucers and sucked it through the cubes of sugar they held between their teeth.

Then she ceremoniously lifted a picture from the wall. It was a group photograph captioned Lower Grades, P.S. 15. "See if you can tell which one is him?" Mrs. Glickstein challenged me playfully.

I looked across the rows of serious little faces, wondering whether I could pick him out. It was a cinch. My finger went right to him. He was on the left end of the first row, standing a little closer to the camera than anybody else. It looked weird to see that same intense ferret face on this little body in short pants and long black stockings wrinkled over the knees. "That's him," I said.

"And also here," Mrs. Glickstein said mischievously, pointing to the opposite side of the same row. I looked more closely. By God, there he was again, only this time his face was distorted in a big grin. "He ran around behind the bleachers so he should beat the camera," Mrs. Glickstein explained.

I studied this second image. I had seen that same exultant look on his face before. The moment he watched his name flash on the screen for the first time, the night of his dramatic triumph when the flashlights flared around him and Rita Royce. His face told you that this was a triumph too. When the picture was posted on the school bulletin board Sammy's achievement must have monopolized the comment, and the triumphant sneer on that dark little puss revealed that this had already become his goal.

Mrs. Glickstein wanted me to tell her how much Sammy weighed and whether he was any taller and if he were a good boy and had he met any nice Jewish girls. And she went on talking about what a fine baby he had been and what a smart, hardworking boy, distilling the story of his youth with the unconscious censorship of a mother's pride. In English she sounded awkward and ignorant, but when she discovered I understood Yiddish (though I had practically forgotten how to speak it) she became articulate with that mysterious sense of poetry all peasants seem to have.

All the time we talked, Israel sat there hardly saying a word, noisily sipping his tea or chewing on the dry bread. But the twisted way he smiled at his mother's naive account of her little Sammele, an occasional comment he could not resist, gave him away. When Mrs. Glickstein boasted of the regularity with which Sammy's check arrived every week, Israel nodded scornfully, mumbled grimly, "Sure, sure, he's very thoughtful." I watched him more and more as Mrs. Glickstein talked, wondering how long this hate for Sammy had been fermenting. He was the one to talk, I thought, this was my man.

At sundown we heard a new sound, a singsong chant of many low voices in weird cacophony. The Orthodox Jews were beginning their evening prayers in the synagogue next door. Israel rose to join them. I said I would like to come along. He nodded, flustered and pleased.

When I left, Mrs. Glickstein blessed me again, asked me to look after her little boy, and pressed a paper bag into my hand. *"Strudel,"* she said, "still hot. I made it today. Sammele used to say I made the best *strudel* in the whole world."

When she tried to control herself, her eyes only moistened more. "And maybe you will tell him some time he should try to come home and see his Momma."

It was like a very little moan for a very deep wound. I went out wondering how many other cruelties of Sammy's she had accepted with the same mild protest.

||||||

The synagogue was a bare, shabby place, airless with all the windows shut, where forty or fifty men, mostly aged and bearded, faced east to the Holy Land, humbled themselves before their fierce, demanding God and wailed their songs of endless sorrow. I stood there swaying with them, but only mechanically, for I was raised in the Reform Temple that these traditional religionists would spit upon, and in recent years I had even strayed from this watered-down Judaism, occasionally doing lip service on the High Holy Days now but coming to believe that if love for your fellow man is in your heart you need no superstructure to dramatize it for you. And if it isn't, no God and no church can put it there. So I stood there swaying and wondering. What is a Jew? The anthropologists have proved it is not a race, since the only scientific category is the Semitic, which includes Arabians and Assyrians, some of the most fervent anti-Jews in the world. And if it were merely a religion, all Jews like me would have to be excluded. And if it is only a unit of national culture, it is withering away in America, for the customs and traditions that the Glicksteins brought over at the end of the nineteenth century may have been inherited by Israel, droning in his *yarmulka* at my side, but were thrown overboard as excess baggage by anyone in such a hurry as his younger brother.

|||||||

Afterward we went across to a little bakery, because that was the most convenient place to sit, and ate potato *knishes* and talked.

The poverty of the neighborhood had swallowed Israel. He had worked for the Settlement House fifteen years. When he was a child he had developed tuberculosis of the skin, and doctors had been telling him to find a better climate, but something held him here, like an umbilical cord between him and his people, which he would not cut.

"It is hard to explain," he said. "I would always be thinking about them. I would worry about them."

He talked without an accent but with the wailing tone and cadence of the Jewish chants.

"How much can the Settlement do?" I said.

He nodded wearily. "I know. Sometimes I feel like I'm trying to bail out the Hudson with my bare hands." The singsong of his voice emphasized the futility. "This one has no clothes to go to school. So, when you get the clothes, he can't go to school because the father has no job. So, when you find the job . . ."

He shrugged helplessly. "The same every day, only worse. The Reds say to me, 'What is the use of your Settlement? It is just a patch on the old tire. What we need is to throw the old tire on the dump heap and start with a new one.' I don't know, sometimes I think maybe they are not so crazy. Only more violence? I have seen too much already. And meantime who is going to get the milk for Mrs. Fleischman's baby, or find someone to take care of little Irving whose mother died yesterday . . . ?"

He stopped short, swamped with the hopelessness of it.

"Israel," I said, "have you always felt this way about it?"

"I guess I got it from the old man," he said. "If he had lived a long time ago they would have written about him in the Bible. Everybody on the East Side called him Papa Glick. I can remember when I was a kid, Papa was always bringing somebody hungry home for supper, even when we didn't have enough to go round. I remember once he even dragged an Irish bum in off the Bowery for the Passover feast, and the ceremony made the mick bawl. Whenever anything went wrong, the neighbors always yelled for Papa. They even called him in the middle of the night like a doctor. Poor Papa Glick."

"Where is he now?"

"He's been dead since Sammy was thirteen."

"How did he die, Israel?"

"He was run over. Coming home with his pushcart one night. Poor Papa. It was like he really wanted to get run over."

"Why?" I said. "What was the matter, Israel?"

"What is the use?" he said. "What's passed is passed. So now that my brother is a big man I would only sound jealous."

"But you really wouldn't want to be Sammy?"

"Me be Sammy!" he said. "May I eat a live pig first."

"How was it with him and your father?" I said. "What kind of a kid was he? You can tell me."

What I was trying to say was that I was on his side and he seemed to understand.

Israel was one of those Jews who cannot look angry. When they want to look angry they only look more melancholy.

"He broke Papa's heart," he said. "He made Papa not want to live any more."

"What happened?" I said. "What did he do?"

"It's a long story," Israel said. "I know it's a terrible thing to say about your own flesh and blood, but, before God, if he should drop dead this minute I would not even sit *shiva.*"

When we finally left the bakery it was dark and the pale kids looked like hobgoblins playing around the lampposts and I had heard Israel's story. It was a sad, angry story, full of tears and curses and, as I walked slowly toward the subway through those jumbled ghetto streets, it made me shudder to pass all those little creatures who might be Sammy Glicks.

Israel's story was just fascinating and unsatisfying enough to make me want to go on playing Sherlock Holmes, only this seemed more important than tracking down a murderer. And there were still large gaps to be filled. But Israel had given me some promising leads. He had told me about Sammy's first teacher, Miss Carr, who was still at P.S. 15. And about Foxy Four Eyes, the degenerate son of a tailor, always the idol of the younger boys who used to hang out at his old man's shop on the corner.

The first chance I had I was down again. I walked through the yard of Sammy's school. The boys had gathered to watch a fight. "Kill the dirty sheeny," they were yelling, "Kick him in the balls." Send him back to Palestine, to Ireland, to the Pope. Blazing with hatreds so quickly inherited, it was easy to make the mistake of thinking they were in the blood.

The little boys did not fight like children. It looked professional. They fought grimly, weaving, jabbing, dancing away. They clinched, pounded each other's kidneys, broke, and punched with perfect timing. These were not children but seasoned battlers, battle-scarred veterans of seven or eight, for the East Side is like one gigantic prize-ring through the ropes of which everyone has to climb at birth.

On the fence at the back of the yard, a child who looked as if he had not been on this earth more than half a dozen years was conscientiously inscribing the usual obscenity in chalk letters, a foot high, which stood there like a desperate challenge to a hostile world, summing up in two brief words the attitude toward life that Sammy had probably begun to learn at the same age and place.

I really hadn't expected to find her, but Miss Carr was still there. Middle-aged, wiry, talkative and not as nervous as you would expect her to be after struggling for control of those hostile, overcrowded classes for so many years.

As she talked on, memory of Sammy sharpened, reminiscences of him she thought she had forgotten began to return, and she passed them on willingly, partly because she took special pride in her memory, partly because Sammy's childhood exploits still had a fascination for her.

One story she said she would never forget. Sammy's first day in school. After she told me, I knew I would never forget it either. And I knew that even if Sammy had forgotten it, it had become a part of him.

As I was leaving, Miss Carr said, "So now he's a famous movie writer. I used to think Sammy might become a brilliant scholar. But as he got up in the higher grades he began to lose interest. That's our problem down here, you know. I'm afraid P.S. 15 is the smallest part of their education. The street is the real school. And that's where Sammy was a star pupil." She took off her glasses and began to clean them carefully and I suddenly saw how old and tired she was. "But I guess there's nothing we can do about it. Sometimes I sit here looking out that window and feel so hopeless—the things they learn out there in the street."

Then back into the street again. Searching for another kind of classroom where Sammy received a liberal education. It was still there too. The old tailor had died and the shop had been handed down to Foxy Four Eyes, whose shifty, crossed eyes leered out at you through lenses half an inch thick. He was chinless and puffy-cheeked and when he started to talk he exhibited a mouth full of bad teeth and a vocabulary that made Sammy sound like the Archbishop of Canterbury. The walls of the little shop were decorated with intimate pictures of female anatomy cut out of *Film Funs* and *Police Gazettes* with loving care.

"I'm a friend of Sammy Glick's," I said. "He told me to look you up if I were ever down this way."

"Well, for Chris'sake," he said, "good old Sammy! He sure was a hot-shot, that Sammy! I always said he'd sock the jackpot, but I sure never thought he'd get his in the movies." His laugh was shrill and indecent. "Boy, I'll never forget the time . . ."

|||||||

I left Rivington Street behind, but not the smell of Rivington Street, not the noise, not the faces. Not Sammy Glick running through Rivington Street. For days after that wherever I was, whatever I was doing, it kept coming back to me. I saw the Dead End Kids in a movie. Oh, hell, I thought, compared to Sammy these are nothing but a bunch of Honor Scouts. Their speech may be a trifle more colorful, but they aren't really evil, not the way I know childhood can be evil now. Oh, the beautiful American dream of childhood, barefoot boys with feet of tan, playing pirate, swimming holes, bullfrogs in quiet ponds and Sunday hats, puppy loves, schooldays, dear old golden rule days, my bashful beau, my ring-around-rosie queen in calico, Tom Sawyer and Penrod and Andy Hardy with America's No. 1 Star, Mickey Rooney, don't miss that heartwarming picture of family life coming to your neighborhood theater on Rivington Street, a sole screenplay credit, by Sammy Glick.

Where was the childhood of Sammy Glick? Step right up, ladies and gentlemen, and see the man who was never young. It was flashing through my mind like a montage nightmare, Sammy's face looming up behind all those quick and terrible scenes of his unchildhood:

Max Glickstein was a diamond cutter in the old country, proud of his trade and his religion. After the pogrom that took his first-born, Max brought his wife and other son to America. The child died in mid-ocean. "We must be brave, Momma," Max tried to console her. "Maybe God is trying to tell us that we will carry none of the troubles of the old world into the new. We will have new sons, little Americans. In America we will find a new happiness and peace."

They found Rivington Street. But no diamonds to cut. In time, Max got a job cutting glass at ten dollars a week. "Glass," he complained. "Glass any jackass can cut. But diamonds!"

For years he cut glass every day but Saturday, when he worshipped his God, and Sunday, when the Christians worshipped theirs. And his wife bore him two sons, first Israel and five years later Shmelka. The midwife did not think Shmelka would live. He weighed only five and a half pounds. "Nebbish such a little one," said the midwife. "Were he a little kitten we would drown him already." But survival of the fittest is a more complex process with thinking animals. Even one who thought as simply as Mama Glickstein. She pushed her great breasts into his mouth until he choked, hollered, and began to live.

Because he was puny, Mama spent so much time with him that his growth was precocious. He walked before his first birthday. Talked before his second. When he was three and a half, he changed his own name. One of Israel's friends always teased him with "Whadya say yer name is, Smell ya?" One day Mama called, "Shmelka, come here," and he paid no attention. She called his name again.

"Shmelka isn't my name any more," he said.

"No," Mama said, "then what is it, please?"

"Sammy," he said.

Sammy was the name of an older kid across the hall whose mother was always yelling for him.

The strike came when Sammy was four. The glasscutters wanted twelve-fifty. Papa was a foreman now, making sixteen, but he remembered how it was to live on ten dollars a week. And now it was even worse with the war boom started and prices rising. He walked out with his men.

"Mr. Glickstein, don't be a dope," the owner said. "In another two, three years you will becoming maybe a partner. To cut your own throat, that is not human. And what kind of foolishness is this when I can get plenty immigrants" (the owner having been here *twenty years could look down on the aliens)* "to take their places?"

Papa Glick's voice was deep and sure as if he were reading from the Torah. "To be a partner in a sweatshop, such honors I can do without."

But the owner was right about one thing. There were too many others. The strike dragged on six months—a year . . . They never saw those jobs again.

Neighbors helped the Glicksteins the way Papa had always helped them. And he picked up a few pennies as the cantor in shul on Saturday. But he would gladly have served for nothing and often had. There in the synagogue, a dignitary with his impressive shawl, his yarmulka and his great beard, there life was rich and beautiful. The rest were just the necessary motions to keep alive.

And this they barely did. Sammy played in the streets without shoes. For his fifth birthday he was given a pair that Israel had outgrown. But they were still several sizes too large for him, and the way they flapped like a clown's made the other kids laugh. Sometimes when Sammy would run after his tormentors the shoes would fly off, and Sammy would pick them up in a rage and hurl them at his nearest enemy.

Papa Glick finally gave up any hope of resuming his trade again. He was too old. America was a land for young men. Finally he got himself a pushcart like all the others. He sold shirts, neckties and socks, nothing over twenty-five cents. But there were too many pushcarts and not enough customers. So Sammy started peddling papers. He was three feet, four inches high. He wanted to play. He couldn't see why Israel shouldn't do it instead. But soon Israel was going to be bar mitzvah. After school let out at three o'clock he studied in the cheder until suppertime. Papa was so proud of him. The melamed had told him Israel had the makings of a real Talmudic scholar. And it was well known that the melamed was a man who never had a good word to say for anyone but God. "God has blessed my son with the heart and brains of a rabbi," Papa boasted.

Sammy lugged his papers up and down Fourteenth Street yelling about a war in Europe. He used to come home with a hoarse throat *and thirty or forty cents in pennies. He would count the money and say, "God dammit, I'm yellin' my brains out for nuttin'."*

Papa Glick would look up from his prayer book. "Please, in this house we do not bring such language."

"Look who's talkin'," Sammy said. "Know what Foxy Four Eyes tol' me—he says I wouldn' hafta peddle papers if you wasn't such a dope and quit your job. He says his ol' man tol' him."

"Silence," said Papa Glick.

"He says that strike screwed us up good," said Sammy.

Papa Glick's hand clapped against Sammy's cheek. It left a red imprint on his white skin but he made no sound. By the time he was six he had learned how to be sullen.

"Papa, please," Mrs. Glickstein pleaded. "He's so small, how should he know what he's saying—he hears it on the street."

"That's so he should forget what he hears," said Papa.

Several weeks later Sammy came in with a dollar seventy-eight. Papa, Momma and Israel danced around him.

"Sammy, you sold out all the papers?" said Papa in amazement.

"Yeah," Sammy said. "There's a guy on the opposite corner doin' pretty good 'cause he's yellin' 'U.S. may enter war.' So I asks a customer if there's anything in the paper about that. So when he says no, I figure I can pull a fast one too. So I starts hollerin' 'U.S. enters war,' and jeez you shoulda seen the rush!"

"But that was a lie," Papa Glick said. "To sell papers like that is no better than stealing."

"All the guys make up headlines," Sammy said. "Why don't you wise up?"

Sammy worked a year before he entered school.

That first day at P.S. 15, Sheik kept staring at him. He wanted to listen to what Miss Carr was saying, but he couldn't concentrate very well because the Sheik's small black eyes kept boring into him. Everybody knew the Sheik. His old lady was Italian and his old man was Irish and the neighbors would always hear them fighting at night over who was the better Catholic. The Sheik was older than anybody else in the class because he had been left back a couple of times. The kids didn't call him the Sheik because he was hand-

some, but because it was whispered around that he already knew what to do with little girls. There was even a story that he had knocked one up already, but this was probably circulated by Sheik himself who was a notorious boaster and had a habit of appropriating all his big brother's achievements.

The Sheik sat there all through the hour actively hating Sammy. Sammy had taken his seat, the seat he had had for the past two years. He had told Sammy, but Sammy had refused to budge.

"O.K., yuh dirty kike," Sheik whispered harshly through his teeth. "See yuh afta class."

It was lunch hour. Some of the kids were getting up a game of ball. Sammy wanted to play. After school there was cheder. And then papers to sell. Sammy was going to be a ballplayer when he grew up. He had a good eye and he was fast. But now he had to fight Sheik. Sheik was two years older, half a head taller. Sammy appraised him. He would probably get the bejesus kicked out of him. But he wasn't scared. Just sorry he couldn't get into that ball game. He followed Sheik into a vacant lot across the street, all boarded up and full of old tin cans and whatever anybody had ever felt like throwing there.

As soon as they got inside the Sheik let one go. It cracked against Sammy's nose, and blood spurted. Sammy's nose felt bigger than his whole face and he couldn't see, but he moved in swinging. Sheik caught him on the nose again. Sammy went down with Sheik on top of him, kicking and swinging, spitting into the bloody face under him, his whole body quivering in a frenzy of hate, shrieking until it became a chant, "You killed Christ. You killed Christ . . ."

When Sammy finally stopped fighting back, Sheik left him there and went to eat his lunch. Sammy tried to stay there until he stopped bleeding, but it wouldn't stop, so he had to walk back to the schoolyard that way. Miss Carr ran over and dragged him into the ladies' room. While she washed off the blood he stood there terribly white and terribly silent. No tears. Just his mouth set hard and his eyes ugly.

"I think your nose is broken," she said.

"It don't hurt much," said Sammy.

"You'd better come into the office and lie down."

"Jeez, look where I am! The guys better not see me in the girls' can."

She didn't know how to treat him. She was new here and she had never seen kids like this before. If he would only cry she could comfort him like an injured child. But he would not let her.

"Hey, what the hell's the matter with that guy sayin' I killed Christ? The dirty bastard."

"You must not talk like that," said Miss Carr. "Christ died so that everyone should forgive each other and live in brotherly love."

"Yeah?" said Sammy. "How about Sheik? Don't he believe in Christ?"

"Well, yes," said Miss Carr, "but . . ."

"I gotta sit down," said Sammy, "my head's spinnin'."

Miss Carr tried to put her arms around him but he drew away. He was like a little injured animal snarling at the hand that is trying to help it.

"You won't have to worry from now on," she said. "I'm going to have a talk with Sheik. And I think I'll ask some of the bigger boys to look after you."

His voice made her sympathy sound patronizing. "Who ast ya to? I'm no sissy. I c'n take care-a myself."

Sheik felt called upon to avenge Christ every day. Sammy accepted his beatings as part of the school routine. He never tried to avoid them, to sneak off after school. He just absorbed it with the terrible calm of a sparring partner. He would come home every night with his eyes swollen or his lip cut and his mother would hold him in her arms and cry, Sammele, Sammele, but he never cried with her, only held himself stiff in her arms, a stranger to her.

After a while, there was no satisfaction left in it for Sheik any more. It had become manual labor, slaughterhouse work. Sheik began to look around for more responsive victims. It even left Sheik with a strange kind of fear for Sammy. Somewhere along the line it had become the victim's triumph. Sammy would talk back to Sheik any time he liked. There was nothing Sheik could do but beat him up again. All the suffering that Sammy had swallowed instead of crying out had formed a hard cold ball of novocaine in the pit of his stomach that deadened all his nerves.

Life moved faster for Sammy. He was learning. The Glicksteins' poverty possessed him, but in a different way from Israel. He was always on the lookout to make a dollar. The way the little Christians put on Jewish hats and mingled with the Jewish boys to get free hand-outs in the synagogue on the holy days gave him an idea. On Saturday he went down to the Missions on the Bowery and let the Christ-spouters convert him. At two bits a conversion. He came home rich with seventy-five cents jingling in his pockets. His father, struggling to maintain his last shred of authority, the patriarchy of his own home, demanded to know why he was not at cheder. Sammy hated cheder. Three hours a day in a stinking back room with a sour-faced old Reb who taught you a lot of crap about the Mosaic laws. You don't go to jail if you break the laws of Moses. Only if you got no money and get caught stealing, or don't pay your rent.

"I hadda chance to make a dollar," Sammy said.

"Sammy!" his father bellowed. "Touching money on the Sabbath! God should strike you dead!"

The old man snatched the money and flung it down the stairs.

Sammy glared at his father the way he had at Sheik, the way he was beginning to glare at the world.

"You big dope!" Sammy screamed at him, his voice shrill with rage. "You lazy son-of-a-bitch."

The old man did not respond. His eyes were closed and his lips were moving. He looked as if he had had a stroke. He was praying.

Sammy went down and searched for the money until he found it.

His mother came down and sat on the stairs above him. She could never scold Sammy. She was sorry for Papa but she was sorry for Sammy too. She understood. Here in America life moves too fast for the Jews. There is not time enough to pray and survive. The old laws like not touching money or riding on the Sabbath—it was hard to make them work. Israel might try to live by them but never Sammy. Sammy frightened her. In the old country there may have been Jews who were thieves or tightwads and rich Jews who would not talk to poor ones, but she had never seen one like Sammy. Sammy was not a real Jew any more. He was no different from the little wops and micks who cursed and fought and cheated. Sometimes she could not believe he grew out of her belly. He grew out of the belly of Rivington Street.

When Papa Glick found out how Sammy made his seventy-five cents, he went to shul four times a day instead of twice. He cried for God to save Sammy.

Sammy remained a virgin until he was eleven. But no storks ever nested in his childish fancy. When he was still in his cradle he could hear the creaking of bedsprings and his parents' loud breathing in the same room. Cramped quarters forced sex into the open. When Sammy ran to find a place to hide from the Jew-hunting gangs with rock-filled stockings who roamed the streets on Hallowe'en, he bumped into a couple locked together in the shadow of the tunnel-like corridor behind the stairs. On sticky summer nights he used to trip over their legs as he raced across the roofs. The first day in the street he learned about the painted women who called out intimate names to men they didn't know. When he was ten he used to turn out the light to watch the lady across the court get undressed. She was fat, and when she let her great flabby breasts ooze out of her brassiere they flopped down like hams as she bent over. Curiosity and then desire began to creep into Sammy's wiry, undeveloped loins.

He even went up to one of the women around the corner and offered her the quarter he had been given to buy groceries, but she just looked down at him, put her hands on her hips, and laughed.

"Send your old man around, sonny, you'd fall in."

A couple of days later Sammy was hanging around Foxy's shop when Shirley Stebbins came in. Shirley was several years older than any of them, maybe sixteen or seventeen. She was tall and thin and only needed a little more flesh to have a voluptuous figure. People said her family was having a tough time because she was going to high school when she should be working. She wasn't hard the way the other girls were hard, boisterous and suggestive. Everybody on the block called her Sourpuss because her mouth was always set in a sullen expression of contempt. Foxy Four Eyes had advanced the theory that she was frigid. He said it happened when her father climbed into her bed one night when his wife was in the hospital.

"Foxy, I'm in a jam," she said. "I need ten dollars bad."

"Bad, huh?" he said, managing to give it an off-color inflection as he put his hand on her. "A guy can do an awful lot with ten dollars."

He winked at the kids as if he had said something witty. A guy called Eddie who was fifteen and knew his way around got it first.

"I'll get in for a buck," he said.

The expression on his face left no doubt about the pun. It had started as a gag, but Foxy egged them on until the nine of them had subscribed six dollars. Foxy's cheeks burned with excitement and his cockeyes looked out at his protégés proudly.

"All right, sister, I'll be a sport," he said. "I'll throw in the other four—just to see ya oblige the boys."

She looked at all of them. They were jumping around her like frantic little gnomes. Sammy hardly reached her shoulder.

"All right," she said in a tired voice. "Let's see the money, you cheap bastards."

In the back room, when it came his turn Sammy was scared. He was sprawled across her, fidgeting foolishly. Foxy Four Eyes could hardly talk, he was laughing so hard. "Hey, fellers, lookit Sammy tryin' to get his first nookey!"

Sammy could feel the blood flushing his head, and her silent contempt, and his panicky impotence.

While he still clung to her ludicrously, she half-rose on her elbows and said, "Somebody pull this flea off me. I'm not going to make this my life's work."

Foxy and Eddie laughingly dragged him off, still struggling for her, like a little puppy pulled from its mother's teats.

Shirley counted the money carefully and left a little more bitter than she came. "Thanks, you cheap bastards," she said.

Sammy ran after her. "Hey, that ain't fair! I oughta get my four bits back."

But that was the initiation fee Sammy had to pay to be inducted into the mysteries of life.

After the war, prices went higher, but there was no change in the pushcart business. The talk at meals was always money now. The Glicksteins were behind in their rent. A newsboy's take was no longer enough to complement the old man's income. The boys had to find regular jobs.

Sammy and Israel both answered a call for messenger boys. There were hundreds of others. For hours they cussed and fought each other for places near the door because their parents had sent them all out with the same fight talk, spoken in English, Yiddish, Italian, and with a brogue—Sammy, Israel, Joe, Pete, Tony, Mike, if you don't get that job today we don't know what we'll do.

Israel was just ahead of Sammy. They had been waiting since six in the morning for the doors to open at eight. They were chilled outside, nervous inside.

When the doors opened at last and Israel was finally standing before the checker, he was told:

"Sorry, kid—ain't hirin' no Hebes."

As Israel hesitated there, crying inside, Sammy suddenly threw himself at him and knocked him down.

"What the hell you do that for?" said the checker.

"That dirty kike cut in ahead of me," Sammy screamed.

The checker looked at Sammy curiously. Sammy stood there, small, spiderlike, intense, snarling at Israel.

"Fer Chris'sake, you look like a Jew-boy yerself."

"Oh, Jesus, everybody's always takin' me for one of them goddam sheenies," Sammy yelled. Then he broke into gibberish Italian.

At twelve years of age Sammy made one bat out of hell of a messenger. For the first few months he just did a good fast routine job. Then he began to catch on to ways of branching out. He started dropping in at the cat-houses on his way home. He would ring the bell—any bell—and tell the maid:

"Willya find out who rang for a messenger boy?"

In a couple of minutes the maid would return and say, "Can't find nobody who says they called you, sonny."

Then he'd put up his squawk. "Mean to tell me I hadda come allerway down here for nuttin'? Somebody in here musta called— the boss sent me down here on the double-quick. Whatta you wanna do, get me canned?"

He'd keep this up good and loud until the madame came out. The kid is probably right, she'd figure. Maybe one of the men did it for laughs or got drunk and forgot.

The gag was almost always good for two bits anyway. And lots of times the madame would yell, "Anybody want the messenger boy before he goes?" Then some of the customers would remember to wire their wives or the girls would want to send out for ice cream or a magazine.

After Sammy got inside he had another stunt that nearly always worked. He would stand in the middle of the main room and start singing a song. His voice was lousy, but he wasn't shy about using it and he usually sang something with a gulp in it, like "You made me what I am today—I hope you're satisfied," which always got the girls. So the guys would toss him something to please them—or to shut him up. Sometimes on Saturday nights he'd take in more that way than from his regular weekly wage.

It made Sammy feel pretty good hanging around with the guys on the corner Sundays with a little dough in his pocket. One Sunday morning Sheik singled him out. Sheik already had the secretive, mannered poise of a racketeer.

"Follow me over tuh the park," Sheik said. "I wanna talk tu ya."

Two years before when they had been the heads of rival gangs, Sammy's men had cornered Sheik on a roof. Everybody knew what Sammy had taken from him and they were all ready for Sammy to tell them to send the Sheik back to his block with a hole in his head. But Sammy just looked at Sheik kind of funny and said, "Go on, get runnin', you bastard, get the hell outa my block."

It meant that Sammy was beginning to understand the secret of power. Having Sheik beaten to a pulp would only have evened the score. *Without ever having thought it out, Sammy seemed to know intuitively how this gesture would leave him one up on Sheik.*

Over in the park Sheik said, "Listen, Sammy, I watched you a long time. You got balls. You're O.K. with me."

"Come on, what d'ya want?" said Sammy. "What's on ya mind?"

"I'm fed up with this stinking hole," Sheik said. "I'm gettin' outa here. I'm gonna pull off one little job and head west. And I wanna cut you in."

Sammy listened to the plan. It was just a glorified version of the old pushcart snitches. Sammy was to go into Levy's and ask for something that would make Levy go back into the storeroom to look for it. Then Sheik would run in and lay one on him and tie him up while Sammy was rifling the cash register.

Sammy listened soberly.

"Not me," he said. "That's sucker stuff. Why the hell take a chance goin' up the river when there's plenty better ways, if you're smart?"

"Like what?" said Sheik.

"Lookit Johnny Maloney," Sammy said. "He's off your block. His kid brother tol' me Johnny makes a couple a hundred smackers every election day—just for takin' people around 'n' votin' 'em. And lookit Salica. He ain't so much older 'n' us. Salica must be gettin' richer 'n' a bastard. Every time a guy gets laid around here it's dough in his pocket. What's the percentage in havin' the cops against yer when you can do something like that and have 'em with ya?"

Sheik succeeded in getting away from there all right. He got three years in the State Reform School. So did Leo Kaplan, the kid Sheik got to take Sammy's place.

Three weeks before Sammy's thirteenth birthday Papa came in too upset to eat.

"Tonight when I come out of shul *the rabbi wants to talk to me. 'Max, my heart is like lead to tell you this,' he says, 'but your son*

Samuel cannot be bar mitzvah. *He never comes to* cheder. *He does not know his bruchas. The* melamed *says he knows no more about the Torah than a goy.'* "

Bar-mitzvah *is the Hebrew ceremony celebrating a boy's reaching the state of manhood at the age of thirteen. He shows off all his knowledge and makes a speech which always begins, "Today I am a man . . ." and everybody gives him presents and congratulates the father and feels very good. It is as vital to the Orthodox Jews as baptism is to the Christians.*

"Oy vay!" Papa cried. "That I should live to see the day when my own flesh and blood is not prepared to become a man."

"Aw, what's that got to do with becomin' a man?" Sammy said. "Just a lotta crap. I been a man since I was eleven."

"Oh, Lord of Israel," Papa said, "how can You ever forgive us this shame? That I, a man who went to synagogue twice every day of his life, should have such a no-good son."

"Yeah," Sammy said. "While you was being such a goddam good Jew, who was hustlin' up the dough to pay the rent?"

"Silence, silence," Papa roared.

"I guess I gotta right to speak in this house," Sammy said. "For Chris'sake I'm bringin' in more money 'n you are."

"Money!" Papa cried. "That's all you think about, money, money . . ."

"Yes, money, money," Sammy mimicked. "You know what you c'n do with your lousy bar mitzvah. *It's money in the pocket—that's what makes you feel like a man."*

The day that Sammy was to have been bar-mitzvahed *Papa went to the synagogue and prayed for him as if he were dead. He came home with his lapel ripped in mourning. He would have liked to lock himself in all week because he couldn't face the shame of it. But the next day he had to be out in the street again, an extension of his pushcart.*

People saw him push his cart through the street with his eyes staring dumbly at nothing. The driver who hit him said he sounded his horn several times, but the old man did not seem to hear.

When he was carried upstairs to his bed Israel and Mama sat there crying and watching him die.

Afterward, Israel didn't know what to do, so he went up on the roof to look at the stars. He found Sammy there smoking a butt.

"Is it over?" Sammy said when he saw his brother.

Israel nodded. He had not really broken down yet, but the question did it. He cried, deep and soft, as only Jews can cry because they have had so much practice at it.

Israel was eighteen, but now he was a little boy crying because he had lost his papa. Sammy was thirteen, but he was a veteran; he had learned something that took the place of tears.

When Israel realized that he was the only one crying he became embarrassed and then angry.

"Damn you, why don't you say something?" Israel said. "Why don't you cry?"

"Well, what's there ta say?" said Sammy.

"At least, can't you say you're sorry?"

"Sure," Sammy said. "I'm sorry he was a dope."

"I oughta punch you in the nose," Israel said.

"Try it," Sammy said, "I bet I c'n lick you." Sammy sat there dry and tense. "Aw, don't work yourself into a sweat," he said.

"Sammy," Israel pleaded, "what's got into you? Why must you go around with a chip on your shoulder? What do you have to keep your left out all the time for?"

"Whatta you take me for, a sap like you?" Sammy said. "You don't see me getting smacked in the puss."

"But we aren't fighting now," Israel said.

Israel was right about not knowing Sammy. There were no rest periods between rounds for Sammy. The world had put a chip on his shoulder and then it had knocked it off. Sammy was ready to accept the challenge all by himself and this was a fight to the finish. He had fought to be born into the East Side, he had kicked, bit, scratched and gouged first to survive in it and then to subdue it, and now that he was thirteen and a man, having passed another kind of bar mitzvah, he was ready to fight his way out again,

*pushing uptown, running in Israel's cast-off shoes, traveling light,
without any baggage or a single principle to slow him down.*

I was sitting in the corner at the end of the bar and, like all
thinkers who are on the verge of a great discovery, feeling miserable.

Henry leaned over the bar and picked up my empty glass.

"Henry, do you know what I've been doing for the past two
hours?" I asked.

"Yes," said Henry, "getting plastered."

"No," I said, "working out a theory that will end hate in the
world."

"That's the same thing," said Henry.

"Now, Henry, I want you to listen carefully," I said. "Because
Fate has chosen you as the first one to hear my message. Do you
remember Sammy Glick?"

"Do you ever let me forget him?" Henry said.

"Okay," I said. "When Sammy Glick first walked into my office
he turned my stomach. But just think if when he walked in I'd
known as much about him as I do now." I punctuated my speech
with thoughtful gulps. "We only hate the results of people. But
people, Henry, aren't just results. They're a process. And to really
give them a break we have to judge the process through which
they became the result we see when we say So-and-so is a heel.
Now the world is full of people hating other people's guts. Okay.
Now, Henry, answer me this, what if each of them took the time
to go down to Rivington Street—I mean each person's particular
Rivington Street, Henry? We would begin to have compassion in
the world, that's what. Not so much soda this time, Henry."

"I don't think you better have any more, Mr. Manheim,"
Henry said.

"Okay," I said, "you patronizing bastard. No great thinker is
ever appreciated in his own time."

I went to the phone and put through a call to Hollywood 3187.

"Hello?" she said.

"Hello," I said, waiting expectantly.

"Hello," she said.

"Remember I said I'd call you if I ever found out why Sammy loves shoes so much?"

"Al, you're drunk!" And then with a slight reprimand: "Darling!"

"And," I gloated, "I know why Sammy hates unions and why he treats all women like pros and all men like enemies. Kit, you gave me a terrific steer. And I haven't only learned about Sammy. I've learned something about the machinery that turns out Sammy Glicks."

"Congratulations," she said. "Don't you think you'd better reverse the charges? You can't afford a long-distance call like this."

"Of course I can't," I said. "Anybody would call you up if he could afford it. But to be unable to afford it and do it anyway— that's love."

"You still haven't changed?" she said.

"No. Have you?"

"No," she said. "If I ever have a husband you are definitely it."

"That will be a very comforting thought to go to my grave with," I said. "Here lies the husband chosen by Kit— if she ever had one he was definitely it."

"You're very clever," she said. "Have you ever thought of coming to Hollywood?"

"Darling," I said, "for Chris'sake! When do we get together again?"

"As soon as our jobs bring us together again," she said. "Jobs you should be doing can make worse ghosts than ex-lovers."

"Now that I've got a line on what makes Sammy run, maybe I should begin on you."

"I'm not running anywhere," she said. "I'll be right where you left me. But you might work on Whither Is He Running?"

"That reminds me," I said. "Whither is he?"

"Well, there's been another shake-up at World-Wide, and Sidney Fineman has his old spot back as head man. And I'll give you one guess who his assistant is."

"How is he making out?" I said.

"So-so," she said. "I mean he hasn't got Fineman's job yet."

"Give him time," I said.

"Give him nothing," she said. "He'll take time. I think he even counterfeits time. Throws a couple of extra hours into every day."

"Your three minutes are up," said the operator.

"Hang up, Al," she said. "Now it will be my turn to call you. These were three of the nicest minutes I've spent in months."

"Do you love me?" I said.

"Would I tell you to hang up if I didn't?"

I hung up and went back to the bar and finally talked Henry into giving me another drink—if I promised not to give out with any more theories.

"Okay," I said, "but I hope you have no objections if I just sit here and think anything I like."

"Not as long as you don't move your lips," said Henry.

I thought about attraction. My attraction for Kit. The attraction Sammy had for us that brought us together. I tried to trace it all through again. I kept wanting to get it straight in my mind.

I thought of Sammy Glick rocking in his cradle of hate, malnutrition, prejudice, suspicions, amorality, the anarchy of the poor; I thought of him as a mangy little puppy in a dog-eat-dog world. I was modulating my hate for Sammy Glick from the personal to the societal. I no longer even hated Rivington Street but the idea of Rivington Street, all Rivington Streets of all nationalities allowed to pile up in cities like gigantic dung heaps smelling up the world, ambitions growing out of filth and crawling away like worms. I saw Sammy Glick on a battlefield where every soldier was his own cause, his own army and his own flag, and I realized that I had singled him out not because he had been born into the world any more selfish, ruthless and cruel than anybody else, even though he had become all three, but because in the midst of a war that was selfish, ruthless and cruel Sammy was proving himself the fittest, the fiercest and the fastest.

CHAPTER 10

was sitting at my typewriter hoping for an interruption when the phone rang.

"Mr. Manheim," a smooth male voice began importantly. "I am calling for Mr. Glick."

"Well, for Chris'sake, when did he blow in?"

The way the important voice ignored my familiarity was a quiet reprimand. "Mr. Glick only expects to be in town a short time and I am making up a list of his appointments for the week. He would like to have you come in this Thursday at six o'clock."

Why not? I thought. Now that I finally have him cross-indexed in my mind, he can't give me mental indigestion any more. I can just sit back and watch him running through the next act as if it were a Greek tragedy. Or rather, an American tragedy.

"Okay," I said. "I guess I can make it. Where do I go?"

"Waldorf Towers," he said. "Suite Thirty-three E."

Twinkle, twinkle little guy, I thought. Up above the world so high.

When I finally found my way up to Sammy's apartment, I was admitted by his Man Friday, Sheik Dugan, who ushered me in with beautiful manners, and I realized who it was I had spoken to on the phone. It was difficult to determine what Sheik's official status was, but from the variety of duties he seemed to perform during my visit I would guess he had become a sort of combination secretary, valet, business manager, companion and procurer.

Sheik's manner made me feel I was being led before royalty as he guided me through the lavish sitting room to an enormous, high-ceilinged bedroom where Sammy was sitting in a silk, initialed lounging robe while some guy was down on his knees in front of him tracing the outline of his foot on a special piece of paper.

I wasn't sure whether he had taken on weight or whether it was just authority.

"Hello, Al," he called. "How's the boy?" He offered me his left hand, the Hollywood handshake. "Be with you in a minute. Just being measured for some shoes."

It wasn't the usual quick job with the sliding ruler. The man was measuring his foot from every possible angle and writing it all down on the chart. I sat there and watched the ceremony.

"Your left foot is eight and three-fifths, width B minus," the fitter announced. "The right is eight and two-fifths, width an even B."

Sammy seemed pleased with the discrepancy. "You see," he said, "that's why I have to have my shoes made to order. They may cost a little more but they wear twice as long. And when shoes don't fit me perfectly, I get headaches."

The shoe man took us both in with a salesman's smile. "No

use telling Mr. Glick anything about shoes," he said. "He knows more about them than I do!"

"Well, in my business shoes are important," Sammy explained. "I must walk nine or ten miles every story conference."

"Now, what we like to do with our regular clients," said the salesman, "is make a plaster mold of their feet. Then our designers can draw up any style shoe you wish and you're sure of getting a one-hundred-percent perfect fit."

Sammy couldn't have been more flattered if he had been asked to pose for a bronze bust.

"Fine," he said. "On your way out check with Mr. Dugan as to when I'll have time for you again."

"Thank you very much, Mr. Glick," said the shoe expert and he salaamed out.

"Well, Al, good to see you again," Sammy said. "How have things been going for you?"

His tone was cordial but no longer chummy. More the democratic employer showing that he still knows the elevator boy's name.

Sheik poked his head in the door. "Better start dressing, tootsie. Rita says she'll be down in twenty minutes."

"That gives me exactly an hour," Sammy cracked. "Are my things laid out?"

"Maybe I better duck," I said.

"No," Sammy said. "Stick around. New York's such a merry-go-round I may not have time to see you again. This trip is one of those quickies. Just in to catch some shows and see a few people and back to the jute mill. Let's talk while I'm dressing."

Sammy had caught the Hollywood habit of putting every waking moment to use. It reminded me of the famous director who even had his secretary go on reading scripts to him through the bathroom door.

"What's this I hear about you and my old lady?" Sammy laughed as he started to throw his clothes on the bed. "You should have heard what she was giving out with about you this morning.

Absolutely *meshugah* for you. You're a sweet guy to go to all that trouble."

The way he said it made me sorry I had ever gone down. It looked too much like sucking around. That was the only way Sammy saw it and it seemed to give him a new respect for me. He felt I was catching on.

He was stripped down to his silk shorts and I had to follow him to the bathroom as he started to shave.

"That was the first time I've seen the old lady since I went out to the Coast," Sammy said. "Isn't she a great character? What the hell, we don't know how to be happy. We don't know we're having a good time until the waiter at the Troc hands us a check for a hundred bucks."

Sammy Glick, I thought, the homely philosopher of the Waldorf Towers.

"I tell you, it was a real thrill," Sammy went on. "But this'll kill you. As I was getting out of the cab, some Hebe who was unloading a fish wagon took a look at me and yelled, 'Well, how d'ya like it down here? Enjoying the sights?' Is that a laugh? Right on the spot where I was born!"

I had the picture, Sammy the conquering hero, returning home in a wraparound camel's-hair and an Eddie Schmidt suit, and some little guy Sammy might have gone to school with, a Jewish workman up since five, smelling of fish and hating his job, suddenly crying out his bitterness at this arrogant slummer.

It was a laugh all right, but only Sammy's kind of laughter. The Jewish fish-boy didn't know it but he was right. The closest Sammy could ever get to recapturing his youth was to go slumming.

Sammy had finished shaving and his beard was replaced by a clean blue shadow. I followed him back into the bedroom again as Sheik began to help him into his evening clothes.

"Well, I'll have to run you out of here in a minute," Sammy began in a new, efficient voice. "So I better tell you what I've got in mind for you. I suppose you know I'm assisting Sidney Fineman with the whole program. But just before I left the Coast I talked him into letting me make a couple of pictures on my own. These have to be B's of course. But I want them to be unusual B's—little pictures with big ideas."

"Little pictures which show that you should be making the big pictures," I said.

"Right!" he said, and then he looked at me searchingly. I tried to look innocent, but I knew he was beginning to suffer just as much about playing second fiddle to Fineman as he had about being a copy boy or only making five hundred dollars a week. Instead of sitting on the roof of the tenement with that terrible hunger to be out of the slums, he was up there on top of the Waldorf going crazy to get out of the B-picture field he was just about to enter.

"I've got plenty of great ideas," he said. "One of them is to make a newspaper picture—only not the usual drunken reporter and madcap heiress crap. The real thing—the way you and I know it. Hoked up of course."

"Something like *The Front Page*?" I said.

I couldn't even get a rise out of him any more. That night at Paine's swimming pool he was pretending to be a big shot. Now he was beginning to be one and the difference was interesting.

"Something like that," he said. "Only more (he snapped his fingers loudly) up-to-date, more of an exposé. And I'm thinking of bringing you out to do the job."

He threw it away, but not quickly enough to hide the gloat. I thought of that day he ran off with half my column. And I thought how funny it was that this latest gesture could spring from kindness, loyalty, shrewdness or sheer perversity.

"It won't be like working for one of those high-powered producers," he was saying. "You'll be able to get to me any time you need help."

"You forget who I am," I said. "Blacklist Bill. Don't let my gentle expression fool you. I am a subversive influence."

"For Christ's sake, I can get on the phone and clean that up in two minutes," he said.

I was so eager to get back to Hollywood and try to win my *H* that I was even willing to let Sammy send me into the game. But since I had no illusions about how long my benefactor would stand by me if he found he didn't need me, I thought I had better hold that need up to the light of reason a moment or two before I rushed for my trunk.

"What makes you so hot for me all of a sudden? I should think you'd want to start playing safe with a top-notch screen writer."

"I've thought it out from every angle," he said. "All I can spend on these pictures is two hundred grand, top. You figure your writing cost shouldn't be over ten percent of the whole nut, so I couldn't afford any of the top guys, anyway. Which is okay with me. What the hell, any halfwit is liable to get a good job out of a Lawrence Paine or a Bob Griffin. Nobody is going to go around saying, Did you see the great script Sammy Glick got out of Bob Griffin? And, anyway, I'd like to start out with somebody congenial. I thought of you first because of that promise I made in the Troc a couple of years ago. You could have done me a lot of harm by shooting off your mouth that night. I like to have people loyal around me."

I think the main reason he picked me out was the one he didn't mention. He was tackling something a little too early—like Shirley Stebbins—and he was just as unsure of himself. He probably wouldn't stay scared very long but just at this moment it was reassuring to have me work for him. It gave him that necessary sense of power.

That made me realize why he was being so generous with Sheik. Israel had told me that when Sheik returned from reform school, he got himself a string of dames, hung around with the East Side gamblers and tried to muscle in on some of the small-fry rackets. But he was just another tough guy in an overcrowded field and about all he got for his troubles were a Heidelberg scar, a dose, and a couple of years in the can.

The second time he got out he heard that Sammy was in the dough out in Hollywood, so he wrote him for a little on account and while he was about it he wondered if there was anything in Hollywood he could do.

He didn't really expect to get an answer but two weeks later a letter arrived with a train ticket and traveling expenses. Sheik would never understand why, but through this he became the instrument of Sammy's endless revenge. Now Sheik was well-fed and well-mannered and elegant in white tie, but he was still the enemy slave brought home behind the conqueror's chariot. He was the measuring stick that was always at Sammy's elbow to remind him of his rise. Here was Sheik, whose fists had broken Sammy's face, living the life of his malevolent dreams, and yet hanging by a hair which Sammy could snap any moment he wanted to drop him back into the ratholes and the flop-joints again.

|||||||

As I was going out, Rita Royce and her party blew in.

"This is one of my writers," Sammy introduced me. "I'm bringing him back to the Coast with me. He's going to do my first picture, *Deadline.*"

While my hand was making the rounds, Sammy said, "Better call the Stork, Sheik, and tell them to hold that table for us—we'll be ready for dinner in about an hour."

At the door Sammy punched my arm twice in rapid succession, Jimmy Cagney fashion. "Well, I'm tickled to death to have you with me, kid. I know we're going to knock them for a row of Academy Awards. I'll have Sheik get a lower for you—right next to my drawing room—so if you get any great ideas in the middle of the night you can run right in and spill 'em, sweetheart."

That night I sat in Bleeck's wondering if I was a heel. Manheim, confess, I thought. The moment you heard that name you thought of Hollywood again. You thought what that name could do for you. You thought of all that Hollywood dough. You thought of getting back to Kit.

I gave myself five minutes for rebuttal.

The trouble with Hollywood is that too many people who won't leave are ashamed to be there. But when a moving picture is right, it socks the eye and the ear and the solar plexus all at once and that is a hell of a temptation for any writer. I felt that when I went back for the fourth time to see *The Informer.* And one afternoon when I happened to catch a revival of the Murnau-Jannings masterpiece, *The Last Laugh.* And even when I saw one of my own jobs, a stinker if there ever was one, but with one scene in it that sang because I happened to stumble onto real picture technique. That is what held Kit there. Hollywood may be full of phonies, mediocrities, dictators and good men who have lost their way, but there is something that draws you there that you should not be ashamed of.

CHAPTER 11

As Kit and I came out of the preview we could see Sammy leaning against the lamppost with his hands in his pockets and his long cigar blowing triumphant puffs like a Roman candle.

"Well, what do you think?" he said with a grin that told you what he expected to hear.

"That's a pretty good movie," Kit said.

"When a sourpuss like you says pretty good, it must really be terrific," Sammy said.

Sheik sailed over, making that circle of approval with his thumb and forefinger as he came. "Well, sweetheart," he said, "it's a killer. Even tops *Deadline* for my dough."

Sheik was still Sammy's shadow but he had been promoted. He

was an agent now. He had just sort of drifted into it by going up to an ingénue he knew Sammy was signing and telling her he would use his influence to have Sammy take her. Other clients followed until now Sheik was clearing around three or four hundred a week. Still in the small-fry class, but between his firm grip on Sammy's coattails and his increasing popularity as a ladies' man, Sheik was definitely on his way.

Word had gotten around that Sheik was an ex-mobster and soon, with Hollywood's talent for self-dramatization, Sheik had become a famous gunman, in fact, Capone's right-hand man. A killer whom Sammy Glick and Hollywood had regenerated. This, along with his other social attributes, had begun to make him a celebrity's celebrity.

"After *Deadline* the second-guessers were saying I could only make mellers," Sammy said. "Now they'll be saying I can only make comedies. It's got a million laughs, hasn't it?"

"Absolutely," said Sheik. "You should have saved a few of 'em for some of World-Wide's other pictures. Outside of your two, this year's program is stinking up the studio so bad you have to have a gas mask to go through the halls."

As Sammy laughed, I noticed that his face was puffing out a little bit. The lean ferret look wasn't gone—it was just beginning to be framed with a fleshy border. Sheik watched Sammy's face too, joining in his laughter like the background people at a cue from the director.

The leading lady knifed her way through, leaving a wake of panicky autograph hounds.

"You were O.K.," Sammy told her.

She made a little curtsy and told him it had been a pleasure to work for him.

"O.K.," Sammy said. "So next time don't try to tell me you don't like the part. Doesn't this prove that we always know what's best for you?"

As her public swallowed her up again, Sammy gave us a wink. "When those babies go soft on you—that's the time to sock it home."

Sidney Fineman came out of the crowd. The herringbone design under his eyes seemed more noticeable these days. His posture was still erect and dignified but you could feel him making the effort to keep it that way.

"That's a good solid writing job, Manheim," he said to me, and then he turned to Sammy with a tired, brave smile.

"Well, my boy, looks like you've done it again."

Sammy shook his hand with a straight face. "Thank you, Mr. Fineman," he said, "let's hope so."

He had learned how to be polite to his superiors now but it would never really become him. He called Fineman Grandma behind his back, when he wasn't being more vivid.

We stood on the curb talking cutting and last-minute story points as the crowd drifted away.

"I have only one real objection," Fineman said mildly. "The action seems to get started too quickly. There doesn't seem to be enough time to plant the characters and the situation. What do you think, Sammy?"

Kit and I looked at each other, and I knew we were thinking the same thing. Sidney Fineman had his own studio in Hollywood when Sammy was still hawking papers on 14th Street. He had been the first one with enough daring to make a classic like *Helen of Troy* when everyone else was making two-reel horse operas. He never asked questions then.

When I first started writing the screenplay, Sammy had told me specifically that you never have to sell your characters or your plot in a farce comedy. For a moment I thought he was going to tell Fineman off about that. But apparently he had decided the time wasn't ripe yet. For all he said was:

"Maybe you're right. Let's have another look at it in the morning."

"Fine," Fineman said. "Perhaps it will look better when we're fresh."

Sammy smiled at him as if to say, Speak for yourself, pal, I never felt fresher. "That's right," he said, "maybe it will."

There was something in Sammy's voice that cut the conference short. Sammy watched Fineman's chauffeur help him into his big black limousine.

"The corpse is climbing back into his hearse," Sammy cracked. Only Sheik laughed.

"Well, where do we go from here?" Sammy said.

"Sunset Club," Sheik said. "They've got a new dinge band there that'll kill ya."

"What did you get for me?" Sammy said.

"Some brand-new stuff," Sheik said. "Punkins Weaver."

"Is she O.K.?" Sammy said.

"Until the real thing comes along," Sheik sang. "Blonde. Willing. Cute kid."

Kit and I stopped in at one of the little bars on Vine Street, just south of Hollywood Boulevard. All along the sidewalk were little knots of poolroom characters who always seemed to be there, holding mysterious conferences. Down the street the playboys were getting out of red Cadillac phaetons or monogrammed town cars at La Conga. There was something savage and tense about that street. Autograph hunters prowled it, and ambitious young ladies in fancy hair-dos and slacks.

"God, this is a tough town," Kit said.

"Why is it tougher than anywhere else?" I said.

"Because it still has the gold-rush feeling," she said. "The gold rush was probably the only other set-up where so many people could hit the jackpot and the skids this close together. It's become a major industry without losing the crazy fever of a gold-boom town."

"What made you think of that? Fineman?"

She nodded. "Sometimes I think the three chief products this town turns out are moving pictures, ambition and fear."

"I felt sorry for Fineman too," I said. "For all his fame and his dough, I still wouldn't like to be in his shoes right now."

"Something tells me there's going to be a lot of traffic in those shoes."

"I don't think Sammy's ready to try them on yet," I said. "Don't forget Sammy likes to have his shoes fit."

|||||||

I sat in while they looked at the picture with the cutter again next morning, stopping it reel by reel to talk it over.

"I guess you're right about the opening at that," Fineman said. "Any more footage would make it drag."

"I'm glad you see it my way," Sammy said.

I don't think Fineman saw anything more to it than that; an older man and his younger assistant working together to tighten up their picture. But I knew that tone in Sammy's voice, the warning rattle. It was like reading a Fu Manchu book and wondering how and when the hand will strike.

After the picture had been run off, the cutter said, "Well, you don't have to worry about that one. I'll run it through again this afternoon and clean it up a little bit. If I nip a couple more hundred feet out of it it'll be tight as a drum."

Fineman seemed to be thinking of something else.

"Sammy, there's something I want to talk to you about," he said. "Walk back to my office with me."

"What's the matter with right here?" Sammy said. "We'd save a couple of minutes."

"No," Fineman said, not quite as soft-spoken as usual. "It's a rather delicate matter."

|||||||

That night I had to go over to Sammy's for a conference on the next picture. Sammy had moved from his apartment to one of those Hollywood Colonial manors in upper Beverly Hills.

The first thing he did was show me through every room, rattling off the names of all the celebrities who had lived there before him and the marquee names he had for neighbors.

"I tell you, there's nothing like having a house of your own," he said. "I get up in the morning and look out at those palm trees and the other big houses and I say to myself, Sammy, how did it all happen?"

I have a couple of ideas on it, I thought, if you really want to know.

"But now I'll really show you something," he said. "My grounds." He turned on the floodlights that illuminated the garden. "I've got my own barbecue pit and my own badminton court. And have I got flowers! Do you realize you're looking at twelve hundred dollars' worth of hibiscus plants?"

"And you're going to live here all alone?" I said.

"Well, the cook sleeps in," Sammy said. "By the way, I've got Claudette Colbert's cook. And, of course, my man."

He must have felt self-conscious about that, for he added, "He's off tonight but he's really something. I think he must have been Ronald Colman's stand-in. It'd panic you to see him bringing my breakfast up in the morning in a full-dress suit. The first time he stuck his puss in the door I said, 'Charles, you look as if I ought to be waiting on you.' And Charles just gave me the business, 'Yes, sir, will there be anything else, sir?' He never steps out of character!"

Neither do you, I thought, neither do you.

For the next couple of hours we sat in the study batting the story back and forth. Sammy's mind drew a blank when it came to originality—but since the same goes for most screen stories, he actually turned this to advantage. What he had was a good memory and a glib way of using it. Our story was like so many others that he could lift ready-made situations from the shelves in the back of his mind, dust them off and insert them into our yarn like standard automobile parts.

"Now, I want you to work night and day on this," he said. "Because MGM is making a submarine picture too, only on a terrific scale, and if we can get out with ours first we can steal a hell of a march on them and cash in on their publicity."

Our work was over and I started to go.

"It's early yet," Sammy said. "You don't have to run. How about a nightcap?"

He had a Capehart and a canopy bed and shiny new sets of Balzac and Dickens and twelve hundred bucks of hibiscus, but he didn't seem to know what to do with himself when he wasn't talking to somebody.

He mixed a drink for me. He was very solicitous. He said, "You know we've been working so hard we never have a chance to talk any more."

I wondered when we had ever talked about anything but the life and works of S. Glick. And while I was wondering, that is just what the conversation drifted to again.

I happened to say that I thought Fineman was one of the best gents in the business.

"I guess everybody in the studio likes him," Sammy said. "But that doesn't mean so damn much. Between you and me, he's just an old woman. He's beginning to lean on me like a crutch."

"He still seems to be able to navigate under his own power," I said.

"That's what I used to think," Sammy said. "Until today."

"The talk you had with Fineman?"

He said, in the way people have of saying much more than they are saying, "The talk I had with Fineman."

Okay, Sammy, I thought, spill it, you predatory genius.

"When I was in there talking with the old man, all of a sudden it hit me—I had him by the balls. You understand, this is strictly between you and me. It mustn't go out of this room."

Strictly confidential between you and the world, I thought, and if you don't tell it to somebody quick your lungs are going to blow up in your face like punctured balloons.

Fineman filled his pipe painstakingly and lit it. It was hard to begin.

"Sammy, we've been working together for over a year now and I think we understand each other. I'd like to feel I can talk to you as a friend."

Sammy's face was what is known as expressionless. A very definite and frightening expression.

"You know you can, sir," he said.

"Good. You may not have learned it yet and I hope you never

will—but this is a business with a very short memory. It doesn't matter what you did last year or the year before. If your last few pictures are lemons, you're in hot water. That's why I've decided to talk to you, Sammy. I know you appreciate how much I've done for you—and I felt you'd be willing to help me."

Help. That was the turning point. That was the moment Sammy had been waiting for. He sat there trying to look noncommittal, like a poker player who has just discovered he is holding a royal flush.

"I'm your man, Sidney," Sammy said. "Just say the word."

"Some of the Wall Street crowd who control our lot are coming out to look over our production set-up."

Sammy had got that tip from Young's secretary two weeks before.

"They want to try to find out why we slumped to third place among the major studios this year. And I have it from a fairly reliable source that Harrington, the chairman of the board, favors a new production chief. Now, these aren't men who know pictures. They've got ticker tapes in their brains. They know the pictures I let you make have been our most solid moneymakers and they'll be interested in hearing what you've got to say. You know what I mean, I want them to know that we're working well together. And, if I'm still in harness, I'll tell you what I'll do for you: Let you make four of the A's on next year's program—even suggest that you head your own independent unit, if that's what you want—and I'll get a new assistant. There's a new lad on the lot called Ross who's supposed to be very promising. How does that sound?"

Somewhere between the time Fineman started that speech and the time he finished, one era ended and another began. Sammy had sneered at Fineman before, but that had been mostly bravado for Sheik's benefit. He had entered the office still in awe of him. Now, as Fineman went on talking, Sammy could see him shrinking as if he had drunk an Alice-in-Wonderland potion. Wondering, what the hell keeps that weak sister in this office at five G's a week? An old-fashioned story mind—a quiet, indirect method of getting his way that's supposed to pass for executive ability—an old-woman-ishness that's won him the reputation of best-loved producer.

"Sid, old pal," Sammy said. "You're in. Just let them come to *me. I'll give them an earful. And it will come from right here."*

He tapped the breast pocket of his camel's-hair jacket reverently.

And while he was tapping it he got a new idea.

Sammy spent hours with Fineman at the office every day, but at night, except for the occasional Grand Central Station parties, there was a barrier. Fineman had never asked Sammy to his dinner parties or his Sunday morning breakfasts. Sammy finally had to give up hinting. It got Sammy sore just thinking about it. So I'm not good enough for the bastard's home, but I'm good enough to save his lousy job for him! And Sammy never just got sore. Nothing so luxurious as that. He always got sore with a plan.

"Look, Sid," he said. "Why wait for these Wall Street guys to come to me? Why wouldn't it be smart for me to start working on them the day they blow in? What if I threw a big party for them at my new house, a swell dinner, and entertainment, with all our stars there . . . ?"

"Don't you think it would be my place to give the party?" Fineman said.

"But if I'm at your party what does it mean?" Sammy argued. "Hell, I'd have to come to my own boss's party. But if I give a party in their honor, also celebrating the first anniversary of our association . . . !"

"If it's handled right it might have a good effect at that," Fineman reflected.

"Don't worry," Sammy said. "It'll be handled right."

"So a week from Saturday I break into the society columns," Sammy said. "And by the way, you and Kit are invited. You two are still an item, aren't you?"

"A permanent one, I hope."

"By God, that's what I need," Sammy said suddenly. "I'm getting fed up with these floozies you're always promising something to—a day's work or a test. A man in my position ought to settle down and get some dignity in his life."

"You mean you're thinking of getting married?"

"Why not?" he said. "Hell, I'm not one of these guys who's

spoiled by getting in the dough. You know I'm just a simple down-to-earth guy at heart. All I want is a sweet, healthy girl to put my slippers on when I come home from work and give me a bunch of kids who can enjoy what I've got—maybe a nice bright kid to take over my business when I retire."

"Have you got anybody in mind for the job?" I said.

"Well," he said, "I've been thinking about it. I'm really thinking seriously of Ruth Mintz. You know, the daughter of the shorts producer on our lot? A nice refined girl. No beauty, but, hell, this town is lousy with beauty, and that's only good for about ten years, anyway. She's got a nice build. And she's nuts about kids. What more could I want?"

"I don't know," I said, "what more could you? Do you love her?"

"Love," he said. "How the hell have I had time to love anybody?"

|||||||

When I finally made a break, I met Kit at the Derby for coffee. She was coming from a Guild meeting. The Guild had risen from the dead after the Nine Old Men decided to cut the nonsense and declare the Wagner Act constitutional. Three or four hundred writers had returned to the fold again and the battle now was to get the NLRB to come in and hang a company-union charge on the Photodramatists.

"How was the meeting?" I said.

"We saw through the night that our Guild was still there," Kit hummed off key, patriotically. "How was yours?"

"Sammy was in a reflective mood," I said.

"Was he sick?"

"No, he was falling in love."

"With whom? Himself again?"

"With the idea of someone to bring his slippers to him when he comes home at night. And someone to give him an heir."

"If that's a pun," she said, "you have to stand in the corner and repeat the name Sammy Glick five hundred times."

"That's the punishment Sammy is always inflicting on himself," I said.

Our ham and eggs arrived and we were hoggishly silent for a minute.

"Did Sammy ever ask you to marry him?"

"Of course not! All Sammy is looking for is a nice simple housewife like his mother told him to marry, who looks like Dietrich, whose only interest in life is Sammy Glick, and whose father is a millionaire who can finance Sammy's company and put him in with the Best People." She laughed and added, "And all I had to offer was the Dietrich department."

"You're a fine figure of a woman, all right," I said. "Nobody could say you were exactly homely."

"Ah, you've hit on it at last—*exactly*. People look at me and say, she's homely all right, but not exactly homely. And there you have the secret of my charm."

"By God, you're right," I said. "I never realized it before. But there's something about your face that's fooled me for years into thinking it's beautiful. It's just your personality shining out like one of Oleson's giant spots. And if you ever switched it off you'd be homely as sin."

"Al!" she said. "You mustn't make love to me like that right out here in the open."

||||||

The night of the party Kit and I saw it happen, saw love come to Sammy Glick, or something as close to love as Sammy will ever know. Kit and I and little Ruth Mintz.

This is the way it began. The other members of the Wall Street scouting party were punctual, but Harrington didn't show until the buffet dinner was almost over.

He came in with a dame on his arm, an amazing-looking dame, who made an entrance like the star at the end of the first act. The first thing that clicked when I looked at her was the horse shows in the rotogravure section of the Sunday *Times*. Only not the smartly tailored horsewoman in derby and cutaway, but the horse itself. She was a show horse with a dark red mane, prancing, beautifully groomed, high spirited, accustomed and proud to be on exhibition.

If Harrington's life were ever screened, he would be played by Lewis Stone, though Stone would have to go easy on the make-up and underplay his scenes to do the role justice.

Sammy spotted them at the door like a master of ceremonies, beckoned Fineman over to do the honors and ran toward them.

"Mr. Glick," Harrington spoke in efficient snaps. "Very glad to meet you, sir. I've been looking forward to this. I'd like you to meet my daughter, Laurette."

Sammy made a nervous little bow and kept on looking at her. She seemed to fascinate him. He went on staring at her with the out-of-this-world look of a monk at the Shrine of the Madonna, or a strip-tease patron.

"I know that girl," Kit said. "Laurette Harrington. She was at Vassar for a little while."

"I think we're on hand for an historic event," I said. "Sammy Glick is falling in love."

"Sammy isn't impetuous enough for that," she said. "He's just falling in love with the idea of being in love with a gal like that."

Kit and I edged our way up to the ringside. Ruth Mintz was standing beside Sammy, but she might just as well have been standing in Outer Mongolia.

"Father hates being late," Miss Harrington was saying. "It's all my fault. I came home frightfully late after looking at pictures all day."

"Perfectly all right," Sammy said in his best party voice. "What pictures did you see?"

"Well, one I've really been chasing all over the world," she said. *"Blue Boy."*

"Blue Boy?" Sammy said. "A foreign picture?"

"Not exactly," Laurette said. "It was done in England."

"Oh, Gaumont-British," Sammy said.

"No, by an Independent," she said. "Gainsborough."

People started to laugh. She began to laugh with them. When

she did, tossing her head back, I had the impression of a red flame leaping up, red hair, full red lips and somehow her voice was red too.

"That," Kit mumbled, "would be a bitch."

Harrington stepped in and stopped the fun. "I'm afraid you're misunderstanding each other. Laurette means the paintings at the Huntington."

By that time the story was on its way toward becoming a Hollywood legend. By the next evening it would be attributed to at least three other people.

I don't think Sammy ever forgave her for that one. I think it was part of his falling in love with her. Like his revenge on Sheik. He stood there in the hallway of his five-hundred-a-month house, hosting his first big Hollywood party and someone had suddenly hauled off and socked him and he just stood there, taking it, looking as he must have looked when he was taking his beatings from Sheik, telling her she could leave her wrap upstairs, staring after her as if he would like to murder or rape her.

Everywhere I looked, Sammy seemed to be running after Laurette. I had the impression of a chunky, gutty pony, stepping way up in class, coming up on the outside to challenge the tall, graceful thoroughbred on the rail. He was filling her plate for her, drinking brandy with her, dancing with her out on the patio to the rhumba orchestra. As they danced she looked a head taller because she danced it professionally, with her shoulders straight and her head tilted up while Sammy tore into it with his head down like a prizefighter. Now and then she would look down and bestow a smile upon him that was cold and too perfect on her lips.

Kit said, "There's Ruth Mintz, looking like the little girl who's lost her mother at the circus. Go and dance with her or flirt with her or something."

When I picked Kit up again she had just run into Laurette in the powder room.

"I should have come here ages ago," Laurette had told her. "Isn't Sammy Glick amusing? Dad says he's a dynamo. After the

Great Danes from Yale and Princeton sniffing around me all summer, it might be fun to know a dynamo."

"How long are you staying?" Kit said.

"I'm toying with the idea of taking a house for the winter," Laurette said. "And I'm going to keep it absolutely jammed with theatrical people. I simply adore them."

Laurette wasn't a particularly witty girl, but she delivered all her lines as if she were, and by pointing them up with laughs she gave an impression of both great wit and vitality.

"Laurette babbles like an idiot," Kit said. "But I don't think she is. I get the feeling she has a good mind which she's been brought up to believe is very poor taste for a woman of her position to use."

On our way back from the patio I found Sammy chatting with Harrington and the other bankers and I paused a moment with Ruth to see if the sight of her would revive his interest in the girl he had chosen to be his slipper-and-child-bearer.

Sammy was talking, and from the way they were listening, he was going over.

"Now, of course, every producer must be first a businessman and then a creator," Sammy was out-yessing them. "First we have to analyze the slump of the industry as a whole. I figure it's ten percent the jump in radio popularity, fifteen percent double features, twenty-five percent the national decline in purchasing power and fifty percent the lack of new ideas in pictures themselves. Too many people are coming out of theaters saying, 'I saw that same movie last month.'"

I recognized the explanation that Fineman had given me when I first went to work for him. Only Sammy seemed to know just how to feed it to them. Knew how they loved to listen to the sound of figures and statistics.

"That's very interesting," said Harrington. "What we need is more men out here who think of pictures as a commodity like any other—and forget this prestige business."

"That's exactly what I've been saying," Sammy jumped in.

"After all, pictures are shipped out in cans. We're in the canning business. Our job is to find some way of making sure that every shipment will make a profit."

I wondered where Fineman was. I wanted to be around when Sammy put in that right word for him.

He could run with these men. They had college degrees and belonged to clubs and had summer homes and knew Herbert Hoover, but he knew what they were after. Laurette was different. She wasn't a whore and she wasn't an extra girl, and she wasn't a star and she wasn't a working girl, and she wasn't a homebody and that perplexed him. Her job was not to do anything and do it attractively and amusingly. Sammy couldn't bribe her with a day's work, or slap her on the fanny, and he couldn't even talk about himself without being heckled. She was someone he had to be polite to and that cramped his style. He felt she was laughing at him because his manners weren't up to her standard and this undermined his confidence. And Sammy Glick without his confidence was not a pretty sight.

"Mr. Glick, can you make a noise like a dynamo?" I heard her say and Sammy just looked ill at ease and let her get away with it. Just looked at her as if to say, Okay, baby, you win the first round, you draw first blood, but it's just enough to make me sore. These are big stakes and I'm willing to let you jab away until your arm gets tired and I begin to catch onto your style.

As Kit and I ducked out early, taking Ruth home and out of Sammy's life, Sammy was leading Laurette out to show her his twelve hundred dollars' worth of hibiscus.

|||||||

At lunch in the commissary next day Kit looked over my shoulder and said, "Well! The Little King and the Red Queen."

I looked around as they were coming in together. They posed a moment at the entrance. Laurette, slightly taller, the chic and haughty queen, with a green suede bag slung over her shoulder, a green turban pulling her copper-colored hair straight back from her face. You felt that everything was pulled tight on her, that her stockings were pulled as tight against her legs as possible, that the waistline was drawn in to the fraction of an inch, that she was rigged smart and snug as a ship. Sammy almost started in ahead of her and then he remembered and stepped aside to let her lead. He followed close behind her, with the preoccupied casualness of one who knows he is being watched. But he was so proud of the effect their being together was having that he couldn't keep the exhilaration out of his face.

They passed near our table and disappeared into the executives' dining room off the main commissary.

"She's an exotic-looking thing," I said.

"You mean those droopy lids and the dark shadows under her eyes?" Kit said. "That's dissipation."

"Just the same," I said, "she looks like quite a dish. How come none of the aristobrats ever grabbed her off?"

"Seems to me she was married," Kit said. "The year she came out. But it didn't take. When she entered Vassar she had just come back from a year in Spain, trying to forget. I think she managed to forget all right, but in the process she got the habit of living as if she were always supposed to be forgetting something. Her mother was dead and I guess the old man was too busy staying rich to do much about it. Everybody talked about the way she came to class the first day with painted toenails. She caused quite a stir, while she lasted. A little bit like Tallulah Bankhead enrolling as a freshman at Smith."

"I wonder what they have to talk to each other about," I said. "I'd love to listen in on that conversation."

"I wouldn't," Kit said. "She's probably telling him of the screaming times she used to have in Biarritz before the Spanish War made the town so horribly political. And Sammy is wondering whether he's making too much noise with his soup. . . ."

"And how much influence she has with her old man," I added.

"I think you're underrating him," she said. "This isn't just business. Didn't you see his face? The bloom of true love is upon him at last."

"But I wonder how goddam glamorous she'd look to him if her name weren't Harrington."

"It can't be broken down like that. Sammy isn't making a mechanical play for her because he thinks he can use her. It's all mixed up together. The fact that her name is Harrington must be just as sexually exciting to Sammy as that moist red mouth or those snooty boobs of hers."

We could follow the courtship in the papers after that. The orchids every day. The places they were seen dancing. The gifts. The photographers even gave us the tender looks on their faces over plates of hamburger in the Derby. A Hollywood columnist included it in her radio discussion of exciting romances of the year.

Once in a while when I was in and out of Sammy's office I heard him talking to her on the phone but he never mentioned anything about it until a month or so later when I was at his house going over the script for the submarine picture. I had finished the job a couple of days ahead of schedule and he was in a good mood. He sent Charles to the bar to make us some highballs and then he turned to me with his preview face.

"Well, Al, what do you think of me and Laurette?"

He seemed to let the sentence drip over his tongue like tasting fine wine.

"Well, it all seems pretty fantastic," I said. "But maybe you'll be fantastically happy."

"Oh, it hasn't gone that far yet," he said. "But it might, by God, it might. Jesus! I can't believe it myself. But it's beginning to look as if I'm going to get her."

This may be love, I thought, but not the fine and mellow kind. It may not be in line of business but it's grim enough to be.

"You know, it's a funny thing," he confided. "When I first met her, I thought she was just another Miss Rich Bitch. Just gave her a little rush because I thought I might be able to get a line on how Sidney stood with her old man. I guess I told you I was trying to do everything I can for him. And she kept taking me up on all my invites, but all the time she was doing it she was giving me the polite finger."

There was the moment after Sammy had taken her to lunch the first day when he squeezed all his savoir faire *into: "And when shall I see you again?" And she answered: "Now I know who puts that line in all the movies."*

Several evenings later he was taking her to an opening. He had even bought a new full-dress suit. Made for the occasion. He had sent out advance notices to the press agents that he and Miss Harrington would be among the notable couples attending.

When he called on her Laurette was in street clothes, having a drink with a hefty dame in a boy's haircut who greeted him with a belligerent stare.

"This is Babe Lynch," Laurette said. "She just flew into town on her way to the air races in San Diego. I haven't seen her in ages, so I knew you wouldn't mind if I passed up the opening tonight."

"If you had told me early enough I could have gotten an extra ticket," Sammy said. "In fact, if you make it snappy I can always find a way of getting her in. It isn't our opening, but I'm a pal of the theater manager."

"That's sporting of you," Laurette said. "But Babe only brought her flying togs. So why don't you run along? Call me in the afternoon."

Sammy swallowed his pride, but it stuck in his throat like a fish bone. Going down in the elevator he tore up the tickets. As they fell around his feet in little pieces he realized he might have given them to somebody, but to hell with everybody . . . They were his tickets and he could do what he liked with them.

He drove home, out Sunset Boulevard from the Beverly-Wilshire, fifty, sixty, seventy miles an hour, as fast as he wanted because he had a captain's badge from the Police Department. Thinking, I'm going to get her. She thinks she's too good for me, but I'm going to get her, me, Sammy Glick.

Nothing she could do would discourage Sammy. This was something worth being insulted for. Sammy was running with Class, and

Class was something strange and wonderful. He had a crazy hunch that if he didn't care how much dust he ate in the early laps, he could snap the tape with his strong little chest.

The next evening Sammy called the Beverly-Wilshire again. Hollywood is a terrible place to be left alone in, he said. She might want someone to show her the bright spots.

"How sweet of you," Laurette said. "Come right over."

When he arrived, she was having cocktails with a young man. The young man stood up, terribly tanned and tall, looking down at Sammy with an easy, attractive, self-assured smile. Sammy found himself staring into a broad and immaculate expanse of stiff shirt. Laurette was in evening clothes too.

"I thought George was on the other side of the globe," she explained, ignoring Sammy's face as she introduced them. "Imagine how thrilled I was when I found out he was back in Pasadena. I thought it might be fun if we all went together."

George didn't seem to mind Sammy at all, which made it worse.

"I haven't seen Laurie since Biarritz two summers ago," he explained with a maximum of white teeth as he poured Sammy a cocktail.

He was sore this time. He was so sore he forgot this was a precious bit of china that a loud word might crack.

"Listen, Miss Harrington, don't let me butt in. Why don't you two kids just run along and have a good time?"

But Miss Harrington would not hear of it. "Mr. Glick is so clever," she told the bronzed face from Pasadena. "He knows everything about making pictures. He's going to tell us all about it at dinner. Aren't you, Mr. Glick?"

Sammy tried to turn the compliment aside, if it were a compliment, or the jibe, if it were that. But he couldn't do it deftly enough. He had always been better with the sledgehammer than he was with the foils. Laurette kept laughing at him, silently and politely, her superiority piercing Sammy's pride like banderillas, stinging, hurting . . .

Sammy sat with them in the Florentine Room, feeling a raw and ugly wound inside, out of place in his business suit—his running

togs. He felt a little better when he beat George to it by ordering
the most expensive wine in the place. But when it arrived, Laurette
looked at it and told the waiter to send it back. "If you haven't
1927, don't bother. That's the only good year left."

The orchestra was playing a tango. Sammy didn't know how to
tango. Laurette and George danced it with their hands and their
heads as well as their feet, like a professional team. Sammy's eyes
took every step with her, watched her dancing with her lips parted,
her eyes half closed, her body swaying to the slow rhythm. He
thought of the tango partners she must have left behind, American
scions and Georgian princes and titled Englishmen. Maybe he
could get a tango expert to come to the house, secretly, and then
he would get up one evening and surprise Laurette, that bitch, the
woman he loved. If it didn't take too much time. Though it might
be worth it to make time. He had finally found a woman worthy
of his ambitions, she was the golden girl, the dream, and the faster
he ran the farther ahead she seemed to be.

Then they returned to the table and Sammy stood up, feeling
challenged and mean, and popped down too quickly again.

"What a beautiful dance," Laurette said. "You feel wild and
free."

She knew Sammy had never felt wild and free.

The music was back to jazz. Sammy rose jerkily. The manners
were gone. Just the speed, the fury, the one-man battle.

"Come on, let's dance."

He held her tight against him, his hand clamped against her bare
back, his fingers tense and strong on her skin. It was a double
satisfaction, the immediate thrill of her refined presence so close
to Sammy Glick and the chance that this would reach the columns.
He danced a dogged box-step which he forced her to follow. Both
of them felt the struggle of it.

"You even dance like a dynamo," she said.

"Okay. Wanna quit?" Sammy said.

He was beginning to find himself.

"No," she said. "I'm enjoying it."

She was. It was terrifying when he held her like that, not trying to be polite any more. *She hadn't been really terrified in a long time. To dance as badly as Sammy and not be ashamed of it set him apart from all the other men she had ever known.*

She had the next dance with George and when she returned, Sammy was gone. The waiter handed her a note:

> *Decided I couldn't waste any more time here so I ducked out to the studio to clean up some work. The bill is taken care of for the rest of the night. Have fun.*
> *Sammy*

"I took a chance," Sammy said. "And my hunch was right. I had gone soft on her and she was taking me for as big a sucker as these studio broads would if you gave them a chance. You know what she did? She called me at the office after that polo player left. Said she wanted me to come back and talk to her. I told her to meet me at my place. And she came. What do you think of that, Laurette Harrington coming over to see me in the middle of the night? We sat up talking until it got light. I had her all wrong, Al. That sophisticated stuff is all on the surface. She's just a sweet, simple kid at heart . . ."

All the running Sammy ever did in his life must have been just the trial laps for those next two months. He wasn't even around the office very often. He was too busy.

One day we had an appointment at three and he finally showed a little after five. Irresponsibility was never one of Sammy's faults so I suspected something colossal must have happened.

When he finally came in I knew it was more than merely colossal. It was so big that even he was overwhelmed. He came in quietly, underplaying the scene.

"Al," he said, "have you ever heard of anybody scoring two holes-in-one the same afternoon?"

He made you play straight for him.

"Well, I'm your man. Only it's a little more important than golf. Harrington and I have been sitting in Victor Hugo's from one until just now. He's one of the sweetest guys in the world,

Harrington. And I'm not just saying that because he's going to be my father-in-law."

"Congratulations," I said. "I hope you and Mr. Harrington will be very happy."

"You should have seen me," Sammy said. "I was as nervous as a whore in church. Thought sure as soon as I broke it to him he was going to run out and throw Laurette on the first plane. You know, fine old Southern family and all that crap. But Jesus, he was tickled to death. In fact he seemed so anxious to marry her off to me that I began to wonder whether he was on the skids himself and figured the head of a studio was a nice little thing to have in the family."

"Head of the studio?"

"Yes," Sammy said. "I did everything I could. But I'm afraid poor Sidney is out after all."

"What do you mean afraid?" I said. "Afraid Harrington might change his mind?"

"Al," he said, "it's a good thing I have a sense of humor. Because if I didn't you'd have been out on your ear long ago. As a matter of fact I really went out there and fought for Sidney this afternoon."

"Arise, Sir Samuel, my true knight," I said.

"Don't give me that," he said. "I've got nothing to apologize for. I kept my word. I told Harrington I'd be willing to work under Fineman. I couldn't do any more than that, could I?"

"How should I know?" I said. "And why should you care what I think, anyway?"

"Listen, Al," he said, "I'm no dope. I know how long those pals of mine would stick around if I couldn't go on doing things for them. You're different. You never asked me for anything—I mean for yourself. You're my only friend. I'm only human. I'm not just a—dynamo. Every man's got to have a wife and a friend."

I still think the guy had something when he said forgive them for they know not what they do. Nine times out of ten that may be a virtue. But there is always that tenth time when a strong stand is needed and softheartedness becomes very flabby behavior.

This was one time when I really had the impulse to break off diplomatic relations with Sammy. When he was knifing his fellow man in the back he performed with such gusto and brilliance that it fascinated me as a tour de force. He was so conscientious about being unscrupulous that you almost had to admire him. But there was something indecent about this new pose. It was a little too much like the tycoon who spends the first part of his life sucking and crushing and the last part giving away dimes and Benjamin Franklin's advice. I could imagine the Sammy Glick of forty instead of thirty, with all the sordid details of his career washed from his mind, reviewing his life like an official biographer, believing that his contribution to mankind has entitled him to friendship, kindness and peace.

Suddenly he felt he had to justify himself. He insisted upon giving me a playback of that historic interview with Harrington.

They were sitting in Victor Hugo's. The orchestra was playing chamber music, soft and refined, but the only music for Sammy was Harrington's voice.

"Sammy, I'm going East tomorrow. I don't know whether you realize it or not, but we're contemplating some important changes in our organization out here. We feel your record entitles you to a say in this reorganization."

"That's very kind of you," Sammy said. "Of course, it's only fair to tell you how much I've learned from assisting Sidney. He's been like a father to me. Everything I know about producing came from him. In fact, he's taught me everything he knows."

"That's just what I've been wondering. Perhaps he has given you all he has to give. He let too many flops slip into the program this year."

"Only a genius can make pictures on an average of one a week without some turkeys, Mr. Harrington. Sidney is a hard worker. He did the best he could."

"I appreciate your sentiments. But, to speak frankly, the purpose of my visit was to determine whether his best was good enough."

"The pictures would have made money if the overhead wasn't so

terrific. But it isn't entirely his fault if production costs have been too high."

"Then you think production costs are too high?"

"You put me in a difficult position, Mr. Harrington. I don't like to speak about my superiors. Especially a man like Fineman, who was such a pioneer in this business. After all, I can remember when I was a kid seeing his nickelodeons."

"Naturally, my boy," Harrington said. *"Loyalty is always to be commended. Always. But our first loyalty is to World-Wide, and I wonder if Fineman isn't becoming a little too old-fashioned to uphold the standard of the World-Wide trademark."*

"You couldn't find a better man than Fineman," Sammy said, *"among the older producers."*

"I've had a chance to watch you both function," Harrington said. *"And I may have some difficulty convincing the Board because you're so young. But I've made up my mind that what this studio needs is new leadership. Young blood."*

The waiter came to the table. *"Will that be all, Mr. Glick?"*

Yes, Sammy thought. *I think it will. I think that is just about it, pal.*

"No," he said, *"bring Mr. Harrington and me another brandy."*

"To you and Laurette," said Mr. Harrington.

"And to World-Wide," Sammy added quickly.

He crossed to the window that looked out over the lot. The studio street was full of the pretty girls in slacks going home in twos and threes and carpenters and painters in overalls carrying their lunchboxes and cat calling to each other; a director exhausted from the day's shooting and already worrying with a couple of assistants about the camera set-ups for the next; a star clowning as he climbs over the door into his silver Cord; the crazy-quilt processional of laborers, extras, waitresses, cutters, writers, glamour girls, all the big cogs and the little ones that must turn together to keep a film factory alive.

"Now it's mine," Sammy said. "Everything's mine. I've got everything. Everybody's always saying you can't get everything and I'm the guy who swung it. I've got the studio and I've got the Harrington connections and I've got the perfect woman to run my home and have my children."

I sat there as if I were watching *The Phantom of the Opera* or any other horror picture. I sat there silently in the shadows, for it was growing dark and the lights hadn't been switched on yet and I think he had forgotten he was talking to me. It was just his voice reassuring him in the dark.

"Sammy," I said quietly, "how does it feel? How does it feel to have everything?"

He began to smile. It became a smirk, a leer.

"It makes me feel kinda . . ." And then it came blurting out of nowhere—"patriotic."

CHAPTER 12

The reshuffling at the studio was announced three weeks later but Sidney Fineman hung around for several months, tying up threads he had begun. Kit did his last picture. She said it was really something to see him roll up his sleeves with the enthusiasm of a kid just breaking in.

"He wasn't working to make money," Kit said. "He enjoyed living well, like anybody else. But that wasn't the main part. He was a picture maker. He had pride in his work, like an artist or a shoemaker. The reason he worked was to make good pictures."

And it just happened that his last picture turned out to be a unique kind of hit. It had only two characters, a farmer and his wife, and somehow it managed to electrify and convince and challenge and entertain just by following them through their ordinary passions and defeats and everyday triumphs without any heavies or comedy reliefs or sub-plots or sub-sub-plots, and the critics didn't know whether to call it comedy or tragedy or fantasy but audiences called it entertainment of a fresh and provocative kind because it had all three, because a little of all their lives was in it. It might have earned Fineman a producing berth at one of the other studios, but somehow or other everybody was saying that it was impossible for Fineman to do anything as modern as that and most of the credit was given to Larry Ross, the kid assistant Fineman had upped from the writers' ranks. As a matter of fact, as Kit discovered, the source of this rumor was none other than young Ross himself and apparently Sammy was glad to give it his stamp of approval because he was already claiming Ross as one of the protégés he had developed.

As soon as Fineman moved out of his office, Sammy had the wall to the adjoining room knocked down, to make it larger. Then he threw out the whole Colonial motif because he said it cramped him. When the office was finally remodeled it had the intimacy of Madison Square Garden. The walls were lined with leather and the solid glass desk looked like a burlesque runway. On one wall was an oil painting of Laurette, which made her look ten years younger, even though it had been painted just a few months before. Opposite her was a large autographed photograph of Harrington.

|||||||

Because he died so soon after his separation from World-Wide, there was some talk that Fineman committed suicide, but the Hays Office hushed it up so fast that it was impossible to track it down. Of course, there are less spectacular ways of taking your life than by gun or gas; there is the slow leak when the will is punctured, what the poet was trying to say when he spoke of dying of a broken heart.

The papers said Fineman was only fifty-six. I would have guessed somewhere in the late sixties. The papers also said that he had recently been forced to resign his post at the studio because of failing health.

The day after he died a whistle blew in all the studios at eleven o'clock, a signal for all activity to cease for a full minute of silence while we rose in memory of Sidney Fineman. At one minute after eleven another whistle sounded, the signal for us to forget him and go on about our business again.

But the soul of Sidney Fineman was not let off that easily. Hollywood likes its death scenes too well for that. A few days later they gave Sidney a testimonial dinner at the Ambassador at ten dollars a plate.

I wanted Kit to go with me, but she held her ground. "I like to give my testimonials to people before they're dead," she said. "I'm going down to hear Hemingway. He's raising money for the Loyalists."

Mrs. Fineman sat at the table of honor between Sammy and Harrington, who had just come back to the Coast again to be on hand for the wedding.

Sammy's speech had women digging frantically for their handkerchiefs. In presenting Mrs. Fineman a gold life pass to all World-Wide pictures, he said, "The greatest regret of my career is that I had to take the reins from the failing hands of a man who has driven our coach so long and so successfully. And I can only say that I would gladly step down from the driver's seat and walk if I thought it would bring Uncle Sid back to us again."

The columnists reported tears in Sammy's eyes as he sat down.

"Perhaps the camera flashlights made his eyes water," I suggested to Kit.

"No," she said. "I don't think it's at all impossible that those were real tears. Sammy has the peculiar ability to cry at phony situations but never at genuine ones."

"I didn't think he had any tears in him for any occasion," I said. "I thought that well had run dry long ago."

"Oh, God, no," she said. "Sammy is an emotionalist. Only

instead of letting himself go he just sounds one note over and over again."

"I know which note that is too," I said. "Mi mi mi mi . . ."

|||||||

The wedding was a beautiful production. It was staged in the garden beyond the lawn terrace of the estate in Bel Air that Sammy had just purchased from a famous silent star who had gone broke after the advent of sound. The wags insisted on calling it Glickfair.

Beyond the garden were the swimming pool and tennis court and just across the private road a freak three-hole golf-course. The house itself was of baronial proportions, an interesting example of the conglomerate style that is just beginning to disappear in Hollywood, a kind of Persian-Spanish-Baroque-Norman, with some of the architect's own ideas thrown in to give it variety.

There were at least a thousand guests milling around—from Norma Shearer to Julian Blumberg, whose first novel had shortened Hollywood's memory of his Guild activities.

People were clustered about the garden like bees, buzzing *isn't it lovely, lovely, just too lovely!* The flower girls were two little child stars and the bridesmaids who preceded Laurette down the terraced steps all had famous faces.

Laurette's white satin wedding gown made her complexion seem whiter than ever. Her red lips and hair against that milky skin, and the solemnity of the moment as she moved to the funereal rhythm of the wedding march added to the unreality of the spectacle. She was a ghastly beauty floating through the Hollywood mist. She and Harrington in his striped trousers and top hat were like a satirical artist's study of the whole grim business of marriage.

Sammy entered the garden from the opposite path, followed by Sheik, both in gray double-breasted vests and afternoon cutaways. Sammy was staring straight ahead of him, a smile set hard on his lips as if it were carved there. Sheik kept grinning, obviously a little lit, taking it big.

All through the marriage ceremony newsreel cameras were grinding. As Sammy and Laurette were declared man and wife for better or for worse for richer or for poorer in sickness and in health till death do them part, a professional mixed chorus suddenly stepped forward and sang, "Ah, Sweet Mystery of Life."

After that the crowd broke, moving over to the terrace, where enormous banquet tables had been set up, manned by the entire staff of the Vine Street Derby. Four office boys staggered in with a six-foot-high horseshoe made entirely of gardenias, across which was strung a white silk banner with gold letters, "Long Life and Happiness Always."

Everybody seemed to agree that this was the greatest wedding Hollywood ever had. "Even bigger than the MacDonald-Raymond," I heard someone say. And I could almost see the *Megaphone* proclaiming: GLICK NUPTIALS HIT ALL-TIME HIGH!

When it finally let out at dusk Kit was in a restless mood. "Let me drive," she said. "I feel as if I want to do something. I wonder how long it will be before the world looks back on that the way we do at African rituals."

We drove out to the ocean and up along the coast. It was quiet, relaxing, good to be alone. "Isn't that our cove?" I said.

We stopped. Without either of us saying anything I took her hand and we started down. It was a night without stars. The tide was high and the wind whipped in off the water.

We stood with our arms around each other, looking out over the waves, cold but comfortable. We discovered one solitary light moving slowly along the horizon. We played with it. It was a rumrunner and we had the plot of a B-picture. It was a ghost ship, a derelict, and we had mystery. It was the Japanese fishermen who put out from Terminal Island before the sun is up, and we had realism.

We lay down on the clean cold sand that trembled with the force of the waves pounding down. There was a long moment when we no longer heard the ocean roar. Then we were listening to it louder than ever.

We didn't feel like going home, going inside anywhere, so we drove down to Ocean Park and strolled out on the amusement pier. Public dancehalls with the girls coming alone in cheap evening dresses, and the barrel passageway where a woman screams with embarrassment and delight as her dress suddenly blows up around her face, the Krazy House full of electric shocks and trap doors in the dark—a ten-cent introduction to a harmless form of masochism—the guy showing off to his girl by knocking all the bottles over with a baseball, and necking in the boat that moves foolishly along through dark tunnels, all the screwy, healthy releases that don't cost too much, the cheap thrills people will probably always get a kick out of.

Kit insisted on going on the roller coaster seven times, sitting in the front seat, rising high over the ocean and then diving down, down past the Ferris wheel and the revolving airplanes and the merry-go-round, past the crowd flashing by like a crazy pan shot, heading straight for the water and then at the last possible moment swishing up into the sky.

"I have a wonderful idea," Kit said, as she tried to get me on for the eighth time. "During my lunch hour I'm going over to Mines Field and take flying lessons."

"The hell you are," I said. "I forbid it."

Those were always fighting words for Kit. "What do you mean you forbid it?"

"I absolutely refuse to let you take the chance," I said.

"Al, you're getting awfully possessive lately," she said. "You're beginning to act as if I were married to you."

"That settles it," I said.

"Settles what?"

"Our marriage."

"Now, Al, if it's just a question of living together . . ."

"It's a question of marrying you," I said. "I am not going to let you take another ride on that damn thing. I'm getting dizzy. I want to marry you. I want you to quit this funny business and come along like a good girl and get married."

"Al," she said, "you have a roller-coaster jag. We haven't even got a license."

"We're going to drive down to Tiajuana. You don't need a license in Tiajuana. All you need is five bucks and a woman. We can come back in the morning."

"That sounds too much like a Hollywood elopement," she said. "And who do we think we're eloping from? People out here are always sneaking off to get married when there's no one around even vaguely interested in trying to stop them. And anyway, I hate Tijuana. It's just a little outhouse for San Diego."

"What do we care what Tiajuana looks like?" I said. "We won't even see Tiajuana. Let's just jump in the car and start down. We can get there in four hours—they may still be open."

"I always feel sorry for couples who have to get drunk in the small hours of the morning before they can work up courage enough to run off and get married. As if they're afraid that any moment they'll sober up and change their minds. Let's just go down quietly to the City Hall and get it over with."

I didn't realize until she was all finished that she had said yes. "Kit!" I said. "Darling! Jesus! Kiss me."

"You fool," she said. "Not out here."

We did.

"Where shall we go?" I said. "We've got to take a week off and celebrate."

"I know a spot down on the Gulf where we can get a cottage right on the beach and swim and drink *tequila* and carry on right out in the open if we feel like it and forget all about Hollywood until we have to come back."

And forget all about Sammy Glick, I thought, the four-star, super-colossal, marriage-to-end-all-marriages of Sammy Glick.

I realized that neither of us had said a word about Sammy's marriage since we left that spectacle behind us. But somehow what had happened to us was bound up with that marriage.

|||||||

It was about one o'clock and we were sitting in the kitchenette talking and drinking beer when the phone rang. Kit went to answer it. She called me, handing the phone over significantly.

"It's for you. And you'll never guess who."

I thought of Sammy, installed in his canopied French Empire bed making love to three million dollars.

" 'Lo, Al. Busy?"

His words came quick and sharp as ever, but there was a hollowness, a ring of humility I had never heard before.

"Sammy! For God's sake! What do you want?"

"Al, I want you to come over. I want to talk to you."

"Tonight? Now? Are you crazy?"

"Do me a favor and come over."

"Jesus Christ, do you know what time it is?"

"It isn't much after one o'clock."

"But what about Laurette?"

"Come on over, Al. Please."

I tried to think if I had ever heard him say that word before.

"Hold on a minute, Sammy."

I looked up at Kit. "He wants me to come over. What the hell does he think I am?"

"He knows what you are, darling. That's why he called you."

"I'd love to know what it's about."

"Go ahead. I ought to be reading a script, anyway. Duty calls, Boswell."

She understood. I could feel that old preoccupation with the destiny of Sammy Glick gripping me again.

"O.K.," I said into the mouthpiece. "Keep your pants on. I'm coming."

I could see the house as I turned in the Bel Air gate. It stood up there on top of a hill like a feudal castle. Bright lights from every room cast their yellow geometric shafts out into the black night.

The big oak-paneled door swung open so soon after I rang that Sammy must have been standing behind it waiting for me. Behind him was a spacious hallway suitable to a public building, with a curving marble stairway and elaborate chandeliers that seemed to dwarf him. He was wearing a silk monogrammed smoking jacket over his dress trousers. In his hand was an almost empty highball glass. I had never seen him drunk before.

As I entered he grabbed my hand feverishly. His palm was damp. "Thanks, Tootsie. What took you so long?"

It had only been fifteen minutes from the time he called.

I followed Sammy through one bright and costly room after another until we reached the bar. He seemed to be suffering from a severe shock, terrifyingly becalmed, like an injured motorist wandering around after a bloody collision.

He mixed my drink in silence and then as he handed it to me over the bar he blurted, "Goddam it, I just didn't have the guts to stick it out here alone tonight. I went through the house and turned all the lights on. I kept the radio going full blast. I sat at the bar and tried to get myself stinko. No dice. I was talking to myself. I was going nuts. Jesus, Al, you're easygoing. You're sane. Talk to me, Al. Keep me from going nuts."

"When did she leave?" I said.

"How'd you know?" he asked anxiously.

"Doesn't take a Philo Vance."

"Oh," he said, and he looked relieved. "I thought maybe it was out already. There's so goddam much talk in this town. You've got to promise not to let it get out. I'll ruin you in this town if you ever let it out."

"Balls with that ruining-me-in-this-town stuff," I said.

He came out from behind the bar and stood in front of me apologetically.

"O.K. Al, forget it. It just came out before I knew what I was saying. I know you're regular, Al. You never tried to bitch me out of anything. I can talk to you. That's why I got you over. If I can only talk it out, I'll feel better, you know, get it out of my system. Like puking."

His damp hands wiped up and down his face. Then his conversation went on jerkily and I had the impression that it was out of sync with the movement of his lips.

"After the wedding, a goddam madhouse. Nothing but champagne. Twenty-five hundred bucks' worth down the drain. People cockeyed all over the joint. Can't find Laurette. Make a goddam fool of myself asking everybody if they seen Laurette. Then upstairs in the guest room . . . Jesus Christ, with that new punk I just signed, Carter Judd . . ."

He emptied his highball, keeping his face for a long time in his glass.

"Judd ducked out as I came in. But she just pulled herself together and waited for me. Just waited for me as if it was nothing at all."

Sammy's face blotched red and white, unable to hide the pain of his wounded pride. His features became so ugly and distorted I knew I was going to see him cry. He started to say, "I can't believe . . . I thought . . ." and the tears came, forming foolishly in the corners of his fierce little eyes. I wondered why I thought of surrealism when I saw him cry and then I remembered the Dali exhibit of rain falling inside a taxicab. This was no less bizarre, no less grotesque. Sammy's tears were rain falling inside a taxicab.

After the tears, came, hideously, the tight, strained, hysterical little sobs he tried so futilely to choke. But he couldn't hold it any longer and the dam broke and the tears flowed over. He tried to blot his face with his handkerchief and when the flow could no longer be checked that way he sat down on the stool with his elbows on the bar and cried into his nervous little hands.

When he got his voice again he didn't want me to see how he looked, so he spoke through his fingers latticed against his face. Before his speech had been nervous broken discords. Now his words came haltingly, absently, one at a time.

"I told her I couldn't understand it. From a lousy casting couch broad, maybe. But when a high-class girl like her, a lady, an aristocrat . . ."

It was no fake. He was devastated. Kit was right. His was no calculating marriage for position. It did not have to be. He had fallen in love with position, with the name and the power of Harrington, and it came to him not as something sordid and cold but as love, as deep respect for Laurette's upbringing and attraction to her personality and desire for her body.

He paused a long time, the glibness gone. In his mouth was the thick, sour taste of defeat, and distress was ugly on him. He was sweating with strain and the shame of it.

"It wasn't so much what I saw. Hell, we were all drunk and kidding around. It was how she spoke to me, just stood there like a haughty bitch, saying . . ." His hands began to massage his face slowly again. "Jesus, I'll never forget what she said . . ."

He balanced a desperate moment on the threshold, swaying, his eyes bulging, terribly sober.

She came forward, straight at him, smoothing out her dress, the lovely cream satin wedding gown that Princess Pignatelli would be gushing over in her society column next morning.

Her voice was vicious and low, drunken and passionate. Ugly and hoarse to Sammy. "Well?" she said.

He waited for her to alibi, plead, weep, swear, apologize. But that was all she said. He waited for her to wilt beneath his righteous (and horrified, and frightened) stare, but she only stood there, proud and composed, stately and perverse and cruelly self-possessed. These were the elements he had loved and admired, and suddenly he hated them, he wanted to hide from them.

"Don't stand there gasping like a fish out of water," she said. "What have you got to gasp about? You've got what you want. And Dad's got what he wants. And little Laurie's going to get what she wants."

"What do you mean?" Sammy said, feeling his words fade off into the air like a skywriter's. "What are you talking about?"

"Now listen, dear," she said. "We're going to see a lot of each other. What's the use of trying to fool ourselves? I know why you married me—for the same reason you do everything else. And don't worry—I won't let you down. I'll be the best hostess this town ever had. I'll handle this part of the business, and I'll be careful, I won't let my private life interfere with your career. Only you and I just signed a contract—the same goes both ways."

He had wanted the devotion of Rosalie Goldbaum, he had wanted the companionship of Kit, he had wanted the domesticity of Ruth Mintz and the glamour of Rita Royce, and he had thought he was getting the drop on all of them (and something more, something indispensable) in Laurette Harrington.

His chin went forward defensively, he stood there drawing in slack sail, tightening up, and when he answered her his voice was screwed down hard, cold and metallic.

"Sure. But the joint is lousy with snoopy columnists, that's all. You want it to look right, don't you? Now go on back to the party and stay out of the two-shots. Unless they're with me."

Then she smiled at him boldly and she seemed to tower above him as she came forward to take his frenzied little face in her hands and kiss it on the forehead as if they had been married twenty years.

"All right, dear," she said.

He was imitating her voice." 'All right, dear.' That was just the way she said it, 'All right, dear.' "

"Where is she, now?" I said.

His shoulders rose and fell in a hopeless shrug. "How the hell do I know? With that Judd bastard, I suppose. I can keep him in louse parts till he's a dead pigeon in pictures. But where will that get me? There'll be others. They'll be around her like flies, the sons-of-bitches. And the night I made her I thought I was the greatest guy in the world. Why, she's a ⋮ . . . Why, she's nothing but a high-class . . ."

Ah, sweet mystery of life, at last I've found you, I sang to myself, in a small clear voice. Ah, at last I know the secret of it all . . .

"I don't know what the hell to do," Sammy said. "What would you do, Al? What would you do if you were me?"

"Sammy," I said, "I'd like to help you, but that's a very hypothetical question. I wouldn't want to be in your shoes."

He studied me quizzically. "You hate my guts, don't you? You hate my guts just like all the rest of them."

It was said without antagonism. Spoken regretfully.

"No," I said, "that isn't quite true. If you want to know what I really think—I think you couldn't help yourself. With you it was a choice of being a nice guy and a flop or the way you are now. No, I guess you didn't even have that choice. The world decided it for you."

"Don't give me that double-talk," he said. "I'm in a spot. No kidding, what would you do?"

"Sammy," I said, "all I can tell you is that I'd pull out of this set-up so fast . . ."

He was back on his feet fast and his energy seemed to be flowing back into his body again.

"By God, I will! I'll start moving out right now. By the time that bitch gets back in the morning she won't even find a collar-button lying around this dump. I'll get Charles out of bed. I'll call the chauffeur . . ."

He started running across the room. Then suddenly he stopped and stared ahead, staring at something that wasn't there, like a sleepwalker.

"Oh, Jesus," he said.

"Now, what?"

"I wonder how walking out on his daughter will hit old man Harrington?"

"What do you care?" I said. "You don't need Harrington. You've arrived."

"But Christ," Sammy complained, "you never know how you stand in this crazy business. Take that kid Ross, for instance. He's got something on the ball. But I don't like him. Don't trust him. He's a smart-aleck. I can see already he thinks he knows more than I do. And who the hell knows, maybe he does. But with Harrington in my corner . . ."

I could see the future running through his mind like ticker tape:

Mr. and Mrs. Glick entertain Morgan partners . . . Mr. and Mrs. Glick fly east to spend Christmas at famous Harrington estate . . . Among those seen at ringside tables after the opening were Samuel Glick and his lovely wife the former Laurette Harrington dazzling in white sequins and er-mine . . . Just good friends says Laurette Glick of Clark Judd of Freddie Epson of Maurice del Rios . . . Utterly ridiculous says Mrs. Glick of

separation rumors . . . Cheap gossip says Samuel Glick in Chicago alone
for studio convention . . . Harrington millions said to be behind Glick
Productions . . . Mr. and Mrs. Glick request the pleasure of . . .

"Sammy," I said as I stood up, "I hope you and Laurette will
be very happy."

I started to leave.

"Stick around," Sammy said, and he picked up the phone on
the end of the bar.

"Hello, Sheik . . . !" He laughed loudly. "I did! Well, bring her
over here, ask her if she's got a friend. . . . No, it's no gag.
. . . Goddam right I mean it . . . No, not her, she always tells me
what a great actress she is and she's all washed up, and she's a lousy
lay, anyway . . . Jesus, what the hell good are you? Sure, sure I
know you can't get me an Academy Winner at two o'clock in the
morning . . . Ha, ha, ha . . . Hey, wait a minute!"

He turned to me energetically. "Hey, Al, remember Billie, the
redhead I fixed you up with at the Back Lot a long time ago? I
wouldn't mind some of that tonight. Haven't got her phone
number by any chance?"

"She's turned pro," I said. "She's working out of Gladys's."

"Hell," he said. "I like to roll my own. I was going to make that
dame open up tonight."

I found myself getting satisfaction out of saying, "You better
be satisfied to take her this way. Because I happen to know the
only way you'd ever get to Billie is pay as you enter. You'll never
be able to understand it, but Billie is folks. Billie is a very moral
lady."

"Okay," he said. "If I have to pay, I'll pay. But, by Christ, I'm
going to get my money's worth!"

I thought of Foxy Four Eyes's back room on the occasion of
Sammy's introduction to the orgasmic mysteries, the day he
learned to value the act of love in terms of money's worth.

"Hello, Sheik," he said. "To hell with your dogs. Drop by
Gladys's and pick up Billie Rand. . . . No, don't pick up anything
else. Ha, ha, ha . . . okay, sweetheart."

He hung up, still laughing with Sheik. Then he saw me, on my way out, and stopped.

"What's your hurry? Hang around a while. We're going to have some laughs."

"No, thanks," I said. "I'm putting my bachelor days behind me. Kit and I are getting married this week."

"Well, I'll be damned," he said. "I thought that was her voice when I called, but I wasn't sure. Well, all I can say is you're a lucky guy, Al. She's a great girl."

He said it with a memory, with a touch of remorse and I knew what he was thinking, that he would have liked to have her, that he would have liked to have someone, but it was impossible, it was absolutely physically, psychologically, economically impossible.

"Well, I'm tickled to death. We'll have to get together and kill a case of champagne some night."

He walked me to the door and then he left the door open and walked me to my car. He could not bear to be alone. He put one foot on the running board and leaned through the window.

"Before you go," he said, "forget everything I told you tonight. I don't know what the hell got into me for a minute. What the hell have I got to kick about? I feel great. I got the world by the balls. Keep in touch with me, sweetheart."

There in the silence I could almost hear the motor in him beginning to pick up speed again.

As I drove off I saw him standing outside on his palatial stone steps, under his giant eucalyptus trees, looking out over his hundred yards of landscaping that terraced down to the wall that surrounded his property. He was a lonely little figure in the shadows of Glickfair, the terrible little conqueror, the poor little guy, staring after my car as it drove out through the main gates, waiting for Sheik to bring the girls and the laughter.

I drove back slowly, heavy with the exhaustion I always felt after being with Sammy too long. I thought of him wandering alone through all his brightly lit rooms. Not only tonight, but all the nights of his life. No matter where he would ever be, at banquets, at gala house parties, in crowded night clubs, in big poker games, at intimate dinners, he would still be wandering alone through all his brightly lit rooms. He would still have to send out frantic S.O.S.'s to Sheik, that virile eunuch: Help! Help! I'm lonely. I'm nervous. I'm friendless. I'm desperate. Bring girls, bring Scotch, bring laughs. Bring a pause in the day's occupation, the quick sponge for the sweaty marathoner, the recreational pause that is brief and vulgar and titillating and quickly forgotten, like a dirty joke.

I thought how, unconsciously, I had been waiting for justice suddenly to rise up and smite him in all its vengeance, secretly hoping to be around when Sammy got what was coming to him; only I had expected something conclusive and fatal and now I realized that *what was coming to him* was not a sudden pay-off but a process, a disease he had caught in the epidemic that swept over his birthplace like plague; a cancer that was slowly eating him away, the symptoms developing and intensifying: success, loneliness, fear. Fear of all the bright young men, the newer, fresher Sammy Glicks that would spring up to harass him, to threaten him and finally to overtake him.

I thought of all the things I might have told him. You never had the first idea of give-and-take, the social intercourse. It had to be all you, all the way. You had to make individualism the most frightening ism of all. You act as if the world is just a blindfold free-for-all. Only the first time you get it in the belly you holler brotherhood. But you can't have your brothers and eat them too. You're alone, pal, all alone. That's the way you wanted it, that's the way you learned it. Sing it, Sammy, sing it deep and sad, all alone and feeling blue, all alone in crowded theaters, company conventions, all alone with twenty of Gladys's girls tying themselves into lewd knots for you. All alone in sickness and in health, for better or for worse, with power and with Harringtons till death parts you from your only friend, your worst enemy, yourself.

But what good are words when not even experience will regenerate? It was too late to hate him or change him. Sammy's will had stiffened. It had been free for an instant at birth, poised bird-free in the doctor's hand that moment in the beginning before it began to be formed to the life-molds, the terrible hungers of body and brain, the imposed wants, the traditional oppressions and persecutions, until at last Sammy's will had curled in on itself, like an ingrown hair festering, spreading infection.

Now Sammy's career meteored through my mind in all its destructive brilliance, his blitzkrieg against his fellow men. My mind skipped from conquest to conquest, like the scrapbook on his exploits I had been keeping ever since that memorable birthday party at the Algonquin. It was a terrifying and wonderful document, the record of where Sammy ran, and if you looked behind the picture and between the lines you might even discover what made him run. And some day I would like to see it published, as a blueprint of a way of life that was paying dividends in America in the first half of the twentieth century.

THE SAMMY GLICK
SHORT STORIES

AUTHOR'S NOTE

What could connect Dartmouth College and a Vermont marble strike with the novel *What Makes Sammy Run?* They would seem to be a continent apart. But actually, without the former, the latter might never have materialized. It happened like this:

In the mid-thirties, as student editor of *The* (daily) *Dartmouth*, I was shoulder-deep if not over my head in the story of the marbleworkers' union's struggle for a living wage against the quarry owners, who turned out to be generous, longtime supporters of the college, the Proctor family of Proctor, Vermont. I wrote and featured on our front page a series of articles describing the lives of the families of the marbleworkers, pulling out all stops and not having to exaggerate, since the kids were hungry, the clothes threadbare, and the company houses drafty through bitter winters.

The series had set off an angry confrontation between spontaneous sympathizers with the strike and indignant defenders of the Proctors. To the friendlies, I was an undergraduate John Reed, and to the opposition a traitor to my college and my class. And I don't mean the Class of '36. President Ernest Martin Hopkins showed me drawersful of letters demanding my expulsion. The right-wing alumni and the American Legion seemed to think expulsion was much too good for me.

In the midst of this storm in a Dartmouth teacup, Bennett Cerf, the celebrated president of Random House, came to Hanover to deliver one of his joke-studded lectures. He phoned me at *The Dartmouth* office and asked if I would drop over to see him at the end of the day. Actually our "day" ended at three or four in the morning, when we put the paper to bed, but the Hanover Inn was a scant hundred yards away, so I dropped over around suppertime to meet the famous Mr. Cerf.

Bennett, as I would soon come to know him, told me he had been reading my marble-strike series, was impressed with both the style and content, and wanted to know more about my work. I told him that I had been writing a number of short stories for the campus literary magazine, and also a one-act play, *Company Town*, based on my experiences in Proctor. The state troopers, blatantly taking the side of the quarry owners, had actually stopped and turned back our trucks delivering food and clothing to the besieged families. (Ah, the bad old thirties!) It was excellent material, and I had made the most of it.

When Bennett asked me what my plans were after graduation, I told him I was going back to Hollywood to work for David Selznick as a reader/junior writer, but I intended to keep my hand in as a short-story writer. "Good," the ebullient, ever-optimistic head of Random House said. "If you ever have a novel in mind, we'd be interested. Come and see us."

Back in Hollywood, while working for the now-legendary Dave Selznick, I got my short-story career in gear very quickly. In my first two years out of college, I managed to sell stories to *The Saturday Evening Post, Collier's, Story, Esquire*—and *Liberty.* It was in that quirky mass-market magazine that I first published, in short-story form, "What Makes Sammy Run?" It was so well received that *Liberty* asked for another Sammy story and I came up with "Love Comes to Sammy Glick."

Shortly after this I met with Bennett Cerf again. He had read the *Liberty* stories and asked if I saw them as the seeds of a Hollywood novel. In truth, I was in the process of making notes along that line. I was introduced to Saxe Commins, a warm and sympathetic editor, who encouraged me to leave Hollywood film-writing and come east to write the book. With a $250 advance (against the munificent total of $500) I was on my way. I holed up in Norwich, Vermont, just across the Connecticut River from Dartmouth, and, with outline in hand, began banging away. In less than a year the job was done.

From time to time, I would run out of money and have to stop for a short story to pay the rent and support a young wife and baby daughter. The novel was published on my twenty-seventh birthday, with pre-pub praise from Scott Fitzgerald and John O'Hara. Bennett had warned me that while he, Saxe, and everybody else at Random House was enthusiastic about the book, I should not expect much of a sale. People who read, they felt, don't buy "Hollywood" novels.

But *Sammy* fooled all of us. With a rave from *The New York Times,* from Dorothy Parker, on coast-to-coast radio from Walter Winchell, and from Damon Runyon, in his salute to Sammy as "the all-American heel," the book went into eight printings before publication and was the choice of book-review editors as "Best First Novel of the Year." The hardcover sale went over fifty thousand and the countless paperback editions have sent the circulation into the millions. To my amazement, Sammy Glick is as well known today as he was in 1941 when he first struck terror in the hearts of the Hollywood tycoons.

The two short stories that follow are republished in their original form, the first using dialogue without quotation marks, a

stylized or stylish experiment I was drawn to, perhaps from reading Saroyan and other groundbreakers in the thirties.

For the sake of literary history, if that doesn't sound too pomp-
ous, I have left the secondary characters' names as they were in
the original stories. Al Manners, the laid-back narrator who
becomes obsessed with Sammy's ruthless climb to the top,
becomes Al Manheim in the novel. Eugene Spitzer, the *nebbish*
whose story Sammy steals for his breakthrough to Hollywood,
becomes Julian Blumberg. Geoffrey Boyce, the dignified studio
head whose place Sammy usurps, becomes Sidney Fineman. I
believe the reason for these changes was to counter the possible
charge of anti-Semitism. Since Sammy is obviously Jewish, I
thought it should be clear that nearly all his victims—Rosalie,
Manheim, Blumberg, Fineman, his brother, Israel—were also
Jewish, suggesting the wide range of personalities and attitudes
under the one ethnic umbrella.

B.S.

"WHAT MAKES SAMMY RUN?"

Al sat with a friend in a booth at the Vine Street Brown Derby watching the people watch each other.

It's a funny thing, Al said, if you watch an animal while it eats, it stops. But here in the Derby several hundred people pay, and pay well, for the privilege of being watched while they eat.

Al is a writer. He writes scenarios, but he could say that because he worked on a newspaper for ten years, and he didn't forget it. He remembered going down to New York and begging for a job, making a pest of himself because he needed twenty dollars a week to be a man in this world. Al was getting five hundred now. That was because he had no push. He seemed content with being small fry. He was lazy. He would never get anywhere. When other writers gave him good ideas for stories he would give them credit. He was a washout.

A big man with a fat body carefully hidden in smartly tailored clothes stopped at the table. He squeezed Al's hand affectionately.

Saw your picture, Al, he said. Tuhriffic!

And he pressed his pudgy hand against Al's as if to indicate that further expression failed him.

That's the original phony, Al said, as the fat man left his table to squeeze somebody else's hand. I happen to know he told Sol Morris my picture stinks.

Al looked around at the new star who had just come in with her husband and her lover, at the too-flattering caricatures of Hollywood celebrities on the wall, at the too-revealing starched uniforms of the waitresses.

Sometimes I feel if I passed my hand over all this it would topple down like a house of cards, Al said. Just like that. Pffffffft.

Whenever I think of it I think of a little kid we used to have on the paper. He was fifteen years old, a little ferret of a kid, sharp and quick. Sammy Glick. Used to run copy for me. Always ran. Always looked thirsty.

Good morning, Mr. Manners, he said to me the first time we met. I'm the new office boy, but I ain't going to be an office boy long.

Don't say ain't, I said, or you'll be an office boy forever.

Thanks, Mr. Manners, he said; that's why I took this job so I can be around writers and learn all about grammar and how to act right.

Get the hell out of here, I said.

He raced out too quickly; a little ferret. Smart kid, I thought. Smart little kid. He made me uneasy. I guess I've always been afraid of people who can be agile without grace.

In three weeks Sammy did more running around that office than Paavo Nurmi in his whole career. It made me feel great. Every time I gave him a page of copy, he'd run off with it as if his life depended on it. I can still see Sammy racing through the office.

I guess he knew what he was doing. The world was a race to Sammy. He was running against time.

Sometimes I used to sit at the bar and say, Al, I don't give a good damn if you never move from this seat again. If you never write another line. I default. If it's a race, you can scratch my name right now. Al Manners does not choose to run. And it would run through my head like that, What makes Sammy run? What makes Sammy run? Does he know where he's going? I asked one of the reporters:

Say, Tony, what makes Sammy run?

You're drunk, Al, he said. How the hell do I know?

But I've got to know, I told him. It's important. Don't you see? It's the answer to everything.

You're nuts, he said.

Three weeks later I had my first run-in with Sammy Glick.

Those were the days when I was writing my drama column and I used to bat it out around four o'clock and then go over to Mac and Charlie's and forget.

One morning a storm from the general direction of the city editor blew at me.

Why in hell don't you look what you're doing? he said.

What's eating you? I said cagily.

That column you turned in last night, he said. It didn't make sense. You left all the verbs out of the last paragraph. If it hadn't been for that kid Sammy Glick it would have run the way you wrote it.

What's Sammy Glick got to do with it? I said, getting sore.

Everything, he said. He read it on his way to the linotypers. So he sat right down and rewrote the paragraph. And damned well, too.

That's great, I said. He's a great kid.

A few minutes later I came face to face with Samuel Glick himself. Nice work, I said.

Oh, that's all right, he said.

Listen, wise guy, I said. If you found something wrong with my stuff, why didn't you come and tell me? You knew where I was.

Sure, he said, but I didn't think we had time.

But you had time to show it to the city editor first, I said. Smart boy.

Gee, Mr. Manners, he said, I'm sorry. I just wanted to help you. You did, I said.

Sammy seemed very satisfied. Don't you think it's dangerous to drop so many verbs? he said. You might hit somebody down below.

Listen, I said. Tell me one thing. How the hell can you read when you're running so fast?

That's how I learned to read, he said—while I was running errands.

It made me sore. He was probably right. Somebody called him and he spun around and started running. What makes Sammy Glick run? I pondered. It must have something to do with centrifugal force, only deeper.

A couple of weeks later I turned in my column and went down to the bar. The telephone rang for me. It was Sammy. He said, The boss says your column is four inches short.

What the hell, I said. Tell him I'll be right up.

You don't have to worry, he said. I took care of it myself.

You, I said stupidly. I knew he had me.

Sure, Al, he said. I dashed off a four-inch radio column to fill, and the boss liked it.

Oh, he's seen it already, I said. Then why the hell did you call me? Why don't you just take over my column?

I just wanted to help you, he said.

Sure, I said, Joe Altruist, and hung up.

But the pay-off came the next morning. I had just started on the column when the city editor came over.

From now on write it six inches shorter, he said.

O.K. by me, I said, if you can give me one good reason.

From now on we're using Sammy Glick's radio column, he said.

You mean Sammy Glick the copy boy? I asked.

No, I mean Sammy Glick the radio columnist, he said. His stuff looked good today.

Maybe you'd like to know he copied the first paragraph from Somerset Maugham, I said.

Maybe that's where you need to go for your stuff, he said.

So that's how Sammy got his start. He was smart enough never to crib from the same writer twice. When it came to wisecracks, he rolled his own. I hated him so much I began to admire him. Every other copy boy was a nice guy. At least if you bent over, they'd ask you to stand up and turn around before stabbing you.

But I began to see what made Sammy run. Though I couldn't see just then where he was running.

After Sammy Glick had been writing his column for a couple of months he came up to me one day and said, Say, Al, next Monday is my birthday, and since you sorta gave me my start I thought maybe you'd like to have dinner with my girl and me at the Algonquin.

I'll never forget that girl, or the day either, and there's a real story in that too. Everything Sammy did was a story. That's why I'm telling you all this. Because Sammy is a genius, one of our big Americans, Napoleon in a double-breasted suit. Some day he's going to lie in a museum, stuffed, labeled: THIS IS SAMMY GLICK. IN AN AGE THAT COULD NEVER STOP RUNNING, HE RAN THE FASTEST.

We met in front of the restaurant. He was standing with a spindly-legged, thin, pale, vague little girl. She would have been an angel, only her face was made up like an actress, heavy red lipstick and eye shadow and too much powder. I wanted to take my handkerchief and wipe it all off. The poor little kid. The blue eyes and the frail body and the sad look were hers. They grew out of the shadow of the tenement right up through the crowded sidewalk. There was a little of the gutter and a little of the sky in her. I could see her staying after school, lost somewhere between the two covers of a book.

And then, later, almost grown up, evening elbows on the dusty sill, looking up at the stars, clean stars, high over a Hundred and Eighteenth Street.

Miss Rosalie Goldbaum, he said, meet Mr. Al Manners. He has the column next to mine.

Oh, Sammy has told me so much about you, she said.

Sammy smiled. We walked into the Algonquin lobby. He was nineteen years old.

Dinner was what I would have called uneventful. Sammy was almost too busy looking for celebrities to pay much attention to either of us. Miss Goldbaum was shy, very sweet and frankly unaffected. Except when she talked about Sammy. And I encouraged her. Perhaps I had been misjudging Sammy, I thought. Perhaps there was another side to him. He was a thoughtful lover, and slowed down to a walk for Miss Goldbaum.

You know, Mr. Manners, she said, writing that column isn't what Sammy wants to do.

Of course not, I said; they forced it on him.

He just does that to make a living, she said.

It's a damn shame, I said.

But he writes *me* the loveliest things, she said, and some day he's going to be a great writer. Because he's a poet.

Sammy was looking across the room at George S. Kaufman. He was lost in thought. Miss Goldbaum edged her hand into his. Sammy played with it absentmindedly, like a piece of silverware.

Gee, Miss Goldbaum said, sometimes when I look at Sammy I just can't believe it, so artistic and everything, and him just a little kid right out of the Bronx.

Her tight little world was bursting with Sammy Glick. All her craving to live and her blood beating to possess and to be maternal found expression in this one little smart ass. She had little pointed breasts, miserable and sad, and they seemed to me to be reaching out for Sammy, the way black-eyed Susans tilt themselves toward the sun. She was boring me. So I caught George Kaufman's eye, and he came over, and was introduced, and had a drink with us.

Sammy was in his element, artificially gay, trying his best to out-wisecrack Kaufman. He was obsequious, sniveling, unsure of himself and very bold. It would have been funny, only I had seen Sammy too long.

Kaufman stayed only a few minutes, and soon Miss Goldbaum yawned, and I said I had a lot of work to do before getting to bed,

and Sammy looked at Miss Goldbaum and said, We both appreciate your celebrating this way with us. She nodded. Yes, Sammy
said it exactly right. And they were gone, walking down the steps
to the subway arm in arm.

When I turned to Winchell's column next morning there it
was, the bold-face print laughing up at me:

**When rising critic Sammy Glick celebrated his nineteenth birthday
yesterday at the Algonquin, Al Manners and George Kaufman were on
hand as principal cake eaters.**

You didn't have to be a mastermind to figure out how Walter
got that item, and when Sammy came in I gave him one of my
searching looks.

I see where Kaufman got himself a plug in Winchell's column,
I said.

Yeah, Sammy cracked, you should have been there.

Listen, Samuel, I came back. You got enough gall to be divided
into nine parts.

Aw, don't be sore, Al, he said. I can't keep hiding under your
desk. I gotta spread my wings a little.

You didn't even give Miss Goldbaum a break, I said. You're a
disgrace to the rodent family.

Listen, he cracked. She gets a break three times a week.

You . . . stink, I ended lamely. I was too sore to be smart.

O.K. by me, he said, walking off. Some day you'll cut off an arm
for one little whiff.

Then another thing happened. It all began when a tall, timid
guy came in with a manuscript under his arm and asked for Mr.
Glick. He had written a radio script, and since Mr. Glick was an
expert on radio he thought maybe Mr. Glick would be so kind as
to read his stuff.

I should be happy to help you, Sammy said, a little different
than he had ever talked before. I could feel at that moment
something loud and strong pumping inside that little guy, like a
piston, twisting him up and forcing him on.

After the tall guy had gone, Sammy sat down and read the stuff. He smiled as he read it, and when he hit the third page he laughed out loud.

Hey, this is good stuff, he said; funny as hell.

What's it about? I asked doubtfully.

Brand-new angle, he said. The guy won't have anything to do with the girl. So *she* kidnaps *him*. But he still says nix and gets her arrested. In the court it looks like curtains for her, but they clinch and decide to get married, and the babe is saved because he's the only witness and a guy can't testify against his own wife. Pretty hot!

The guy who wrote it came back the next week.

You have an idea here, Sammy told him. Of course it's rough, and it needs developing, but maybe with a little work we could fix it up, he said.

You mean you'll help me! said the dope.

I think I can pull something out of it, Sammy said, and then I'll give it to my agent.

Say, I didn't expect all *this*, said the dope.

When the guy had gone, Sammy asked me, Say, Al, who's a good agent for me? I want to sell this story to Hollywood. I got the title all doped out—*Girl Steals Boy*.

Why not Leland Heyward? He only manages Hepburn and a couple of dozen other stars, I said.

Is he good on stories? Sammy asked.

Pretty fair, I said. He makes a couple of thousand a week out of them.

Well, I'll think it over.

I thought that was the end of it. It should have been, if life didn't confound us ordinary sleep-and-eat people by producing geniuses like Sammy Glick. Life is choppy, full of rip tides and sudden breakers, and some guys scream once and go down, and others fight their way to the surface and still go down. Some have water wings; they have a genius for self-preservation. It's them we see when we raise our water-logged heads above the foam, floating, just floating over us as nice as you please—Sammy Glicks, every one of them.

Two weeks later Sammy rushed in, exultant and jumpy.

Shake hands with God's gift to Hollywood, he said, grabbing my hand before I had time to stick it in my pocket.

Don't use the name of the Lord in vain, I said. You mean you sold that story?

Five thousand dollars, he said. We should have had a better price, but this is my first story.

It's a disgrace, I said, five thousand.

Well, that's just the first, he said, and there's plenty more ideas where this one came from.

You mean from the guy who wrote this one, I said.

Aw, he said, he had nothing on the ball but a prayer. He's lucky I bothered with him.

Like Miss Goldbaum, I said quietly.

And all of a sudden I hated Sammy Glick. Before, I had been annoyed, or disturbed, or just revolted. This was one hundred percent American hatred.

The next morning I read something in the film section of the morning paper that revealed the fine Bronx hand of Sammy Glick:

Sammy Glick, prominent radio columnist, has sold his first screen story to Colossal for $10,000. Titled *Girl Steals Boy,* this is the first of a series Colossal has contracted for, according to Mr. Glick. Collaborating with him was Eugene Spitzer.

What I can't understand, I thought, is how Eugene Spitzer ever got mentioned at all. I was very bitter. All of a sudden I was jealous of Sammy Glick, and congratulating myself on not being like him.

One day, a week later, Sammy didn't show up at all. Maybe he's sick, I thought at first, but I quickly discounted this optimism. Guys like Sammy Glick don't get sick, unless it helps them get out of a contract, or lands them an insurance payment. The afternoon passed.

Sammy came in around suppertime. He wore a new suit. He also wore a new expression. I liked it even less than the old stock. He had a blue check shirt and a red carnation in his buttonhole. He held a cigarette loosely between his fingers. My Sammy Glick, my little copy boy.

Hello, Obnoxious, I said.

I came in to say good-bye. Sammy said. I'm off for Hollywood.

How did this happen? I asked. Metro wire that they just couldn't get along another day without you?

Not exactly, said Sammy seriously. My agent sold me to Colossal on the strength of that story.

And that's strength, I said. How about Eugene What's-his-name? Does he go too?

Colossal just wanted me, Sammy said simply.

Well, I said, our gain is Colossal's loss.

No more of these pebbles for me, Sammy said. It's two hundred and fifty bucks a week for me, starting a week from Wednesday.

There was a short pause, during which time I reviewed the history of Sammy Glick, complete from fifteen a week to two hundred and fifty. It was America, all the glory and the opportunity, the push and the speed, the grinding of gears and the crap.

|||||||

See you in the Brown Derby, Sammy was saying.

Then I got nostalgic. I was always a soft guy, and I said:

Sure, kid, and remember, don't say ain't.

That was too much for Sammy. He didn't like it. He didn't like to be reminded. There are two kinds of big shots: those who tell as many people as they can that they started out as newsboys at two dollars and peanuts a week, and those who take every step as if it were the only level they knew, those who drive ahead in high speed and never bother to look back to see where they've been. I began to have a strong hunch that Sammy fell roughly into the latter category, only more so.

I watched Sammy walk out of the office that day, and then I stood at the window and watched him as he appeared on the street below and jumped into a taxi. I sound like a sucker, but I felt just a little sorry for Sammy Glick. I felt the way I did on the commencement platform, the last day of college, watching the guys; thinking, You poor uneducated guinea pigs, you're smug, you've got no springs, and you're going to take some awful bumps. And it's not your fault; they've poured you into a mold, like Jell-O. *They* is the villain, but don't get me wrong.

I never said Sammy Glick wasn't arrogant, deceitful, four-flushing, crude, cruel—well, I could go on like this all day. But that's what Sammy learned. He learned it on the sidewalks in the Bronx and he learned it well. He knows where he's going, and he's running fast. And when you know that, when you know what makes Sammy run, you know something.

A couple of months passed, and then I got *my* break. I don't know yet how it happened; you can bet dollars to supervisors I didn't get it by stealing any stories from Eugene Spitzer. One of the Warner brothers must have got the idea to round up all the drama columnists in New York, and when they pulled in the net, there I was, floundering with the rest.

The day after the news broke that I had "surrendered to Hollywood"—it certainly wasn't a battle—a girl's voice came trembling over the telephone to me.

You probably don't remember me, she said. This is Miss Goldbaum—Rosalie Goldbaum.

Her voice sounded funny to me. It was shrill but dead, like a high note on a cheap piccolo.

I told her I was glad to hear from her again, which was a lie. I've got to see you, she said.

Oh, hell! I thought. Meet me at the Tavern at seven, I said.

I got there fifteen minutes late, and she was sitting in a booth. I noticed that her shoulder blades stuck out. Her eyes were red. When I took her hand and said, Gladtoseeyou, it was rubbery and soft, like a half-blown balloon. She said, Oh, it was so good of you to come.

There was something too intimate and uncomfortable between us.

You're looking swell, I said.

I read you were going to Hollywood, she told me. You'll see Sammy Glick.

Somehow I sensed I shouldn't wisecrack about that. I can, I said guardedly.

Will you—Mr. Manners, would you see him for me?

Sure, I said. When I run into him I'll say hello for you.

I knew it was more than that. I wanted to find out.

It's not that, she said. You could find out why he never writes, she said. Never, not once, not a single letter, and she kept mumbling it as if trying to make herself believe it was true.

Sure, I said, I can ask him; but after all, it's new to him out there, and, getting adjusted and all, it's hard to write.

||||||

Can you imagine me, defending the slob? It didn't sound convincing.

You don't understand, she said. He promised to send for me the second week he was out there. I got rid of everything I couldn't take along. I was all set. He told me not to worry; he'd send for me in a couple of weeks. He told me the only reason we couldn't go together was he didn't have the train fare. Said he'd send me his second week's salary. Now I don't know what to do.

Skunk, I said.

Tell him I don't understand, she said. Ask him why. Ask him why.

She was crying. The waiter was standing over us impatiently. It was embarrassing.

Do you want yours with onions? I asked.

She wiped her eyes with her napkin. Her mascara was running.

Before I left, I slipped her twenty-five bucks. Just to salve my conscience for knowing a slime like Sammy Glick. She put it into her purse as quickly as possible, as if her hand was trying to put something over on the rest of her.

Give me your address in Hollywood so I can pay it back, she said.

Write me care of Warner's, and tell me if you hear from him,
I said.

I looked after her as she turned down to Broadway and the
crowd sucked her in like an undertow. And I stood, thinking what
New York and Sammy Glick had done to Miss Goldbaum, this
little female toothpick of humanity, thin and straight and strong
for its size, but easy to break for a grown-up man, or a grown-up
city.

All the way out to Hollywood, Miss Goldbaum kept running
through my mind, and when I got out there, the first thing I did
was go over to Colossal and look up Sammy.

His secretary had a bigger office than our city room. She said
Mr. Glick was in a story conference.

I waited an hour and fifteen minutes. I was all steamed up about
this thing. Finally Mr. Glick made his appearance. He didn't wear
a tie. Instead he wore a big yellow scarf, with a big yellow handkerchief to match. If you put his suit on a table you could have played
checkers on it. He was no longer the thin, pale, eager little kid that
used to say, Thank you, Mr. Manners. He had one of those
California tans, and he was beginning to bulge at the waist. But
he hadn't stopped running.

Well, Al, he said, so they finally pulled you into the racket. I
didn't think you were smart enough.

We sat down in his office. His desk looked as long as the runway
in a burlesque theater. He swung his feet on to it. I noticed he
was wearing camel's-hair socks.

How's the gang? he asked. Still selling their souls for twenty
kopecks?

They all send regards, Sammy, I said.

Great old bunch, he said meaninglessly; but once you get the
Indian sign on the producers out here the dough comes rolling in
so fast you use it for wallpaper.

|||||||

Miss Goldbaum was asking for you too, I said. Sammy stopped
running for a moment. He looked at me and I knew he was

wondering how much I knew. Even through that sunburn he paled.

How is she, Al? he asked.

Swell, I said, just swell. High and dry.

I couldn't help it, he said.

He was frightened. And it's a funny thing, the poor guy meant it. He had to come out here. He had to move along. There was something in him that wouldn't be checked, something that had to run loose. And sometimes it was so strong it ran way out ahead of him. That's what Miss Goldbaum got for loving a guy like that. I guess it can happen to anyone up in the Bronx, and the Bronx is just like any place else these days, only faster and harder.

Al, he said, I'll write her. I'll tell her it just isn't the place for her: I'll send her a thousand bucks. Damn it, you know how those promises are; it could've happened to anybody.

Give her a break, Sammy, I said. And then, for no reason at all, I said, Give everybody a break.

Sure, he said, sure. What are you working on over at Warner's?

I don't know, I said. But I've got a hunch it's the ninth episode of the Mr. Wu series.

Don't be a sucker, Sammy said. Turn down the first three stories they give you. They'll think more of you.

I guess I'll be seeing you around, I said, getting up.

I sold five stories last month, said Sammy, under a different name, because I'm under contract over here.

He made no bones about it. He was glorifying the American rat. He put his arm around my neck affectionately as he walked me to the door.

Here's a hot one Lubitsch told me, he said.

I heard that three weeks ago in "21," I told him when he finished.

Just one more tip, he said. If you want to get into the real dough out here, write something on the outside. Write a play. Like me. When I get it produced it will be twenty-five hundred a week and my terms.

I'll do it tonight when I get home, I said.

Eight weeks later, when I was still waiting for an assignment, I get a little printed notice in the mail: Mr. Samuel Glick requests the pleasure of my company at the opening of his play, *Live Wire*, at the Hollywood Playhouse.

Sammy's car picked me up that night and brought me to his apartment. He was having a cocktail with Public Beauty Number One. Sixty million people would hock their lives to shake this girl's paw, and here was Sammy gurgling champagne with her.

Well, the play was really pretty good. The scene was a radio station and there was plenty of excitement and fireworks. All the time I keep thinking this seems awfully familiar. And then I think maybe I just dreamed it, like people do sometimes.

One or two people yell, Author, author! and Sammy takes a bow, and someone sets a basket of roses on the stage, and all of a sudden it is a big success and I am sitting next to a hit author, and everyone is stepping over me to shake his hand, and he is modestly denying that he must have worked very hard on it, saying it just came easy, three or four nights' work, and then every one is amazed, and someone says a new genius has come to Hollywood, and Sammy says, Oh, I wouldn't say that exactly.

Going out the lobby, Sammy said he was thirsty, and I said come up to my place and have a drink; but Sammy said, How about the Brown Derby? because he wanted to see more people.

And the Beauty said, The Vine or the Beverly Hills? I guess she would have liked to go to both.

So we got to one or the other, and it took Sammy ten minutes to get to a table, so many people flocked around him and his favorite star, and all the time I'm trying to think where I saw this play before.

Finally, when the Beauty said, Excuse me, I have to comb my hair, and went out to the ladies' room—even movie idols do—Sammy said, Well, Al, you haven't told me what you think about the play.

||||||

I think it's just like something else I've seen, I said.

You're pretty smart, he said.

All of a sudden it came to me: *Five-Star Final*!

As long as you know, he said. I might as well tell you. I used exactly the same construction as *Five-Star Final,* scene for scene, only I changed the characters, and I made it funny.

Those people don't know what a genius you are, I said.

The star came back, stopping at three tables en route.

Sammy, she said, when will you write a play for me?

When he can find one, I said.

I don't want to write for you until I feel something great, Sammy said, something that's—you.

She moved closer to him.

I gotta go, I said. Thanks for everything. It was an evening I'll never forget.

Good-bye, Mr. Masters, she said, feeling very proud and democratic that she had remembered my name.

I didn't see Sammy for six months after that. But I used to read about him in the papers. *Live Wire* went to New York and he sold it back to Colossal for a hundred fifty thousand. Then Parsons carried a story that he and the Beauty were secretly married, but both their agents denied it, and finally they said, We're just good friends, very good friends. Then DeMille got him to write his recent epic.

The next time I saw him was at the preview of my first picture at Pasadena. I ran into him in the lobby on my way out.

Hello, Sammy, I said.

You've got some smart stuff here, Al, he said, but the story line isn't straight enough.

||||||

No, I said; it isn't exactly *Five-Star Final.*

He didn't bat an eye. After all, he said, there's only one *Five-Star Final.*

I was about to say something, but Sammy's limousine was at the curb and he was gone. I got involved in a story conference on the sidewalk, but I couldn't keep my mind on it. The more I thought about Sammy the more I realized he had more drama than all my characters put together. My little office boy was going up. He was a human rocket. Would he reach the moon, or would he break like a Fourth-of-July firework, splattering his sparks into the sea?

By the time Al had finished his story, the Derby was completely empty. He and the other guy looked at each other in silence. Al stared at the caricature of President Roosevelt above the door. As he stared, an aggressive little man, a little dark ferret of a man, pushed the door open energetically and stood expectantly awaiting the headwaiter. He was followed by four others, all of whom seemed to be talking to him at once.

There he is now, Al said.

Speak of the devil, said his friend.

Of course everything I told you is confidential, said Al, strictly on the q.t.

Hollywood is a jungle and the smaller animals have to run for their lives.

Mr. Glick and his party came down the aisle. He saw Al, and stopped.

Hello, Al. How's tricks?

Can't complain. You're looking good, Al said.

That's the funny angle on this whole thing, said Al, studying his glass, after Sammy had passed. My agent tells me I may go to work for him next week. And I'd still rather have my name on a Sammy Glick production than any picture in town.

"LOVE COMES TO SAMMY GLICK"

Leaning against a lamppost outside the theater, Sammy Glick could hear them. The preview had been over for three minutes. They were still clapping. He had done it again.

His pal Tony Kreuger came over. Tony was an agent, his clothes were made on Bond Street, and he sent his sainted mother two hundred bucks a week. He spent the rest on broads and night-clubs. He had a talent for showing Sammy a good time. Sammy wasn't exactly backward, but he never had time to learn how to talk to women, he took them as they came. He had enough to do, just getting ahead.

"Well, kid," Tony said, blowing him a kiss, "it's a sweetheart!"

Sammy nodded, ahead of him. "I clocked a hundred and six-teen laughs."

"Some of World-Wide's other pictures could have used a few of them," Tony said. "Outside of your three the program stank up the studio."

Sammy watched the people as they squeezed out into the lobby. The stars of the picture cut their way through to him, leaving desperate autograph hunters rocking in their wake.

"You were O.K.," Sammy told the stars.

They smiled. They were modest and gracious. They told him it was a pleasure to work with him.

"O.K.," Sammy said, "so next time don't try to tell me you don't like the part."

He grinned after them. "When they go soft on you—that's the time to sock it home!" he said to Tony.

Out of the crowd came a middle-aged man who wore his clothes like someone who had been successful a long time. He was one of those tall, aristocratic men just beginning to lose the glow of handsomeness.

"Well, my boy," he said, "I'm afraid you've done it again."

Sammy shook his hand seriously. "Thanks, Mr. Boyce," he said, "let's hope so."

He had learned how to be polite to his superiors now. He still called the studio production chief Mr. Boyce. He called him Grandma behind his back.

They stood on the curb talking cutting and last-minute story points as the crowd drifted away.

"I have only one real objection—that it gets started too quickly," Boyce said mildly. "What do you think, Sammy?"

"Let's look at it again in the morning," Sammy said.

Boyce walked on toward his big black Packard limousine. "The corpse is going back to his hearse," Sammy cracked to Tony.

Boyce sank into the back seat and closed his eyes as the car started. Sammy stood on the curb looking after him.

"Where do we go from here?" he asked Tony.

"Swing Club," Tony said.

"Who've you got?" Sammy wanted to know.

"Same old Peggy," Tony said.

"Don't you ever get tired of it?" Sammy asked. "That's all she's good for."

"That's just the point," Tony agreed. "She's nothing but a hayride and she knows it. At least she never bugs me about auditions and screen tests like the other broads."

"And what did you get for me?" Sammy said.

"Something new," Tony said. "Sally Ann Joyce."

"Is she O.K.?" Sammy asked.

"I picked her up in the beauty parlor at the Roosevelt," Tony said. "And when she gives you a facial . . ."

It was like every other evening, a montage of hot riffs, champagne, wisecracks, Swing Club, come-ons, feelies, promises. The music had been loud and distorted, it had taken old melodies and twisted them like hairpins, it was a symphony strictly from hunger, the four of them beating their feet to anguish and festered ambition, rocking to the beat of a selfish muse.

When it was all over, Sammy's girl kissed him at the door. "So long, baby," he said, patting her, "you were swell."

"Thanks," Sally Ann said, "it takes two. We'll do a repeat."

"You're the boss," Sammy said.

"Sure," she said, "and I know you—you're the cute little blonde who wants a screen test."

Sammy grinned. She was a good kid. The town was full of good kids.

Sammy was right on time for his appointment with Boyce. They met in the projection room. Sammy asked him how he was.

Boyce said he was fine. He didn't look fine. He was beginning to look tired when he got up in the morning. He looked at Sammy's stocky, concentrated figure. It was taking on weight, but it was taking on power, too. Somehow, he was glad when the lights went out.

They looked at the first reel of the picture.

"You're right about the opening, any more footage would kill it," Boyce said.

"I'm glad you see it my way, Mr. Boyce," Sammy said.

Walking back to their offices, Boyce said to Sammy, "Will you drop down to my office for a few minutes?"

The office was spacious, though it wasn't exactly Sammy's idea of the real place for a big shot. Full of English antiques and real books.

Boyce filled his pipe, trying to begin.

"I won't beat around the bush," he said. "I like to think I can talk to you like a friend."

"You bet you can," Sammy said.

"I'm in a spot," Boyce went on, "and I think you can help me."

"Shoot," Sammy said confidently.

"I don't suppose you know that the bankers are coming out next week," Boyce said. "They've got control of World-Wide now and they want to look over our production set-up."

Sammy had found that out from Boyce's secretary weeks before. "No," he said, "I didn't know that."

"Well, then, I'll level with you," Boyce said. And he told Sammy the whole thing. Boyce's pictures had been falling off. There was something in the wind about the bankers coming out to choose a new production chief. They wanted to know why the only three real moneymakers on the program had been Sammy Glick's.

Boyce paused. He couldn't tell anybody he knew Sammy's record was a thousand percent because he had managed to slip his name off every picture that was going sour.

"Money talks," Boyce said. "The right word from you may do the trick. And if I'm back in harness again, you'll handle the five biggest properties on next year's program."

Sammy's expression didn't change. "You're in, Geoffrey," he said. "Let them come to me. I'll give them an earful. And it will come from right here." He tapped his heart dramatically.

Sammy had been just barely listening. When Sammy first came to World-Wide, he was a smart kid and Geoffrey Boyce was a dignified genius. He had made up his mind to be Boyce's assistant if it killed him. Now in ten unexpected minutes he had wriggled up out of his respect for Boyce, leaving it behind to blow away like a snake's skin.

But then, as Boyce went on speaking in that quiet, cultivated way, Sammy remembered that there was a difference. There was a reason why Boyce had never invited him to his home socially, there was a reason why Boyce's friends were brokers and horse-women and civic leaders while Sammy trucked to swing music with Tony and the Peggys and the always Sally Anns. This was a new world into which Sammy couldn't run. He would have to crawl.

"You're giving a party for those bankers, aren't you?"

"I suppose I have to," Boyce said.

"Then get a load of this," Sammy said. "Why let the bankers search me out? Why not have me right there, smacking them in the face, showing them you and I are like this?"

"Of course," Boyce said. "Thanks, Sammy."

"Forget it," Sammy said. "I should thank you."

When Sammy returned to his office, his secretary showed him a clipping from the morning edition of the evening paper. *Is Sammy Glick's heart Suzy-Q-ing for filmcutie Sally Ann Joyce?*

"Get that dumb broad on the phone," he told his secretary, "and tell her to lay off the press releases. And next time they juggle my name with any of those floozies, get them to deny it. And if Tony Kreuger calls me, tell him I'm out."

"Turning over a new leaf, Mr. Glick?"

"Yeah," he said, unabashed, "and don't forget to burn the old ones. Glick marches on."

The night of the dinner party, Sammy arrived just on time, but he didn't feel as sure of himself as usual. He felt subdued. Sammy recognized Harrington from his pictures. A. J. Harrington. The brains of the company. And Sammy was going to meet him right here in this room. Harrington was perfectly cast for his part. Tall, athletic, early fifties, a sort of Charles Evans Hughes still able to wield a polo mallet.

While Harrington was shaking hands, a woman came into the room. She was something to stare at, tall, handsome, elegant. To Sammy she seemed like something that had just stepped out of a Saks Fifth Avenue window.

"Mr. Glick, I want you to meet Miss Harrington," Boyce said.

She was the most untouchable woman he had ever seen. He stood there staring at her, and bowed stiffly.

"My father has talked about you," she said.

He saw that she was taller than he was.

"I'm very glad, Miss Harrington," Sammy said.

"Why?" she laughed. "You don't know what he said yet."

"That's right," Sammy said. "How stupid of me." He knew that wasn't just what he meant to say.

"As a matter of fact," she said, "You're not being stupid at all. Father raved about your pictures." Her eyes were laughing at him. She knew how to make him feel small and uncomfortable.

Sammy said, "I hope you did, too."

"I haven't seen them," she said. "I've been in Europe all summer."

"I'm afraid you'll never miss them," Sammy laughed weakly.

"You shouldn't be so modest," she said.

"After all, they're just moving pictures," Sammy said uncomfortably. "I mean they won't live, or anything."

"I have a feeling modesty doesn't become you," she said.

He offered her his arm as they went in to dinner. He wondered if she was smiling because she knew he had never done that before.

The only one who seemed to have a good time at dinner was Miss Harrington. To the Boyces it was too obvious that this was only the lull, the seven-course, elaborately served lull before the storm. Paine, the other banker, and Harrington knew it, too. Sammy sat next to Miss Harrington, trying to think of the right thing to say, conscious of her smooth white arms close to him, watching her all the time out of the corner of his eye, casting a quick glance now and then at the revealing semicircles that plunged seductively into her low-cut dinner gown, trying to see behind the pride and the elegant aloofness of that face.

Mr. Harrington frowned, watching them. Laurette had found another victim. He hoped Mr. Glick wasn't the sensitive kind.

Laurette went on talking, went on mocking, asking Sammy how pictures were made, what he thought of the medium as an art form, whether he thought Gainsborough would have made a good cameraman.

But nothing she could say could insult Sammy, it would only give him a line on how to proceed; he was beginning to get ideas. He thought back to the women he had known, Rosalie Goldbaum, scrawny and sincere, lost track of years ago; then all the Sally Ann Joyces. This was something new, worth being insulted for. This was Class, and Class was something strange and wonderful to Sammy.

After dinner the men assembled in the den.

"I hope my daughter didn't upset you," Harrington remarked.

"Upset me!" Sammy said. "Nothing upsets me. She's been charming."

Then they talked business and Sammy made a fine showing. If the box-office drop was due partly to general recession and partly to double features, he had a solution for both problems. He had a way of talking fast that sounded so sure.

"It's young men like you who are going to lick this thing," Harrington said.

"I wish there were more of them," Paine snapped. "In my time there were more men who wanted to get rich fast. It made them hop."

"It's slower going these days," Sammy said. "You've got to be tougher."

When the guests had gone, Boyce asked Sammy to stay on.

"Good work, Sammy," he said. "You made a fine impression."

"It's a cinch," Sammy said. "It's like choking babies."

"I suppose they made an appointment with you," Boyce asked.

"No," Sammy said, "but Miss Harrington is having lunch with me at the studio tomorrow."

"Good idea to have her on our side," Boyce said. "Harrington thinks a lot of her."

"Same here," Sammy said. "She's like the beautiful heiress in pictures whom the boy mistakes for a working girl. I didn't know there really were any dames like that!"

Laurette kept him waiting thirty-five minutes for lunch next day. Then she came in, apologizing carelessly, and they shook hands. Her suit was mannish, but to Sammy there was nothing masculine about her. The cut of her jacket implied a subtle sex appeal. He looked her over from head to foot as she came toward him, completely satisfied that his first impression of her was justified. Maybe it was better to come out of the Bronx because Class meant something to you when you finally hit the real thing.

Laurette wasn't very hungry. A salad would be sufficient. It seemed barbaric to eat anything more on these hot Hollywood afternoons. Sammy said he supposed she was right. He had just ordered frankfurters and sauerkraut.

Sammy could feel her watching him intently while he ate. He felt himself trying nervously to eat as neatly as possible.

"How do you like Hollywood?" Sammy asked between mouthfuls.

"I can't tell yet," she said. "We have better restaurants in New York and more fun in Newport. I mean, I can't tell until I get to know you people better."

"You don't talk at all like I expected," Sammy said.

"That's because I'm one of those new models," Laurette said. "Custom-made. Not for the general public."

"They should be," Sammy said.

"Why?" she asked. "You're not in the market for one, are you?"

They walked back to the office without saying much.

At the main entrance Sammy held her hand a moment too long. He wanted to see what she would do. Her only reaction was a smile. He felt like the little boy in Sunday School who has just brought the young teacher flowers.

"Thanks," she said. "You were really charming."

"When will I see you again?" he asked.

"Now I know who puts that chestnut in all the movies," she said.

Sammy tightened up. He had thrown himself across every puddle instead of the cape, and it wasn't paying off. He started up the stairs toward his office. "O.K.," he said. "You win, lady."

The next evening, Sammy called her. She was alone in Hollywood, he said. She might want someone to show her the bright spots.

"How thoughtful of you," Laurette said. "Come right over."

When he arrived at her apartment, Sammy's enthusiasm froze. She was having cocktails with a young man. The young man stood up. Sammy found himself staring into a broad expanse of stiff shirt. Laurette was in evening clothes, too.

"George was on his way to the air meet at Albuquerque. I thought it might be fun if we all went out together."

George didn't seem to mind Sammy at all.

"I haven't seen Laurie since Biarritz last summer," he explained.

They talked about Biarritz. Had Sammy ever been there?

Sammy said, "Listen, Miss Harrington, don't let me butt in. Why don't you two kids run along without me?"

"We wouldn't think of it. Mr. Glick is so clever," Laurette said. "He knows everything about making pictures. He's going to tell us all about it at dinner. Aren't you, Mr. Glick?"

Sammy tried to turn the compliment aside, if it was a compliment. But he couldn't do it deftly enough. Laurette kept laughing at him silently and politely, her superiority piercing Sammy's pride like *banderillas*, stinging, hurting, forcing fiercer fighting.

They found a table downstairs in the Florentine Room. Sammy felt better when he beat George to it by ordering the most expensive wine on the list. But when it was brought, Laurette said, "If you haven't got the 1931, don't bother. That's the only good year."

The orchestra was playing a tango. George asked Sammy if he would be good enough to excuse them. "Go ahead," Sammy said, "don't let me stop you." Sammy didn't know how to tango. He wasn't surprised to find that Laurette could dance it like a pro. He sat there like a stupe, burning, deciding that Laurette had only asked him up here to show him up. Perhaps the thing to do was to take a powder and deprive her of this satisfaction. But he couldn't, his eyes took every step with her. When she danced she closed her eyes, that lithe, graceful body swaying, poised a tempting moment, swaying on again to the sensual rhythm.

Then they returned to the table, and Sammy stood up, feeling challenged and sore, and popped down too quickly again.

"A beautiful dance," Laurette said. "You feel wild and free."

She knew Sammy had never felt wild and free.

The music was back to jazz. Sammy was going to show her. He nodded toward the dance floor, and they rose together. He held her tight against him, frankly and crudely, enjoying the double satisfaction, the feel of her so close to him, and the chance that this would hit the columns.

Sammy was a stiff, crude dancer but he was a strong leader. She knew from the moment he pressed his hand stubbornly on her back, forcing her to follow all his mistakes. She saw how insistent he was, how unapologizing, uncompromising when she tried to press him out of the simple box step he refused to vary. It was a struggle, both of them felt it, and Sammy was enjoying it at last.

"You dance divinely," she said.

"Listen," he said. "You don't have to hand me that. I know how I dance." He was beginning to find himself.

"Have it your way," she said. "You'll never be Fred Astaire."

"Wanna quit?" Sammy said.

"No," she said, "I'm enjoying it."

She was. He was terrifying when he held her like that, not trying to be polite any more.

At twelve o'clock George said he had to go.

"Nice fellow," Sammy said. "Old friend?"

"The world is full of nice fellows."

They talked until three o'clock.

Sammy told her what he expected to do in the world.

She told him it must be marvelous to want to do anything.

"You don't have to try," Sammy said. "You've got everything. I want everything, too."

Sammy was pleased, knowing he was getting to her. She must have realized it, too, for suddenly she said, "I don't know why I'm telling you all this. I really don't like you very much."

"And me just sitting here with you all night to make a hit with your old man!" Sammy said. "How do you like that?"

Sammy drove home seventy miles an hour. I'm going to get her, he thought. She's Class and I'm going to get her. Me. Sammy Glick.

Mr. Harrington invited Sammy to lunch with him at Victor Hugo's next day. "My daughter's told me a lot about you," he said cheerfully. "You've made quite an impression."

"What a marvelous girl," Sammy said. "You must be very proud."

They talked about business. Harrington didn't waste words. "Only three pictures really made any money this year," he said. "Your three. How do you account for it?"

"I don't know," Sammy fenced. "Boyce did the best he could."

"The reason we're out here," Harrington continued, "is to find out if his best is good enough."

"It isn't entirely his fault if production costs are too high."

"Then you think costs are too high?" Harrington pounced.

Sammy hesitated just long enough. "You put me in a difficult position, Mr. Harrington. I don't like to talk against my boss."

"Naturally, my boy," Harrington agreed. "But this is serious. Think it over and we'll get together later in the week."

That evening Boyce called Sammy in. "You lunched with Harrington today. You're not double-crossing me, are you, Sammy?"

"Hell, no," Sammy said. "Christ, I fought for you."

"How does it look?" Boyce said. "I'm depending on you. You know how it is in the studio. You're the last friend I have."

"All I need is more time, Geoffrey," Sammy said.

Every time Laurette came home from an evening with Sammy she was too bored ever to want to see him any more. Every time he called again, she accepted. He called every night. He never let up. He was always the same.

For Sammy Glick these were unforgettable days. In his most ambitious flights of ambition, he had never looped so many loops so high.

Then came the evening when Sammy invited Laurette to his home for dinner. Just the two of them. She wore a strapless, crimson evening dress that clung to her bare powdered shoulders. There was more splendor to her than Sammy had ever known in the world.

Sammy's butler served martinis. They drank together, feeling important, mellow and alone. Tension between them was evaporating.

"This reminds me of a night I spent in Venice," Laurette said.

"Why?" Sammy said. "It sure doesn't remind me of the Bronx. Forget about Venice. Everything I ever heard about Venice sounded like a lot of crap."

"Mr. Glick, how romantic," she said.

"How about thinking about us?" Sammy said.

She only smiled at him, and he trembled, determined to get her. She was so beautiful. It was romance. She was gorgeous, she was refined and irresistible, and—he kept cheering himself on—Sammy Glick was going to get her.

It was even better after dinner.

"Look at that garden," Sammy said. "I've got a swell garden."

They walked down the steps. His arm went around her waist. She drew away and he moved with her. She smiled at him and the arm remained, holding her tightly at the hip.

"How do you like those big red flowers?" Sammy asked.

"Hibiscus," she said. "Lovely—'Rose red, princess hibiscus, rolling her pointed Chinese petals!' "

"Christ!" Sammy said. "What's that?"

"A poem I like about hibiscus," she said.

"Princess hibiscus," Sammy said. "That's swell. Just like you." He suddenly kissed her lips. He felt like a million bucks. Her million bucks.

They had reached the teahouse at the end of the lawn. "Let's go in here," Sammy said. "It's getting cold."

"No," she said. "There's still a warm breeze. No, Sammy."

But he was kissing her again and she was only *saying* no and don't. That meant she couldn't stop him. They went into the teahouse. It was an old rule of Sammy's: When they go soft on you—that's the time to sock it home!

Chalk up another victory for Sammy Glick. She had been terrified, she had clung to him, he was stronger and he had won, as he had always won.

It was getting colder. "We'd better go inside, baby," Sammy said afterwards. He felt dizzy with his achievement.

"I must go home," she said. "Call me a taxi."

"I love you," Sammy said. "I know it sounds screwy to say it. You're the first thing I ever loved."

Then she was gone.

He stood there in awe of himself. Sammy Glick in love. He felt important, released. His whole life had been a dare. This had been the most outrageous of all. Who could stop him now? Sammy Glick and Laurette Harrington—Laurette Harrington and Sammy Glick, Sammy Glick . . .

Next day Sammy had lunch with Harrington again.

"I have something important to tell you—to ask you. I'll give it to you straight. Only way I know how to deal. I want to marry Laurette."

"You love her?" Harrington asked. "You're sure?"

"A thousand percent," Sammy said. "I'm the kind of a guy who doesn't fall in love easy—but I was sold on Laurette right off the bat. I was afraid I wasn't good enough for her. But then I got to thinking nobody gets anywhere by blushing and tossing in the towel. So here I am, banging on the old door."

Harrington was thinking it over. There were crazier ideas. He knew that times were changing. He was still on the board of directors, but he had a feeling things were not really safe. Not even Laurette knew how worried he had been. And any fool could see this Sammy kid was on his way. Sammy might be a sound investment.

"Of course, it's not up to me," Harrington said. "Laurette's always done everything she wants."

"I'm asking her tonight," Sammy said positively.

"Fine," Harrington said. "I see no objection. Have you thought any more about the studio set-up? Paine and I have more or less decided Boyce isn't right for it any more."

"You couldn't find anyone better than Boyce," Sammy said. "Among the older producers."

"But maybe the studio needs young blood," Harrington said. He wondered what Laurette would say to Sammy. Things had moved quickly. A son-in-law in power in Hollywood might not hurt him on the board.

That night Sammy proposed to Laurette.

"But I haven't even told you I loved you," Laurette said.

"But you couldn't have done what you did if you hadn't loved me," Sammy argued. "I would never have tried if I wasn't sure you did."

"You're always sure, aren't you?" she asked. Her father had already told her he thought the marriage was a good thing. But she knew it was more than that. She would never have known how to turn him down. He was so set on it she had the feeling a tidal wave would sweep up across Hollywood if she said no.

"This is the greatest day of my life," Sammy said. "Baby, you and me are going to have everything we want in the world."

The next afternoon Boyce called Sammy in. He had aged. Sammy was startled to see how old he looked.

"Well, Sammy," he said, "I want to thank you."

"Thank me!" Sammy said. "What for?"

"I just got through talking with Harrington," Boyce said. "He told me you did everything you could for me—but the board back east had already decided. They want you."

"I'm sorry, Geoffrey. If there's anything I can do . . ."

"Thanks," Boyce said. "Nobody can really help anybody else these days. You've got your own worries."

"Sure," Sammy said. "We all have." He knew he didn't have any worries. The world was his kite. All he had to do was let out more string. Up, up, up!

Then Harrington and Paine announced that Mr. Samuel Glick was the new chief executive of World-Wide. The first thing Sammy did was remodel Boyce's office. He wanted something much bigger, and much more modern.

One week later Harrington had the honor to announce the engagement of his daughter Laurette to Mr. Samuel Glick.

The day of the announcement Sammy wrote the first letter he hadn't dictated in two years. It was to his mother in the Bronx.

Dear Mama—

I can hardly believe it is your little Sammy writing you, so many wonderful things have happened to me. Now I'm the whole boss of the studio. But that isn't what I wanted to write you about. Mama, don't be worried, I am going to marry the finest girl in the world. Oh sure, she may be rich and ritzy but I just want you to know that I never forget what you told me about getting married when I left home—that a good, simple wife meant more than anything I might ever do. But Mama, no matter how perfect this all is for me, it wouldn't be right if you weren't here to meet the bride and be at the wedding. So I am enclosing a thousand bucks. Buy some nice clothes and start out here on the Super Chief. I want you to be as happy as I am. Your loving son,

Sammy

The next morning Sammy's secretary called in and said Tony Kreuger was on the phone.

"Hello, Tony," he said. "What's new, kid?"

"Same old merry-go-round," Tony said. "You seem to have a corner on the news these days."

"I know it," Sammy said. "I guess I'm a lucky guy."

"All kidding aside," Tony said with a sudden note of sincerity,

"I think it's swell, pal, I'm tickled to death for you, and the beauty of the thing is you deserved it."

"That's damned nice of you, Tony—anything else on your mind?"

"I was wondering if I could throw a stag for you Saturday night," Tony said. "Get some of the old gang in."

On the morning of the stag party, Laurette called Sammy for lunch. "I've just bought a new sport dress, darling," she said, "so I thought we might go Vendoming."

Sammy was sorry—he was working so hard now he only had a sandwich and a milkshake sent in. But he'd drop in for cocktails.

"All right for you," Laurette chided. "Throw me into the arms of other men."

"They know me well enough to throw you right back," Sammy said.

That afternoon, as she smiled across the table at Gordie Melville, the Australian who ran a local fencing school and doubled for swashbucklers like Errol Flynn, she wondered if Sammy was right. She wondered at the way his insolence had first amused her, then overwhelmed her—and now? She studied Gordie carefully. He would smile when she smiled, and if she leaned forward he would meet her at the middle of the table. She liked to do it. It brought back that necessary sense of superiority. She would not let Sammy crush it. Maybe, if she laughed with Gordie, she could rediscover her kind of pride again.

Late that day Sammy dropped in for cocktails at Laurette's. She met him in a green satin lounging robe. They kissed. "Couldn't you possibly stay tonight?" she asked.

"No chance, honey," Sammy said. "Can't let the boys down."

"I wish you didn't have to go," she said.

"There'll be thousands of nights from now on, huh, honey?" He patted her affectionately. He still couldn't picture himself doing that, but there it was.

The stag turned out to be an elegant affair at the Ambassador. It was the final victory dinner, with two hundred of Hollywood's more prominent males doing him homage. And Sammy was king of them all. As he came in, they all stood up, raised champagne glasses and droned, "Poor Sammy, poor Sammy," but Sammy could laugh because he had met the enemy and they were his.

Sammy took the seat of honor, with Tony at his right hand. It was the beginning of a dizzy, exultant, triumphant evening. Over and over again, Sammy told Tony and every other willing listener how he rose from newsboy on the east side. Sammy was feeling great. He got up and made a speech. Then the lights went blue and purple and a gorgeous stripper took off the last bead. Sammy drank more champagne in the dark, smiling to himself. This was what he wasn't going to marry and he felt cocky inside and out.

"How about dropping up to the apartment for a while? Remember Peggy and Sally Ann?—I told 'em to meet me there—said I might bring you along." It was Tony.

"You can take Peggy and Sally Ann both and . . ." Sammy began and stopped. "Sorry," he finished. "Not tonight."

"One little nightcap," Tony begged.

"Not tonight," Sammy insisted. "Thanks, Tony."

"Not going moral on me?" Tony asked.

"I'm afraid it's too late," Sammy said, more stubbornly. "Maybe some other time, huh?"

"Sure," Tony agreed, changing his tone. "We'll be seeing each other."

Sammy was gladder he hadn't given in when he hit the fresh air. He had to see Laurette, cool, refreshing and clean like the wind that whistled past his car as he raced to her. It was two-thirty in the morning, he swayed up the steps to her door, drunker now on backslaps and self-approbation than anyone would ever be on champagne.

He let himself in with his key. She had given him a key. Something seemed wrong with the house. Maybe he shouldn't have come. But hadn't she asked him to spend the night? One little reassuring *shtup* and he'd be on his way.

Then he noticed what was wrong. The lights. They were all on, and the radio blaring. He stopped still, like any animal, listening. He heard laugher, a duet, low and intimate.

Not alone. He swayed there in the hallway, eyes bulging, suddenly sober. Yelling, "Laurette—Laurette!"

She came straight at him from the living room, pulling her robe tighter around her, that green satin.

Her voice was vicious and low. Drunken and passionate, ugly and hoarse to Sammy. "Well?"

He waited for her to alibi, apologize, plead, curse, weep. But that was all she said. He waited for her to go on, beg forgiveness; he wanted her to wilt beneath his righteous stare, but she only stood there, not bothering to hold the robe so closely around her any more, stood there proud and composed, stately and cruelly self-possessed. These were the elements he loved and admired and aspired to, and he hated them, he wanted suddenly to hide from them. He would make no scene, he would never ask her who was there. And she had been ready to tell him, she was all set to say, "Gordie Melville, dear," and look at him, and watch him wilt like yesterday's gardenia, knowing he could not crush her any more, letting him know the Gordon Melvilles would be her barricade.

Sammy only stared, their future running through his mind like ticker tape:

Mr. and Mrs. Glick held a house-warming at their charming Bel Air home Mr. and Mrs. Glick are celebrating their fifth anniversary with a three-month European tour Please tell Mrs. Glick not to expect me home tonight Mrs. Glick is calling from Honolulu, sir Mrs. Glick and I are only too glad to accept your weekend invitation Among those at the opening were Mr. Glick and his charming wife dazzling in white sequins and ermine Mr. and Mrs. Glick . . .

They were going to have everything they wanted.

"I'll call you in the morning," Sammy said almost in a whisper. "We have to meet my mother at the train at six."

She smiled at him boldly. "I was planning on it," she said.

Then she came toward him, calmly took his face in her two hands, and kissed him as if they had been married twenty years.

He never remembered walking down the stairs out into the open again. The sobbing came only when the door was shut behind him. Tight, strained, hysterical little sobs he tried futilely to choke. And then he couldn't hold it any longer. He sat down on the last step and cried into his nervous little hands.

It was all over in a minute. He wiped his face with his silk initialed handkerchief, got behind the wheel of his roadster, and the next stop was Tony's apartment.

Ten minutes later he was with Tony and Peggy and Sally Ann. The all-night station was booming. "Here we are—back in the Swing Club," the announcer said.

Sally Ann jumped up and did a funny little dance to it. "Remember, honey? It's just like last time!"

Sammy didn't smile. Then Tony came over and stuck a drink in his hand.

"Well, kid," he said, "I told you so—only even I didn't figure it's happening this fast. What a man!"

"You called it all right," Sammy admitted.

"Just since that night in the Swing Club!" Tony marveled. "In charge of all production, and married to big money. Eastern money. Baby, I've got to hand it to you."

"You said it, Tony, I got Hollywood right where I want it—on its back!" Sammy whacked Sally Ann on her pretty little ass and she laughed appreciatively. He told Peggy to turn the radio up loud, the all-night jazz station. "Stompin' at the Savoy . . ." He tossed off his drink and brought his live little hands together in a sudden clap of defiance. "Fuck 'em all! A one-way ticket on the fast express! I'm sitting pretty!"

AFTERWORD

In 1939—no, it can't be almost fifty years ago!—this writer took his leave of Hollywood to go east, specifically back to his *second* alma mater, Dartmouth College, to write a book about his *first* alma mater, Hollywood. He had been taken there when he was four. His father, B.P., a twenty-six-year-old pioneer photoplay-writer, had worked himself up the movie ladder to producer and partner of L.B. Mayer in the now-forgotten, downtown Los Angeles Mayer-Schulberg Studio. By the time I was running the *Blue-and-White* daily, and a mediocre half-mile for L.A. High, Mayer and my old man had become bitter rivals, L. B. running MGM and B.P. running Paramount.

After Dartmouth and three years as apprentice screen writer for three legendary moguls, David Selznick, Walter Wanger and Sam Goldwyn, I was ready to leave Hollywood because I had learned from years of watching and a few years of personal frustration that in the dream factories the writer was low man on the totem pole.

Whether you made $100 a week or $2,500, you and your story ideas, your scenes, your completed screenplays, were shuffled like cards by the studio heads and their usually sycophantic assistants then known as "supervisors."

Everyone who goes into the writing life has hopes and dreams. But *Sammy* was to endure beyond my rosiest fantasies. In 1952, it was included in the Modern Library, and I wondered if the name listed between Schopenhauer and Shakespeare belonged to me. In 1960, NBC presented a two-part television version starring Larry Blyden as Sammy and John Forsythe as his Boswell, Al Manheim. Then a musical version starring Steve Lawrence ran for two years on Broadway. Year after year, paperback editions continued to appear, most recently in the late seventies with an Author's Afterword speculating as to whether a Sammy Glick, greedy for political power, had taken over the White House a few years earlier.

Despite its long life in other forms, once the all-powerful Mayer put it on his *ex cathedra* list, *Sammy* had remained a Hollywood untouchable. But now, after all the years of ostracism my father had predicted for the book at the hands of the original moguls, *What Makes Sammy Run?* has finally broken through the studio gates. A new generation of studio heads, fresh out of film schools or rock music, have practically forgotten Louie Mayer and his Doge-like taboos.

Today, as we begin to address the problem of putting *Sammy* on screen, and to reappraise the contemporary significance of Sammy Glick, I find myself challenged by the question: What has happened in America—or is it *to* America?—that has so drastically changed our perception of Sammy Glick from dread repugnance to upwardly mobile acceptance, if not actual admiration and emulation?

When I first took the book to Random House almost half a

century ago, Sammy's chances for enduring fame, on a scale of one to ten, seemed to hover around zero. Bennett Cerf, my publisher, warned the neophyte novelist to expect the worst. Even if it enjoyed good reviews, Cerf went on, the chances for commercial success were virtually nil. It was the cold verdict of the publishing world that there simply was no market, and precious few readers, for a Hollywood novel. The horror stories abounded. Only the year before, *The Day of the Locust* had not earned back its $500 advance to Nathanael West—that premature absurdist and avid hunter—who had to keep on grinding out western-movie scripts at Republic to keep food on the table and shells in his shotgun. The popular hobo writer Jim Tully, the up-and-coming John O'Hara . . . all had come a cropper on the Hollywood novel. Even when *Sammy* won enthusiastic advance notice from a trio of literary heavy hitters, O'Hara, Dorothy Parker and Scott Fitzgerald, Cerf stood by his first printing of twenty-five hundred copies, and promised if the book sale exceeded what he considered a rosy estimate, he would wine and dine me at "21."

"The problem is that people who read novels have no interest in Hollywood, and the people who go to movies don't read books," Cerf pontificated. It sounded reasonable. I was prepared to paste the O'Hara and Fitzgerald letters in a scrapbook for my young family while going back to screenwriting to support them.

But soon after publication, I was at "21" with Bennett Cerf not once but month after month, as the book took off in a way none of us had foreseen. *The New York Times* gave it the equivalent of four stars: "Best first-novel of the year." In Hollywood, it was the *succès de scandale* my veteran producer/father had feared. "You'll never work in this town again," he had written me after reading it. "How will you live?" From the moment the book dared show its face in Hollywood bookstore windows, I was marked "traitor." Sam Goldwyn, literally turning purple with anger, fired me. Hedda Hopper, the columnist who could make or break careers, accosted me in a popular Hollywood restaurant with "Humph! I read that book! How *dare* you!"

But the ultimate blow came from the tycoon of tycoons, Hollywood's boss of bosses, Mayer, my no-longer-benevolent "uncle Louie," of MGM. At a meeting of the Motion Picture Producers' Association, L.B. turned on my father: "B.P., how could you let your own flesh and blood write such a book?" And before my beleaguered father could answer, L.B. intoned, "You know what we should do with him? We should deport him!" The only member of the powerful MPPA who dared the wrath of L.B. was my liberal and maverick old man. "For Christ's sake, Louie, he's the only novelist who ever came *from* Hollywood. Where the hell are you going to deport him, Catalina Island?"

|||||||

With Mayer wanting to deport me, I had the unusual distinction of being attacked simultaneously by the Communist party and John Wayne. Although it was the first book in the history of Hollywood fiction to side with the Writers Guild in its bitter struggle against Mayer, Thalberg & Co., it failed to meet the Hollywood Communists' high standards for social realism à la Stalin. But to John Wayne—Big Duke, the USC football lineman transformed into an all-American movie star through the magic of John Ford—*Sammy* was the personification, or novelization, of the *Communist Manifesto*.

Encounters with Wayne at parties, or in famous watering holes such as Chasen's, Ciro's and Romanoff's, became Beverly Hills versions of *High Noon.* In Wayne's superpatriotic eyes, an attack on Hollywood (or the Sammy Glicks of Hollywood) was an attack on Free Enterprise, Mother and The Flag. I was verbally abused, publicly denounced, and if flogging had been permitted in Hollywood along with tongue-lashing, I would have been as bloodied as Kunta Kinte in *Roots.*

If *Sammy* went on running into the fifties and sixties, so did John Wayne's righteous indignation. One of the happiest moments of my life was sailing into Puerto Vallarta in the mid-sixties on a ninety-foot schooner with my wife, Geraldine Brooks. The timing was perfect, a Mexican Pacific sunset, the company of friends we could laugh with and exquisite margaritas. If I cashed in my chips at this moment, I felt, I'd be ahead of the Dealer. Then Gerry was saying, "Budd, try not to get upset, but look who's coming in with us." I looked, and lost a little of my Baja California tan. Side by side with our *Double Eagle* was the John Wayne yacht. When the Great American Hero and I stepped ashore almost shoulder-to-shoulder, we were welcomed by the mayor. To celebrate this historic moment—the arrival of a legendary American film star and a prominent American writer, who still lived part-time in Mexico, Puerto Vallarta was planning an official reception/fiesta that evening. Big Duke and I as co–guests of honor! While I could honestly admire his hulking presence on the screen, he and Louis B. had drummed me out of Hollywood. Now he was lousing up Puerto Vallarta for me—and PV was still an appealing, largely unspoiled fishing village in those days.

At the Hotel Dorado I sulked. I'm not going down to that *pachango* and have Wayne shoot me down for *Sammy* again the way he wastes Injuns in those westerns of his. Said the ever-practical Gerry, "We'll put you at a table across the room from his—with your back to him. You love Mexico, the music, the *tequila viejo,* the people—just forget Wayne's there. Enjoy yourself."

Which I was trying to do when I felt a muscular arm around my neck. John Wayne—with his rough-and-ready entourage behind him—was ready to drag me to the nearest jacaranda tree and string me up as a traitor. More than a score of years had passed since *Sammy* first appeared on the scene—but the great defender of the Alamo and the American Way (with the exception of the First Amendment) had never forgotten or forgiven. After a brief scuffle—when the guests of honor were separated, and the mayor was ready to run for cover rather than high office—the hero of *Fort Apache* fixed me with that famous look and lines only a natural like Duke could get away with: "How about you 'n' me settlin' this once 'n' for all? I'll be back at midnight. An' I'll be waitin' for ya!"

ELEVEN-THIRTY: In my room at the hotel I started warming up, Walter Mitty throwing furious combinations that would render *hors de combat* the mighty warrior of *Iwo Jima* and *The Longest Day.* I had been around boxers all my life. I liked them better than actors. I had watched them get ready. This was my moment.

QUICK DISSOLVE: Two old beach masters lunge at each other—but there's an obstruction somewhere between them. It's the invisible, five-foot-two, 110-pound Gerry making it impossible for either of us to throw a punch without hitting this uninvited but insistent "referee." "Gerry, *please* get out of the way," I beg. Wayne was trying just as hard to remove this unexpected obstacle to his heroics. So, as our corners pulled us apart, the only winner was Gerry. It went into the record books, like most Hollywood fisticuffs, as ND—no decision. Or maybe that should read "double TKO"—the *T* standing for tequila.

If Sammy Glick had been perceived as strictly and narrowly a product of Hollywood, if the character and the novel as a whole had been viewed as myopically and self-protectively as had Louie Mayer and John Wayne, my career might have been over and I would have been down and out in Beverly Hills. But the perception of Sammy Glick by the critics and the public was far broader and deeper than we could have anticipated. I had written about Sammy Glick because I had been brought up among Sammy Glicks, and I had used Hollywood as a background because Hollywood was my hometown and, until I exchanged palm trees for pine trees, the only community I knew.

But the Sammy Glick I had chosen as my prototype was not linked only to Hollywood hucksterism. *The New York Times Book Review* welcomed him to the select company of American anti-heroes from Simon Legree to George Babbitt. In review after review, Sammy Glick was described as "aggression personified," a "conquistador from the gutter." In time, Sammy Glick was to creep into the language, and even into some dictionaries. A "Sammy" might become rich, powerful and famous, but you wouldn't want him to marry your daughter. In fact, you wouldn't want to turn your back on him for fear he'd cop your watch, your story, your company, your wife, your life. The trouble was, Sammy lived by different rules from the rest of us; as the moralizing narrator Al Manheim puts it to him, "You never had the first idea of give-and-take . . . It had to be all you all the way. You had to make individualism the most frightening ism of all."

The reason the book enjoyed such spontaneous success, we were learning, was that I had touched a nerve—not a Hollywood nerve, not a Jewish nerve, but something flawed and dangerous in our national character—some upside-downing of the Golden Rule that resulted in its brutal opposite: "Do it to him before he does it to me!"

That was Sammy's compulsive creed, that was his pirate flag, that's what made him—in the words of one reader—"part of the established folklore of America." "What Made Sammy Run?" became a subject not just for literary critics but for historians and psychiatrists.

As mentioned in our introduction, the eminent Dr. Franz Alexander, head of the Psychoanalytical Institute at the University of Chicago, in his provocative book *The Age of Unreason*, thought he had found his answer in Sammy's being the ultra-aggressive, ruthless and belligerently self-centered type rather common among second-generation Americans from impoverished immigrant families. Their fathers have lost their prestige and their influence due to their inability to cope with their new environments.

While it was flattering to have Dr. Alexander devote an entire chapter to Sammy Glick, his answer made sense only up to a point. Was the Sammy Glick syndrome really limited to children of impoverished immigrants? "Detribalization," Alexander had diagnosed the disease. The son has lost respect for his father's (tribal) values, but has yet to be affected by the mores of his adopted culture. So he is left and lost in a moral no-man's-land.

|||||||

But if that were so, how would you account for the mail *Sammy* drew from all over the country? From insurance companies in Hartford, from chain stores in the South, from mail-order houses in the Middle West, people were writing that I could not have written *Sammy* without personal knowledge of their own mail-room boy who had run over their backs to become office manager, and in some cases company president. Teenage white boys in Atlanta, third-generation sons of the middle class in Boston, no ethnic group, geographical area or economic stratum seemed to have a lock on Sammy. He was not from Rivington Street alone, or from Sunset and Vine. He was made in America.

Through the forties and fifties, Sammy endured as the quintessential antihero, the bad example, the free-enterprise system at its meanest, brass-knuckle, kick-in-the-groin dirtiest. By now the book had sold into the millions, read by people who loved to hate Sammy Glick.

It was in the early seventies that I began to feel the first disturbing shift in what was to become a 180-degree turn in our national attitude toward Sammy. Following a talk I had just given at a local college on the impact of success on American writers, a young man came up to thank me for creating Sammy Glick. "He's a great character. I love him. I felt a little nervous about going out into the world and making it. But reading *Sammy* gives me confidence. I read it over and over. It's my bible."

He put out his hand, the hand that would soon be knifing friends and colleagues in the back. As I took it hesitantly, I asked myself, What have I done? Or what has a changing, greedier, more cynical America done to Sammy Glick? Speaking on other campuses through the seventies, I found to my dismay that the first young man hitching his star to Sammy Glick's was not at all an aberration but the harbinger of a trend. Now all the young people in college reading a new edition of *What Makes Sammy Run?* were reacting to him as if he were a positive guide to their futures onward and upward. The book I had written as an angry exposé of Sammy Glick was becoming a character reference: How to succeed in America when really trying!

What had happened, of course, is that we had left the sixties behind, with its hippies and flower children and their communal dream of sharing and loving, and had moved on to the Nixon generation, the Bebe Rebozo generation of deal-makers and Do-

It-to-Them-Before-They-Do-It-to-Us. In that context, the Watergate break-in was no accident, nor was Attorney General Mitchell's Glickish boast, "When the going gets tough, the tough get going."

Nor the blanket apology for immoral acts or immoral behavior, "Everybody does it."

No, not *everybody* does it; conscience and social responsibility are still alive if not too well in America. But the dramatic transformation of Sammy Glick from the antihero of the forties to the role-model hero for the Yuppies of the eighties is a painful reminder of the moral breakdown we are suffering without even seeming to realize that suffering is involved. This is a new nation, created in ambivalence, with idealistic individuality contending with selfish individualism. From the very beginning it was Jefferson versus Hamilton, the democratic dream versus the autocratic reality of hard money and the bank, social justice vs. a narrow interpretation of law and order.

|||||||

Individualism run rampant, an arrogant disregard for the views and the welfare of our fellow man, was the root of the Iran-contra debacle, which brought the Great Communicator down from his mythic high. Small wonder in such an atmosphere that a lieutenant colonel in the U.S. Marines became his own CIA and State Department, wheeling and dealing with foreign countries, international arms dealers, Swiss bank accounts and rebels in Miami who dreamed of the good old days of Somoza while they gobbled up those mysterious millions.

In the closing lines of *What Makes Sammy Run?* I had described his meteoric career "as a blueprint of a way of life that was paying dividends in America in the first half of the twentieth century." Well, with our takeover artists, our inside traders, our Ivan Boeskys and Mike Milkens, our Ollie Norths, our college football heroes on the take from filthy rich alumni, our New York City commissioners compromised almost to a man (and woman), all signs point to even bigger dividends for the Sammy Glicks in the remainder of this century, and on into the next.

The book I had written as an attack on antisocial behavior has become a how-to book on Looking Out for Number 1. Change that line of the old hymn to read, "America, America, God shed His grace on me." Let's hear it for me, me, *me*!

Who needs free milk and hot lunches for poor kids in school? Who needs loans and assistance for high-school graduates who can't go on to college for lack of bread? It's Darwin Time: survival of the fittest! Sure, all people are created equal. Only Sammy Glick is created more equal than the *schleppers*, get it?

O.K. That's how they're reading it in 1989. And if that's the way they go on reading it, marching behind the flag of Sammy Glick, with a big dollar sign in the square where the stars used to be, the twentieth-century version of Sammy is going to look like an Eagle Scout compared to the twenty-first.

BUDD SCHULBERG
Brookside, Quiogue, New York
June 1989

BUDD SCHULBERG's career as a novelist began with the meteoric success of *What Makes Sammy Run?* Among his other novels are *Waterfront, The Harder They Fall, Sanctuary V,* and *The Disenchanted,* which Anthony Burgess included in his *New York Times* list of "The Ninety-nine Best Novels of the Twentieth Century."

Schulberg won an Oscar for his screenplay *On the Waterfront,* several awards for his film *A Face in the Crowd,* and a Tony nomination for his Broadway adaptation of *The Disenchanted.* He attributes his ability to adapt his own work to stage or screen to his upbringing in Hollywood, where his father ran a major motion-picture studio.

Currently he is writing the screenplay for *What Makes Sammy Run?* scheduled for production early in 1990, coinciding with the publication by Random House of the anniversary edition of his celebrated novel.

"It has understanding, pity, savagery, courage and sometimes a strange high beauty. It is written with a pace that rushes you along with it and a sureness that comes only of great skill. It is good to be present when such things happen."

—Dorothy Parker

Fifty years ago, Budd Schulberg accomplished that rarest of literary feats: introducing a character whose name entered our language. We have all known a Sammy Glick, a man so driven, so consumed by his ambition and his work that he leaves everyone around him wondering about the source of his obsession. Just as shocking and relevant now as it was on publication, *What Makes Sammy Run?* delves into the psychology of a man reliant on his success as a Hollywood producer.

What Makes Sammy Run? is the unremitting story of a young man in such a hurry to hide his ghetto past that his present—and future—becomes a blur. Loud and abrasive, Sammy Glick uses, abuses, lies and cheats his way to the top—only to find he's faced with a horde of little Sammy Glicks trying to take him for a ride.

This anniversary edition of a classic novel includes a new afterword by Schulberg and the republication of the magazine short stories from the late 1930s that developed into *What Makes Sammy Run?* Throughout, Schulberg paints the picture of a detestable man in compassionate colors, making a nearly inhuman character seem worthy of our sympathy.